ANTONIA WHITE

THE LOST TRAVELLER

The Dial Press
New York

To the memory of
HUGH KINGSMILL

"In the sojourning of this carnal life each
man carries his own heart and every
heart is closed to every other heart."
—*St. Augustine*

Published by
The Dial Press
1 Dag Hammarskjold Plaza
New York, New York 10017

Copyright 1950 by Antonia White

Copyright renewed 1978 by Antonia White
Introduction copyright © 1979 by Carmen Callil

Manufactured in the United States of America

First Dial printing

Library of Congress Cataloging in Publication Data

White, Antonia , 1899–
The lost traveller.
I. Title.
PR6045.H15634L6   1980   823'.914   80-20016
ISBN   0-8037-4935-X

INTRODUCTION

It is unusual for the publisher of a book to provide its preface. Antonia White wanted to write a new introduction to the three books – *The Lost Traveller*, *The Sugar House* and *Beyond the Glass* – which complete the story she began in her famous novel *Frost in May*. Now eighty years of age, and a novelist whose small output reflects the virulent writer's block which has constantly interrupted her writing life, she preferred to talk to me. For though separated by age, country of birth and nationality, we share a Catholic upbringing which has been a dominant influence on both our lives. What follows is based on a long conversation I had with Antonia White in December 1978, and on the many times we've talked since Virago first re-published *Frost in May* earlier that year.

'Personal novels,' wrote Elizabeth Bowen in a review of Antonia White's work, 'those which are obviously based on life, have their own advantages and hazards. But we have one "personal" novelist who has brought it off infallibly.' Antonia White turned fact into fiction in a quartet of novels based on her life from the ages of nine to twenty-three. 'My life is the raw material for the novels, but writing an autobiography and writing fiction are very different things.' This transformation of real life into an imagined work of art is perhaps her greatest skill as a novelist.

Antonia White was the only daughter of Cecil Botting, Senior Classics Master at St Paul's School, who became a Catholic at the age of thirty-five taking with him into the Church his wife and seven-year-old daughter, fictionalised as 'Nanda' in *Frost in May*. This novel is a brilliant portrait of Nanda's experiences in the enclosed world of a Catholic convent. First published in 1933, it was immediately recognized as a classic. Antonia White wrote what was to become the first two chapters of *Frost in May* when she was only sixteen, completing it sixteen years later, in 1931. At the time she was married to Tom Hopkinson, writer, journalist and later editor of *Picture Post*.

'I'd written one or two short stories, but really I wrote nothing until after my father's death in 1929. At the time I was doing a penitential stint in Harrod's Advertising Agency . . . I'd been sacked from Crawfords in 1930 for not taking a passionate enough interest in advertising. One day I was looking through my desk and I came across this bundle of manuscript. Out of curiosity I began to read it and some of the things in it made me laugh. Tom asked me to read it to him, which I did, and then he said "You must finish it." Anyway Tom had appendicitis and we were very hard up, so I was working full time. But Tom insisted I finish a chapter every Saturday night. Somehow or other I managed to do it, and then Tom thought I should send it to the publisher – Cobden

Sanderson – who'd liked my short stories. They wrote back saying it was too slight to be of interest to anyone. Several other people turned it down and then a woman I knew told me that Desmond Harmsworth had won some money in the Irish sweep and didn't know what to do with it . . . so he started a publishing business and in fact I think *Frost in May* was the only thing he ever published . . . it got wonderful reviews.'

Between 1933 and 1950 Antonia White wrote no more novels. She was divorced from Tom Hopkinson in 1938, worked in advertising, for newspapers, as a freelance journalist and then came the war. Throughout this period she suffered further attacks of the mental illness she first experienced in 1922. This madness Antonia White refers to as 'The Beast' – Henry James' 'Beast in the Jungle'. Its recurrence and a long period of psychoanalysis interrupted these years.

'I'd always wanted to write another novel, having done one, but then you see the 1930s were a very difficult time for me because I started going off my head again. After the war and the political work I did I was terribly hard up. Then Enid Starkey, whom I'd met during the war, suggested to Hamish Hamilton that I should have a shot at translating and they liked what I did. After that I got all these commissions and I was doing two or three a year but I was completely jammed up on anything of my own, though I kept on trying to write in spite of it. I always wanted to write another novel, and I wanted this time to do something more ambitious, what I thought would be a "proper" novel, not seen only through the eyes of one person as it is in *Frost in May*, but through the eyes of her father, her mother and even those old great aunts in the country. Then suddenly I could write again. The first one [*The Lost Traveller*] took the longest to write. I don't know how many years it took me, but I was amazed how I then managed to write the other two [*The Sugar House* and *Beyond the Glass*]. They came incredibly quickly.'

In 1950, seventeen years after the publication of *Frost in May*, *The Lost Traveller* was published. In it Antonia White changed the name of her heroine Nanda Grey to Clara Batchelor. 'Of course Clara is a continuation of Nanda. Nanda became Clara because my father had a great passion for Meredith and a particular passion for Clara Middleton (heroine of *The Egoist*). Everything that happened to Clara in *The Lost Traveller* is the sort of thing that happened to me, though many things are changed, many invented. I wanted *The Lost Traveller* to be a *real* novel – *Frost in May* was so much my own life. So I changed her name . . .' In every other respect this novel begins where *Frost in May* ends. It is a vivid account of adolescence, of the mutual relationships of father, mother and daughter as Clara grows to maturity and comes to grips with the adult world.

* * *

Two years later Antonia White continued Clara's story, in *The Sugar House*.

Carmen Callil, Virago, London, 1979

PART ONE

Chapter 1

ON every ordinary weekday in term-time, Claude Batchelor stepped out of his house at exactly twenty minutes past nine, slammed the door and set off at a furious pace in the direction of St Mark's School. People who lived in certain West Kensington streets timed their watches by the sturdy, immaculately dressed figure which hurried past their windows as punctually as a train. But on a certain Tuesday in March 1914 it was well after eleven when Claude Batchelor left his house. He shut the door softly behind him and stood hesitating on the steps as if he could not decide which way to go.

He was as carefully dressed and shaved as usual but his blue eyes were bloodshot and his clear skin dulled to a greyish yellow. His was one of those faces that suffering caricatures. The firm, fleshy features, Saxon in colouring, late Roman in cast, were trained to express humour and anger; under the stress of grief they merely looked dissipated.

For three years Claude had known that his father might die at any time. He had accustomed himself to say to his wife, "We must realize that my father cannot live indefinitely" and even "When my father dies, we might do so-and-so". Now that his father was dead, he knew that never for one moment had the idea been real to him.

Certainly he had behaved as he had always intended to behave. Ever since the nurse had said "Poor man, he really has gone now" and competently closed his father's eyes, Claude had done everything expected of him. For the past few hours he had been calming and directing with stoical efficiency, making neat lists of what must be done and who must be informed. Now, standing alone in front of the shrouded house, his will collapsed. It cost him a huge effort to remind himself why he had come out and to order his legs to carry him in the right direction.

By the time he reached the post office he had recovered enough mechanical awareness to write out several telegrams. His small upright hand, the writing of a man who constantly uses Greek characters, was as lucid as usual but his mind was still clouded. When he came out into the street again, the spring sunshine seemed as unnatural as the electric light and drawn blinds he had left at home and people as remote as figures on a stage. North End Road was filling up with the miscellaneous crowd that took possession of it when the city men had gone to work and the two great schools drawn in their population. It was the hour when the young actresses, with smears of last night's make-up still on their eyelids, sauntered out to have their hair waved or to exercise their little dogs; when the old actors, pretending they were on their way to rehearsal, converged in the direction of the "Three Kings." Wives were doing their shopping, frowning over their lists and demanding that the joint or the whiting be sent "in time for lunch, without fail, please". Girls, newly grown-up and taking tiny self-conscious steps in tight skirts that clung to their black silk ankles were staring into drapers' windows or ordering cakes for their mother's bridge parties.

Perhaps because from now on there would be only women in his home he looked at the actors and the yellow-faced men retired from the East almost wistfully. Had his sense of fitness not been so strong, he would have crossed over to the "Three Kings" and, leaning on a counter spotted with wet rings, unloaded his misery on a stranger. Instead he stood by the pillar-box, clutching his bundle of black-edged letters and staring. His jaw, which he had consciously thrust forward for so many years that it was now underhung, dropped open as it used to do when he was a boy. The blow had momentarily cracked the shell of Claude Batchelor the successful schoolmaster and exposed a long-forgotten Claude, dreamy, uncertain and awkward. Standing there on the pavement he lost for a time, as in childhood, the sense of separate existence. Nothing marked him off from the girl staring into the hatshop window, the man leering at her, the errand boy on the green bicycle, the old woman stuffing a cabbage into her string bag. He was so merged in them that he knew when a head would turn or a foot falter. Suddenly he was touched by an old fear of which he had never spoken to anyone, the fear that one day he might lose all control of his mind. Against that there was only one weapon; his obstinate will. With all his might he called it into play, holding his breath as if forcing himself into a tight jacket. Then he shot his letters in the box, clenched his teeth and set off at his usual quick pace towards home.

Valetta Road was one of the older streets of West Kensington. Built of stucco and sparrow-coloured brick, it was modelled on the plan of more ambitious neighbourhoods but the houses were so narrow that they looked overloaded by their pillars and balconies. Along the tops of either row ran a balustrade decorated at intervals with spiked urns shaped like policemen's helmets. Each house owned a pillar and a half so that when occasionally a tenant repainted his stucco, it produced an odd piebald effect. No two façades were the same colour but showed greys, biscuits, ochres and hot browns in various stages of dinginess.

Sixteen years earlier, when Claude had come to live in Valetta Road, it had been one of the "best" streets. Now, though it was going downhill and he could well afford to move, he stayed on from habit and a kind of loyalty. Several houses still had well-cleaned steps and shining brass and were inhabited by a single family. But, year by year, one or two more sank to the degradation of a blistered front door flanked by three or four bells with a buckled card beside each. In summer there appeared on the balconies of such houses people of whom the permanent inhabitants disapproved; young men who played banjoes, Indian students and girls who sat about in flowered kimonos drying their hair in the sun and calling "Coo-ee" to their friends in the street.

Among the long-term tenants were men who worked in the city, doctors, army coaches and retired civil servants. The houses of all these were arranged, as if by agreement, on exactly the same pattern. The ground floor windows had curtains of heavy dark material, the first floor blue or rose brocade and white lace draperies and the second floor casement cloth or chintz. If the blinds of Number 18 had not been drawn, its curtains would have appeared perfectly correct except for those of the top floor bedroom. These were of pink satin and people who disapproved of Claude Batchelor's wife saw in them one more proof of her extravagance and oddness.

Usually the whole household knew when its master arrived home. Claude's key grated loudly in the lock, the door banged and the clatter of his stick, as he rammed it into the pottery stand, reverberated on every floor. But today he came in as noiselessly as he had gone out. Isabel, his wife, who was sewing in the darkened dining-room that opened off the hall, gave a little shriek when he appeared in the doorway.

"Claude! I didn't know you were in the house."

"I'm sorry if I startled you."

His voice, harsh with exhaustion, sounded angry rather than apologetic. The dimness was soothing to his eyes after the glare of the street. A single cone of light fell on the table where Isabel sat, removing a crimson feather from a black velvet hat; beyond its radius everything seemed blurred in fog. He remained in the shadow on the far side of the table, looking down at her.

"All the essential telegrams have gone," he said. "I shall send others as soon as we know the exact arrangements for the funeral."

"So efficient even today," she sighed. Then, more alertly, but without looking at him, she asked,

"What have you done about Clara?"

"I asked the Reverend Mother to send her home at once. Presumably she will arrive during the afternoon."

Isabel raised her great eyes and stared at him.

"Oh."

"Why that voice, my dear?"

"You never told me you'd decided."

Her face, unlike his, was perfectly designed to express tragedy. Even when she was gay, the slight droop of her mouth and her large brown exposed eyes gave her an air of sadness. Her soft, stricken voice and the look that matched it accused him, as so often before, of being insensitive.

"I took it for granted you would want her to be there."

"Poor little Clara," she wailed. "It seems so dreadful ... a child at a funeral."

"Nearly fifteen is hardly a child, surely."

"Your mother's idea, I suppose."

He showed that he was hurt by thrusting out his jaw and speaking in his classroom tone.

"As it happens, I did not consult my mother. I assumed ... rashly it appears ... that you would agree with me."

Isabel made a few vague snips at her feather.

"Of course, if you've made up your mind, there's no point in my saying anything. Though how you can expose a little girl to all these horrors ..."

4

"What exactly do you mean by horrors?"

She dropped her hands in her lap and shut her eyes.

"Really, Claude. Today of all days I didn't think you'd bully me."

"Bully you? Oh, my God!" he said wearily.

"Or swear at me." It was hardly more than a whisper. Her eyes remained closed.

He looked at her in silence. Once again she had defeated him. From his boyhood to this day his natural preference had always been for golden-haired women; plump, good-tempered and insipidly pretty. Yet the moment he had set eyes, twenty years ago, on a sallow, brown-haired girl whose beauty was only one degree removed from ugliness he had been fascinated, and fascinated he remained. The sickly light exposed her face to him now wan and lifeless. Her hair, carelessly done, hung limply, revealing the babyish, undeveloped forehead and eyebrows so faint as to be nearly invisible. The smooth arched eyelids were beginning to wrinkle; the perfect lips, pale today and slackly parted as if in sleep, showed teeth that were even but no longer white. The curves of cheek and jaw were still intact but the skin which had once had the satin texture of her arms now showed a roughened grain to which drifts of powder clung unevenly. He was reminded of a gardenia, just turning brown at the edges, its perfume intensified by the first touch of decay. His anger melted into resentful tenderness.

Feeling his eyes on her, she slowly opened her own and her soft high voice was no longer aggrieved as she lisped.

"What do I mean by horrors, dea'est? You've only to look round this room."

The room was sombre enough at any time with its dark red walls and greenish-brown curtains. Today it was muffled in black draperies which blotted up the weak light. Black garments trailed everywhere over the chairs; even the mirror over the fireplace was swathed in a black shawl.

"When a family is in mourning, one expects this surely."

"Not in all families, Claude. My father insisted we weren't to wear black even at his funeral."

"Your father, my dear, as you have repeatedly told me, was a highly unconventional man."

"I don't see why we should have to go to the other extreme. I doubt if anyone draws the blinds down now except in the East End."

"My mother would be upset if we didn't."

"Your mother again. Of course, what I want counts for nothing in this house."

"Isabel, be reasonable. Can't you just for once …?"

She ignored him.

"Your father would have agreed with me," she persisted. "He had all the right instincts, dear old man."

Usually any praise of his father, however patronizing, softened Claude at once. However, he said nothing and, glancing at him, Isabel saw that his face was set. She said coaxingly,

"I think it's a beautiful idea of yours to have him buried at Rock-field."

"I'm glad you approve. I only hope that the sight of so many of my relatives won't be too much for you."

She began to pluck once more at the feather with the uncertain movements of a woman who seldom uses her hands.

"Really, Claude, is it my fault if ugliness of any kind jars on me so dreadfully? I hope for her own sake that Clara isn't as sensitive as I am."

"I'm quite certain she is it. As you often say, she takes after my family."

Isabel pushed her hat away and stared into space.

"Father always thought I was born with a skin too few. I daresay it's literally true."

"My dear, no one attempts to compete with you in the finer feelings. No doubt I myself was born with several skins too many."

"Claude, how can you be so cruel and sarcastic today of all days? Don't you realize how all this brings things back to me? You seem to forget that I lost my father too. Oh, I know it's fifteen years ago. But it seems like yesterday."

Once more she had beaten him. In sign of surrender he crossed the room and sat down beside her.

"I'm sorry, Isabel. I'm shockingly irritable this morning."

She turned her eyes vaguely in his direction, looking at a point somewhere over his shoulder.

"I know it's dreadful for you, Claude. I can sympathize. But at least you were prepared."

He said blankly,

"Oh yes. I was prepared."

"I had no warning. We hadn't the faintest idea that he had a weak heart. Yet that morning when the telegram came I knew at once that it was Father. I've often wondered if I'm not a little psychic."

"Very possibly."

"You, Claude, at least still have a mother. Just think, I can't even remember mine. I was only three months old when she died."

She had told him these things many times before in almost identical words. When she did so her eyes always became fixed and she spoke in a high faint monotone. With exasperated tenderness, he took her hand. She yielded it vaguely and the needle she was holding pricked his finger. At the sight of the blood she started and cried out too late,

"Oh, dea'est, be careful."

She made a little grimace as he dabbed his bleeding finger. Then suddenly she smiled.

"Do you remember? When we were engaged. The pin in my belt. You were so furious because you thought it was untidy of me to have a pin in my belt at all. But the next day you sent me a poem in Latin all about the thorny rose."

He did remember, as if from another life, Isabel with her hair in soft puffs and wearing a pink blouse, standing under a lilac tree in her father's garden.

"You had to translate it for me," she went on. "I was so proud of having a poem written to me in Latin and so ashamed not to be able to make out a single word except 'Rosa'. Such a foolish Belle. And then you did try to teach me Latin and had to give me up as hopeless. I've often wondered why, because my French is so good."

"You can't teach when you're in love with your pupil."

"Then I hope I was your only failure."

He had to smile.

"Positively my only failure."

"All the same, I expect you'd have been much happier if you'd married a female don or something."

"Heaven forbid!"

"You and Clara between you sometimes make me feel a complete idiot. If one of your pupils sent Clara a love poem in Latin, she'd be able to understand every word, wouldn't she?"

His face stiffened again.

"If any of my pupils had the impertinence ..." he began fiercely.

She interrupted,

7

"Yet you were just saying that she wasn't a child any more."

"From that point of view, the longer we think of her as a child the better."

"You needn't worry. I daresay you'll make Clara so learned that no young man will ever dare come near her." She frowned. "No one ever asked me if I wanted my pretty daughter turned into a bluestocking."

"The child has good brains. Why shouldn't she use them? Apart from the fact that she will almost certainly have to make her own living."

"I still think it was overdoing it to make her puzzle over declensions and things when she was seven."

"She enjoyed it." His face cleared. "Ah, at that age she was a joy to teach."

"Isn't she now?" said Isabel innocently. "She's always so desperately anxious to please you."

Again he frowned.

"Hmm. I wonder. When she was younger, yes. But now ... this last year or two ... I wonder."

"More than ever now, Claude. I'm in a very good position to judge." She snapped her fingers. "For ages I haven't counted *that* with Clara."

He thrust his jaw forward.

"If I thought that were true, Isabel, I should have to speak to her. And in no uncertain terms."

"Please don't, dearest. Certainly not today when she's just had such a shock. I daresay all clever daughters are critical of their Mammas at her age. Yet when I think how I used to long for a mother when I was beginning to grow up! But I wasn't a bit like Clara. I was such an absurd romantic little thing, living in a sort of fairy-tale world of my own."

"I'm by no means satisfied with Clara myself," said Claude. "It seems to me that lately the child has become hard and self-centred."

"Yet she was so sweet and affectionate when she was tiny, wasn't she? I can see her now in her big white bonnet, trotting along beside her Grandfather, holding his hand and looking up at him so adoringly."

"Ah," he sighed. "If we could go back to those years!"

She touched his hand lightly.

8

"Poor Claude. I was almost forgetting. I'm sure no one will miss him more than I shall."

"He was so fond of you, Isabel."

"Wasn't it touching, the way he took such an interest in my clothes and so on? He really had quite a flair for such things. It's strange when you think of ..."

She broke off in time and he, knowing perfectly well what she had been about to say, made no comment. To cover it, she gave the feather a tug and it came away with a crackle of ripped stitches.

"There, now I've deliberately ruined his favourite hat. He would have been the first to see it's nothing without the feather."

"I think he would have been touched by your sacrificing it."

"What good can it do him, poor dear? I think there's something positively unchristian in all this gloomy attitude to death. After all, we *are* supposed to believe he's gone to a happier place."

He half smiled.

"As Catholics, we usually expect a certain delay."

"You mean purgatory and all that? I think purgatory's a wonderful idea. So consoling for people like me. And so logical when you come to think of it. All the same, in the east they wear flowers at funerals and make quite a festival of the whole thing."

"I've no idea what they do in the east."

Isabel stroked her cheek with the crimson feather and said dreamily,

"If I died first, you'd have to make all the arrangements for my funeral, wouldn't you, Claude?"

She ignored his "Dear girl ... for heaven's sake!" and went on:

"I should like everyone to wear their nicest clothes. And no funeral march. Just that Chopin nocturne I used to play you when we were engaged. And don't give me a tombstone. I should feel crushed under it. I'd like you to plant a rose bush and a cypress tree on my grave."

"Will you kindly stop, Isabel."

She looked at him with a childish wonder that might or might not have been simulated.

"I've always prayed," he said, "that you would outlive me."

"Isn't that rather selfish, dearest? It's so much worse for the one who is left."

"Of course it is selfish," he said angrily, suddenly pulling her close to him.

There was a knock at the door and they quickly composed their faces and attitudes. Zillah the housemaid came in, carrying an enormous cardboard box. She wore her black afternoon uniform instead of her morning print and her handsome grey eyes were swollen.

"Mr Shapiro's chauffeur left this for you, sir."

"Even the servants loved him," Claude said when the girl had gone. "Poor Zillah was in tears this morning."

"Servants love deaths and funerals. Even a pretty girl like Zillah doesn't get much excitement in her life."

Claude methodically untied the box. From layers of tissue paper, there emerged an immense wreath of lilies of the valley and mauve cattleyas.

"Oh, how exquisite," said Isabel, staring greedily.

Claude's eyes filled.

"If only he could see them!"

"When we're alive," said Isabel, "no one thinks of sending us orchids. All the time he was ill, Becky Shapiro never sent him so much as a bunch of violets."

"Really, it is too much. They shouldn't have done it."

"Why? It's nothing to these rich Jews."

"Plenty of rich Christians wouldn't even have thought of it," he said sharply.

"The Shapiros owe it you. Look at all you've done for their little Izzy and their little Sam. All right, my dear, I admit it is nice of them. But I can never help smiling when I think of those boys, born over a fried fish shop, going to Oxford."

"Is it any odder than my sending Clara to Mount Hilary. Why shouldn't the Shapiros want things for their children that they haven't had themselves?"

It was her turn to stiffen.

"You seem to forget," she said coldly, "that Clara is half a Maule. If my grandfather hadn't lost his money, if my father hadn't been eccentric and cut himself off from society ..."

"Yes, yes, my dear," he said hastily to avert what must inevitably come next; the Maule coat of arms; the Lawrence portraits; the snuff-box presented by George III. "No one realizes it better than I. And no one is gladder for Clara's sake."

Easily propitiated, she smiled.

"It's the *only* trace," she said. "Your being so impressed by money and the Shapiro kind of vulgar success."

"I like Shapiro for himself."

"You always say he's very intelligent. He certainly plays an extraordinary game of bridge. But I can't get over that accent and those fingers."

She stroked her nose appreciatively with her own impeccable hand. The nose too was impeccable; straight and thin, with finely incised nostrils.

"Such a pity about Clara's nose," she said. "You couldn't call it ugly but it has definitely spread a trifle."

Her eyes wandered again to the flowers.

"Lovely, lovely things. Doesn't it seem criminal to think of them mouldering on a grave."

He got up abruptly and moved towards the door.

"I must go, Isabel. There are still innumerable things to do."

"All these ghastly formalities. They can't even let one die and be buried in peace. Will you be in to luncheon?"

"No. I shall get some lunch at my club."

Her eyes were still on the flowers.

"If he had been alive, the very first thing he would have done would have been to give me one."

"No doubt, my dear."

She looked at him innocently.

"I think that eastern custom is a charming idea, don't you?"

"Eastern custom?" he asked in bewilderment.

"I told you just now, dearest. About wearing ..."

"Goodbye, Isabel," he said and left her. She heard him collecting his hat and stick in the hall and this time he did not leave the house noiselessly.

Chapter 2

ISABEL waited till she heard the front door close. Then she took the scissors from her workbox and carefully snipped off two of the largest orchids from the wreath. Going over to the mirror, she lifted a corner of the black shawl. Finding it was still impossible to get a good view of herself, she pulled the shawl off altogether. She switched on the centre light and returned to the mirror. No sooner had she pinned the orchids to the shoulder of her dress than the door was stealthily pushed open and someone came in.

"Oh, it's you," she said, swinging round "I do wish you wouldn't creep about so quietly."

Old Mrs Batchelor advanced slowly into the room, having switched off the main light and closed the door as carefully as if she feared to waken a sleeper.

"I'm sorry, Isabel. I thought you would wish everything as quiet as possible today."

"Please put that light on again."

"I didn't mean any harm," said Mrs Batchelor meekly. "I was only thinking of Claude's purse."

"I want it on, please."

Mrs Batchelor turned on the light and stood hesitating by the door.

"Do come and sit down," said Isabel.

"You're sure I shan't be in your way?"

"No, no. Is there anything you want? Shall I tell Zillah to get you a cup of tea?"

"No, thank you, dear. I wouldn't like to give the maids extra trouble."

"That's not the point. Do you *want* some tea?"

"No, really, Isabel. I couldn't touch anything."

Mrs Batchelor sat down in the hardest chair and dabbed her eyes.

"I'm afraid I shall be more of a burden than ever to you now that he's gone," she sobbed.

"Oh, please try not to cry. You'll only tire yourself out. Do you mind if I just arrange your hair a little?"

It was only with great effort that Isabel could bring herself to touch her mother-in-law. After living in the same house with her for over ten years, the morning and evening kisses were still an ordeal. The very appearance of the old woman was an affront to her eyes. Ellen Batchelor was barely five feet high and cruelly misproportioned. Her large flattened head was dumped down on the narrowest of shoulders; her enormous stomach thrust forward in a solid mound below the tiny bust which she had compressed since her girlhood in iron stays. Her broad plump face was as white as lard and the irises of her dull brown eyes were rimmed, like onyx stones, with bluish white. She always wore a wig of rich deep chestnut curls, pulled so far forward that wisps of her own grey hair escaped at the back.

"There, that looks better," said Isabel, settling the wig at its proper angle. "I can't think, though, why you don't have a white one. It would be far more becoming. Claude thinks so too."

"I had beautiful chestnut hair when I was a girl," said Mrs Batchelor. "I know I've nothing to be vain about now. But poor Fred always admired my hair."

"You could order a white one in time for the funeral. It's a very good moment to make the change, don't you think?"

Mrs Batchelor's violet lips began to tremble again.

"It would be so expensive. And somehow I don't feel inclined to think about hair at such a time. It's all very well for you, dear. You still have a husband to care how you look."

She craned her head forward and peered at Isabel's orchids.

"Excuse me asking. But are those real blooms you're wearing?"

"My cattleyas? Yes, of course they're real."

"You will pardon my remarking on them, won't you?"

Isabel said nothing.

The old woman glanced round nervously and, in doing so, caught sight of the wreath.

"Oh, what lovely flowers. They must have cost a fortune. Did Claude? Poor boy, he shouldn't have afforded them with all the other expenses."

She went over and fumbled the orchids with her puffy, veined hands.

"Oh, please don't," cried Isabel. "You'll bruise them. If you want to know, they're from Claude's friends, the Shapiros."

"How very kind of the Shap—Shapers. ... Oh, dear, I never can pronounce that name right. I must remember to thank them."

"Claude will do that. They were sent to *him*."

Mrs Batchelor sat down again. After a moment she said with timid boldness, "I would like to ask a favour of you, Isabel."

"What is it?"

"You've so much influence with Claude. He won't listen to me, I know. But I do wish he could be persuaded not to go to so much expense over the funeral."

"He's quite definitely made up his mind. And you should know better than anyone what Claude is when his mind is made up."

"All the same, I wish you'd try, dear," Claude's mother went on with dull courage. "If you could even get him to give up the idea of having the burial at Rookfield."

"But why? It is a beautiful idea. What could be more appropriate? His father came from that part of the world. People should always be buried in those charming little country churchyards if there's any possible excuse. There's something so sordid and impersonal about these great hideous London cemeteries."

"I don't deny that Rookfield is a pretty spot," said Mrs Batchelor without enthusiasm, "but all the same, Isabel ..."

"I wish you'd say straight out what's on your mind."

"Well, it's something one hardly cares to mention."

"Oh, for goodness' sake, say it!"

With a great effort Mrs Batchelor approached the point.

"It's like this, Isabel. I know you don't think much of some of Claude's relations on his father's side. And I'm not saying for a minute they've got a position like Claude has. But some of them have done quite well in business. And they do notice things so. I'm sure you wouldn't want them to have any opportunity of looking down on Claude."

"What on earth do you mean?"

"I don't know how to put it without you misunderstanding me. But my sisters, the little aunts, as you call them, they're very countrified. And Paget's Fold ... it's hardly more than a cottage and not at all stylishly furnished. Then Cousin John Hoadley ... he does speak so very broad."

"I suppose you mean," said Isabel, "that you're ashamed of your relatives."

"There, I was afraid you'd misunderstand me. It's only that I wouldn't wish anyone to feel embarrassed."

14

"I've always found the aunts and John Hoadley perfectly charming."

"I know, dear. It's always surprised me that you thought so much of them," murmured Mrs Batchelor.

"But apparently, though they're good enough for me, they're not good enough for people like Sidney Gould and Horace Batchelor. Really, you have the strangest ideas."

"Don't mistake my meaning, Isabel. You make allowances for their being simple people. But Horace Batchelor, he always was jealous of Claude from a boy and he judges everything by show. He fancies himself a lot now that he's bought himself a motor-car and is so intimate with Sir Rex Popham."

"Popham," exclaimed Isabel, closing her eyes as if the name made her feel faint. "You can hardly expect *me* to be impressed."

But Mrs Batchelor stuck to her point with surprising obstinacy.

"Horace has never been to this house where everything's so nice. Now if the funeral were to take place in London …"

Isabel cut her short.

"I tell you Claude has made up his mind. And I entirely agree with him."

Mrs Batchelor sighed and folded her hands in resignation.

"Then there's nothing more to be said."

The old woman looked so meekly hopeless that Isabel said more gently,

"He really is right, you know. There are some things you don't quite understand."

"No. I daresay not."

"Just as some people have no ear for music or can never pronounce a foreign language."

"We all know you have a great many advantages, dear. You could have looked much higher than Claude."

Isabel was silent.

"Still you couldn't have a truer, kinder husband," the old woman went on. "I hope you'll never find yourself placed as I am, all alone in the world."

"You can't say you're alone while you have Claude."

"Yes, indeed, Isabel. I know I should be thankful. But poor Fred and I … we were together nearly fifty years." Her onyx eyes filled again. "I can't get used to the idea that he's gone."

The fat face under the wig was that of a stupid child who has been cruelly used. Isabel tried to feel pity for her mother-in-law. But she could only feel sorry for the situation, not for the person.

"Do lean back and be comfortable," she said, putting a footstool under Mrs Batchelor's feet. "I'm sure Claude would like you to have a glass of sherry."

"No, really, please. Is Claude gone out?"

"Yes."

"Poor Claude. It all falls on him. And he feels this so much, though he doesn't show it. He did so worship his father, ever since he was a little boy."

"He was certainly a wonderful son."

"To both of us, Isabel. No one will ever know all Claude's unselfishness. In the bad times when we had the shop and things went wrong, not through any fault of Fred's ..."

"I know, I know," said Isabel, trying desperately to be patient.

Mrs Batchelor blew her nose.

"I know you don't like my mentioning the shop. But trouble does bring things back so."

"I wish you could stop thinking once and for all about those awful times."

"Claude says he wants me to stay on here just the same. But I shouldn't want to be a burden."

Isabel was silent a moment. Then she said very amiably,

"Have you ever thought of going to live at Paget's Fold? It's so lovely and peaceful down there. And it would be so nice for you to be with your sisters."

But Mrs Batchelor's obstinacy returned.

"Somehow I never did seem to care for the country. And I don't think it's good for my rheumatism. I've always thought Paget's Fold was damp."

"The aunts never complain."

"I daresay you get used to it if you've lived there all your life. And then Sophy and Leah have got very set in their own ways. I doubt if they'd really want me."

"Oh well, it was only a suggestion. Of course if you don't want to go ..."

"I'm not in the habit of consulting my own wishes. May I ask if Claude has mentioned such a thing?"

"We haven't discussed it."

"Oh dear," said Mrs Batchelor, tearful again, "how much better if it had been me that had been taken."

Isabel began to put her needles and cottons very carefully back in her workbox.

"I suppose most women want to die before their husbands," she said in a neutral voice. There was a pause during which Mrs Batchelor sniffed and composed her trembling face.

"You've been doing a lot of sewing, I see. Mourning makes so much work, doesn't it?"

"I think the whole idea of mourning is horrible," said Isabel. "I was saying so to Claude just now. I shall wear black till after the funeral and not a day longer."

"I know you have very modern ideas, Isabel. Yet I seem to remember that when the King died in 1910, you wore black for quite a long time."

"That was court mourning. There are still one or two things my family expect me to do. Perhaps you have forgotten that my grandfather had a post at court."

Mrs Batchelor was silent, but not because she had forgotten about Isabel's grandfather.

"In my day, things were different," she said. "We went into deep black even for quite distant relations. Someone in my family or Fred's was always going so after I was thirty I took to wearing black always. My looks had gone by then and it saved the dyeing."

Isabel shuddered.

"How horribly depressing. Didn't Mr Batchelor object?"

"He didn't altogether like it but he was glad of any little money I could save. He tried to comfort me by saying I looked slimmer in black."

"Poor Mrs Batchelor. Of course black is kinder to some figures," said Isabel, unconsciously running her hands over her own beautiful body. "Personally I look my worst in it. It doesn't suit my skin."

"It's wonderful how you've kept your youthful figure, my dear. Of course you didn't have to be on your feet directly after your confinements as I did."

"For heavens' sake," Isabel burst out, "aren't there enough ghastly things at the moment without remembering all that?"

"I'm sorry, Isabel. I didn't mean to say anything to grieve you."

"Birth and death! One's as crude and horrible as the other!"

The old woman looked frightened.

"You say such strange things sometimes, Isabel. I don't always follow you."

"Claude's father would have understood. He hated ugliness of all kinds."

"Yes, indeed, so he did. Poor Fred," Mrs Batchelor sighed. "You remember we had to get rid of one of the nurses because he objected to her teeth. And what a handsome man he was. I've even heard you say, Isabel, how distinguished he looked. Ah, all the girls were in love with him when he was young. I never expected him to choose me, even though there was the little bit of money. Still, I suppose not everyone was willing to marry a deaf man."

"He couldn't have had a more devoted wife," said Isabel politely.

"I certainly studied to please him. But then in my day women took it for granted they should give way to their husbands."

"Didn't that make the men rather selfish?"

"I'm sure I don't know, dear. Certainly Fred didn't pay me all the attentions Claude still pays you after all these years. Ah, you're lucky in your husband, Isabel. No doubt it's natural for a mother to think so but it isn't only me that says it."

"I who say it," said Isabel absently.

"I beg your pardon. I often wish for Claude's sake I'd had more education. But we thought it enough for a woman to be able to cook and sew and run her husband's house economically."

"My mother," said Isabel, stifling a yawn, "spoke four languages perfectly and couldn't so much as boil an egg."

She stood up, gathered up her hat and her workbox and moved towards the door.

"Forgive me. I must go and arrange about Clara's room."

Mrs Batchelor's dull eyes brightened.

"Then dear little Clara *is* coming home for the funeral."

"That's what you wanted, isn't it?" said Isabel smoothly.

"It wasn't for me to say. Her Daddy wished it, I know. But I thought perhaps you ..." Suddenly she noticed something and broke off.

"Isabel," she said in a frightened voice, "the shawl. It's fallen off the looking-glass. And I'd made sure I'd put it up so it couldn't."

"I took it off, if you want to know."

"But, dear, surely you know it brings bad luck to the whole

family. A looking-glass uncovered when there's a corpse in the house."

Isabel's suppressed rage broke out at last. Her face turned dead white and her nostrils quivered as she said in a voice of fury,

"This is beyond anything. I am not to look in a mirror for three days because of some absurd peasant superstition. Am I mistress of this house or am I something rather less than a housemaid? Yes, go and whine about me to Claude. As if I cared!"

She swept a heap of clothes off a chair and flung out of the room.

Mrs Batchelor's face, at first terror-stricken, assumed a look of patient malice. As soon as she was sure Isabel had gone upstairs, she went over to the fireplace and, with clumsy movements of her short arms, replaced the black shawl over the glass.

Chapter 3

FOR the next few hours, Claude had no time to think of his grief. Yet all the time he was interviewing registrars and undertakers, ordering flowers or writing letters at his club, he was preparing for the moment when he would have to feel its full weight. One commission he left to the last and, just as the sunny, windy spring afternoon was beginning to fade, he presented himself at the door in the bleak façade of Oratory House.

It was nearly eight years since he had taken the decisive step of his life and become a Catholic. His colleagues at St Mark's had been amused, dismayed or bewildered. None of them had thought of him as a man likely to go through any kind of spiritual crisis; he had seemed, at thirty-five, too comfortably settled in his profession, his opinions and his general way of life. Till then, like most of the other masters he had professed a tolerant agnosticism, talked rather daringly in the Common Room and lived blamelessly. From the point of view of his career his conversion was sheer insanity. He had already been approached with offers of headmasterships by two or three minor public schools and the governors of St Mark's had their eye on him as a possible successor to Doctor Cavell. As a Catholic he could never hope to be more than an Assistant Master for the rest of his days.

There had been no question of his having to leave St Mark's; he was far too valuable an asset. He was a good classical scholar, he was popular and presentable and, above all, he had a genius for coaching. Year by year scholarships and exhibitions were won by Marcians who had seemed the most unlikely material till they had passed through "Batchelor's mill". Doctor Cavell had dealt with the matter with great diplomacy. As a clergyman of the Church of England, he had mildly, but firmly, deplored Claude's step. As a headmaster, he decided that it was now safe to offer him a rise of only fifty pounds instead of the hundred he had been contemplating.

Claude's conversion had seemed at the time sudden and even dramatic. It was in fact neither. Ever since Cambridge, where, to his mother's puzzled distress, he had given up all religion, he had been fascinated by the Roman Church. It had fascinated him then by the very things which gave it such a sinister aura in the eyes of his family. Intoxicated with Wilde and Pater, it had glittered for him with decadent splendours. He had occasionally gone to High Mass with a sense of delicious daring and had even read a paper to a College Society in which he had connected it with the Eleusinian Mysteries. It was not till he was well over thirty and had long ago abandoned this romantic attitude that he came to study it seriously. One of his favourite old pupils became a Catholic and induced Claude to come with him to a course of sermons by a Jesuit who was simply concerned to show the reasonableness of his Church's doctrine. Claude was impressed. He made up his mind to go into the whole subject but he did not, as his friend had hoped, ask for an interview with the Jesuit. It was not till three years later that he decided to put himself under instruction.

Night after night during those three years he had sat in his smoky study in Valetta Road after his last pupil had gone; a glass of whisky at his elbow and books of theology and controversy littered about his desk. As a boy, without any outside encouragement, he had set himself to master Greek and Algebra. With the same patience he now set himself to tackle the Christian religion. He compared the claims of Lutheran, Calvinist, Anglican and Catholic as carefully as he had once studied the arguments for and against the unity of Homer.

Gradually it became clear to him that if he were to be a Christian at all, nothing would satisfy him but the Catholic Church. If its first premises were granted ... and he could find no positive grounds for not granting them ... there seemed to be no flaw in its deducions. His mind was delighted by the subtle interrelation of its doctrines; he saw that nothing could be changed or mutilated without altering the delicate balance of the whole body. More and more it appeared to him as a living organism that had grown and was still growing according to a mysterious inner law. It was this principle of life that most impressed him, surviving and renewing itself through so many centuries in spite of weakness, corruption and greed. If, as it claimed, the source of that life was divine, then the Church had the right to speak with that scandalizing authority and he had no choice but to submit. Yet still he continued to hesitate.

The prospect of spoiling his career hardly weighed with him. If this was the truth about the nature of things, he must accept it and act upon it, whatever the consequences. Yet suppose that some day he should be convinced that, after all, it was not the truth? He knew himself well enough to realize that if he committed himself, it would be for life. All his loyalties had originally been based on convictions. Sometimes the convictions had wavered or vanished, but the loyalty had always remained. In becoming a Catholic he would be involving other people. Isabel, who would never have come to such a decision on her own, was willing to follow him. Catholicism seemed to her a poetical and aristocratic religion. Nothing would have induced her to wrestle with historical or doctrinal problems but she had already gone so far as to buy herself a crystal rosary and a black lace mantilla. There was the still more acute problem of Clara who was still under seven. The whole responsibility of "bringing them over" rested on him.

There were grounds enough to make him hesitate, but the real cause of his delay went deeper. His mind was satisfied but his heart remained cold. He felt nothing that could be called a religious impulse; no craving for God, no awakening of faith. And so for months he had stayed suspended, tired with his years of collating evidence, convinced in his reason but impotent to act.

One Sunday evening he went alone to Benediction in the French church in Soho. Although he now knew its meaning, the service no longer impressed him as it had done in his Cambridge days. Usually insensitive to details, he was annoyed by the perfunctory movements of the fat, blue-jowled priest who gabbled the Latin in a strong Marseilles accent. In front of him knelt two old Italian women in black, stinking woollen shawls and the whole church reeked of stale incense and garlic. Bored and distracted, he became acutely aware of a girl beside him, a sallow, sullenly handsome girl in a suit which fitted her so closely that it seemed to be worn next to the skin. When she slowly peeled off her white kid gloves, the ringless hands against the dark stuff gave him the sense of deliberately exposed nakedness. Mixed with the smell of benzine from the gloves came the smell of sandalwood soap. She repelled and disturbed him; unable to attend to the droning of the rosary his mind fastened on her. With her deep-lidded eyes and pale lips she had a look of Isabel and he guessed that the body under the severe suit would have the same fluid softness. Suddenly, without warning, the demons of his imagination leapt on her, stripping her, using her with a cold brutality of lust. He was not looking at her, but, as if she had guessed his thoughts, he felt her shift further away from him.

At that, his fever left him. His flesh turned cold; he was weighed down by an enormous oppression of guilt. For the first time in his life, he seemed to grasp the meaning of evil. He was conscious of something corrupt in the depths of his nature; something at once frigid, impure and violent. Hitherto he had thought of sin mainly in terms of lust and rage but the quality of this had a peculiar malignancy that tainted the very source of the spirit. He felt as if he were isolated from every human contact; locked in a dark cell that was both icy and suffocating.

The service came to an end. An acolyte put out the candles one by one till only the red sanctuary lamp burnt on the altar. The Italian women shuffled out in their felt slippers; he stood up mechanically to let the girl pass him; he heard her high heels tapping down the aisle. The last footsteps died away; the door creaked to; he was alone in the empty church.

For half an hour he knelt in a rigidity of despair that was like death, not attempting to pray, unable even to think. Then, very gradually, a faint warmth began to penetrate his numbness. He relaxed a trifle, unclenched his clasped hands and noticed that the knuckles were white. Slowly the faint thawing warmth grew in his heart as if someone, far away down a long passage, were bringing a light. He stared at the sanctuary lamp as if its red bead of flame were the one point of contact with the world of sanity and hope. Then he became aware, not with his mind or his senses but with some faculty never awakened before, of an intense personal presence in the church. Words formed themselves so clearly in his brain that it was as if someone had spoken. They were words he had read a hundred times in the Gospel without attaching more than the most general meaning to them. "I am the way and the truth and the life." Now they broke on him like an illumination. It was as if the living Christ offered Himself here and now for his acceptance or refusal. Christ was the key that could unlock his prison of frozen isolation and the key was his for a single act of faith. He buried his face in his hands, muttering over and over again, "Lord, I believe, help Thou mine unbelief."

His moment of experience had quickly passed but he had had no more doubts or hesitations. The next day he asked for a priest to instruct him and six months later he was received into the Church.

Isabel was conditionally baptized with him and Clara a few weeks after. Since then he had behaved with a steadiness unusual in converts, showing no fanatical fervour in his early days and no relaxing when the novelty had worn off. His religion had profoundly influenced his habits and opinions, he was minutely faithful to all its observances but never again had he experienced that direct touch on his soul.

Neither of his parents had followed his example. Even his mother's blind adoration would not carry her as far as that though, after his conversion, she took to going to a very high church. His father had regarded religion as entirely a matter of nationality. Claude's step had seemed to him as peculiar as if he had decided to become a naturalized Italian. In vain his son had reminded him that, up to the time of Henry VIII, England had been Catholic. Frederick Batchelor had merely reiterated, "All Roman Catholics are foreigners. I can't see why the Church of England isn't good enough for you. I don't hold with these foreign religions and never shall."

In spite of his misery, Claude could not help smiling as he rang the bell of the presbytery to think how violently his father would have disapproved of his errand. For he had come to ask a priest to say Masses for the repose of his soul.

He was shown into a gloomy parlour furnished with a table, two straw-seated chairs, a prie-dieu, some Arundel prints and a "Spy" caricature of Cardinal Newman. It reminded him inevitably of the still gloomier parlour at Farm Street, furnished on the same pattern, where, eight years ago, he used to go for his weekly instructions.

After a long wait, an old Oratorian father appeared. Claude explained, with the shyness he had never been able to shake off in the presence of priests, that, as his father had not been a Catholic, he presumed Masses could not be said for him by name but only for his own "intention".

"Oh no. We can mention his name. But they cannot be actual Requiem Masses, you understand. Are you by any chance a convert, Mr ...?"

"Batchelor. Yes, Father."

"Forgive me for asking," said the old man kindly. "I am a convert myself. I know how one feels at such times. My own father was an Anglican clergyman. When he died I kept thinking, 'Here am I, a priest, and I could not give him the Last Sacraments.' But I remember him every day in my Mass."

Claude felt his throat contract. He could only nod and take the warm, shrivelled hand the old priest held out.

"There is nothing I can say to comfort you," said the other, "except what you know already, that every man who sincerely follows what lights God gives him belongs to the soul of the Church."

"I don't think my father ever asked himself questions. He was a very simple man."

"Well, we know what Our Lord said about children."

After a few minutes talk, Claude asked if he could go into the church.

They walked down a gloomy stone passage and entered the Oratory by a side door. After the austere parlour, the great ornate church with its coloured marbles, its silver lamps and its mounds of lighted candles seemed almost theatrical. He felt exposed and ill-at-ease as, having made a stiff genuflection, he stood fidgeting with his hat and muttering some kind of thanks in a whisper to the priest. The other replied in exactly the same voice he had used in the parlour. This and the way he came into the church, as if merely passing from one room of a house to another, gave Claude a peculiar reassurance. Here was a man whose life was all of one piece. Their conversation had lasted only a few minutes, he had been offered in words no more than pious commonplaces, yet when the old man left him, the reassurance lingered like a track of warmth in the air.

Walking slowly down the church, looking for an empty side chapel, he came to the bare black and white altar of Our Lady of Sorrows. There he knelt down, put his face in his hands and at once broke into the painful choking tears of a man who has almost forgotten how to weep. After a time he no longer attempted to control them; they rose, collected and fell in a regular rhythm as blood wells from a wound. For the wound was deep, deeper than anyone he knew realized. No one else would weep like that for Frederick Batchelor. For three years he had been hardly more than a living doll and most of his life he had been a total failure. But he had been the one person whom Claude had loved without asking for any return.

It was an incurable love for it had been born in disillusion. Until a certain summer afternoon not long after Claude's eighth birthday, he had merely admired his father as a powerful, all-wise being. Even his deafness had seemed a splendid and mysterious attribute, giving something oracular to his irrelevent replies to a small boy's questions.

On that particular afternoon he had been sitting under the counter of his father's shop and playing his favourite game of pretending that he owned it. He could not see the customers but he knew them by their voices and amused himself by guessing what each had come to buy. His father seemed even more deaf than usual that day; he moved uncertainly, often knocking a tin or a bottle off its shelf. The customers too seemed to be behaving oddly; never had he heard so many complaints and impatient raps on the counter. Even his father's voice sounded strange. Not only was he talking a great deal and laughing when there seemed nothing particular to laugh at, but he was running all his words together just as Claude himself did when excited. Suddenly an indignant woman left the shop, slamming the door behind her so that the bell rang like an alarm; then he heard young Goatcher the assistant and Harry the errand boy giggling together and muttering something he could not catch. The next moment there came a heavy thud and the boys stopped giggling. Claude jumped up and peered over the counter. His father was lying full-length on the floor, his eyes closed and his face ashy. Claude was too frightened to say anything. When his mother came fussing in from the parlour behind the shop, he crouched down again in his hiding place. Harry and Goatcher carried his father through into the parlour while Mrs Batchelor mounted guard over the street-door. When they came back, he heard her say "It's a kind of attack your master has sometimes. I daresay the heat has been too much for him."

Claude had guessed from her voice that she did not believe what she said and from the way Goatcher answered "There's no denying it's a hot day" that he did not believe it either. No one talked of sending for a doctor. When his mother had gone, Goatcher and the errand boy began to talk.

"What she ought to have said was 'It's a thirsty day', eh?"

" 'Taint no business of yourn, young Harry."

"Reckon it's most people's business. I warn't born yesterday, Bert Goatcher. Everyone round here knows what old Batchelor's trouble is. Long before I come into this shop, I knew all about it."

"Well, there's no call to screech so. The Missus 'ull hear you."

"Why don't she do what my mother does to my Dad Saturday nights? Puts him out in the yard and turns the pump on him, that's what she does."

"It's like this, Harry," said Goatcher patronizingly. "Mr Batchelor, he's a poor, feeble sort of chap. Can't hold a tiddly drop no more than a woman hardly."

Harry snorted.

"Proper drunk he was, eh? My Dad'll laugh outway when I tell him."

Claude had listened, shocked and fascinated. He could only grasp that his father was in the habit of doing something that gave people like Goatcher and Harry the right to jeer at him. At last he jumped up and shouted, "I heard you ... I heard every word."

"Little pitchers has long ears," sneered Harry.

"You shouldn't dare ... you've no right," Claude spluttered.

"And you ain't got no right to spy on your elders and betters, Claudie," said Goatcher.

"You wait ... you just wait," Claude was nearly choking with rage and misery. "No one's going to laugh at my father. When I'm grown up, I'll show you, I will."

"Go it, Claudie," mocked Harry.

Goatcher gave him a cuff. "Leave the kid be. Claudie, you run along to your Ma."

Still muttering, "I'll show you," Claude had run, not to his mother but out into the garden. Up and down the lawn where he played his endless solitary games of croquet, the blue ball against the red, he had stumped with his eyes screwed up to keep the tears back and his hands clenched in the pockets of his home-made jacket. It was a blazing June day and he had never again been able to smell sweet peas or the faint reek of manure from a strawberry bed without remembering that afternoon. He had not been angry that day or any day since with his father, only with anyone who dared to jeer at him. Pacing furiously up and down the tiny parched lawn, he made up his mind that he would show, not merely Harry and Goatcher but the whole world, that Claude Batchelor's father was not to be laughed at. He would grow up as soon as he possibly could; he would work very hard so that he could look after his father and make everyone respect him.

He had kept his promise. The business at Hamling went bankrupt. Claude won a scholarship to Dulwich and his father, in partnership with a brother, opened another grocer's shop in the neighbourhood of the school. By the time Claude was sixteen the second business had also failed. While still a schoolboy himself, he set up as a coach to younger or less bright ones. He was so successful that he was soon able to raise his fees from a shilling to half-a-crown an hour.

After his second bankruptcy, Frederick Batchelor thankfully decided that he was not cut out for a business man. For some years he managed to get intermittent jobs in city offices. The exquisite copperplate writing which was his one accomplishment and the deafness which stopped him from wasting his employers' time in conversation made him an ideal copying clerk. But, after a few months in any firm, he would have one of his drinking spells, insult someone in authority and be dismissed.

As soon as Claude was established as a master at St Mark's, with a regular flow of private pupils, he had made his father give up all attempts to work. Long before he afforded himself any luxuries, even in the days when he had expected Isabel to dress on twenty pounds a year, it had been his joy to buy expensive things for Frederick Batchelor; silk socks, handmade shirts, good cigars to smoke after his Sunday lunch. No sooner had his father entered on this career of being spoilt and cherished than he gave up his drinking bouts. He thoroughly enjoyed an occasional glass of port or madeira but he never again touched spirits. Gradually he became exactly what Claude had always dreamt he should be, an extremely distinguished-looking old gentleman, known and respected throughout the neighbourhood. Tall and thin, with small bones and delicate hands, he had always seemed as out of place among the stocky, coarsely-built Batchelors as a crane in a flock of geese. As his hair grew white and his features still finer-drawn with age, the freakish elegance of his appearance l ecame more and more marked. He and Isabel took a connoisseur's interest in each other's looks and clothes. His wife, who had grown plainer and heavier with every year of marriage, he had regarded as an ugly, but indispensable piece of furniture. He did not share her almost idolatrous devotion to their son. He was fond of Claude, he was grateful to him, but there had always been a cool detachment about his gratitude. The only person for whom Frederick Batchelor had really put himself out was his granddaughter Clara. He had stood up for her, right or wrong, against parents, nurses and all other authorities. She had revived in him the one passionate affection he had ever felt, which had been neither for Ellen nor Claude but for his first child, a girl, who had lived eighteen months and died the day before his son was born.

It was to Clara that Claude's thoughts turned first when his tears had spent themselves. Would she be able to understand anything of what he felt? He banished the thought as a distraction and, staring with dry, aching eyes at the picture of the Virgin over the sombre altar, he tried to pray for his father's soul. But he was too exhausted to pray. He was no longer even aware of his grief. Weariness gave him a counterfeit peace. Where his heart should have been, there was nothing but a cold empty space. He forced himself to recite set prayers for the dead, saying them as if for a stranger. While one part of his mind carefully spelt out the De Profundis, another hunted distractedly for something to fill that cold space under his ribs. Again and again it came back to the thought of Clara. How would he find her when he returned home? Would she be unhappy? Would unhappiness melt the ice that had so imperceptibly formed between them? Would she turn to him for comfort as she used to do when she was a child? His forced prayer petered out. Images began to compose and dissolve in his mind as they do on the edge of sleep. He saw Clara shaking back her fair hair, smiling up at him, slipping her arm through his as she used to do long ago on their walks. Innocent images, yet suddenly he forced himself to check them. There is a point at which a dream, while still sweet, becomes menacing. He made himself inhabit the cool, scentless black and white chapel, for, in another second, he might have been kneeling in a different church.

Chapter 4

LATE in the afternoon, Clara arrived home. Isabel, whose quick ears had caught the first sound of the cab wheels, had slipped out of the room without warning Mrs Batchelor and was waiting in the hall.

"Darling," she exclaimed gaily, throwing her arms round her daughter. "How lovely to see something young and fresh."

Clara, still clutching her luggage, stood stiffly in her mother's embrace. All through the long drive from the Convent she had been nerving herself to face a grief-stricken family. Relieved, but a trifle shocked, she could only say lamely, "Hullo, Mummy." Then stooping down and fidgeting with her bag she muttered, "Is Daddy very upset?"

"Yes, darling, of course. But don't let's think about all those sad things yet. Come along up to my room where we can talk properly. It's so wonderful to have you home."

"Oughtn't I to see Daddy and Granny first?"

"Daddy is out," said Isabel, adding untruthfully, "Granny doesn't want to be disturbed."

Whispering, "Leave your luggage for Zillah", she almost ran up the stairs, pushing the child in front of her. On the second landing, Clara stopped outside her grandfather's room.

"Is he there?"

"Yes, pet, but don't go in."

"I know what dead people look like. I saw Mother Veronica at school."

Isabel shuddered.

"Really. I didn't know nuns were so morbid."

As she was hurrying Clara up the next flight, a plaintive voice called from the hall below,

"Is that little Clara?"

Isabel put her hand over Clara's mouth.

"There's no need to answer. You'll see her soon enough. I deserve to have you to myself for a moment after all I've been through."

In Isabel's bedroom the blinds were not drawn. After the gloom of the rest of the house it looked wantonly bright. The last sunshine poured in like shafts of limelight, striking prismatic sparks from the litter of silver and cut glass on the dressing-table and showing up the worn places on the carpet. Isabel had modelled the room on a description of a French actress's boudoir that she had once read in a novel. Now the satin-striped paper was yellowish with age and its blue garlands unevenly bleached; the veneer on the imitation Sheraton had begun to blister and the pink satin curtains sagged from their rings. During the time that Isabel had coloured her daydreams with Loti and Lafcadio Hearne, she had put fans and kakemonos on the walls and an incense burner among the china shepherds on the chimney-piece. On a small table in a corner stood a crucifix festooned with a rosary, an empty holy-water stoup and a dusty strip of blessed palm. Near it was a prie-dieu over which was flung a négligée trimmed with matted swansdown. The windows were open, for Isabel believed in fresh air, but the room still smelt of scorched hair, camphor and Shem-el-Nessim.

Isabel, breathless from her climb, went straight to her dressing-table and considered herself in the mirror as if scanning the face of a beloved invalid. She seemed to have forgotten all about Clara as she plunged a puff in a bowl and shook it out so vigorously that a cloud of scented dust mingled with the motes in the sun-shaft. Between dabs at her face she said defiantly:

"If I want to have the blinds up, I shall *have* the blinds up. If anyone is shocked, they can *be* shocked. Anyhow, she can't climb four flights."

Clara, who had taken up her stand by the bed, said nothing. She began to screw and unscrew one of the brass knobs of the bedstead. The huge bed with its black bars and polished rails was aggressively out of keeping with the rest of the room. It was an uncompromising middle-class late-Victorian bed, solid in workmanship and repulsive in design; planned to bear the weight of pregnancies, long illnesses and dead bodies.

Isabel wrenched herself from the mirror and faced Clara.

"Don't you think I'm perfectly right, darling?"

Clara blinked.

"Right about what?"

"Don't you ever listen to anything I say?"

"Sorry. I didn't realize you were talking to me. Yes, I expect so."

"Why on earth don't you sit down instead of standing there like a stranger?"

Clara bit her lip and went on screwing and unscrewing the brass knob.

"I'd rather not. I've been sitting for hours in that cab."

"I wish you wouldn't frown like that, darling. You'll ruin your nice forehead. Do you know you've got two quite definite lines over your nose already? And you're only fourteen."

"Nearly fifteen," Clara corrected her, still frowning.

Isabel gave a whimsical sigh.

"Imagine my having a daughter who's nearly grown-up ... or thinks she is. But I'm not going to be one of those horrid mothers who are jealous of their daughters. I want you to be as pretty as possible."

Clara blushed and made a face.

"It's no good, Mother. I'll never be pretty."

"You could be if you'd take a little trouble."

It was Clara's turn to sigh. The conversation was taking an all too familiar turn but she could think of nothing to say to deflect it.

"What's the matter, Clara?" Isabel asked impatiently. "Is it Grandfather or what? Of course it's very sad for *us* but we ought really to be glad for him."

"Yes, I expect so," said Clara politely without raising her long fine eyelashes.

"It's quite right and natural you should be sorry. He adored you. But I assure you you don't feel it any more than we do."

"Daddy will really mind most, won't he?"

"Yes, I daresay. It's such a dreadful thing to lose a parent. Of course I never knew my mother. She died when I was a tiny baby, poor thing. But I've felt the loss all my life. And I was only ten years older than you when my father died and I had no one. After all, Daddy still has Granny."

"You were married, though, weren't you?"

"Ah yes, darling. But no one can ever replace a parent. You'll realize that yourself some day. A *long* time hence, let's hope."

Clara became very intent on the knob.

"We shall both have to be very kind to poor Daddy, shan't we?"

Clara seemed not to have heard but she gave the knob such a violent twist that it came right off.

"Sorry. I can put it back." She began to do so.

"That wretched bed. I wouldn't mind if you pulled the whole thing to bits. But it seems to be indestructible like all ugly things."

"Granny and Grandfather gave it you for a wedding present, didn't they?"

"Of course they did. I've told you so a hundred times. It's got Granny's appalling taste written all over it. Really, darling, you seem very absent-minded today."

Clara made a great effort and brought her mind into focus. For the first time she opened her eyes wide and looked intelligently at her mother. The eyes were neither blue like Claude's nor brown like Isabel's, but a changeable grey flecked with hazel. When she opened them (she had a habit of keeping her lids half-closed) her whole face came to life.

"I suppose," she said, "that on the whole you'd really rather it was Granny who died."

Isabel looked away. "Clara ... what a wicked thing to say. As if I'd wish anybody dead!"

"Still, if one had to choose," said Clara undaunted, "I've been thinking the same thing myself."

"You naughty little thing."

"Not that I've anything against Granny. But if someone had to ..."

Isabel smiled.

"Well, darling, since you've said it. If someone had to ..." She gave Clara a confiding look. "It's very alarming sometimes to have an intelligent daughter. But sometimes it's rather nice. It's something we'd never dare to say to Daddy, isn't it? Though I shouldn't be surprised if he felt just the same."

"Was it Daddy who wanted me to come home? Or everybody?"

"I didn't want it, darling. I longed to see you, of course, but if I'd had my way, you shouldn't have been let in for all this. Mothers understand some things better than fathers, don't you think? I've always said, in spite of everything, you were just as sensitive as I am."

Clara was staring out of the window. She watched a pigeon flapping across the sky. The cement urns on the balustrade opposite were a rosy ochre in the late afternoon light.

"It's still missing," she said suddenly.

"What? What's missing?"

33

"The urn that fell off last holidays. Don't they ever put them back?"

"Nothing is ever put back in this neighbourhood. West Kensington is going down and down. But of course I can't persuade Daddy to move. There's a charming little house in Edwardes Square that I've got my eye on. Only there wouldn't be room for Granny. So that's out of the question. I *had* hoped that now she would want to go and live at Paget's Fold with the aunts."

"I don't think they'd get on very well, would they?" said Clara cautiously.

"They're her sisters. They're her own generation. Why should I have to put up with it all the best years of my life? Just think, Clara. Never to be able to have one's own way in the smallest thing. It's not as if I wanted much. A little white house with green shutters and window boxes and furnished as I like it instead of with their horrible old things."

"Yes, it would be fun," Clara agreed.

"I knew you'd understand. You've got my artistic tastes. The Batchelors haven't the faintest feeling for that kind of thing."

Clara said with sudden anxiety, "Will Daddy be home soon?"

"Not till dinner-time, I expect."

"We should hear the door if he did, shouldn't we? Even up here?"

"Certainly. If he makes his usual clattering. But he's not at all like himself today. It's rather dreadful to see him."

Clara turned white.

"What on earth am I to say to him?"

"Just be your nicest, most natural little self. You can be a very sweet Clara when you want to be."

"I'd better go down and get washed and changed, hadn't I?"

"There's heaps of time. Why are you always so anxious to run away from me? All this time you've been standing there like a statue, obviously dying to get away. You haven't so much as taken off your hat and coat."

Clara obediently pulled off her outdoor clothes and threw them on the bed. Her face was blank and set. The tight felt hat had flattened her hair and left a jagged red mark like a scar across her forehead. She stood there stiffly in her high-necked, long-skirted uniform dress of navy serge as if before a tribunal.

"Why on earth are you wearing your school uniform?" Isabel demanded.

"The nuns made me. That bright blue thing I went back in doesn't exactly look like mourning, does it?"

"That awful serge. It's dreary enough to wear at the funeral."

"Oh, Mother. It's dark blue, not proper black."

"I suppose Daddy will insist. Whatever *can* you wear?"

"There's my new best dress, the black velvet. Only we'd have to take off the red sash and the lace collar."

"Ruining it, of course. Still, I've had to ruin my lovely hat from Cécile's."

"I'll go and get it, shall I?" said Clara, brightening at the thought of even a brief escape. For the last few months it had been misery for her to be alone with either of her parents. It was all the worse because she had no idea why this was and Clara was always frightened by anything she could not explain. There seemed to be a new creature growing up inside her, something still unformed and skinless that could not bear to be exposed to the light. The thoughts that nourished this inner self were too sacred or too silly to be told to her father or mother and the mysterious creature was insistent, resenting interruptions and demanding constant attention. When she heard her mother say "All right, darling," she gave a radiant smile of gratitude on behalf of the mysterious creature and almost danced out of the room.

No sooner had she gone than Isabel opened a drawer in her dressing-table and pulled out a paper-covered book from its hiding-place under a heap of crumpled underclothes. The book was called "The Diary of a Lost One". On the cover was the picture of a man wearing evening clothes, an opera cloak, and the ribbon of an order, embracing a woman whose blue kimono had slipped off one bare shoulder. Quickly she found the page she had turned down and began to read. Immediately she was absorbed. She had read nearly a chapter of the cramped, broken print before she heard Clara's step on the stairs. In a flash another corner was turned down, the book slipped under the heap of underclothes and the drawer closed. When Clara came in with her dress her mother was sitting staring into space, her hands clasped in her lap.

"Sorry I was so long. I ran into Granny."

"Were you long, pet?" said Isabel with her sad smile. "I was thinking. I'm so used to sitting alone and thinking that I sometimes forget all about time."

"It will be quite easy to alter," said Clara briskly. She spoke more stoically than she felt. The black velvet dress meant a great deal to her; it was the first she had ever been allowed to choose for herself. For once she had enlisted her mother's support against her father. Claude had wanted her to have a childish blue cashmere. The old Clara would cheerfully have agreed but the mysterious creature had a craving for something grown-up and sophisticated and the mysterious creature was unscrupulous when it wanted something. The dress was cut almost like one of Isabel's, in a proper 1914 fashion, tight-fitting and short-sleeved with a frill of creamy lace at the neck and a vivid crimson sash. When Clara put it on, she felt at least nineteen and walked and spoke quite differently. In her bedroom she had even tried the effect with her plaits wound round her head, and, in a glass that did not show her legs, it seemed to her that she looked completely grown-up.

"The lace, the dash of colour, they're the making of it," said Isabel with real concern. "Poor Clara."

Clara assured her carelessly that it didn't matter and she didn't mind. But, though nothing would have induced her to show it, she was glad of her mother's sympathy.

"You're my daughter in one thing, anyhow. You do like pretty clothes."

"Most of us do at the convent," said Clara, withdrawing again. "I expect it comes of wearing ghastly uniforms all the time."

"Take the horrid thing off and we'll try your frock on."

"There's no point, is there? I've only got to unpick the trimmings."

"I want to try the effect of a rather nice piece of black frilling I might let you have."

"I'm sure it will do beautifully. There's no need to try the thing on."

"Darling, you really are maddening, the way you argue over every tiny thing. You'd never dream of behaving like that with Daddy. Do as I tell you at once."

Clara frowned and flushed as she began very slowly to unhook her high stiff collar.

"Absurd child. I believe you're shy of your own mother. It's these convent ideas I suppose. Nuns must have very peculiar minds."

"It's nothing to do with the nuns," said Clara uncomfortably. "I'm sure to have a hole in my petticoat or something."

She finished unhooking her uniform and stepped out of it in her

36

white cotton petticoat and black woollen stockings. Isabel studied the immature body as if measuring it against her own finished curves. She herself was not tall, but she was so well-proportioned and held her head so high on her long neck that she appeared so. Neither was she slight. Her small bones were cushioned with flesh firm as just-ripened fruit. But her tapering wrists and ankles, and the light way she moved all helped to give an impression of slenderness.

There was no sign that the child standing there so stiffly, dangling her long frail arms would ever develop that sleek, harmonious shape. Though Clara was still thin, she was squarely-built, like her father, with broad shoulders and hips. The slender arms and legs were oddly matched with the heavier bones of the torso; she seemed to have the body of one person and the limbs of another. There were the same elements of lightness and heaviness in her face. Its contours, compared with Isabel's perfect oval, were carelessly drawn and her features contradicted each other. Her hair, brushed severely back, showed a high masculine forehead and small feminine ears. The modelling round the eyes was delicate but the dented obstinate chin and the blunt tip of the otherwise well-drawn nose seemed to have been added by a coarser hand. According to her mood, her face could look vivid, almost beautiful, or dull. The transformation was sometimes so sudden that in a moment not only the contours, but the size and colour of the eyes and even the texture of the skin would appear entirely different.

Now, as she stood exposed to her mother's critical stare, her body looked its most awkward and her face its most sullen and lifeless.

"You've grown," Isabel said at last after surveying her daughter point by point. "Just as well, perhaps. You'll need to be tall to carry off those hips and shoulders. Why, oh why, my pet, did you have to inherit the Batchelor torso? Thank goodness you've got decent arms and legs. You've got me to thank for those."

Clara put up a slender, ill-kept hand and fidgeted with her shoulder straps. Against the whiteness of her arms, the rough, reddened skin was as conspicuous as a glove.

"You must do something about your hands," Isabel scolded. "You can't have been using that lotion I gave you to take back to school."

"Not allowed to," said Clara with a gleam of a smile.

"Oh, these nuns ... these nuns ..." wailed Isabel, rolling her splendid eyes. "And look at the dreadful way they do your hair. A noble brow is all very well but there are limits. Your hair's easily your best point."

She pulled off the ribbons and untwisted the two thick plaits and drew the long rippling strands forward all about Clara's face and shoulders. The hair was thick and silky, almost pure gold in colour.

"Now you look more like my pretty child. But you'll deform your lower lip if you keep biting it like that. That petticoat needs letting out. You'll spoil your figure for life if you go on wearing it so tight across the chest."

"I'll put the black dress on," said Clara, blushing. She struggled ungracefully into it before her mother could make any more criticisms. When her head emerged, pink-cheeked and tangled, she looked an entirely different creature in spite of her red hands and heavy shoes and stockings. Against the black velvet sheath her arms and neck were very white and the mass of hair made her face seem small and soft.

"And people say clothes don't make a difference," cried Isabel. "Just come and look at yourself."

Clara let her mother drag her to the long glass. She wanted to go on looking sulky but the dress would not let her. In spite of herself, she smiled. She had an attractive, mischievous smile and a dimple in one cheek.

"Go on. Look at yourself," insisted her mother.

Clara looked with pretended indifference but found she wanted to go on looking. The flushed girl in the glass with the loose, shining hair and the white neck was like a stranger.

"Of course it looks ridiculous with these shoes and stockings," she said in a new grown-up voice.

"Thank goodness you're not *all* brains, my pet," said Isabel kissing her. Clara accepted the kiss without flinching.

From downstairs came the faint crash of the front door. Clara froze like a scared rabbit.

"It's Daddy," she said. All the life and colour had gone out of her face. She made for the door. "I must fly. He might be coming up here."

"Don't be so silly. Whatever does it matter?"

"I couldn't possibly let him see me like this. Not today."

"Clara! Really, you're behaving as if you were out of your mind. Anyone would think you'd been doing something disgraceful."

But Isabel found herself protesting to an empty room. She went out on to the landing and called angrily "Clara". There was no answer.

38

In a burst of fury she took the girl's hat and coat and flung them after her down the stairs. Then she went back into the room and, having exchanged her usual questioning glance with her reflection, drew the curtains. She returned to the mirror again and sat for some moments, staring at herself and fingering the orchids on her dress. At last, with a sigh, she unpinned them, went over to the washstand and splashed some water into a glass. She took the orchids over to the little table in the corner and with a face, half penitent, half mischievous, placed them in front of the crucifix.

Chapter 5

OON after dinner, Isabel yawned and said she was too tired
to stay up any longer. Old Mrs Batchelor had already gone to
bed and the three others were sitting in Claude's study. Clara
tried to make her escape at the same time but her father held her back.

"I won't keep you up long," he said, as he closed the door behind
Isabel and sat down again at his desk. He signed to her to take the
armchair near him that her mother had left empty but Clara, appearing not to notice, went back to her corner. Barricaded from him by
the two great desks that stood back to back and half-filled the room
she felt safer.

"You'll forgive me if I just finish correcting this prose?"

"Of course, Daddy," she said, thankful for the respite.

He nodded, shook some red drops from his fountain pen and went
on ringing and underlining words in the exercise book before him.
There was no sound but the ticking of the clock and the soft scratching
of the nib. Clara sat rigidly in her corner between two bookshelves
and wondered why she had not the courage to tiptoe over to the door
and slip out. This was the moment she had been dreading ever since
the arrival of the telegram. She was hardly yet able to feel sorry that
her grandfather was dead. All her affection was overlaid with resentment at his having exposed her to this unbearable situation. She shut
her eyes, trying hopelessly to persuade herself that the whole thing
was a dream. She even prayed wildly for a miracle. She knew perfectly
well that her crazy prayer would not be heard, yet, in spite of herself,
she held her breath and strained her ears to catch some sound from
her grandfather's room overhead; the impatient tap of his stick on the
wall or his muffled cry of "Ellen!" She still heard nothing but the clock
and the metallic whisper of the pen.

When she opened her eyes again, the room, hazy with smoke, swam
a little. Objects which she had known ever since she could remember
seemed threatening, like things distorted in nightmare. The shelves
filled with dingy bindings and black files, the dusty plaster casts of
Plato and Athene, even the great faded plush armchair were all hostile.

The smell of tobacco, ink and old leather which made up the permanent atmosphere of the study oppressed her like a drug. She felt her arms and legs growing thick and heavy and her eyes stiffening in their sockets. But why, she kept asking herself, should she be in such a state simply because she was alone with the person she cared for more than anyone in the world? Only a few months ago they had been companions and conspirators; her greatest delight had been to steal half an hour with him when her mother was not there. She had even wished that something terrible would happen to him so that she could prove how much she loved him. Now it had come and she felt nothing but terror and distaste. She glanced at his tired face, bent over the prose he was so methodically correcting. Why could she not get up this minute, go over and put her arms round him and say the perfect comforting words?

As if he felt the impact of her look, he stopped writing and raised his head. Then he screwed the cap on his pen and, with the gesture she knew so well, planted it upright in the bowl of lead shot in front of him.

"Come and sit over here, Clara."

Reluctantly she moved into the great armchair that stood beside his desk. Its high padded sides hedged her in like a prisoner's dock; the light overhead poured mercilessly down on her face.

"You look white, my dear," he said, considering her with kind, glazed eyes. "This is a sad homecoming for you."

It's much worse for you," she said in a high, artificial voice. To avoid his look, she stared straight ahead at the row of photographs on the mantelshelf. They stared back at her like the cardboard audience in a toy circus she had once had and their familiar faces seemed to have the same disquieting look of expectancy. They watched her with cynical interest, waiting for her to fall from the trapeze. The one that mocked her most was a photo of herself at seven which she had always hated. Isabel, wearing flowing skirts and a great feathered hat, sat gracefully on a property balustrade and she herself stood beside her mother, stiff as a sentinel in her kindergarten gym tunic and an absurd hussar cap. The sight of that cap always embarrassed her though once she had been so proud of it that she had slept with it on her pillow. Now the stolid, glowering child, whose only trouble had been that she could never be a colonel of hussars, sneered at her from her security.

"Are you wondering where *his* photo is?" her father asked kindly.

"I know it's very weak of me. But just for a day or two I felt I couldn't bear it."

His voice faltered. For a moment she feared that he was going to break down in front of her. Anger and reproaches she could bear but not that. Clutching the arms of the chair, she held her breath and began to count slowly as she always did when undergoing an ordeal. She knew she was expected to say something but no words would come. Why couldn't he understand without being told that there was nothing she would not do, cut her hair off, hold her hand in the fire, if it would give him any comfort? Why couldn't he realize that the one impossible thing was to speak?

The whirr of the clock striking half-past nine gave her a scrap of courage. Time was still moving on, however slowly. At some point it must release her. She glanced at her father; he was apparently absorbed in stuffing tobacco into his pipe. He pressed the shreds down firmly with his short white fingers, using, as he always did when he handled things, a little more force than was necessary.

"Your mother," he said, after the long pause, clearing his throat, "Your mother does not agree with me."

"What about, Daddy?"

"That you are old enough to be with us all just now. She thinks it would have been better to leave you at the convent. What's your own opinion?"

"Of course I'd rather have come," she lied.

"I hope you like the idea of his being buried in Sussex."

"Oh, yes, I think it's a very nice idea." She was lying again. Ever since she had heard it discussed at dinner, she had been hating the thought that the funeral was to be associated with Paget's Fold, the one place she connected only with happiness. Worse still was the thought of a slow, fifty-mile drive, sitting in silence, watching his miserable face.

"After all, he was a Sussex man. The churchyard at Rookfield is full of his and your grandmother's people. It seems only right for him to be with them."

"Yes, of course. How will the aunts manage with all those people?"

He eyed her a trifle severely.

"They will rise to the occasion as they always do. You know how wonderfully unselfish they are. They seem to take a real pleasure in putting themselves out for other people."

"Yes, don't they?" she said almost brightly. She went on to ask some perfunctory questions about the arrangements, hardly listening to the answers. What was it he had really kept her back for? Soon she could feel that her careless questions were beginning to irritate him. Perhaps it would be a good thing to let him get angry with her. After all, she was used to that. When he was annoyed, he spared her no more than his other pupils. She had been through plenty of bad moments of that kind in this very room and she could bear those. She whispered to herself *"un mauvais quart d'heure"*, unaware that her lips were moving, though she felt a muscle twitch in her cheek and put up her hand to hide a silly, nervous smile.

"Were you going to say something, Clara?"

"No, Daddy, really."

Try as she would, she could not control her face. She knew it had taken on the expression he most disliked, with her eyelids drooped and her lips, in the effort to keep from trembling, set in a superior smile.

"You were looking at the clock. Perhaps you would like to go to bed."

Not daring to say "Yes" she shook her head.

He sucked at his pipe.

"I'm inclined to think your mother was right after all when she said you were too young to understand the meaning of death."

Caught off her guard, Clara said contemptuously,

"As if Mother knew everything about me."

"That is not the tone to use when you speak of your mother."

He drew fiercely at his pipe. When he spoke again he had mastered his annoyance.

"I was thoughtless enough at your age, heaven knows. And long after. But it wasn't till today that I realized how bitterly one regrets the things one might have done for a person and didn't do."

"But you were always so good to Grandfather," she said warily. "Everyone said so. He was always saying so himself."

"Never good enough. Never good enough." He sighed, "My dear child, if I only knew how to spare you that kind of remorse."

She made a great effort to meet him.

"It's so difficult sometimes," she said, speaking almost naturally, "to know what other people *do* want."

He re-lit his pipe.

"It's usually obvious enough if one takes the trouble. I don't want to give the impression that your mother has been complaining. Far from it. But couldn't you make a little more effort?"

Clara froze again.

"I'll write oftener from school if you like."

"I know she would like you to be rather more affectionate in your manner towards her. She is devoted to you and often, I am sure, she feels lonely. I have so little time to give her. You're old enough now to be a real companion for her."

Was it possible he had kept her back only to talk on the old theme of her behaviour to her mother? In her relief she said warmly,

"I *will* try to be nicer."

"There's another thing, Clara. Your grandmother. Life is going to be difficult for her now."

Without stopping to think, she said,

"Because of Mummy, do you mean?"

He frowned.

"I certainly meant nothing of the kind. That was a singularly uncalled-for remark."

"Sorry."

"Granny had never had much to make her happy. Now she is a widow, there isn't much for her to live for. She's so pathetically grateful for every half-hour you spend with her."

Clara began to long more than ever for the day when she could get back to school. Though the discipline was strict and every minute of her time parcelled out and supervised, she felt free there. In the enforced silences of the convent day the mysterious creature could breathe and grow. At home, to be silent was taken for a sign that one was sulking. However full, however empty one's mind, one was expected endlessly to be making conversation. Forgetting everything but herself for the moment she said out loud:

"It must be rather a blessing sometimes to be deaf."

He glared at her.

"That would be an extremely impertinent remark at the best of times. But with my father lying dead ..."

"Oh," she broke in, appalled, "I'd forgotten about Grandfather's being deaf. Truly I wasn't thinking about Grandfather. Or Granny either."

Claude's nostrils expanded with anger.

"Apparently not. Or about anything that I have been saying to you

44

tonight. You seem to be incapable of thinking of anyone but your-self."

"Oh, Daddy, please, I didn't mean it."

"You had better to go bed, Clara. I apologize for having kept you up."

She tried to speak but her lips began to quiver uncontrollably. Without warning, she suddenly burst into loud childish sobs. For some moments she cried so convulsively that she did not hear him come over to her or feel his hand on her hair.

"Clara, my dear little girl," he said in a shy, gentle voice, "Clara, my dear."

She let him soothe her but she would not rest against his shoulder. She sat rigid, fumbling for her handkerchief, as wary as an animal that submits to fondling from fear.

"Don't cry any more." He smiled wanly. "Or should I say do cry? They say it helps."

She blew her nose violently and rubbed her fist over her eyes. Her forehead was covered with red blotches and her eyelids swollen as if they had been stung by wasps. Clara had never been able to weep otherwise than awkwardly and explosively.

"I *hate* crying," she gasped.

"Don't be ashamed of your feelings, my dear. They're right and natural. You were really fond of him, weren't you?"

She groaned inwardly. How could he imagine she was crying about her grandfather? There was nothing to do but nod her head and mutter,

"Awfully fond."

He sat down once more at his desk. Taking one of the three pens from the bowl in front of him he began mechanically to jab it in and out of the shot.

"He was a remarkable man," he said softly. "Too delicate in all his tastes and instincts for the kind of life he was born to. When I was a little boy I used to think of him as a prince in disguise."

Clara's tears were locked back now. She could trust herself not to break out again. But she was beaten and could now only play for favour.

"I've only seen a prince once. Hedwig von Eisenspach's father. He was awfully disappointing. Very short and fat. Grandfather looked as they ought to look."

She was vile, she told herself, seeing her father's face brighten. She

45

had said nothing about some quality in the little fat man which made her grandfather's brittle handsomeness and his famous "manners" show up as mere gimcrack.

"It pleased him so much," said Claude, "to think you should be at school with a real princess. Often I can hardly believe it myself when I think of my own childhood."

"She's not a bit exciting really. Oh, I know what you mean. It seems queer to me too. Everyone's awfully nice to me but I know I don't really belong."

She looked at him anxiously, wondering if, once again, she had said the wrong thing.

"Perhaps I made a mistake," he said thoughtfully. "Perhaps I should never have sent you to a school where the other children have such a much more impressive background. Ever since we became Catholics, it was my dream to send you to Mount Hilary. But was it fair? I should be very much distressed if you came in any way to look down on *his* people. Or your grandmother's."

"I'm awfully fond of the aunts and Uncle John Hoadley. And Blaze. Oh, lots of them," she said evasively.

"I'm counting on you to be your nicest, most natural self on Thursday. With everyone, even Aunt Louie and Cousin Horace. I don't deny I find those two a little trying, myself."

"Am I usually so awful with them?" sighed Clara, deflated by the image of that nicest, most natural self she could never recognize well enough to impersonate.

"No, of course not. I just wanted to ask you to make a special effort ... for *his* sake. Thursday will be a particularly trying day for your mother. You know how sensitive she is. So many things jar on her."

"I do understand," she said, realizing that he was appealing to her. "I'll make an extra special effort."

In spite of herself, she could not help yawning.

"You seem very tired." It sounded like an accusation.

Swallowing another yawn she brought out bravely,

"Was there something special you wanted to say to me, Daddy?"

"As a matter of fact there was. But, as you seem so sleepy, perhaps we'd better leave it. It was just an idea I had."

"Please do tell me."

It was his turn to be embarrassed.

46

"I didn't quite like to suggest it even to your mother. You see, on religious matters, you're my authority. You are being trained in Catholic ways as neither your mother nor myself were able to be."

Clara waited apprehensively. Only last year she had still been quite unselfconscious with him about religion. Lately in the holidays she had tried to avoid going to church alone with him. Religion had become part of her most secret life; it was deeply concerned with one aspect of the mysterious creature.

"And how happy it makes me," he went on, "to know that you are being so well grounded in the Faith. I don't know when I've felt so grateful, so deeply impressed as on the day of your First Communion. If ever I were to suffer from doubts, I think it would be enough to remember the look on your face that morning."

"What did you want to ask me, Daddy? she said stolidly.

"Even though he wasn't a Catholic, would there be any objection to reciting the Office of the Dead for him?"

"Oh no. I can't see any reason why you shouldn't." Her voice was quite cheerful with relief. Whatever it was she had feared was not going to happen after all. She had worked herself up into a panic for nothing. She stood up. "Do you mind if I say good night, now, Daddy darling?"

He looked disappointed.

"Not, of course, if you're too tired. But my idea was that the two of us should go up and say it together ... beside him."

She was so horrified that she could only echo blankly,

"Say it together beside him?"

"Isn't that what you did at the convent when your Mother Veronica died?"

How could she explain the difference? She thought of the noble impersonality of that office chanted by the whole community in the chapel and she pictured the two of them kneeling in the cramped space by her grandfather's great bed. They would share a book; they would mutter the psalms self-consciously and stumble over the responses. She had a cruel impulse to cry out "You have no sense of fitness."

"Well, Clara, what do you say?"

She could only stare at him beseechingly.

"What is it, my dear? Are you afraid? He looks so peaceful, there is nothing frightening. But the last thing I want to do is to harrow your feelings."

Her look of desperation was almost impudent as she said, "No, of course I'm not afraid."

He stood up, pulled open a drawer and took out a black-bound book. Then, drawing her arm through his, he said,

"Thank you, my dear. We'll go up at once, shall we?"

Chapter 6

OLD Mrs Batchelor's two sisters, the Misses Sayers, did not attend the funeral. They stayed behind at Paget's Fold to put the last touches to the cold luncheon which had taken them two days of anxious work to prepare. Cooking over oil burners in their dark stone-flagged kitchen, they had baked hams, roasted chickens and strained jellies till they were nearly worn out. It was the responsibility rather than the work that had tired them. They felt that Claude had conferred a great honour on them and had a custard been burnt or piecrust heavy, Miss Leah and Miss Sophy would have blamed themselves all the rest of their lives.

Though the old ladies were sixty-eight and sixty-seven respectively and had lived at Paget's Fold since they were born, they never forgot that the house was not their own. Ellen had made it over to Claude on his twenty-first birthday and they looked on themselves simply as his caretakers. As he would not hear of their paying rent, they went to endless trouble to save him money on repairs. If a pane broke or a door came off its hinges, Miss Sophy got out her grandfather's old tools (he had been the village carpenter in the eighteen-thirties) and mended it according to the directions in "Enquire Within Upon Everything". Their joint income was about forty pounds a year but, sooner than accept the help Claude was only too willing to give them, they made a little extra money by teaching and dressmaking. Miss Leah, the elder, taught spelling and arithmetic to the children of the vicarage and the bigger farms; Miss Sophy made dresses for the women for miles around. Her knack of fitting even the clumsiest figure and the beautiful finish of her work (her stitching was as neat and firm as a Frenchwoman's) kept up the demand in spite of the alluring ready-mades to be bought in Horsham and Brighton. Farmers driving in to Steyning market from other parishes would drop their womenfolk at Paget's Fold to plan or try on their new clothes. The dresses took her many evenings of hard work, for she was busy in house and garden all day, but, even for the most elaborate, she refused to charge more than five shillings. She and Leah could therefore never relax from the minute economy they had practised ever since they could remember. Their economy had nothing dreary about it for they had long ago turned it into an ingenious game.

They managed to find a use for the humblest and most unpromising objects. Old cotton reels were painted and converted into blind-cord tassels; corrugated paper was cut into strips, varnished and stuck round the walls as a dado or made into frames for pictures cut from the Christmas annuals. Even a cork had possibilities; fitted with a crochet jacket it became a decorative wasp-crusher. If Claude sent his aunts a box of chocolates, the chocolates themselves (eaten at the rate of two a day) were only part of the treasures they found in it. Each piece of tinfoil was carefully smoothed out to be used later to adorn a mirror-frame or hair-tidy; the paper shavings were kept for packing flowers, the ribbon trimmed their hats or tied back their lace curtains and the box itself did duty for years.

Leah, the elder, was thin, tense and earnest. She loved to store her mind with pellets of information from old encyclopaedias and magazines. In looks she was quite unlike either of her sisters. Her face, worn down almost to the bone, was narrow and well-shaped; her eyes, set in deep, shadowed sockets, were large and still bright and she had beautiful hair of a colour between flaxen and silver. Even when she was wearing her shabbiest working clothes and her garden clogs, she managed to preserve an air of frail elegance. When she was not looking anxious or disapproving, she had a charming faintly mischievous expression which was apt to mislead people into thinking that she had a great sense of humour. They soon found that the point of every joke had to be carefully explained to her and that she usually found it either cruel or ill-bred.

Miss Sophy, on the contrary, was plump, lively, quick-tempered and fond of a joke, good or bad. She thought Leah a paragon of learning and greatly admired her though she pretended to despise "bookishness". She read a great deal herself but in a way she never dared to own to Leah. Her one delicious indulgence was to retire to the bedroom they had shared since they were children, take a novelette and bury herself, till she was interrupted, in the loves of dukes and mill girls and the sins of high society.

Now and then the two old sisters pecked each other. Sophy would scold Leah for her didactic slowness and Leah Sophy for her frivolity but these birdlike scuffles did not affect their content with each other.

They had become like a devoted, long-married couple, more amused than disturbed by their differences and resigned to the fact that neither could share the other's most passionate interest.

As the passing bell sounded, now clear, now muffled, carried on the gusts of the March wind from the church half a mile away, Miss Leah sighed.

"You should have gone to the service, Leah," said Miss Sophy. "I could have managed perfectly well by myself."

"I don't deny I should have liked to go. But I couldn't leave you single-handed."

"Two hands are better than four sometimes. I know you meant kindly, Leah, but you've been absent-minded all morning."

"I'm sorry about the jelly glass," said Miss Leah with dignity. "I forgot how rapidly glass expands and that if the expansion occurs unevenly ..."

"You poured the jelly in too hot, dear," said Sophy briskly.

"No doubt I was careless, Sophy. Yet little accidents like that always make me think that a genius might have made them the occasion of some great discovery. If James Watt's mother had not let the kettle overboil ..."

"I know. I know. We might never have had railways. A good thing too. Look at all the poor people who get killed because of them. I don't believe God meant us to go prying and peering into every-thing."

"God would not have given us the faculty of discovery, surely, if He had not intended us to use it," said Leah with mild severity.

"You clever ones have an answer for everything," retorted Sophy. She was shocked to find herself scrapping with Leah on such a morning but she was tired and nervous. "What about Adam and Eve? They wanted to know more than was good for them and look at the result of that."

"Sophy, dear, I don't think we should let ourselves get involved in argument just now, do you?"

"Very well, Leah. Though you always say that when I'm getting the best of it." Sophy put her head on one side, like a listening bird. "Hark! The bell's stopped ringing."

"It stopped many minutes ago," asserted Leah.

"No. Only a moment. Your hearing isn't what it was."

"My hearing is still excellent, Sophy," said Leah, nettled for the first time. Sophy smiled but the smile vanished immediately and her faded, violet-blue eyes turned moist.

"Poor Fred," she said softly. "Sometimes when the wind was in the south like it is today he could just make out the sound of the church bells. Oh, the wickedness of that schoolmaster. Fancy boxing a little boy's ears so hard as to make him deaf for life."

Her round face, crumpled yet glossy like a yellow apple that has only just begun to shrivel, was streaked with indignant pink.

"I am sure he never meant to do such dreadful harm. One has occasionally to punish children, boys especially. I myself ..."

"Nonsense, Leah. As if you'd ever done more than rap their knuckles with a pencil."

Miss Leah sighed. "I daresay I have often hit harder than I should. I have no right to judge."

"And it's not only the deafness that man will have to answer for," said Miss Sophy, roused as she always was by any injustice: "Who knows but what Fred's little weakness may have come from that? Think how cut off he must have felt. I wouldn't like to be that school-master in the next world."

Miss Leah sighed again. After a moment she said timidly,

"Sophy, if you meant what you said just now ... that you can do the little finishing touches without me ... would you mind if I went up to our room and read the burial service to myself?"

"You couldn't do anything better. Go along, dear."

When she had gone, Sophy slipped back into the pantry, lifted the huge trifle from the cool brick floor where it had been standing all night and began decorating it with almonds and angelica. They had made just such a trifle for Fred and Ellen's wedding. She could see Ellen now with her plump narrow shoulders emerging from the frilled white petticoat and smell the hair-oil and the hot tongs on the chestnut ringlets as her sister bent down, stabbed a finger in the cream and licked it.

"Oh, you greedy," Sophy muttered, just as if Ellen were still stand-ing beside her. She had made Ellen's wedding dress; even at twenty that figure had been a problem to fit. Leah had been the pretty one, slender and white skinned, with big grey eyes and silky flaxen hair, yet no one had ever come near making her an offer. Sophy had often wondered why. Perhaps it was because she looked so delicate (their father had died young of consumption) and men did not want a sickly wife; perhaps merely because she frightened them with her air of aloofness and her bookish talk. Ellen was the only one who had determined to get a husband and succeeded. No doubt the tiny property had helped. Paget's Fold belonged to her and she owned fields and cottages that brought in about a hundred a year; she had flirted confidently till the day she set eyes on Fred Batchelor, the handsomest young man any of them had ever seen. How plain, how dull, how crushed she had become after all these years of marriage. When they were girls, Ellen had been bold and jolly, always giggling and tossing her chestnut ringlets, endlessly in trouble with Mamma over her behaviour with young men. She read the poems of Byron in secret; she got love-letters from the most unsuitable people; she made Leah and Sophy blush with her speculations about marriage and childbirth. Now not a trace of the old Ellen was left. Coarseness and liveliness alike had vanished with her flushed cheeks and bouncing curls, leaving a dreary pasty-faced old woman in a brown wig. In their childhood, Leah had been the one with the daring imagination. It was she who had planned their wildest escapades and practical jokes. Sophy could see her now, thin and long-legged, fearless as a gipsy, with her red cloak flying and her arms and legs always covered with bruises and scratches. She had become her present serious self almost overnight when she was fifteen, after Papa's death. Nothing remained of that other Leah but the faint mischievous expression that puzzled people so much. Carefully arranging the angelica in a lattice pattern (it had been circles for the wedding and, you never knew, Ellen might remember), Sophy realized that she had changed as much as her sisters. For, as a child, she had been quiet, shy and dull, tagging mutely after the others, not understanding their jokes and games, happiest sitting alone in her little chair with a picture book or a kitten. Now of all three she was the liveliest, hating to sit still, longing for someone to share her sense of fun, gay with people she knew though the old fits of shyness and melancholy often caught her in the company of strangers. Oddest of all, she had become the one to whom Leah and Ellen deferred on practical matters. Characteristically she put this down to her own faulty nature and often scolded herself about it. "It can only be because you're so obstinate" she told herself. "If Leah weren't so unworldly and Ellen so meek, they'd never give way as they do."

The trifle was ready and she carried it carefully to its place of honour on the sideboard. Paget's Fold had been built for a small farm-house and the room they used for meals and all ordinary purposes had once been a large, stone-flagged kitchen. The front door, shielded by a threefold screen pasted all over with scraps, opened straight into it, as did also the doors to the stairs, the tiny dim green parlour, the dark kitchen that had been bakehouse and washhouse and the brick-floored pantry that still looked and smelt like a dairy. In spite of the draughts that eddied through these five old ill-fitting doors, the main room was as cosy as years of loving accumulation could make it. Layer on layer of wallpaper padded the walls till they were soft to the touch though the hardness of the stone floor could still be felt under the rag and patchwork rugs that almost covered the faded carpet Isabel had discarded ten years ago as too shabby for Valetta Road. Every chair had a flat plush cushion tied on with tapes to conceal its bareness; the old sofa was heaped with cushions stuffed with feathers laboriously collected from the green outside. Miss Sophy, straightening spoons and knives for the last time looked round it with affectionate pride. There was not an object in it which she did not love, from the pot of musk on the bamboo table in front of the hermetically sealed window to the spotty steel engraving of the execution of Strafford that hung over the sideboard. But at the thought of the strange eyes that would be soon looking and criticizing, her shyness returned. She was seized with a panicky desire to run away and avoid the whole thing. Then she reminded herself that Isabel and Clara would be there and her courage came back. They were her special favourites; Isabel even more than Clara now that the child was growing up so quickly. Claude's wife seemed like one of the heroines of her paper-backed novels come to life and Isabel repaid her devotion with an uncritical tenderness she showed to no one else. Isabel would support her and snub those loud-voiced Batchelor relatives who were "rising" in the world and inclined to treat herself and Leah as figures of fun.

She glanced at the old grandfather clock; its dial, duck-egg green with age and covered with fine cracks, showed that it was nearly one. At any moment now the funeral party might return. The clock was still a person to her as it had been when she was a child; its heavy resonant tick sounded through the house like the beat of a heart. Last Monday night, without warning, one of the great leaden weights had dropped with a crash that woke both herself and Leah. She had brushed aside Leah's "scientific" explanations; she was convinced that the clock had stopped at the very moment of Fred's death. Had it not stopped in the same mysterious way the night their mother died and only a little while before they heard the news that poor Bertie Hoadley, the good-looking cousin who had disgraced himself and been packed off to the colonies, had fallen over the ship's side and been drowned? As the hand jumped, she was oppressed by the thought that for the next two hours or more she would be imprisoned in a room filling with the fumes of wine, smoke and human beings. Recklessly she trotted into the kitchen, pulled on her heavy wooden clogs and slipped out through the back door into the garden.

She pattered up the wet brick path like a little hoofed animal, sniffing the sweet air. It had rained earlier in the morning and bright drops shook down from the trees on to her face and hair. This was the time of year she loved most, the middle of March. After weeks of heavy snow, the wind had shifted suddenly; the thaw had run quickly, followed by two days of sunny, languid spring weather. Trees and hedges budded almost while you watched them though tufts of snow still lingered on the withered hemlocks in the ditches and in sheltered pockets on the roof. Clouds, in fleecy puffs or beaten out into long thin rifts, floated in a sky washed the purest, most transparent blue; high up a lark bubbled and just above her head a pair of thrushes flew busily to and fro, collecting twigs for their nest in the great walnut tree. She looked with a gardener's practical delight for every sign of green shoot or swelling bud. Her crocuses were out under the old apple tree; there was still a patch of snowdrops by the kitchen garden hedge. Forgetful of her best black skirt and the damp earth, she knelt down to touch them, the wind blowing her soft scanty hair, that she had pinned up so carefully for the occasion, into wild wisps. She picked a few snowdrops for Isabel, admiring their untarnished whiteness and delicate green scallops. Isabel loved flowers and, better still, she looked at them, which was more than most people did. In the summer holidays Sophy always ran out into the garden before breakfast to pick a rose or a pansy or a sprig of lemon thyme to lay on Isabel's plate. She was searching in her pocket for a wisp of bast to tie up her bunch when she realised that she was wearing, not her working skirt but her best, and that she had forgotten all about the funeral. Perhaps at this very moment, they were treading down the raw earth on the grave of a man she had known for nearly fifty years and had once been timidly inclined to love. She was shocked at herself but, out here with the wind blowing and the wet grass shining, try as she would, she could not focus her mind on death. It was almost the first good gardening day of the year; she ached to grub about the beds and plan her spring sowing. Why should that be more disrespectful to Fred's memory than to sit interminably in a stuffy room watching Fred's odious nephew Horace overeat himself and listening to Louie's spiteful, jocular complaints? Gardening was out of the question, but, holding her snowdrops as carefully as if they were butterflies, she could not resist taking one more turn round the beloved half-acre. It was a rebellious act for Leah must by now have finished her Service and be hunting for her in every room.

She skirted the big oblong vegetable patch, bordered with currant and gooseberry bushes, and came down the path by the thatched shed against whose wall grew an espaliered nectarine and two or three pears. Pushing through the gap between the drenched laurels and a clipped hedge of arbor vitae she stepped on to the mossy lawn at the far end of which stood the walnut tree. Her mother had planted it when she was a little girl, nearly ninety years ago, and now, from a trunk like a triple pillar, it swelled out into a vast semi-circle of lichenous branches and twigs. Every year the leaves grew a little scantier but still each summer it formed a huge symmetrical cloud of green so that the house could be identified more than a mile away by the walnut tree, the biggest in the parish. She could not bear to think, that, however slowly, it was beginning to decay. Every winter now the gales split off dry branches and the common in front of the house was littered with broken twigs. Sophy rarely prayed for anything for herself but she often prayed that she would die before the tree had to be cut down. Paget's Fold would never be the same without it. It was a person to her just as the clock was a person; the spirit of the garden as the other was the spirit of the house. As she passed under it, she patted its trunk and tore away a strip of the choking ivy as a mother might tuck back a lock of a child's hair. Beyond the walnut tree, some broken brick steps under a tangle of lilac and laburnum led to the two uneven strips of green in front of the house. A brick path divided them running from the gate in the iron palings that fenced them off from the common to the ricketty wooden porch that was hardly more than a prop for the jasmine and French honeysuckle that climbed all over it. Beyond the gate, so old and loosely hung that the cows often pushed it open and walked into the front garden, the common, dotted with gorse bushes, sloped down to the main road and the scummy pond with its ring of elms. Paget's Green was large enough to give ample space to two farm-houses and half a dozen cottages and to pasture innumerable geese, cows and old horses. At all times of the year it was strewn with feathers; there was old Mrs Goatcher even now filling her apron with them. Miss Sophy had meant to slip past the house to her flower garden and the tiny orchard but, catching sight of Leah's profile at an upper window, she decided it would be wiser to move back to the gate and pretend to look down the road for the funeral party.

Her eyes fixed themselves not on the road but on the downs of sallow green and purple-brown fields beyond the ridges. Nye Timber, the one high point in the smooth swell, always took the light differently from the rest and seemed to her to be made of a different material, of fine pale sand instead of worn green velvet. Today it was just that pearly lilac that had made her call it, as a child, the Heavenly Mountain. So it seemed to her still. She could not imagine a heaven that was not furnished with all the things she loved on earth. It was the downs she pictured when she said "I will lift up mine eyes unto the hills". Yet, though she loved them, she found them a little remote and frightening. As always, after gazing at them, she glanced back over her shoulder, to look at the house. She loved it, down to its very defects and discomforts; it shocked her to realise if Leah were to die she would suffer less than if the two of them had to leave Paget's Fold. In front the old pink brickwork, meshed in beams, was almost hidden by creepers and climbing plants. The box tree was much too high; it grew right up to one of the bedroom windows, blotting out all the light from the parlour so that you sat in a green gloom that smelt like a damp wood. The ivy was too thick; people were always warning her that it would pull the bricks apart. Often indeed it drove long sprays right into the rooms, through the deep walls and all those layers of paper. But she hated to cut it back; there was nothing she disliked so much as a naked-looking house. She thought with annoyance of all the people about to intrude on the old house's privacy and as she did so, she heard the sound of an approaching motor. Hurrying in, she was met by an indignant Leah.

"Sophy, what can have possessed you? Quick, take off your pattens. Your hair's all awry. And look—you've a great splash of mud on your good skirt. Sophy dear, how *could* you? Whatever will Claude think?"

Chapter 7

THE funeral guests, crammed elbow to elbow round the small table, had automatically herded into family groups; the Batchelor connections at Claude's end and the Hoadleys at Miss Leah's.

Clara had managed to attach herself to the Hoadleys. She wanted to be as far away as possible from her father for she could not forget the horrible thing that had happened in the cemetery. As he had stepped forward to throw the earth on the coffin, he had burst into tears in front of all those people and stood with his shoulders heaving and his face buried in his hands until her mother had taken him by the arm and led him away. She could not help feeling shame as well as pity. It was bad enough that Horace Batchelor and Aunt Louie should have seen him cry. It was worse to remember how he had stumbled away, blindly clinging to her mother.

Now, out of the corner of her eye, she could see him forcing himself to eat while the aunts coaxed him like a sick child.

"Claude, do let me give you a little more pie. I daresay you had a very small breakfast."

"No, really, thank you, Aunt Leah."

"I trust you don't find the pastry heavy," she said anxiously.

He managed to smile.

"I assure you it is delicious. No one ever made such pastry as you and Aunt Sophy. But today you've surpassed yourselves."

His cousin Horace scooped up a huge mouthful of pie and, with his cheek still bulging, held out his plate.

"If Claude can't do justice to it, here's someone that can. And I wouldn't say no to a slice of ham while you're about it, Claude. Time someone made a breach in it. Unless you've got it on sale or return of course."

"Ah, there's no one could carve like my poor Fred," said Ellen Batchelor, as Claude cut the ham. She had had two glasses of sherry to revive her after the ordeal of the long drive and the funeral and was in a state of melancholy benevolence. "It was a pleasure to watch him with a ham."

"Sliced it a shade too thin for my taste," said Horace. "That's right, Claude. Give her a good old hack."

"Such carvers as Frederick are born, not made," said Leah. "Though I'm sure Claude carves very well. That was your father's favourite knife, Claude. I'm afraid I could never put such a fine edge on it as he could."

"If the provision trade was a matter of slicing ham, poor old Uncle might have made a pile," said Horace.

There was an uncomfortable silence; a few people looked anxiously at Claude's mother. But old Mrs Batchelor's air was almost as remote as Isabel's.

"Wonderful, Fred was with his hands," she said, as if she had not heard. Everyone, except Horace and Aunt Louie Batchelor, put down their knives and forks and murmured agreement. "I daresay some of you have seen those walking sticks he used to make. Dog's heads and so on to the life. And done with nothing but an ordinary penknife. Then think of his handwriting. Everyone said he would have made a wonderful writing master."

"We have a beautiful specimen of his work upstairs," said Miss Leah. "You remember, Clara dear, in your bedroom?" Clara nodded. "I often bring it down to show people and it has been greatly admired. The Lord's Prayer, with every petition written in a different script. Copperplate, Gothic, and what I believe is called Italiano. There was no style he could not copy."

"Lucky he was honest, eh, Auntie?" said Horace.

Miss Leah stiffened her spine and seemed to grown an inch taller.

"Strictly speaking, Mr Batchelor, I am not your aunt. Your father, Mr Edgar Batchelor, was only a connection of ours by marriage."

"Does that mean I could marry you if I hadn't got a better half already? And I would too, for the pastry alone."

The blood rose under Miss Leah's transparent skin. Unutterably offended, she pinched her lips and looked down at her plate.

"Haha, she's blushing," went on Horace, delighted to see that Claude was frowning at him. "Bet it isn't the first proposal she's had."

"Horry, you shouldn't," said his mother admiringly. "He just can't help it," she explained to the company. "He's got such a sense of humour." She was a small tight shrivelled old woman in an old-fashioned jet-trimmed bonnet tied under her chin. Her greedy black eyes and the way she held her head on one side made her look as if she were always guessing the price of something. "After all, it doesn't always pay to put a long face on your troubles. Look where Horace has got with his jokes. Sir Rex has just promoted him chief sales manager, no less."

"No call to let that out, Mother," smirked Horace. "You'll have me blushing too. Besides, it's still sub-rosa, as you might say. Didn't know I was a Latin scholar, did you, Claudie?"

Claude raised his glass.

"Congratulations, Horace."

"Thanks, old boy. I don't say I shan't miss being on the road at first. Free and easy life. Suits me. Lot of responsibility, this new job. Have to mind my p's and q's. Going to have a lady secretary too." He dug his wife Ada in the ribs. "Probably have to work late at the office while she's new to the job. *You* won't mind, will you, old girl?"

The anaemic wife smiled uneasily, revealing her pale gums.

"No, of course not, Horace."

"There's a nice wife for you! Only too pleased to get her old man out of the way."

Ada flushed. Claude came to her rescue.

"How is your little boy, Ada?"

Before she could answer, her mother-in-law exclaimed,

"A picture, isn't he, Horace? And the image of his dad. Just like Horry at his age, the things he comes out with."

"Let's hope he'll be as successful," said Claude.

"He'll have a better start in life," said Aunt Louie ominously. "Horace has got where he is by his own exertions. Through no fault of his own he had to start at the bottom of the ladder."

Isabel shifted her chair and closed her eyes.

"I suppose," said Claude, "it's early days to think about a school for Georgie?"

"Trying to land one for the old firm, Claudie?" Horace shook his head. "Nothing doing. Not even if you got him in wholesale. Sound commercial education and come into the business at sixteen. That's what I plan for Georgie."

"No doubt you're right," said Claude.

"And mark you, it's not a question of fees. It's a question of principle. Don't think I'm crabbing your old Eton and Harrods, Claudie." He raised his glass and took a long draught. "A schoolmaster's got to live. No offence meant, but I doubt if you'd be worth more than three quid a week in business."

Ellen's dull eyes brightened.

"I don't agree. Claude is so clever and so hard-working he'd have made a success of anything."

"Come on, Auntie. I was only having a bit of fun. Didn't I say 'No offence meant'?"

There was a moment's embarrassed silence. It was obvious that old Mrs Batchelor was not appeased. Ada plucked up courage to speak. She was a faded blonde who quirked her little finger as she handled her knife and glass.

"I'm sure," she said in a shaking, ultra-ladylike voice, "Horace would never wish to hurt anyone's feelings."

She glanced nervously at him as she spoke. She could never forget that she had been only a shopgirl when he married her. Her life was an agony of apprehension that she would not be able to keep up with him as he pushed and elbowed his way towards the heights of the drapery world.

"Thanks, old lady, but I can speak up for myself." He winked at Isabel who stared past him as if his chair were empty. He was determined to make her notice him.

"Pardon me, but that's a remarkably nice gown you're wearing. Paris model, I shouldn't wonder."

"I bought it in London," said Isabel from a great distance.

"Looks like Paree on you. It's the figure, no doubt." He leaned over the table.

"Look here, Cousin Isabel, next time you want something pretty, you come along to Cousin Horace. I'm great pals with our gown buyer. Get you anything you want, straight from Paree, cost price ..."

"Very kind of you, Horace," interrupted Claude, "but we couldn't think of putting you to so much trouble."

"No trouble at all, old boy," said Horace. "Pleasure. Give me a ring any time and I'll take you down to the warehouse, Isabel."

"Would you care for some trifle, Mr Batchelor?" said Miss Leah. "It is made from our mother's special recipe."

"Thanks, Miss Sayers, since I mustn't call you Auntie.

When he tasted the trifle, he smacked his lips.

"Ah, I haven't had a tipsy-cake like this since I was a boy. You and me made ourselves sick on it once, Claudie. Remember?"

Miss Leah coughed with disapproval.

"We can both hold our drinks better now, eh, Claudie? Pretty good claret you've got here. Reminds me of some Sir Rex brings out when he's after a big order. Present from one of your Iky friends?"

"I bought a few dozen some years ago."

"Glad you can afford it, Claude," said the hollow voice of Sidney Gould, a distant relative of the Batchelors who kept a chemist's shop in Norwich. He was a cadaverous man of fifty-five with an expression of determined melancholy, like an undertaker's. His clothes too were like an undertaker's; a ready-made black suit and a dingy stiff collar of some synthetic material that could be sponged instead of laundered. He had been eating large quantities of food with slow concentration; intent on re-imbursing himself as far as possible for the fare from Norwich to London. If he ate sufficient, he would be able to save the price of his supper; if he ate too much or too quickly he would bring on his indigestion.

"I assure you I bought it very reasonably," said Claude meekly. Once, in his hard-up days, he had borrowed fifty pounds from Gould and, though he had long ago repaid it, he had never been allowed to forget it.

"If you asked my advice," said Gould gloomily, "not that you'd take it if you did, you'd look on that wine as an investment. In ten years' time you'd make a very handsome profit on what you originally paid. However, it seems you can afford to be extravagant.

"At my Edgar's funeral," said Aunt Louie suddenly, "there was no claret wine. Nor any other kind of wine either except some home-made cowslip. Ah, Ellen, you may be thankful you do not find yourself a widow in such case as I was."

Two uneven red stains appeared on her yellow cheeks. She looked balefully at Ellen and added with meaning,

"And through no fault of my husband's."

"I know what you refer to, Louie," said Ellen with dignity. ' But I don't think we want to talk about all those bygone things today, do we?"

"Funerals jog the memory," said Louie darkly. "Very different for me the outlook was, the day *my* husband was laid to rest."

"I know, Louie. It was a very difficult time for all. You forget my Fred lost everything too when the ... er ..." Mrs Batchelor caught Isabel's eye, "the *business* failed."

"Failed," snorted Louie. "It was killed stone-dead. If Fred had taken Edgar's advice ..."

"Aunt Louie," interposed Claude. "We all know that my father had no head for business. It was a great pity he was ever persuaded to go into it."

"A pity for others besides himself," said Louie.

"I think it is out of place to refer to such subjects at all today," said Miss Leah. "If we must, would it not be better to remember that all the debts were fully and honourably discharged?"

Louie turned on her. The red stains spread like a blot and her eyes glittered under their granulated lids.

"Now there was a bit of high-falutin' nonsense if you like. They could have got away with six bob in the pound easy but for Claude's notions." She shook her bonnet at her nephew. "Oh, I know it came out of your pocket in the end. But if you wanted to throw money away, what about your own kith and kin? Charity begins at home, I say."

"You'll never teach Claude the value of money any more than you'll teach a hen to swim," said Sidney Gould. "Miss Sophy, I wonder if you could oblige me with a glass of water?"

Sophy, glad of an excuse to leave the crowded room, the flushed and quarrelling faces, jumped up and disappeared into the pantry.

"In my business," Gould went on, "I allow myself exactly three pounds a week for board, lodging and incidentals. Everything over and above that goes back into the business or into my deposit account. Occasionally I invest a trifle. Not speculate, mark you. Invest."

Miss Sophy dumped a glass of water in front of him.

"Much obliged, I'm sure. Excuse me, all." He took a small cardboard box from his waistcoat pocket, selected a couple of pills with bony yellow fingers and swallowed them with a gulp of water. "I have to be particularly careful with my dyspepsia."

Isabel stood up and pushed back her chair.

"It's fearfully hot in here, Claude. I must have a breath of air."

"Come and take a turn round the garden with me," said Horace. "I'm feeling a bit stuffed up myself."

Isabel promptly sat down again. She laid the little bunch of snowdrops against her cheek and turned to Claude.

"Aren't they exquisite? Aunt Sophy picked them for me."

"Charming, my dear."

She tucked them in the neck of her dress.

"You usually prefer showier flowers, Isabel," said old Mrs Batchelor meaningly.

"I love all flowers," Isabel's voice was calm; "especially the ones Aunt Sophy chooses for me." She slipped her arm round the back of her neighbour's chair and touched Miss Sophy's shoulder.

"Everything's so late with the snow," said Miss Sophy. "I should have had some daffodils for your father's wreath, Claude, instead of having to make do with winter aconites. I did feel so sorry."

"It was the nicest of all, your little yellow and white cross. Wasn't it, Claude?"

Claude looked at her with sad affection. He could forgive her many humiliations for her fondness for his two old aunts.

"Someone must have spent a pretty penny on that wreath of orchids and what d'you call 'ems," said Horace. "I meant to have a squint at the card."

"It was a Mr and Mrs Shapiro ... I think I've pronounced it right," said Ellen proudly. It was her day and not even Isabel was going to put her down. "Jewish people they are. Very rich. Claude teaches their son privately and they think the world of him."

"Not by any chance Shapiro the big fur people?" asked Horace. His grin had vanished; his heavy face was alert and serious.

"As a matter of fact, yes," said Claude.

Horace looked at him almost with respect. When he spoke, his voice was quite subdued.

"Look here, I say, Claude. Sending a wreath that size to Uncle's funeral. What, old Izzy himself? Of course I realize it's nothing to them as cash. Still, you must be on pretty good terms with them."

"Mr Shapiro and his wife often come and play bridge with Claude and Isabel," said Ellen triumphantly.

Horace sucked his teeth.

"H'm. They do, do they? I'm fond of a game of bridge myself. Ada's no earthly use of course. What I like is a real men's four."

"The Shapiros always come together," said Isabel firmly. "We make a very good four."

"I'd be the last to shove myself in where I wasn't wanted. All the same, I don't mind admitting I'd like to meet old Izzy in private life so to speak. Look here, Claude. I'll make you a proposition. I don't expect anyone to do something for nothing in this world. If someone were to put me in the way of meeting him, informally, you know, and anything came of it, I'd be very willing to give that person a bit of commish."

Isabel bit her lip and Claude looked embarrassed. At last he said, "I doubt if a business introduction from me would do you any good, Horace. Shapiro, like you, has the poorest opinion of my business abilities."

"I'm not asking for a business introduction. I can send Popham's card up to him any day of the week. What I want is to meet him in a free-and-easy social way. Not a word of 'bithneth'."

He hunched his shoulders and spread his hands like a third-rate comedian telling a Jewish story.

"I think it's the least you can do for Horace, Claude," said Horace's mother. "It ought to be a pleasure to you to oblige. For the sake of justice, if nothing else."

Suddenly from the end of the table came the unexpected voice of Miss Leah. Her white face was flushed and she was quivering with nervous indignation. "Mr Batchelor," she said, confronting Horace like a moorhen facing up to a turkey cock, "this is not my house and Claude must forgive me for interrupting. But I must say I do not think this is the right moment to worry Claude with your private business affairs. And, Mrs Edgar, it is not respectful to poor Fred's memory to keep harping on the past. We all have our failings. I am sure none of us would wish them recalled on the day our friends carry us to the churchyard."

Horace stared at her open-mouthed. He began to mumble something, thought better of it, poured himself out a glass of claret and turned away with a shrug. At a glance from him, his mother, who was obviously about to reply with considerable heat, compressed her lips and glowered at her plate. There was a moment's silence; then an awkward, half-hearted general conversation broke out. Under cover of it, old John Hoadley spoke for the first time.

"You said no more than was right, cousin."

Too shaken by her outburst to utter another word, Miss Leah could only give the old man a grateful look.

Even in his own home, John Hoadley's silence was proverbial. Among all these people he was so shy that he had hardly raised his eyes from the table. When he did so, it was to give a glance of intense sympathy at any face that seemed sad. Though he was just on seventy, his blue eyes were as bright as those of his nineteen year old son Blaze who sat beside him. His wrinkled, sunburnt face in its frame of old-fashioned whiskers would have been insignificant but for those innocent, ageless eyes. Blaze had them too, as kindly but less calm, their blueness exaggerated by the violent red of his complexion. Sun and wind had permanently dyed the exposed parts of his fair skin to the colour of new brick; from his wheat-coloured hair to his collar he seemed to be one fiery blush. People often thought that "Blaze" was a nickname given him on this account, but actually it was his real name. His mother, who was of French descent, had christened him after her grandfather Blaise Meunier but since she spoke no French and had never seen the name written, she spelt and pronounced it Blaze. Working in the fields, with his shirt rolled up over his splendid arms, Blaze had the charm of anyone at ease in his surroundings; today in his tight black coat whose sleeves shot back with every movement exposing his enormous red hands and wrists; with his hair plastered flat above his flaming face, he was the picture of awkward misery.

On either side of Clara sat two of his many elder sisters, both undeniably pretty in spite of their dowdy black dresses and work-roughened hands.

Protected on all sides by Hoadleys, Clara tried to ignore the conversation at the other end of the table. She saw the Horace Batchelors so seldom that she had not realized till today how awful they were. Every time Horace opened his mouth she burnt with shame. For the first time in her life she sympathized with her mother's snobbishness and even drew support from the Maule coat of arms. But she never dreamt of criticizing the Hoadleys; they were part of the enchanted summer holiday life which had no connection with London and Mount Hilary. She had known Throcking since she was four years old; some of her happiest memories were of trotting round the byres and fields with "Uncle" John, helping to feed the calves and the chickens, wriggling through the heaped-up hay in the barns and being lifted on to the backs of the huge quiet horses. Inside a house John Hoadley always relapsed into silence but in his own fields and cattle-sheds he answered all Clara's questions with careful deliberation, teaching her the difference between Shorthorns and Herefords and Friesians and explaining the merits of various breeds of poultry. Sometimes he would seem to forget that she was a child and advise her seriously never to buy a Jersey bull or to plough up a good piece

66

of pasture and Clara, munching a piece of grass, would nod wisely. She was more flattered when John Hoadley said, "Why, I reckon you've quite a good notion of stock, Clara" than by any of her mother's irritated praise of her "cleverness". Up at Throcking she was a different person, a person whom her mother and even her father would not have recognized. Sometimes she fancied she would like to be that simple and stolid person always. Looking at the faces of Horace and Aunt Louie and Sidney Gould, she felt a rush of affection for the Hoadleys. Blaze, in his tight Sunday suit, might be ludicrous; he could never be vulgar. She thought how good he was; how kind, how genuine. Even as a small boy he never bullied or showed off. He wasn't soft; he was stronger than any of the men on the farm and when he gave an order in his quiet, slow voice, it was obeyed at once. He knew and loved his job; he had no ambition to be anything else than a good farmer. Clara had always liked Blaze though, away from Throcking and Paget's Fold, she had hardly given him a thought. Now she glanced across at him and smiled, with a touch of self-satisfaction at being able to appreciate him. His eyes were already on her, but he did not smile back. No blush could have deepened that complexion yet she had the impression that he was embarrassed. Embarrassed in her turn, she looked past him into the dim greenish mirror of the sideboard. For a moment she did not recognise herself. All through the meal she had been so conscious of being the one child among the grown-ups that she was startled to find a reflection that did not look childish at all. Was it only the velvet frock that made her seem at least two years older and quite different? Even in the tarnished glass which dulled all colours, her hair shone and her skin was theatrically white against the black.

"Blaze," she said petulantly, "why do you look as if you didn't recognize me?" She wanted to establish some connection between this brilliant person in the mirror and the Clara Blaze knew, an untidy child in a crumpled holland frock, with a shiny nose and scratched knees.

Blaze looked down at his plate.

"I recognize you all right, Clara," he said with his Sussex drawl. "It's just, well, reckon you've grown a lot since last summer. You're quite a young lady."

"I'm *not* different," she pleaded, half sincerely. "Am I, Uncle John? Everyone looks older in black, don't they?"

The old man considered her gravely.

"I'm sorry to have to see you in mourning, my dear. But what Blaze says is right. You're not a little lass any more."

Suddenly she wanted to disown the girl in the glass.

"But I haven't changed. I know I'm older. But I still like the same things."

"Come on, Clara," mocked Violet. "Would you still like Blaze to give you a ride in the wheelbarrow as he used to do?"

Clara sighed.

"I admit I'm old for that. Did Heather's calf come on all right after all, Uncle John? And did the landlord put up a new gate between Sweetacre and the Bottom?"

"Yes, that little heifer, Pansy we call her, she's a picture now. I was all for selling her, but Blaze, he said no, let me try my hand; and he brought her on wonderful. As to the gate, well, Mr Vernon he won't say yes and he won't say no in a manner of speaking."

"Can I come up and see everything, quite soon in the summer holidays?"

"Why, you're always welcome, Clara. You know that," said John Hoadley. "But the time will soon be coming when you won't want to be spoiling your pretty clothes in a dirty old place like a farm."

"Oh, how *can* you? You know I'll always love Throcking."

Violet patted her hair. "Same old Clara, eh?" The volume of Horace's talk was rising again and she spoke quietly so that her father and Blaze could not hear. "You always were a quaint child. We could never understand how you took to it so, being brought up in London. Dad used to say you were more of a farmer's daughter than I ever was."

"You do like the farm, don't you, Vi?"

"I don't stop to think whether I like it. I'm there and the work's got to be done."

"Still, you must be awfully proud of your dairy. It's so lovely ... just like Mrs Poyser's."

"Who's Mrs Poyser? Someone at Bellhurst?"

" No, just someone in a book."

Violet sighed.

"Sometimes I don't open a book for weeks on end. There's wonderfully little time for reading on a farm. You'd hate that, wouldn't you, Clara?"

Clara considered.

"I know one has to work awfully hard. And I've only seen Throcking in summer. All the same, I do sometimes wish ..."

"You're luckier than you know," said Violet. "Think of the education you're getting. You're clever, we all know that. Only some girls never get the chance to find out whether they're clever or not."

"I hadn't thought of that."

"Look at me. Twenty-two and I don't know a quarter of the things you do. And you're not fifteen. It won't be long before you find your old country cousins very dull company."

"Oh, Vi, I won't."

"Don't tease her," said the gentle Beatrice. "You'll always keep a place for us, Clara, won't you?"

"Of course I will, Bee," Clara's eyes were smarting childishly. "Oh dear, everything's so horrid today. Everyone's different. I'm sure it's all because of those frightful people. Why don't they go? They don't belong here."

"Hush, dear, they'll hear you," said Violet. She added with a touch of mischief, "They're much nearer relations to you than we are."

"Did I hear you pining about education just now, Miss Hoadley?" broke in Horace Batchelor. "If you ask my opinion as a man of the world, it's waste of time sending girls to school. There's only one thing a woman needs to learn and that's how to get a husband."

"I suppose you'd allow us to be taught to read and write," said Violet, flushing.

"No objection to that. Nor to a bit of figuring. Keep her accounts and read her love-letters, that's all a girl wants."

"Claude isn't at all of your mind, Horace," said Ellen Batchelor." He wants Clara to go to a university, just like he did."

"Of all the crack-brained notions!" exclaimed Horace. "What, a pretty kid like Clara stewing over a lot of rotten old books just when she ought to be having a bit of fun? You put your foot down, Clara. Don't let your Dad get away with it."

"There's no question of forcing her," said Claude coldly. "It depends entirely on Clara herself."

"I probably won't be good enough to get a scholarship, anyway," Clara's voice was peevish.

"She will if she sets her mind to it," said her grandmother. "She's always top of her form at school."

"Class," muttered Clara under her breath.

"Chip of the old block, eh?" said Horace. "Claude was always the brainy boy, wasn't he? Even in the old Young Gent's Academy days before he got a schol. to his classy public school. Didn't cut much of a figure out of lesson-hours, as I remember. Ever heard the saying, them that can *do*; them that can't, *teach?*"

Suddenly Clara lost all control of herself.

"You're always sneering at my father," she burst out, her cheeks flaming. "It's simply beastly. I wish you'd stop."

The whole table was suddenly silent. Everyone looked delighted, uncomfortable or shocked.

"Clara, whatever are you thinking of?" It was said in Claude's sternest voice. "Apologize at once or leave the room."

"I won't say I'm sorry, Daddy; I can't."

"Ooh. Temper, temper!" mocked Horace, delighted. "'Pon my word, it suits you. My goodness, what a fine colour!"

Aunt Louie, equally delighted, snapped out,

"The impertinence! If you were a daughter of mine, Miss, I'd put you across my knee and spank you."

Miss Leah cleared her throat unhappily.

"I'm sure Clara didn't mean ..."

Aunt Louie cut across her.

"Nice manners, I *must* say. Is that what you learn from your princesses and duchesses at your Roman Catholic school?"

"Claude, the child was only ..." began Isabel.

"Leave this to me, please," he interrupted her. He turned an iron face to Clara. "Did you hear what I said?"

"Yes, I did." She tried to keep her voice from trembling. "I'm going." Her legs felt like paper but she managed to get up. Quickly and unsteadily she made for the nearest door and left the room.

Chapter 8

IN her blind haste, Clara had taken the door that led straight into the garden. After the stuffy room, the March wind struck like cold water on her face and half-bare arms. In a moment she was shivering in her velvet dress. It was impossible to go back and expose herself to all those staring faces and she dared not slip through the back door into the kitchen in case the old woman from the village who was coming to help with the washing-up had already arrived. She knew Mrs. Twiner all too well; her disgrace would be known all over Rookfield by the evening and remembered and discussed for years.

Avoiding the windows, she ran round to the back of the house and up the overgrown path to the orchard and hid herself among the furthest trees. She was furious at having made such a fool of herself. Why couldn't she have had the sense to keep quiet? Nowadays it was always the same. When her father wanted her to speak, she was dumb. When she should have been silent, some imp prompted her to blurt out the wrong thing. This time, she muttered, angrily tearing strips of lichen from the bark of a tree, he really had been unfair. She had stood up for him and he had humiliated her. Her mother would never have done it quite in that way ... *She* would probably have gone to the other extreme and done something embarrassing, such as calling her "my loyal little daughter" or kissing her in front of everyone. But then she would never have attacked Cousin Horace on her mother's account. Supposing it had been her mother who had done the attacking? Probably her father would have been delighted. The scene in the churchyard came back to her. She thought jealously, "I love him much more than *she* does." If it had been her own funeral, would he have broken down and cried? It was very chilly in the orchard. If she got a cold and neglected it, it might turn to pneumonia. Then he'd be sorry. "Darling child, it was all my fault. Can you ever forgive me?"

The minutes went by. A cloud came over the sun and the wind struck colder than ever. What should she do? She had wild thoughts of running away. She pictured herself stumbling on and on for miles and being picked up exhausted by the roadside, delirious perhaps, her velvet dress covered with dust. Common sense came to the rescue. She'd never get far in her thin best shoes; she would just be making herself ridiculous again. Why couldn't she have been more dignified? The girl in the glass would never have been rude in that shrill, clumsy way. She would merely have given Cousin Horace an ineffable look that would have silenced him. But the girl in the glass didn't exist any more. With her hair blown into tangles, her eyes watering and her nose turning blue with cold, Clara was just Clara again, an idiotic schoolgirl who had once again made an exhibition of herself.

A man's step sounded on the path behind the orchard hedge. Joy, terror and an impulse to run leapt up together. Just how angry would he be? Or was it possible he had come to forgive her. "In front of all those people, dear, you understand, I had to pretend." How gladly she would agree, and, entering into the conspiracy, apologise to Cousin Horace with the best grace in the world. The footsteps came nearer. She stood still, hiding her face against the apple tree. Close by her, the footsteps stopped. When she turned round she saw that the man was not her father but Blaze Hoadley.

"Clara," he said in voice hoarse with shyness. "Excuse me, won't you."

She stared at his crimson face and thought she had never seen anyone who looked so kind. Did that mean good news?

"Have they sent you to fetch me?"

"No, I just slipped away on my own. You don't mind, do you, Clara?" He cleared his throat. "I thought ... well ... fact is I was bit worried about you."

"Awfully nice of you, Blaze. But I'm quite all right. Really I am."

"It's a bitter wind. You must be cold out here with no coat on. Here, if you don't mind ..."

Before she could object he had taken off his black jacket and wrapped it clumsily round her shoulders.

"No, Blaze, really." She said it half-heartedly. The coat, warm from his body, was very comforting. "But what about you?"

"Me?" he grinned. "I need a bit of cooling off after that room."

In his shirtsleeves and with the wind ruffling the unnatural smoothness of his hair, he was more like the Blaze of the farm.

"Now you look almost your old self," she told him.

"Reckon you do too, Clara."

Muffled in the big black coat, with her ribbon off and her hair whipped all over her face, it was no good trying to be dignified any more. She appealed to him, as in the days when she had torn her frock or lost her shoe scrambling about the farm.

"Blaze, what *am* I to do?"

"I'm sure your father didn't mean to speak so sharp," he said soothingly. "He's upset today and no wonder."

"Yes, I *know*," she wailed.

"Don't take it to heart so. Remember how fond he is of you. And proud as Punch, too. I daresay he didn't like seeing you giving way in front of that fellow. He can't bear to have you criticized. Mother's just the same with us. She flies out at us rather than anybody else shall."

"But I only flew out because he was being so beastly about Daddy."

"He asked for it all right. Don't fret yourself, Clara. It'll all smooth out."

"Do *you* think I ought to go back and apologize?"

"It's not for me to judge. That'd mend it sooner than anything."

"It's no good, Blaze. I can't. I'm *not* sorry."

"Well, you know best. Dad and I always give in to Mother for the sake of peace. She's a bit unreasonable sometimes. But your father. He didn't act like himself today. I've never heard him speak anything but kindly to anyone."

"Oh, but he can be absolutely ruthless, Blaze. You don't know him."

"He couldn't be hard on *you* for long. No one could." He looked at her ardently.

"Why do you say that, Blaze?"

He looked down at his thick black boots. When he spoke it was with an obvious effort.

"Well, Clara, when you were little, I thought you were the nicest kid I knew. Not to mention the prettiest. And now you've gone and changed into a young lady overnight. Only, you see, my ideas haven't changed, that's all."

Clara did not know what to say. They were both relieved when a rabbit darted out a few yards from them and streaked away towards the field beyond the orchard.

"Oh, look, Blaze."

"Wish I'd got my old gun. He's been at your Aunt Sophy's cabbages I shouldn't wonder."

73

"I'm glad you haven't. I hate any animal being killed."

"I don't hold with killing for killing's sake. But a farmer's got to keep the rabbits down. Terrible damage they do."

"Yes, I know. And you're an awfully good shot."

"Middling. Anyway, I always make sure they're finished off proper. I remember how upset you were years ago when we picked up one with a broken back."

Clara winced.

"I've never forgotten that. Or Jerry the pig being killed."

"Reckon there's a lot of things about farming that wouldn't suit you, for all you were saying just now in there."

"Yes. I suppose so. But truly I'm not pretending when I say I love Throcking."

"Maybe. Most kids like playing about on a farm." He looked at her intently. "But could you fancy yourself being content living all your life at Throcking or some such place?"

"How can I tell? I'm not likely to have the chance, am I? Sometimes, yes, Blaze, I do really think I could."

"Hmm. I wonder." His clear eyes under their reddened lids continued to search her face.

"Why do you look at me in that funny way?"

"Oh, nothing." He stared at his boots again.

"Why, you're shivering, Blaze. Do have your coat back. I'm beautifully warm again."

"Keep it on. I like seeing you in it," he muttered.

"I must look awfully queer," she said and giggled.

He raised his eyes.

"D'you know, that's the first time I've heard you laugh today."

She became instantly gloomy.

"Oh, goodness, I'd forgotten. I certainly haven't got anything to laugh about at the moment."

"I hate seeing you so put out, Clara. I wish I could say something to cheer you up. But I'm like Dad. Always got a knot in my tongue. Yet when you're not there, it's surprising how easy I talk to you."

"I know *that* feeling," Clara said with a wan smile.

Suddenly he stepped forward and, before she could move, put his arms round her and kissed her.

"There," he said as he drew back. "I know I oughtn't. But I just couldn't help it."

Clara did not know whether she was pleased or angry. It was the first time a young man had kissed her. She could do nothing but stare at him in dismay. Blaze caught her two hands in his and held them tightly.

"Say you'll forgive me, Clara. I know I haven't the right. I never will have. I've lain awake at nights telling myself not to be such a fool. I thought I'd got more hold on myself. Forget all about it."

Still he did not let go her hands. He lifted them up and pinned them against him so that she could feel the hard, warm flesh under his cotton shirt. She stood there awkwardly, not liking to draw away. It was not at all how she had imagined her first kiss. She was both moved and affronted. He was a ridiculous figure in his shirt and braces, with his hair half plastered down, half standing on end above his crimson face. But there was something in his expression that was not at all ridiculous.

"Oh, Blaze," she said miserably. "I *am* awfully fond of you."

"I'd forgotten you were only a kid. You looked deceiving today. And I'm not a kid any more, Clara. I have the feelings a man has. It shan't ever happen again. Unless," he broke off, looking down at her almost sternly.

"Unless?" she said, in spite of herself.

He shook his head. "No. I've got that much sense left. Even if you ever ... No, we've been bred to different ways and that's the end of it. But leave your hands be just this minute, Clara."

They stood for some moments, searching each other's faces, their eyes watering in the wind. It was Blaze who moved first. With a curious dignity he bent his head, put her hands one after the other to his lips and gently let them go. In that one gesture, he seemed to grow up before her eyes. She realised the immense distance between them. He was at that moment a man, all that he would ever be. And she was nothing but a half-baked, pretentious little girl.

"That's all, Clara," he said quietly. "Only remember I'm your friend. If ever I can serve you in any way ..."

"I'm your friend too, Blaze," she said, feeling miserably inadequate.

"If you take my advice, you'll go back in and make it up with your Dad. Things only get worse if you put them off. I reckon I'll take a turn round the field."

He took the coat she offered him, slung it over his shoulder and strode quickly away. She watched him jump the hedge and make off down the field without looking back, almost with a sense of grievance as if he had unkindly deserted her. Moving reluctantly towards the path she saw her father a few yards away standing perfectly still, watching her.

Her heart turned over. How long had he been there? What had he seen? She must have been too absorbed to hear his footsteps. She stumbled towards him on legs weak as a baby's.

"Oh, Daddy," she stammered. "You shouldn't have ... I'm so sorry ... I was just coming in to say ..."

"Indeed," he said coldly as she came up to him. "Not on your own initiative, I think."

He had heard Blaze's last words then. But how much else? He walked away and she followed meekly behind him down the path. The few yards through the orchard seemed interminable. At last he said over his shoulder,

"You'd better go in through the back door and do something to your hair before you go into the sitting room. You're not fit to be seen."

She could bear it no longer. Catching up with him and tugging at his sleeve, she burst out:

"Please, please, Daddy, don't be so angry. I am sorry, truly I am."

He made a few steps as if he neither heard her nor felt her dragging at him. Then abruptly he turned, shook off her hand and looked at her. His face was pale and stern but, besides the anger which she expected, it had an expression she had never seen and could not read.

"Sorry for what, Clara?" he said sharply. There was an odd shrill note in his voice that reminded her of her mother.

She felt herself turn crimson.

"I'm sorry I was so rude to Mr Batchelor."

"Oh, *that*." He gave a half-smile that was like a grimace of pain. "I had decided to overlook it. I came out here to tell you so. An ironic situation, don't you agree?"

She said nothing.

"I was idiot enough to imagine you might be unhappy," he went on. "I fancied I had been too harsh with you. There's no fool like a father."

She looked at him wretchedly.

"I suppose you are going to tell me it is the first time?"

She nodded.

"If it is ... which I doubt ... you might perhaps have chosen a more suitable day, don't you think?"

This time he had gone too far. Suddenly his sarcasm ceased to wound her. She was still terrified but for the first time in her life, she felt almost equal to him.

"I didn't *choose*," she said sullenly.

"Can I believe anything you say?" Angry as he was, he seemed to be almost pleading with her. "There was a time when I would have trusted your word against anyone's. You were a truthful child."

Clara said nothing.

An access of rage seemed to choke him. His face was distorted; his eyes narrowed as if the flesh round them was swelling and silting them up.

"You ... you of all people. Kissing and giggling like a common servant girl. How that young oaf dared to touch you. The swine."

"Blaze isn't a swine." It took all her courage to say it.

She could no longer bear to look at him. The sun was still shining, a clump of daffodil buds nodded in the wind at her feet but a tainted mist seemed to have come over the spring day.

"He didn't mean ... it wasn't his fault," she muttered, hardly knowing what she was saying.

"Ah," he gloated. "There at least we have the truth. A young man doesn't ... unless he is a scoundrel ... if the girl doesn't lead him on. I've no right to blame Blaze Hoadley. You were fair game."

She burst into tears.

"You're so cruel," she sobbed. "You never give me a chance to explain."

"What excuse do you propose to make? I watched with my own eyes. If I did not interfere at once, it was because I wanted to make sure I was not suffering from hallucinations."

He paused. After a moment he said,

"So I am cruel?" His voice was bitter but there was a hint of weariness and uncertainty in it. "I thought you were an innocent child. Do you expect me to be pleased to find you are nothing of the kind?"

She turned away from him and hid her face against a tree. Enclosed in her misery, she was hardly any longer conscious of his presence. A very long time seemed to pass. At last, from a great distance she heard him say, as if to himself,

"I wanted one thing in my life to be perfect."

When she dared to raise her head, he was gone. She saw his square black figure moving slowly down the path towards the house. His head, which he usually carried so stiffly erect, was sunk forward. She watched with stinging eyes till the black figure disappeared behind the angle of the wall. Bewildered and resentful as she was, there was one clear point in the confusion of her mind. Some part of herself seemed to have broken loose and to judge differently from the rest. Had he beaten her, the original Clara could not have felt more humiliated. But someone else ... was it the girl in the glass? ... had the strangest sense of triumph.

PART TWO

Chapter 1

A FEW months after Frederick Batchelor's funeral, his daughter-in-law came very near to dying. Clara, at school, was merely told that her mother had had to undergo a serious operation and asked to pray for her. Half-way through the summer term, she received a letter from her father, saying that Isabel was out of danger and slowly recovering.

"This is my good news; now for the bad. We had always agreed that in the autumn of 1915 you should go to St Mark's Girls' School so that you could take your exams. But I fear that, owing to the expenses of your mother's illness, we shall have to make the change this coming September instead. So this, alas, will be your last term at Mount Hilary. I cannot possibly manage to afford another year for you at the convent. You will know how very distressed I am to have to take you away but your mother's life was in the balance and I had no alternative but to get the very best advice. She is still too weak to write but sends you her fondest love.

Ever your affectionate father,
C. F. B."

When Clara first glanced through this letter in the refectory, she hardly took it in. During recreation she managed to slip away to her favourite hiding-place under the weeping ash. There she read it again slowly, absorbing the full shock. When she was at school, events at home always seemed remote and this illness of her mother's, with its atmosphere of secrecy, had hardly been real to her. Even now it was hard for her to believe that Isabel had been in danger of death. Only one thing in her father's letter struck home; the fact that she had to leave Mount Hilary in a few weeks' time. It was so overwhelming that she had no pity to spare for anyone but herself.

It was a still, softly-burning day in June and Mount Hilary was at its loveliest. From the cricket pitch came the lazy slap of bats and bird-like cries of "Oh *played*, Theresa" and "Well *held*, Adèle." All the smells of summer were in the air, drifting from the limes in Community Alley, the drying hay in the paddock and the azaleas by the lake. Through the showering branches of the ash she had a glimpse of the water and an island of lilies. The Junior School were playing with the boat; she could hear splashes and the grind of the loose old rowlocks and shrill squeals from the bank—"It's our trio next Mother." "No, *honour*, Mother, it isn't. It's Philomena's." Across the lower meadow passed a silent band of First Communicants in retreat, carrying flowers to decorate an altar for the Corpus Christi procession to-morrow. It was as if everything that most charmed her at Mount Hilary had been gathered together on this summer afternoon to remind her of what she had to lose.

If only she had known this was to be her last term, how she would have hoarded every minute. Now she had barely six weeks left. The careless voices from the pitch and the lakeside became an irritation. This time next year they would be calling "I was *miles* inside the crease, Mother" or "My pink ribbon's gone overboard." Voices of people whose fathers did not have to worry about school fees; of people who would never be expected to earn their own living. Tears of self-pity rose in her eyes so that, when a figure pushed through the tent of boughs, she only saw a blur of striped cotton and black serge. When she had dashed away the tears with her fists, the blur resolved itself into her best friend, Nicole de Savigny.

"Hullo," she said with relief, "I was afraid it was a Child of Mary or something."

"Almost as bad," said Nicole, "I've got a message."

"Go back to Rec. I suppose? Well, I won't."

"Neither will I. This is much more civilised." Nicole flung herself on the grass, selected a blade with care and began to chew it, keeping her eyes averted from Clara's face. When Clara had had time to dab her eyes and blow her nose, she said:

"Mother Lovell wants you to go to her room after Rec. What is it? Bad news from home?"

"Well—yes."

"Your mother's not worse?"

"No. She's going on quite well."

Nicole, still chewing her grass-blade, looked at her thoughtfully,

The light, filtering through the leaves that enclosed them like a tent made her flecked, changeable eyes appear green—

"Rather I went?"

"For heaven's sake, *no*."

"Good. I wanted an excuse to stay. Who but the English would waste this weather playing cricket? I wonder our sainted foundress didn't forbid it in the rules. Being French, I suppose she didn't legislate for barbarians." Nicole pushed up the fringe from her damp forehead, "*Ciel*, it's hot."

"She did legislate against fringes," said Clara, smiling for the first time, "I've always wondered how you managed to get away with yours."

"Probably because my great-aunt gave the Order a house when they were on the rocks."

Clara studied the handsome exposed forehead.

"You look ten times better without it."

"Of course. It's entirely a matter of principle. I won't be browbeaten. This time next year, when you and I leave this prison-house I'll ceremonially cut it off. If you want a lock as a souvenir, I've got the perfect locket. Hearts, forget-me-nots, *ewige Freundschaft* ..."

Clara broke in:

"I shan't be here next year. Not even next term."

Nicole sat up.

"*Mon Dieu*, you haven't been expelled?"

"No. Just a sudden notion of my father's."

"Well, he must give a reason."

There was a pause during which Nicole sampled two or three more grass stalks. Then Clara burst out:

"I wish there was no such thing as money."

"Oh, it's *that*. Rotten luck. Haven't you any useful relatives?"

"Not one."

"Quite sure? I thought everyone had."

"Well, I haven't."

Nicole shrugged her shoulders with an angry sigh.

"I wish he'd never sent me here," said Clara miserably. "This place isn't meant for people like me."

"Don't blither."

"I'm not blithering," said Clara with unusual conviction. "Look at you and me. Here we wear the same uniform, eat the same food ..."

"Unfit for human consumption."

" … but in the holidays we go back to different worlds."

"I can do what I like with my money when I'm twenty-one. We might go to China. Or Africa. It would be amusing to go somewhere uncivilised, don't you agree?"

"I've never been on so much as a day trip to Boulogne," said Clara bitterly. "Anyway you won't be twenty-one for five whole years. And you know as well as I do what will happen. We'll keep up writing to each other for a bit. We might even go to a concert or a theatre now and then. And it'll end by our sometimes turning up at the same Old Children's meeting and giving each other a sheepish grin."

"We live in a changing world, my child," said Nicole piously. "How many of us here may live to see great upheavals and social landmarks swept away. Even in this world, how rash to trust to mere earthly fortune. Some of you here today, daughters of fond parents who hoped to shelter you from every worldly care, may even find yourself under the painful necessity of earning your daily bread. Should such be the case …"

"It's jolly well going to be the case with me. It's been rubbed into me ever since I can remember. When you step into your fortune I shall probably be deciding between the dazzling alternatives of being a schoolmistress or a clerk in the Post Office."

"I may never step into it," said Nicole placidly. "Papa says there will definitely be a war between France and Germany in the next few years. If France were defeated, which Heaven forbid, I might be begging you to use your influence to get me a job as Mademoiselle in a broad-minded English boarding school."

Clara laughed but Nicole's face suddenly became serious.

"You know," she went on, chewing her grass-stalk, thoughtfully, "It would be far better for me if I *had* to work for my living. I'm bone lazy. I work in this place because it annoys my vanity not to come out first and because if I didn't, I'd go melancholy mad from *ennui*. As soon as I've left, I shall just run to seed."

Clara forgot her troubles for a moment.

"Nic, what nonsense," she said with angry affection. "You … with every talent in the world. You can't just waste it all. You won't."

Nicole rolled over on her back and stared up at the sky through the branches, with narrowed eyes. Her thin sallow face, whose beauty was all in the modelling of the bones, never looked girlish; now it seemed to be that of a woman of thirty.

When she spoke at last, Clara was struck, as so often before, by the oddness of Nicole's voice, at once hoarse and musical. "You speak like a very good singer with a very bad cold," she had told her once.

"Oh yes," Nicole said. "There's practically nothing I couldn't do ... if I wished to. But I shan't wish. People will always give me everything I want without my even having to ask for it. I'm the cat that will always find its saucer full of cream even though it might prefer skim milk."

"You're awfully cynical," said Clara admiringly. "But you're right. You always will get what you want."

Nicole sat up and grinned. She was sixteen again.

"Except, apparently in this case."

Clara grinned in her turn.

"Skim milk? Thanks for the compliment."

"The whole thing's ridiculous," said Nicole, with unusual violence. "How do they expect me to get through three whole terms without anyone to talk to?"

"Nicole, ... do you *really* mind?" Clara ventured.

"Yes. I mind considerably," said Nicole coolly.

Clara was too pleased to be delicate.

"But why?" she said recklessly.

Nicole merely yawned and glanced at a wrist-watch, which, like all her possessions, had something incongruous about it. The watch itself was tiny and exquisite. Nicole wore it on a broad, battered strap obviously meant for a man.

"Five minutes before the bell. If you've got to face Mother Lovell, you'd better go in and tidy your hair and all that rot."

They walked in silence past the cricket pitch and up the alley of limes to the terrace. Clara found herself staring at the familiar building as if she had never seen it before. In spite of the wings of grey Victorian Gothic that had been tacked on at right angles on either side, the original creamy stucco house with its pilasters and broad shallow bows kept its eighteenth century elegance.

"I've never thought of Mount Hilary as a house before," she said. "It's always been just school. But the old part is really lovely."

"Yes. Except for grisly associations, I wouldn't mind living in it."

"You've got a château in France, lucky beast. It must be heavenly."

"It's very agreeable to look at. But frightfully damp and the central heating never works."

"I don't believe you appreciate anything you've got. Even your name. If I'd been born Clara d'Ellébeuse instead of Clara Batchelor ..." She stopped and sighed.

Nicole's face became suddenly almost stern.

"*Viens toute nue, O Clara d'Ellébeuse*," she said softly and critically. "I wonder if it's really as good as we used to think it."

"Oh, *surely*, Nic." Clara was deeply disturbed. "It's *magical*."

"Well, just listen to this.

> *Je trône dans l'azur comme un sphinx incompris*
> *J'unis un coeur de neige à la blancheur des cygnes,*
> *Je hais le mouvement qui déplace les lignes*
> *Et jamais je ne pleurs et jamais je ne ris.*"

Clara gasped.

"Where did you find that? Who is it? Go on."

"Baudelaire. I've just got on to him."

A dark girl, carrying a great brass bell by its clapper ran past them, the ends of her blue ribbon streaming behind her.

"Oh damn. There goes Luz to ring for the end of rec.," said Clara, whipping off her apron. "I must fly."

Nicole shrugged her shoulders.

"We *would* be interrupted just when we were beginning to talk sense."

A few minutes later, smooth-haired and wearing the dark cotton gloves required on formal occasions, Clara knocked on the door with the beautifully-written inscription "Mistress General." For once she was not nervous when she heard Mother Lovell's quiet voice say "Come in." She guessed why she was wanted: there was no reason to tremble or to examine her conscience. Nevertheless, from force of old associations, her knees were a little weak as she advanced into the room and made her curtsy.

Mother Lovell was sitting as usual, pen in hand, at a desk covered with piles of orderly papers. She laid down the pen, smiled and signed to Clara to sit on the only other chair in the small bare polished room. Then she put out a white, strong-looking hand and touched the tightly-clasped gloved ones.

"My poor Clara," she said, considering her with an expression at once affectionate, pitying and a trifle amused. "Yes ... I think I know how you feel."

Clara looked back miserably into the pale face framed in the crimped white bonnet. Mother Lovell must have been a beauty in her youth but, as with almost all the nuns, Clara could not imagine her face in any other setting. The jutting white bonnet which hid the profile and the black band which covered most of the forehead gave a peculiar definition to the features they left exposed. Even the plainest face took on a certain dignity under the coif but Mother Lovell with her pallor, her large eyes, her sweet mouth, a trifle compressed when she was not smiling, might have posed for the portrait of the ideal nun. Her other-worldly beauty was, however, anchored to earth by a pair of prosaic steel-rimmed spectacles, neatly mended at the bridge with cobbler's thread and the luminous eyes behind them could be uncomfortably shrewd.

"Yes, my dear. Yes indeed," she said, smiling in sympathy and deprecation as if Clara had spoken. "You don't have to tell me. But it is God's will. We must both remember that."

"Yes, Mother," said Clara shyly and without enthusiasm.

The nun folded her hands in her black sleeves and gazed kindly yet critically at her through the steel spectacles.

"It's such a shock," said Clara, finding her tongue at last. "I thought I had a whole year more."

"I know, I know," said Mother Lovell, with a kind of humorous despair, "but what can we do, Clara? Your dear father wrote to Reverend Mother first. I had a long talk with her this morning.

Clara flushed, guessing what they must have talked about.

"Try not to be too sensitive about that side of it, dear child," said Mother Lovell. "It might happen to anyone, you know. My sister, for example. Her husband is in the army, and the pay is *very* little for a large family. She had to take her two girls away from one of our houses and send them to a day school."

"How rot——", said Clara, trying to be interested in Mother Lovell's unknown nieces ... "I mean how sad for her."

"Perhaps I'd better tell you what Reverend Mother said." Again she patted the gloved hands clenched so tightly in Clara's lap. "And you mustn't let it hurt your feelings. For, dear Clara, you are a little too sensitive."

"Am I?" said Clara. "At home they think that I'm awfully thick-skinned."

The nun considered her shrewdly.

"You are very frightened, my dear, aren't you, of giving yourself away? Which isn't," she tilted her head sideways again and spoke almost apologetically, "quite the same thing as controlling one's feelings. But at fourteen ... or is it fifteen now?"

"Yes, Mother. I've just had a birthday."

"Of course. I should have remembered. Well ... one doesn't expect people to be very proficient in that at fifteen. I remember that when I was fifteen I was all prickles inside and out."

"Were you really, Mother?" said Clara, trying vainly to imagine Mother Lovell at fifteen.

"Yes, indeed," the nun smiled. "But we're here to talk about *you*. Now ... and, again, I beg you not to have hurt feelings ... Reverend Mother said that if you had been going to finish your whole education with us, she would most willingly have found means. You understand?"

"Oh yes," said Clara, blushing again. "That was awf ... *most* kind of her."

"*But* ... as your dear father, for one reason and another, had decided that in any case you were to leave us in a year's time ... well, you understand, Clara?"

"Oh yes, Mother," said Clara, with a heart of lead. She was silent for a moment, then she broke out.

"I almost wish I'd never come here. I don't belong. And yet I'd come to feel as if I did."

"Of course you belong. Our children are always our children ... wherever they go. Don't forget that. You must come back and see us often, often."

"Thank you, Mother."

But Clara did not see herself coming back often. She would not be the right kind of "old child". The nuns would be very sweet, very tolerant but she would not belong like the others whose mothers and grandmothers had been to Mount Hilary and who would one day send their own children there as a matter of course. She thought of one girl who had left and taken a job on a provincial newspaper and who came back faithfully for prize-givings and reunions. The nuns always spoke of her as "Poor Mary". She did not want to become "Poor Clara".

"I hope," said Mother Lovell, "that you and I will be able to have many talks before the end of the term. We shall be very sad when that day comes. Still, from the point of view of prizes, I am sure you will leave in a blaze of glory. You've always done very well in work ever since you were in the Junior School. You've inherited your dear father's brains."

"Sometimes I wish I hadn't."

"Clara, that is a foolish thing to say. We must not quarrel with what God chooses to give us. And he gave you a good understanding to be used in His service." She shook her head a little. "Oh, my dear, I wish we could have kept you a little longer. You are going out into such a very difficult world. Here you have had Catholic surroundings, Catholic friends." She smiled. "Don't think I fear for your faith in a Protestant school. You can be a pugnacious young person. Your very obstinacy may help you there."

Clara blushed. She could never understand why people called her obstinate when to herself she seemed the most jelly-like and amorphous of creatures.

"No," the nun went on, removing her spectacles and polishing them with an enormous handkerchief. "I am thinking of later on; of a far subtler kind of attrition. It is so difficult for a convert's child. You have not had to make sacrifices for your faith as your father did. And you have not the deep-rooted habit which becomes almost an instinct with children with generations of Catholic blood. I had hoped in this last year to drive your roots so much deeper into what can never fail ... the very sources of our spiritual life." She breathed on the glasses and frowned. "You have done so well in your religious instruction. Our prize little apologist ... the Canon was specially pleased with your papers. And yet ... and yet ... I feel as if we were sending you out on a long, rough stormy journey with a hat and an umbrella but no shoes." She replaced her glasses and looked questioningly at Clara. "Do you see at all what I mean?"

"Yes, I think I do. But I'm sure I'll always be a Catholic, Mother."

Again the nun considered Clara with her head on one side. She seemed to be about to say something but did not. Clara, embarrassed, stared out of the window. Already the room, even Mother Lovell herself, seemed to belong to another life. The french windows, framed in stiff serge curtains and frosted half-way up, looked out on a dull yard at the back of the house. On the far side was a twisted yew equally dark in June or December. Only the blue sky, faintly ashen as if consuming in its own heat, indicated that it was summer. From the yard came the slop and splash of water where the lay-sisters were washing the vegetables for supper in huge galvanized tubs. Six weeks. Forty-two more suppers.

"Your faith ... my dear," the nun's voice seemed to come from a distance, "of course you will hold fast to that. And we shall all pray for you. But perhaps that wasn't quite what was in my mind."

Suddenly she leant forward and took both Clara's hands.

"Ah, my dear child," she said, her face radiant with affection. "Be simple ... be happy. Remember what St François de Sales said to Ste Jeanne de Chantal ... 'Do not turn in upon yourself ... do not philosophize about your troubles. Go straight on.' When you first came to us, you were such a happy child. Lately ... you don't have to tell me ... I have seen it from your expression ... something has clouded all that. And it comes from inside you, nowhere else. I feel you are no longer simple with yourself—with others—with God."

Clara longed to respond. "Oh, Mother ... if only ..." she began.

Far away, the Community bell rang. Mother Lovell immediately dropped Clara's hands and stood up.

"I must go and say Office now. We will talk another time."

*　　*　　*　　*　　*　　*

Clara did not, after all, have her six weeks. There was an epidemic of scarlet fever and the school broke up early in an atmosphere of flurry. As Mother Lovell was one of the victims, their interrupted talk was never resumed. There was a maimed prize-giving with no bishop, no tableaux, no ceremonial white dresses and crowns of flowers, so that, though Clara had never received more prizes, she did not have her 'blaze of glory'. There was not even the comfort of a last walk with Nicole for Madame de Savigny descended suddenly and removed her daughter a day before the others. Nicole had only time to mutter "Au revoir, ma chère. I'll write," and to thrust into her hands a copy of *Les Fleurs du Mal* and a magnificent ivory card-case, slightly chipped, before she was hurried away.

Clara's last day at Mount Hilary was a dismal anti-climax. The nuns seemed too harrassed to remember that she was leaving. She did not even receive a summons from Reverend Mother for the ritual "going out into the world" advice. Feeling forlorn and neglected, she slipped the Baudelaire into her pocket and set out to walk round the grounds and take a final farewell of the lime alleys, the lake and the shrines. But just as she was escaping, she was stopped by the nun in charge of the linen-room.

"Ah, the very child I was looking for," said Mother Damaris. "You have not handed in your white veil and your *tablier*, Clara. Go and do so at once, will you? And don't forget to remove your number ... neatly, mind."

Sulky and aggrieved, she went back to the study-room and obeyed. She had come to regard the white veil, symbol of Sundays and feasts, and the faithful old black serge apron of working days, as her own property and had hoped to take them home as relics. As she unpicked her number, she was overwhelmed with self-pity. Nothing ever went right for her as it did for other people. She was always being cheated and disappointed and misunderstood. They might at least have made a little fuss of her on her very last day.

"I'm nobody ... nobody at all," she reflected, surveying the two detached bits of tape, "not even a school number now." Next term some unknown child would listen anxiously for "43" in lists of privileges or punishments. A year from now, when Nicole too had left, no one would even remember that "43" had once been Clara Batchelor.

Chapter 2

THE cheerfully submissive letter Clara had written on Mother Lovell's advice must, she supposed, have been a success. Otherwise how could she account for the warmth with which her father welcomed her home? Since the day of her grandfather's funeral (neither of them had ever spoken of it) he had treated her with cold formality. Now he seemed not merely friendly, but strangely anxious to please her. He gave her money to buy clothes, told her to order a bookshelf for her prizes and even hinted at a special treat for the two of them when Isabel should be a little better.

Her mother still lay all day in bed with a nurse in attendance. When Clara first saw her face, shrunken and yellow between the two plaits that made her look like a girl suddenly aged, she was filled with remorse. She could not remember ever having loved her mother and what she felt now was mainly pity, but she tiptoed out of the room full of good resolutions.

Out of gratitude to her father, she spent more time than usual with old Mrs Batchelor. Nothing pleased him more than any attention to his mother and she could be sure that her virtue would be faithfully reported. Clara had never shared Isabel's loathing of the old lady. She was too used to her ugliness to feel it as a constant irritation and she had always found Mrs Batchelor the most reliable of allies. When she was little, her grandmother had defied Isabel's rules whenever she had the chance and Clara was still grateful for forbidden sweets and for hours spent in warm teashops when she was supposed to be having a brisk walk in the park. Now, though her grandmother bored her, she was easier in her company than in Isabel's. Mrs Batchelor's uncritical adoration was like a feather bed. At times it was stifling but, when Clara's vanity was chilled or bruised, she sank into it shamelessly. Sometimes, though she despised herself afterwards, she confided to her things she would not have dreamt of telling her mother. Such moments were intoxicating to the old lady. Her dull eyes shone and her heavy white face became almost animated. She responded with "secrets" of her own, abortive flirtations of fifty years ago or malicious little tales of her parents' courtship.

Isabel's illness had been a great event for old Mrs Batchelor. Not only were illness and disaster of all kinds meat and drink to her but, with her tyrant and rival out of the way, she blossomed into new confidence. Though she refused to take Isabel's place at the table, she ruled the house, paid the bills and ordered the food she liked. Mealtimes, without Isabel's sighs when she dropped gravy on her bodice or mishandled her knife, became pleasure instead of torture. Each week she presented a meticulous statement of her accounts and each week Claude said, "Really, mother, it is astonishing how far you make the housekeeping money go."

Even in this new luxury of importance there was one thing she dared not do and that was have her tea in the drawing-room. She liked to invite Clara to a ceremonial tea in her own room and, on these occasions, she provided special cakes out of her own money.

"It gives me such a nice feeling of independence, dear," she would say. "When you're my age, if by any sad chance you're not well off, you'll realize how much that means."

Isabel regarded Mrs Batchelor's room with such horror that she went into it as seldom as possible and never without wishing to burn every object in it. Into its small space were crammed all the pieces of furniture that old Mrs Batchelor had managed to save from the shabby homes of her married life. A vast double bed, even more hideous than the one she had given Claude and Isabel, occupied most of the floor; the walls were lined with rickety wardrobes, piles of dusty cardboard boxes, chests of drawers with missing handles, and tattered trunks only half concealed by faded bits of cretonne. Though there were two bathrooms in the house, Mrs Batchelor refused to part with a huge, marble-topped washstand on which there always stood, behind the ugly jug and basin, ranks of stained medicine bottles and a tumbler containing her spare set of false teeth. Even when the window was open, which it seldom was, the room retained its peculiar smell of gas, stale clothes, and camphor balls. Sometimes these dense permanent layers were thinly superimposed with the scent of lavender water. But, instead of freshening the air, this merely gave it the peculiar sickliness of perfume on unwashed flesh.

Clara, like everyone but old Mrs Batchelor herself, found the smell oppressive, but she was inured to it almost from babyhood. She could even bring herself to smile and nod when her grandmother, on winter afternoons, drawing the plush curtains and turning the leaking gas fire full on, would say happily, "Now we're really cosy, aren't we, dear?"

However, as it was July, she was spared the torment of the gas-fire and, though she longed for the coolness of the airy drawing-room, she bore these intimate tea-parties tolerably well. During the first of them her grandmother said reflectively:

"I don't expect Daddy ever told you—he is so thoughtful, he wouldn't want to upset you—how nearly we lost your dear mother."

"He did in one letter. Till then I didn't realize she was as ill as all that."

"Oh, very ill. Very ill indeed."

Clara saw from her grandmother's secret, yet inviting look that she would tell her all about it if pressed. But, for some reason, Clara decided not to press.

"Ah well," said the old woman, disappointed, "there are some things it's better for you not to know yet awhile. Something internal, your mother had. She was always delicate internally, you know."

"Was she?" said Clara, uninterested.

"Yes, indeed. Though I've my ideas on that subject. But I keep them to myself as I keep many things. Still, how thankful we should be that she was spared. Your dear Daddy would have been broken-hearted."

The idea of her mother's dying had never seriously occurred to Clara. Now, in the very effort of putting it out of her mind, she found herself toying with it. It was impossible not to think how much more peaceful life at Valetta Road was at the moment. Then she remembered that, if her mother had died, she would have had to face her father's misery.

"Yes," she said sincerely. "I don't think I could have borne *that*.

"You do love your Daddy, don't you?" purred Mrs Batchelor. "And how he does love you. Ah, I know how it feels to love an only child. I never forgot my dear baby Helen that I lost, but your father was everything to me. And one of these days his little girl will grow up and get married and leave him. I've often thought it was a pity you had no brothers or sisters. You'd have liked them, wouldn't you dear?"

"They might have been rather fun," said Clara stolidly. Just how much she wanted them, brothers especially, was a secret too personal to be told to any member of her family.

"It's sad," sighed Mrs Batchelor, "but we mustn't blame anyone, must we? Though from the first I never did think she looked healthy. Such a sallow skin. No, she wasn't at all the type your Daddy admired as a rule. He always thought so much of pink cheeks and golden hair Like yours, dear."

"I hate them myself," said Clara.

"You naughty little thing. Why it's the real English type of beauty. Now, Ada, Cousin Horace's wife ... you'd never think it to see her now, poor thing ... was quite a picture as a girl. Golden curls she had and quite a perfect complexion. I've been told someone wanted to paint her likeness for the Royal Academy. Still I must say your mother's worn better. But she's had a kind husband and an easy life."

"It must be awful to be married to that man."

Mrs Batchelor sighed and wagged her head:

"Ah, I daresay she often wishes things had turned out otherwise."

"You're looking mysterious, Granny. Tell me all."

"Well, if I do, dear, you must promise never to mention it."

Clara pursed her lips and nodded, pretending an interest she was far from feeling.

"I'm afraid there's no denying your Daddy was a bit of a flirt in his day. Fancy, people used to say the same of your old Granny. You'd never think it now, would you?"

"I know you were a heart-breaker. Aunt Sophy's told me things. But I shan't give her away."

"You mustn't believe all you hear," said the old lady with a smile at once fatuous and touching. "Well, as I was saying there was a time when your Daddy was quite sweet on Cousin Ada. Of course she wasn't married then. And she was very taken by him; no girl could have helped being. I know poor Horace had many a twinge of jealousy. There's no knowing what might have happened if your mother hadn't come along. But after he'd met Miss Isabel Maule, Daddy stopped having eyes for anyone else. I know Ada was more than a little upset. The funny thing was it seemed to make Horace all the keener to marry her. Men are very peculiar sometimes. I've an idea he's paid her out in all sorts of little ways. And of course, right from a little boy, he's been jealous of your Daddy."

The horrible lunch party at Paget's Fold came back into Clara's mind with new significance. She realized for the first time that her father and mother had had a life before she existed and that all those dull relatives whom she could never imagine otherwise than middle-aged had once been young and capable of feeling.

She said thoughtfully:

"If Daddy *had* married Ada, I wouldn't have existed. At any rate I wouldn't have been the same person."

"No doubt there's a Providence in these things," said Mrs Batchelor piously. "I often say to myself, 'at least there's dear little Clara.'"

"I suppose no one ever understands really why any two people get married."

Mrs. Batchelor looked frightened.

"Oh, please don't misunderstand me, Clara. Don't get the idea that I would ever dream of criticizing your mother." She raised her voice as if she thought Isabel might be listening at the door. "I wish you could have seen your mother when she was young, dear. Really, she was very striking looking girl. Quite fascinating, many people thought."

Clara smiled.

"Don't be so desperately charitable, Granny. We all know she's awful to you sometimes."

"I daresay it's my fault. I'm sure I never mean to vex her. But every little thing does seem to aggravate her so."

"I often think I was born with a skin too few," quoted Clara.

"You naughty, naughty little girl," said Mrs Batchelor comfortably. "Well, we all have our faults. I often blame old Mr Maule. He really did spoil her shockingly. He was very strict with his other children, but he gave in to Belle, as he called her, in everything."

"Her sisters must have been awfully jealous."

"I don't know, I'm sure. If they were, they were too frightened of their father to show it. A really terrible temper old Mr Maule had. I've seen him threaten your poor Grandpa with a poker. Of course he didn't at all care for her marrying into a family that he considered so much beneath him. With her looks he'd hoped she'd marry a title or at least a very rich man."

"I suppose she did have lots of admirers?"

"Oh certainly, dear, by all accounts. But she hadn't a penny you know. And, though it was a very old family and all that, her father couldn't afford for her to have what you call a society life. Besides he'd quarrelled with all his relations. There was only one Lord I ever heard of wanted to marry her and he was a wicked old man with one foot in the grave. I'll say to her credit she wouldn't have *him*."

"I suppose she was awfully in love with Daddy."

"Oh yes. I'm sure she was. In the nature of things it had to be a very long engagement. Four whole years. It must have been very trying to anyone of her impatient disposition."

"Didn't Daddy get impatient too?"

"No doubt. She always expected so much attention. And your Daddy was working so hard. Many a time when he ought to have been resting, he'd go all that way down to Norwood to see her for an hour. And of course they had their ups and downs. It was wonderful how he put up with all her little tantrums. Often I thought he ought to have been firmer with her for her own sake but it wasn't for me to say. And as I was telling you just now, we ought to blame old Mr Maule rather than her. If she'd been the only one, he couldn't have spoilt her more."

An old grievance flared up in Clara.

"People always say only children are spoilt."

"I'm sure that's not true of you, dear," said her grandmother. "Quite the reverse."

"They always say it though," said Clara resentfully. "I get absolutely sick of it at school. They just assume if you're an only child you're a kind of monster. Even if they don't think you're particularly spoilt, they assume you're bound to be queer in some way."

"In my opinion you could have done with a bit more spoiling when you were little. Your Grandfather thought the same. Many's the time your Daddy hasn't dared show how fond he was of you for fear of ... well, I won't say it. I daresay you can guess what I mean."

Without knowing why, Clara suddenly felt disgusted with herself. The room seemed to have become unbearably stuffy. She glanced at the clock and gave a false start of alarm.

"Heavens, I'd no idea it was so late. I've only just time to get up to Mudie's to change Mother's book."

"You've plenty of time for another éclair," said Mrs Batchelor. "I know how you love them. The clock's ten minutes fast. In any case, you've lots of time if you take a bus."

"No, Granny, really. I've had far too many éclairs already. I'd better go and walk them off."

She stood up and shook the crumbs from her skirt.

"Well, if you insist," sighed the old woman. "I daresay the walk will do you good. But you must be tired of going the same way every day to change your mother's library book. Daddy appreciates what a good girl you've been since Mother was ill. It's wonderful the number of books she gets through lying there, isn't it?"

"I don't blame her," said Clara. "I always long for new books when I'm in the infirmary. We have to make some ghastly saint's life last for days.

"You're an unselfish little thing, aren't you? Just like your Daddy. Don't think for a minute I'm blaming your mother. I'm sure I like a good read myself when I've the time. Poor Mummy, she must miss her bridge parties. Though, even when she's well, she's a great reader, isn't she?"

"So am I," said Clara, driven for some reason to defend her mother.

"Yes. But you haven't got household duties. I often wonder if your mother wouldn't be happier if she took some interest in household things. It doesn't seem natural, somehow, a woman spending so much time lying on a sofa and reading, the way she does. Still, it's not for me to criticize. At any rate you can't lose money while you're reading as you can at bridge."

Clara kissed the cheek the old woman offered her. She had never noticed before how damp and flabby it was.

"Thank you for a really lovely tea, Granny," she said, impelled suddenly to assume her best Mount Hilary manner. "I've enjoyed myself so much."

Her grandmother looked up at her admiringly, yet with a touch of fear.

"Dear me, how you're growing up. It comes over me with quite a shock that you're not just a little thing any more. But you'll always be Daddy's girl, won't you?"

* * * * * *

In spite of the unusual peace at home, the days had never dragged so heavily for Clara as they did that July. She pined for Mount Hilary and woke up each brilliant morning longing for the sight of its trees and meadows and the sound of its bells. All the children she knew were still at their schools; even at week-ends she dared not invite anyone to tea for fear of disturbing her mother's rest or the nurse's. Sickness brooded over the house, upsetting its routine. Rooms grew dusty and silver tarnished, for the two servants were tired and cross from overwork. The endless carrying of trays up five flights of stairs had made even the friendly Zillah sulky. Clara spent most of her time running errands in the baking streets or reading aimlessly in her bedroom. The one or two brief notes that came from Nicole only sharpened her feeling of isolation. Though Nicole was in London and only a mile or two away, she might, as far as Clara was concerned, have been on the other side of the world. She seemed to be immersed in dressmakers, dances and theatres. In a letter she wrote, "I am seriously thinking of entering. It would at least save one from the boredom of having to have one's hair done and changing one's clothes three times a day. The only thing that seriously deters me is the thought of Community recreation. I could easily yet used to a hair shirt but not to 'cheerful, edifying impersonal conversation' twice a day with the same women." In another she suggested that she should slip away from her chaperone and meet Clara "in the National Gallery or the British Museum like a guilty couple in Henry James". But Clara, struck with panic, had made the excuse that she could not leave her mother. In all their three years' friendship she had never met Nicole outside Mount Hilary. Though in one way she longed to see her again, it was not only shyness that made her refuse. Since she had come back home, a kind of inertia had settled on her. She felt dull and stupid; she no longer expected, hardly even wanted anything interesting to happen. Monotony came to have an oppressive charm. She almost dreaded any break in the chalk circle in which she found herself stuck like a hypnotized bird.

Chapter 3

ONE morning at breakfast her father said carelessly:
"Are you by any chance free on Thursday evening, Clara?"
As she had been in every evening since she came home, she
answered, wondering:

"Yes, of course. Why?"

"Only that they've extended the Opera season and I've managed to
get two rather good seats for *Tannhäuser* if you'd care to come."

Realizing this must be the promised treat, she said excitedly: "Care
to? I'd *love* to. Do you really mean it?"

He beamed at her.

"Certainly I mean it. I always promised to take you to *Tannhäuser*
when you were fifteen."

"Daddy always keeps his promises," purred old Mrs Batchelor.
"Fancy your going to the Opera at night like a grand lady, Clara.
She must wear her best frock, mustn't she, Claude? Granny'll wash
and iron it for you, dear."

Clara saw that this was to be a great occasion. The only cloud was
the fear that she might not rise to it and thus disappoint him once
again. For *Tannhäuser* was his one musical passion. He never went to
concerts and music for him was almost entirely an affair of associations.
He was fond of Gilbert and Sullivan because he had first heard them
at Cambridge and he was deeply moved by certain old German songs
and Chopin nocturnes because Isabel had played and sung them
during their courtship.

Larry O'Sullivan, his great friend at Emmanuel, had been an ardent
Wagnerian and, under Larry's influence, he had gone so far as to buy
all the scores. But, except for *Tannhäuser* which was kept in the piano
stool and tattered from use, they had gathered dust for twenty years
in the darkest corner of the study.

He had fallen in love with *Tannhäuser* at the first hearing and each
time he heard it he fell more in love than ever. He never missed a per-
formance if he could help it and he always returned in a state of
extraordinary elation. Almost always he went alone, for Isabel had
never been able to understand why anyone should wish to see a play

or hear an opera more than once. On this subject he was proof against Isabel's jeers. If she went too far he jeered in turn at her beloved Ibsen and Maeterlinck.

"I've no patience with your chlorotic adulteresses and your Don Juans in goloshes," he would say. "I am prepared to tread the primrose path to the sound of flutes but not to limp to perdition to the wheeze of a harmonium."

For years he had been preparing Clara for her solemn initiation. When she was a small child, he had told her the story over and over again and she had hardly learnt her scales before he gave her a piano arrangement of the score. Now that she could play reasonably well, he listened patiently to Beethoven and Mozart on condition that she would give him "just a morsel of *Tannhäuser* for a *bonne bouche*." Invariably, after this, he would say, "Ah, my child, you don't know what pleasure that gives me," and, once or twice, she had seen actual tears of happiness in his eyes.

Sometimes, if he had a pupil-free half-hour on a Sunday morning, he would go himself to the old yellow-keyed piano and thunderously vamp out the Pilgrim's March or even sing extracts in odd transpositions he had made to fit his pleasant, short-ranged tenor. All her life, Clara associated the Sunday mornings of her youth in London with High Mass at the Carmelites, the smell of a roasting joint and her father's voice solemnly chanting:

> "The light of heaven o-hon the pi-hil-grim glow-eth
> In holy freedo-hom and pea-eace now he go-eth"

or crying with full-throated fervour:

> "The wi-hi-hill I sing,
> Oh Goddess young and te-hender."

"You are too young yet to appreciate all it means," he had often told her. "I don't think I did myself until I became a Catholic. Now *Tannhäuser* seems to me the perfect expression of the whole problem of good and evil."

When the great night came, Clara dressed herself in her white muslin party frock and the soft pale blue cloak from Liberty's that Mrs Shapiro had sent her the Christmas before last. Her newly-washed hair, adorned with a blue bow, hung in a shining mass over her shoulders. When she went up to say goodbye to her mother, she felt almost guilty for being so young and fresh and healthy. Isabel, lying among crumpled pillows with her limp hair pushed back anyhow from a face yellow as wax, seemed to have no connection with the sleek beauty of a few months ago.

"Darling, how charming you look," she said wistfully. "The picture of youth. I wish I could have a portrait of you, just as you are at this moment."

From force of habit, and for once unreproved, Clara fiddled with one of the brass knobs of the bed.

"It's only my old white muslin," she said awkwardly. "It's a shame you can't come too. You really must hurry up and get better."

"Sometimes I wonder if I ever shall," Isabel sighed.

"Of course you will," said Clara heartily. "The doctor says you're going on splendidly."

"Doctors don't know everything." The great dark eyes stared hungrily. "Still, it does me good to see you. I've always loved everything young and gay and pretty. Oh why is life so cruel to women? But I shouldn't talk like this when yours is only just beginning. Come and kiss me, pet."

Clara did so. Isabel, always so fresh, so perfumed, now had a sickly smell.

"Like a flower you look and feel," she said, stroking Clara's bare arm. "What a lovely cool white skin."

The faint invalid voice became stronger.

"Don't grow up too fast. Something tells me you'll be attractive to men, just as I was. And whatever you do, don't be in too much of a hurry to get married."

Clara laughed.

"Oh, I'll most probably be an old maid."

Her mother smiled wanly.

"I can't quite see you as that. Though perhaps they're happier. Marriage can be so dreadfully disillusioning if one is at all romantic." She sighed. "And I *was* romantic."

Clara waited for the usual sequel; the story of how, the first Christmas after their marriage, her father had gone out to dinner with some old friends from Cambridge and come home drunk. But it did not come. Instead her mother said hurriedly, almost guiltily:

"Don't think I am saying anything against Daddy. No, no. He is far better than most of them. It is what men are in themselves or what marriage is. Call it nature if you like." She looked intently at Clara. "I wonder, darling, have you any idea of such things?"

Clara frowned and clutched the brass knob. Her idea of "such things" was of the haziest. The nuns, naturally, never mentioned them and at Mount Hilary it was not the fashion to discuss them, even with one's most intimate friends. But lately she had been reading *Adam Bede* and *Tess of the d'Urbervilles* and these had raised a very puzzling question. Her mother was, however, the last person she was inclined to ask for the answer.

"Oh yes, of course," she said off-handedly.

"Really dear? Do you mean to say you know *everything?* Somehow I never thought the nuns ..."

"I think things out for myself," said Clara grandly.

"You're so clever, pet," said her mother. "All the same ... But perhaps modern girls are different." She lay back and, relapsing into her invalid voice, went on:

"I knew nothing. Absolutely nothing. Never, never shall I forget the appalling shock, the dreadful disillusion. And when a woman has a child, she goes down to the gates of hell."

"Clara," sounded Claude's voice from downstairs. Never had interruption been more welcome.

"I must go, Mummy. You know he hates to be kept waiting."

With a hasty kiss and "have a good night" she made her escape. She went downstairs, feeling obscurely angry with her mother as if, in some way, she had spoilt the evening. But when she saw her father standing in the hall and looking up at her with an almost mischievous smile, as if they were fellow conspirators, all her sense of freshness and gaiety came back.

"Ah, I'm glad you're in white, my dear," he greeted her. "Nothing suits you so well." From behind his back he produced a spray of pink carnations. "And here is something to match your cheeks. I have even remembered a pin."

"Oh, *thank* you, Daddy. You do look magnificent," she said, pinning on her flowers and gazing at him with admiration. Evening clothes suited him; they set off his fairness and made him seem taller. Never, she thought, had she seen him looking so young and handsome.

She giggled with sheer happiness.

"I never thought I'd go to the opera with you in your opera hat, I *do* feel grand."

He offered his arm.

"Your carriage is waiting."

To her amazement, it was no mere taxi but a hired car with a chauffeur in livery. A hired car was the very greatest of luxuries, associated only with the most solemn family feasts such as her parents' wedding anniversary. Never before had he ordered one just for Clara.

"Daddy, you *are* spoiling me," she said, leaning back on the thick grey cushions.

"Ah well, I am spoiling myself too. Once in a while, I like to enjoy the illusion of being rich."

She nodded, too excited to speak. The chains of street lamps slid by in the July dusk. She felt as if London were illuminated in their honour.

"Do you mind if I smoke?"

He had never asked her permission before.

"Of course. Or does one say, of course not?"

"I take it I may?" He took out a gold case, presented by a grateful pupil, which he hardly ever used. To see him smoking a cigarette instead of his eternal pipe added to the delightful strangeness of everything. Glancing at his face, shining with pleasure among the blue wreaths of smoke, it was impossible to realize that this was the father who had paralysed her with terror. Their last drive together in a hired car, those appalling journeys to and from her grandfather's funeral, seemed as unreal as someone else's nightmare. Hardly noticing what she was doing, she tucked her arm through his as she used to do when she was a child. For several minutes they drove in blissful silence. Then he turned his face to her.

"Happy? Not bored at the thought of an evening alone with your aged parent?"

"Fisher," she mocked him. "Shameless fisher. I won't bite. And how dare you say you're old?"

She meant it. For the first time it occurred to her that he was probably not so very old after all. Until then, all grown-ups had seemed to her much the same age. They did not grow older as one did oneself; they simply belonged to a different species of human being. Very old people, like her grandmother, were merely another kind of grown-up.

He squeezed her arm.

"I'm perfectly willing to forget the question of age if you are. In fact I'm only too willing to forget everything tonight. Let us ignore the fact that I am a beggarly usher. Let us spend too much and be monstrously irresponsible."

"I hate responsibility," said Clara recklessly. "*Carpe noctem.*"

"Precisely. *Lente, lente, currite noctis equi.*"

"Oh, they don't run *lente* enough," she breathed. "Why do nice things go so fast? We're nearly there."

It was the first time Clara had been inside Covent Garden. From their seats in the front row of the circle, the whole house opened before them like the interior of a vast gold and crimson shell. She had never imagined anything like the great tiers, the massed flowers and the blazing chandeliers. Each box was like a tiny limelit stage with its curtains parted to reveal dazzling creatures from another world. She was so entranced that she almost forgot she had come to hear *Tannhäuser* and her programme lay unopened on her lap.

"I wanted you to have a proper first impression," he said, revelling in her dazed delight. "When I'm alone, I often go in the 'gods'. But your first *Tannhäuser* must be something to remember."

He had even brought opera-glasses which he directed for her from box to box, telling her names to which she barely listened. The pleasure of being able to turn the brilliant puppets at will into human beings was interest enough. It was fascinating to bring a face so close that she could watch the play of every feature; to guess what made a woman smile or suddenly unfold her fan.

"Oh, it's wonderful," she said. "It's like seeing hundreds of novels all coming to life at once."

"Probably not a quarter of them have come for the music. You'll see how the boxes empty after the first act. But I love to see them. Heaven forbid that Covent Garden should ever be filled with Jaeger suits and djibbahs."

"Amen," said Clara fervently.

"All the same, if a duchess chattered during the first bars of the overture, I should have not the least hesitation in shooting her." He took the glasses from her and swept them round the boxes.

"Ah, my dear, there is something you really must look at. Yes, there is no mistaking *her*—Lady Sybil Clavering—the Duke of Westmorland's younger daughter. The gold and white, the goddess type. A Greek nymph with the English dew on her. But it would take Meredith to describe her."

Clara took the glasses and searched obediently for the famous beauty.

"Third box ... on the left ... wearing something soft, white and clinging as male novelists say. No, you are looking at the wrong box."

She found Lady Sybil and said warmly: "Oh yes, she really is lovely," but in her search she had seen something far more interesting. After a decent interval, she switched the glasses back to the wrong box.

"Daddy, there's a girl I know there. I wasn't sure at first, but now I am."

"Really? Who is that?"

"Nicole de Savigny."

"Your great friend at the convent. How interesting. May I look? Certainly a remarkable face, my dear. Not perhaps what one would call pretty, but piquant, undeniably piquant. And is that extremely distinguished-looking woman her mother? The Comtesse de Savigny, I believe you said."

"Yes, I think so. But I've only seen her in the parlour and in a hat."

"Do you know the Comtesse at all?"

"Oh no. We don't talk to other people's parents unless we know them at home."

She glanced at him, afraid she might have hurt his feelings. But the glasses masked his expression. She wished he would put them down. Suppose Nicole should see them staring at her?

"I fancy you told me the Comtesse de Savigny had been an ambassadress. I must say she looks the part."

At last he put down the glasses.

"Like all the low-born, I have a passion for the aristocracy," he said. Clara was too fond of him tonight to wince.

"Darling Daddy, I wish I could make you a duke."

"And destroy my passion? My dear, you are too young to appreciate the exquisite taste of discontent." He laughed. "I agree it would have to be a duke. I haven't the figure for an earl. But dukes are often short and bucolic."

"*You're* not bucolic," she said indignantly. "Blaze Hoadley is, if you like." She stopped and bit her tongue. Now she had wrecked everything. But to her amazement he merely smiled and said:

"Ah, your rustic swain. My Chloë should have a prettier Daphnis."

Clara had no time to brood on the incomprehensibility of parents for already the lights were lowered. There was a hush; then the first grave chords of the overture sounded in the darkness. Her father gave a sigh of pleasure and leant back with closed eyes.

In spite of all his warnings she could not help being disconcerted that both Venus and Tannhäuser should be so elderly and so very fat.

But the smell of scent and dust, the glimmer of white shirt fronts and creamy shoulders in the vast dim house, the sense of being present at some extraordinary ritual soon produced a kind of intoxication. She forgot everything and let herself drown in the sensuous, easy music.

When the lights went up, she and Claude blinked at each other as if waking from the same rapturous dream.

"Well?"

"Oh, *Daddy!*"

He patted her hand.

"Ah, my dear, I'm so glad. I hoped you would feel as I do. Certainly I've heard better Tannhäusers. But what does that matter? In heaven, no doubt, de Reszke will sing it for me. Meanwhile, imagination bridges the gap."

He began to talk of the genius that could so perfectly express in music the conflict between the two sides of a man's nature.

"Every man," he said, "is both Wolfram and Tannhäuser. But women are different. They are either Venus or Elizabeth."

Clara listened with parted lips and shining eyes, as he talked on. She felt she was being initiated into a new world and abandoned herself completely to this extraordinary, transformed father. She thought with his mind, heard with his ears, until both his talk and the music she had just heard seemed a revelation of something at once subtle, exciting and profound.

Suddenly, in mid-flight, he broke off.

"I had forgotten, for the moment, you were only a child."

"Oh, *please* go on forgetting."

He shook his head, smiling.

"Let us take a turn and have a look at the lions."

Reluctantly she followed him out to the foyer. Brilliantly dressed women, gay as tropical birds against the magpie elegance of their escorts sauntered to and fro chattering, fanning themselves, staring through their lorgnettes. At close quarters Clara found them less glamorous than in the frames of their boxes. When her father left her to get her some lemonade, she leant rather disconsolately against the wall, bewildered by the hubbub of shrill and languid voices and the glitter of jewels and sequins. Never had she felt more of a stranger than among this chattering, parading crowd of people who all seemed to know each other. Suddenly a hand was laid on her arm and a familiar husky voice said:

"Well, are you going to cut me?"

"Nicole!"

"I've escaped. Half the German embassy has invaded our box and I can't stand Germans. What luck to find *you* here."

In a sophisticated pink evening dress, with a pearl comb in her unnaturally tidy hair, Nicole looked five years older. However, she wore her fine feathers as carelessly as her school uniform. She had obviously been dressed by a maid but already wisps were straying from the elaborate coiffure, a hook had come undone and the camellias on her shoulder had a battered look. Her hands, manicured and artificially whitened, fidgeted in search of non-existent pockets and her silver-shod feet were planted in her usual masculine stance.

"I feel like a circus-horse on these occasions," she said. "I'm not the type that can appear in public, in white muslin with its hair down. You can, my dear Clara, most successfully. The perfect English *jeune fille*. Who are you with?"

"My father. But I've lost him for the moment."

"If you find him, you must introduce me," said Nicole. "You know how I long to meet this *parent terrible* of yours. Did you come to *Die Meistersinger* last week?"

Clara blushed.

"It's the first time in my life that I've been to the opera."

"Pity you've chosen such a rotten night. I'm not mad on Wagner even at his best but *Tannhäuser* really ought to be prohibited. It's musically indecent. Thank goodness, we are going after the next act."

"Don't say that to my father," said Clara in agony. "He adores it." She had not the courage to say, "I'm adoring it too."

Nicole shrugged her shoulders.

"Oh well. Each man to his own poison. I wonder why the English have this passion for Wagner. I suppose because, like the Germans, they've never been properly civilized."

Clara sketched a curtsy.

"*Merci bien.*"

"Idiot, I don't mean you. Besides, I've a German grandfather if it comes to that."

As they talked, Nicole once or twice broke off to smile or wave her fan at an acquaintance.

"It's so strange, meeting you here," sighed Clara. "I suppose you know lots of these people."

"Oh, one runs into them everywhere."

"I don't.'

"Well, you don't miss much. Thank goodness we go to France the day after tomorrow.

"Lucky wretch. I wonder if I shall *ever* go abroad."

"What's the matter, *mon vieux?* I seem to have a depressing effect on you. You have a hunted look as if you expected to be arrested any moment."

Nicole had hit exactly on Clara's state of mind. She was in an agony in case her father would join them. How would he appear to Nicole's merciless eye?

"Fickle creature. I don't believe you are a bit glad to see your childhood's friend."

Clara clasped her hands together in misery.

"Oh, I am, Nicole, I am. If only there weren't all these people. I feel so stupid and bewildered. If you knew how I'd missed you. It might be five years instead of five weeks."

"Well, I did my best to lure you to an assignation," Nicole smiled with faint malice. "I presume your mother is better since you and your Papa are both here."

"Oh, much better." Clara could feel herself blushing.

"Otherwise," said Nicole, prodding her with her fan, "I might be tempted to think you were shunning me. Now I don't see much hope. I hardly get a second to breathe since *Maman* decided to drag me through the fag-end of the season. I suppose she thought I mightn't have another chance if there's a war."

"A war? Do you really think there might be?"

"You seem very surprised. Don't any rumours reach you in your remote tower?"

In the distance Clara caught sight of her father working his way towards them through the crowd. Nicole followed her look.

"Is that your Papa? The fair one with the moustache? He's absurdly like you."

"Is he?" said Clara, faintly.

"*Ma chère,* you've completely misled me. I expected a tyrant with beetling brows. He looks like a cross between a cherub and one of the later Roman Emperors, the mild ones. The chin's slightly intimidating I admit. I insist on being presented to him."

He was only a few yards away when, to Clara's relief, a majestic woman bore down on Nicole.

"Ah, te voilà enfin, Nicole. Ta maman m'a envoyée te chercher. C'est même un peu fort ce que tu fais là. Même à Londres, les fillettes ne se promènent pas toutes seules à l'Opéra."

With a freezing glance at Clara, she clutched Nicole's arm.

"Viens donc, ma belle."

Nicole shrugged her shoulders:

"D'accord, ma tante. Mais permets d'abord que je présente une grande amie du Pensionnat, Clara Batchelor. Clara chérie, Madame la Marquise de Vuillaume Grandpré."

The aunt coldly inclined her head: *"Mademoiselle."*

"Connais pas ce nom là," she whispered audibly to her niece.

"Au revoir, mon vieux. I'll write to you from France," said Nicole glancing back with a grimace and a wave of her fan as she moved off under escort.

"Au revoir, Nicole."

With a sigh half sad, half relieved, Clara watched Nicole's rose-coloured dress disappear into the crowd. When she looked up her father was standing beside her with a radiant face.

"How charming of your friend to seek you out like that. I was watching you but didn't want to intrude."

"But you should have, Daddy," said Clara. "Nicole was saying how much she wanted to meet you."

She chattered on recklessly, as she sipped the lemonade he had brought, trying to make up to him for her cowardice. "She kept on saying so. And she picked you out at once. She said we were exactly alike."

He could not hide his pleasure.

"Come, come, my dear, that is hardly flattering to you, though extremely gratifying to me."

"Oh ... and she said you looked like a Roman Emperor."

"Indeed. That, again, can hardly apply to you. But I must say I take it as a compliment. I almost regret that I did not come forward. I should have liked to meet this charming young person. But I got a peculiar pleasure from watching the two of you together. Will you be seeing her again in the next interval? Then, perhaps ..."

"No, they're going after this act. Isn't it a shame?" She added a lie. "Nicole is furious. But she has to go on to some embassy dance or other."

"Noblesse oblige. What a price to pay, though, to miss the last act

of *Tannhäuser*. Still, no doubt she has heard it often. I think you told me she was musical."

"Oh yes. Tremendously."

"And who was that rather alarming but extremely impressive lady to whom she introduced you. Not, I think, the Comtesse de Savigny."

"No, an aunt of hers. The Marquise de ... sorry I can't remember the name."

"My dear, you give me glimpses of a brilliant world," he said as they made their way back to their seats.

Clara roused herself loyally and put her hand on his sleeve.

"And who brought me to Covent Garden?"

"My child, I have no illusions about myself. But when I saw you just now with your friend, I could not help feeling proud. I have always cherished the fancy that one day, to quote the immortal Carter, 'from the top of my bus I shall look down on your carriage.' "

The second act was ruined for Clara. Try as she would, she could not help being aware of Nicole's presence. One half of her still shared her father's uncritical ecstasy; the other half was imagining Nicole's amused distaste. Over and over again her eyes strayed from the stage, searching the huge darkened house for a particular box. Not till the lights went up and she saw that it was already empty, could she settle down to enjoy herself again. During the third act she tucked her arm penitently into her father's and he gave it a little squeeze. Once or twice she glanced at him, fearing that she might have broken the bond between them, but each time his head turned at once to meet her look and, in the dimness, she could see that his expression was one of solemn rapture. To her relief, he smiled when the blossoming staff, laid across the convex mound of Tannhäuser's stomach, began to sway up and down like a see-saw.

"The sublime certainly has its ridiculous moments," he said as they stood up to go. "Personally I adore them. Opera wouldn't be opera without them."

As he settled the blue cloak on her shoulders, he smiled mysteriously.

"Not too sleepy, I hope? Because I have a mild surprise for you."

Clara opened her eyes very wide.

"Of *course* I'm not sleepy."

"Then I suggest we go and have a little supper."

Chapter 4

IT was evident from his manner that he was taking her somewhere special, but Clara had been to few restaurants and the name he gave the chauffeur meant nothing to her. When they were ushered into a single room not very large and rather dim, she was at first disappointed. She had expected something with bright lights and a band. Here there were only a few tables, lit with shaded lamps, though she noticed that the people sitting at them looked extremly elegant.

The room was so quiet, the curtains so heavy and the lights so subdued that the place might have been designed to protect delicate creatures from glare and noise. She walked behind the waiter on tip-toe till she found that her feet made no sound on the thick carpet. She and her father seemed to be expected. The table to which they were led had a vase of Clara's favourite pink carnations and beside it stood a gold-necked bottle in a pail of ice. She returned from leaving her cloak in charge of an alarming Frenchwoman, feeling absurdly young and self-conscious in her white muslin. One or two men gave her a languid, faintly amused stare. To her relief their own table was in a corner and from her place she could see no one but her father.

"I took the risk of ordering our supper beforehand," he said as she sat down. "I hope I have guessed what you'd like. I thought you would prefer cold *consommé* to oysters. Though we can eat them safely here even when there is no 'r' in the month. I propose to do so. Then a little salmon, with asparagus tips. Chicken, with a rather special cream sauce you get nowhere else, and *omelette surprise* for a sweet. Does that sound all right?"

"It sounds wonderful," Clara murmured, her eye on the waiter who was busy with the gold-necked bottle. When the cork flew out with a soft explosion, she managed not to look surprised.

"Yes ... a little champagne for Mademoiselle," her father nodded. "If you don't like it, Clara, no doubt François can find you something else."

"Of course I like it," she said grandly, though she had only had occasional sips at weddings and much preferred fizzy lemonade. The waiter filled their glasses and, to her comfort, disappeared.

"It's lovely and cold," she said, sipping it carefully and trying not to make a face. "*Much* nicer than any I've had before."

"I ordered it partly for your sake. Though I admit I have a weakness for champagne myself. Strictly speaking, *Tannhäuser* calls for one of the Rhine wines ... 'the silver harp and the stained legend'. But you might be a shade too young for a still wine."

To show that she could at least appreciate champagne, Clara took a large gulp and tried not to wish it were sweeter. But when she tasted her *consommé* there was no need to pretend. Never had she imagined mere soup could taste so delicious.

"I see you have the makings of a *gourmet*."

"I certainly do love luxury and nice things," she sighed happily. "We're being wickedly luxurious tonight, aren't we?"

"Ah well," he smiled. "The old hack must get out of harness once in a while. I confess I should like to be able to do this a little more often."

Watching his face, it was impossible to imagine that he could ever be other than genial and expansive.

"You're a different person without your harness," she risked. "Oh, I do wish you could be awfully rich."

"Riches are bad for the soul. We all subscribe to that ... in theory. Yet sometimes I wonder if it isn't just as bad for the soul to be endlessly worrying about how one's going to pay one's bills."

"I'm sure it is," said Clara enthusiastically.

"But let's forget bills for tonight. By rights every penny we are spending should be going into some doctor's or draper's or tax-collector's pocket. After all, should I enjoy all this so much without the lurking sense of guilt? The only way to overcome a temptation is to yield to it."

Between mouthfuls of delicious salmon, Clara stared at him fascinated. Was this really her father, the slave of duty, the stern disciplinarian who scolded her when she overspent her pocket money?

"I don't often break out," he said, half apologetically. He lifted his shoulders as if shaking off a weight and looked about him. "I hope you like this place. I came here first when I was an undergraduate. It is always associated for me with poor Larry O'Sullivan." He sipped his champagne with half-closed eyes. "I haven't been here often since his death."

"He was your great friend at Cambridge, wasn't he?"

"The greatest friend I ever had in my life. No one could ever take his place. He died in Egypt when he was only thirty-two." He sighed. "I wish you could have known him. There never was such charm."

"I've always liked his face."

Ever since she could remember, Larry O'Sullivan's photo had stood in the place of honour in the study; a young face with a witty mouth under a drooping moustache and deep-lidded eyes that looked both melancholy and amused.

"He was a romantic figure to me," her father mused. "It was not only his charm: everyone felt the spell of *that*. He stood for everything I never had and he had the gift of turning life into a fine art. He sighed. "He took things lightly. I have never been able to do that."

"Nicole does too."

"Yes, as soon as I saw your friend, for some reason, my mind flashed back to Larry. The French and the Irish ... they know instinctively how to live. Perhaps you and I are attracted by the same types. It is an odd thing perhaps but I have never brought your mother here. When we occasionally celebrate we go to the Carlton or the Savoy. Now and then, very seldom indeed, I come here alone."

Clara's glass of champagne had produced a slight exhilaration. She and her father seemed to be floating together in some wonderful element, entirely detached from their daily life.

"Nineteen, I was," he went on—"only a few years older than you, Clara, when Larry and I had our first supper here. It was always he who took me, of course. I was very hard up in those days. I know it was a Friday for he didn't remember till after he'd eaten his *caneton pressé*. And then he said to old Moulinot ... it was in the father's time of course ... "*Votre caneton vaut bien un brin de purgatoire.*"

Clara nodded.

"I can just imagine Nic saying that."

"Catholics born, the two of them. He took that lightly like everything else. How amused he would have been at my conversion." He pulled himself up and said with a touch of his old manner, "No doubt it went deeper than he admitted. I'm sure he made a good end."

"I wish I could have known you when you were nineteen," Clara said, to lure him back.

"I suppose it is inconceivable to you that your parents were ever young."

"Well, it *is* difficult," she admitted. "Of course I know from photos what you both looked like. I know you had curly hair and wore a coat with funny short lapels. Only I can't imagine knowing you ... as I know Nicole for example."

"As your father, I should certainly have forbidden you to know me in those days. At nineteen I was a cynical young atheist. No, my dear, I should have been a shockingly bad influence."

"I can't believe you were anything but good *ever*," she said, sincerely.

"Can't you, my dear? Perhaps it's a fortunate illusion." He seemed about to say something more but stopped. Instead he looked at her intently for a moment and then sighed: "Ah, Clara."

"What is it, Daddy?"

"Nothing. I was toying with a wild notion I sometimes have."

"Tell me."

"Well, now and then, I try to fancy how it would be if you and I were not father and daughter."

She took it up eagerly.

"Oh, I've often thought that too."

His eyes grew bright.

"*Have* you? That's remarkably interesting."

"Of course I don't mean I want anyone else for a father. But just that now and then ..."

"We could forget," he nodded. "Exactly. Sometimes the idea is so vivid to me that it is almost like a memory. We meet, you and I, in a lonely tower. I don't know why a tower. And by some spell, we have forgotten our own identities. We talk without any self-consciousness."

The waiter interrupted them, bringing the *omelette surprise*.

"No, don't wait. Eat it at once," he smiled, as she paused, eager for him to go on. "You'll find it a new experience, I think."

"But it's magic," she said, tasting the hot *soufflé* and the ice simultaneously. "It's like something out of the *Arabian Nights*."

"A paradoxical sweet. Like these absurd dreams of ours."

Half-way through her enormous helping, Clara laid down her spoon.

"I *am* having a lovely time," she said blissfully. "If only those horses would stand still now, for ever."

"Happiness is remarkably becoming to you, my dear. I don't think I've ever seen you look so pretty. My instinct was right when I named you Clara after my beloved Clara Middleton. But I forgot, you haven't yet read *The Egoist*. I wonder if you will ever share my passion for Meredith."

"I did find the style difficult when I tried," she said humbly. "But I'm longing to try again now I'm older."

"Larry always used to say that your true Meredithian loves the master, not in spite of his obscurities, but because of them. It was Larry, of course, who introduced me to Meredith, as he did to Pater and to Wilde. I never discovered anything on my own; everything came through Larry. Except the one, the most important of all. Odd that the Catholic faith should have been the one thing he never tried to communicate to me." He seemed to have forgotten all about Clara and to be talking to himself. "Well, perhaps, not so odd," he said with a peculiar smile and added "It was a comfort to me that Wilde died a Catholic." He pulled himself up and addressed Clara once more.

"Yes, my dear, I long for you to read *The Egoist*. If it won't make you vain to know how I see you in my imagination. You will find Larry's portrait in it too. In his last years he was Horace de Cray to the life. De Cray with a dash of Lord Henry Wootton."

"Are you in it too," she asked, rather shyly.

"Alas, no, my dear. I should like to be able to see myself in Vernon Whitford. But I could hardly be described as 'Phoebus Apollo turned fasting friar.' Perhaps I have a touch of Dr Middleton ... and, I fear, more than a touch of Sir Willoughby."

"That's the Egoist himself, isn't it?" asked Clara. "But you're most frightfully unselfish."

"Another of your charming illusions, my dear."

He seemed to have withdrawn a little. Already she fancied she could see the shadow of tomorrow faintly clouding his face, though they talked eagerly about books and *Tannhäuser* while he sipped brandy and smoked a cigar. Gradually Clara became aware that the room had become almost silent and that she was sleepy. The waiter hovered discreetly.

"*Eheu, fugaces*," her father sighed, putting out his cigar. Without looking at the bill, he shook out a little pile of sovereigns on to the plate.

"Wha-at?" she said, on a not-quite-suppressed yawn.

"*Eheu, fugaces.* Or, as the immortal Carter translates, "The oysters are eaten and put down in the bill."

They spoke little in the car as it hurried them back to West Kensington and ordinary life. By the yellow tiled umbrella stand, he kissed her goodnight, more lingeringly than he had done for many months, stroking her hair while she tried to tell him what a wonderful evening it had been. The dining-room clock struck half-past one with a fretful ping. The afterglow vanished from his face.

"Hurry up to bed, Cinderella." Then he added, almost with everyday sternness: "Shut your door quietly so as not to wake your mother."

She tiptoed upstairs to a room that semed to have shrunk since she had left it only a few hours ago. Never had the sallow, once-white furniture seemed so shabby, the Indian cotton bedspread so faded. She tore off the white frock, crumpled now, and flung her other clothes in a careless heap. But she rescued the wilted pink carnation and laid it on her pillow so that she could feel its petals against her cheek and smell its bruised sweetness in the dark.

PART THREE

Chapter 1

ST Mark's breaking-up day came at last. Clara, doing last-minute repairs to her cotton frocks, wondered if it were really possible that she and her parents would sleep that night at Paget's Fold.

There was a routine connected with the beginning of the summer holidays. Traditionally the whole family attended the prize-giving at St Mark's, leaving barely time for them to change before the taxi was hooting at the door and old Mrs Batchelor, helpfully getting in everyone's way, was assuring them they would miss the train. Traditionally, too, it was the hottest afternoon of the year and Claude's white forehead glistened as, wearing his hood and gown over his morning clothes, he sat with his perspiring colleagues on the daïs behind the cups and calf-bound books. Clara had come to take a perverse pleasure in this ordeal. The stuffier the hall, the prosier the speeches, the longer the Greek play, the more she appreciated the dash home and the annual transformation of her father. He would slam into his dressing-room in a state of dramatic irritability and emerge ten minutes later in an old tweed suit and a faded Panama, wearing an expression of blissful calm.

This year Clara was let off 'Speechers' so that she could help her mother to get dressed and packed. Though it was a boiling day, she was sorry to miss the ritual torment and envied her grandmother as she drove off with Claude, proud as a Queen Mother in her black satin mantle and parma violet toque.

In her mother's bedroom the pink curtains were drawn to keep out the July sun. Isabel, already dressed for the journey, lay back in a chair with her feet up, giving languid directions. In the fortnight since the *Tannhäuser* evening, she had almost recovered.

That fortnight had seemed endless to Clara and, now that the longed-for day had come, something took the edge off her joy. She had not been to Paget's Fold since the day of the funeral. Would the place ever be quite the same again?

"My little girl is looking pale," said Isabel as Clara paused in her packing, sat back on her heels and sighed. "I daresay she needs some good country air almost as much as I do."

"I'll be glad to get away from London anyway."

"Your voice sounds tired. You've been such a sweet child lately, doing things for Mother. I'd no idea you could be such a good little nurse."

"Oh well, it was mainly trays and errands—anyone can do that."

"But you moved so nice and quietly. I feel I never want to hear the crackle of a nurse's apron again. When I was so dreadfully ill, it nearly drove me mad. You know how sensitive I am at the best of times."

"Yes."

"You can't think what a difference it makes, having someone who cares for you to look after you instead of people who are just paid to do it. For I really believe you are fond of your silly mother, aren't you darling? Sometimes when I felt oh so, so weak and tired, I was tempted just to slip away out of it all. And then I'd say to myself, "There's Clara. I must think of Clara and be brave. You're glad I did, aren't you, pet?"

"Of course," said Clara, vigorously resuming her packing. "Shall I put in two pairs of walking shoes?"

"One will be plenty. I'm afraid I shall do very little walking this year. You don't know what it is to be left without a mother. I do."

"One, then," said Clara efficiently. "The great thing is you're better now. You must take great care not to get ill again."

"It's a comfort to hear you say that. You know, sometimes I used to think it was all for Daddy. But I do believe there's room in your heart for both of us."

"Certainly," said Clara, with a bright grin. "There isn't room for another pin in this trunk, though."

She shut the lid and sat on it.

"Careful, pet. You'll strain the hinge. You're quite a weight, aren't you? I was a sylph at your age. Much too thin and frail of course They were afraid I might be consumptive."

"I'm uninterestingly healthy, like the Batchelors," said Clara. She wrote a label with extreme care. "Now there's only your little last-minute case."

"How beautifully you pack, darling. It always surprises me because you're so slapdash and untidy about most things. I suppose they taught you to do it so efficiently at the convent."

"Mother Damaris—she was Mistress of the Linen Room—was a dragon. At least I'll never have to pack under her ruthless eye again."

"I daresay you were sorry to leave in some ways."

"Oh well, it had to come sooner or later."

"I suppose you feel it was a little bit my fault. I'm sure I didn't want to be ill."

"No, of course not."

"You've got an accusing look. You do blame me," Isabel's face contracted. She said with sudden fierceness: "If you only knew, it's the Catholic Church you ought to blame."

Clara stared.

"The Catholic Church?"

Her voice was so startled that Isabel looked alarmed.

"I shouldn't have said that, Clara. Forget all about it."

"What *did* you mean?"

"Nothing, darling. At least nothing you could understand."

"How do you know?" said Clara, piqued and curious. "I'm not a complete idiot."

"Far from it. But there's no point in your knowing yet. It would only upset you."

"I'd be much more upset not knowing."

"Oh dear," said Isabel helplessly. "It's so hard to be always on my guard. I'm so weak. My poor head gets confused. I don't know what Daddy would say. He'd be furious with me." She seemed on the verge of tears.

"Don't get so upset, Mother," said Clara soothingly. "I won't breathe a word to him."

Isabel said in a low, troubled voice:

"The Catholic Church is terribly unfair in some ways. Especially to women. Oh darling, I often think for your sake it would have been a good thing if Daddy had had his way and you'd been a boy."

"*Did* Daddy wish that?" asked Clara.

"Not after you'd arrived," said her mother hastily. "And of course now he wouldn't change you for worlds. And I definitely wanted a baby girl. You know what they say. 'Your son's your son till he takes a wife: your daughter's your daughter all your life.'"

"I certainly wish I'd been a boy."

The idea was so old and ingrained that she brought it out automatically. But, as she said the words, she remembered the *Tannhäuser* night and wondered if they were still true.

"Oh darling," wailed Isabel. "Doesn't your mother's pleasure count for anything?"

Clara did not answer, being too busy with a pain of her own. Had he never thought of her as anything but a substitute? She hastily filled the suitcase and snapped it to.

"There! All finished. Mind if I go now? I've got lots of my own odds and ends left."

She had quite forgotten whatever it was she had wanted to know. Just as she was about to escape, Zillah came in with their tea.

"You've time for a cup of tea surely? You look as if you needed it after all that labour."

For some minutes they ate and drank in silence. Isabel had a preoccupied air. At last she burst out:

"Well, if you absolutely insist on knowing, darling. And if you'll swear not to tell Daddy."

Clara nodded.

"Have you ever thought you'd like to have little brothers or sisters?"

To her fury, Clara blushed. The question hit without warning on a sore spot. Ever since she could remember, she had privately longed and prayed for them; brothers especially. Her defences went up immediately, but behind them was a wild hope.

"I suppose so. In a vague sort of way."

Almost in a whisper, her mother said: "You might have had three little sisters."

Clara was so startled that she dropped all her armour.

"Mother! what do you mean *might*? What happened to them? Why wasn't I told?"

"Two were born dead, darling. The other poor little thing only lived twenty minutes. Such a lovely baby, too."

Clara was breathless with the effort of trying to take it in.

"Three. I just can't believe it. Why ever didn't you say anything about it? All younger than me? But how can you be born dead? It doesn't make sense."

It was Isabel's turn to look startled.

"But Clara ... you told me only a little while ago ... I thought you knew how children came ..."

Clara tried to retrieve herself. She said with her most worldly air: "Idiotic of me. I forgot for the moment. Quite usual, isn't it, being born dead? Saves a lot of trouble if you come to think of it."

Her bluff succeeded so well that her mother sighed: "What a hard matter-of-fact child you are sometimes. And all these years we've never told you for fear of upsetting you."

"Tell me the whole thing. In detail. Did they have names?"

"Darling, how could they? You can't be baptised when you're dead."

"Didn't the living one get baptised?"

"There was no time to get a priest."

"Why ever didn't you do it yourself?"

"My *dear* Clara. I was dreadfully *ill*. I wasn't even conscious."

"I do think someone might have thought of it. Now she's in limbo and she might have been in heaven. Why ever didn't Daddy?"

"He was much too worried about me to think of anything else. You really are the most extraordinary child. You haven't even given a thought to poor Mother. Just imagine going through all that three times—for nothing."

She checked herself from asking "All what?" and said: "Sorry. Yes, it must have been rotten for you."

"You're so young," sighed her mother. "I suppose I ought to be glad you can't even imagine it. I shall never forget what I suffered when you were born. I was so ill they daren't give me chloroform, even at the end. And of course the first is nearly always the worst. You might think of that sometimes, all that agony I went through, when you are inclined to look down on me for not being clever. You know how Daddy loves you. But he's never had to *prove* his love. A mother has to go down to the gates of hell for her child."

It was the phrase she had used on the *Tannhäuser* night. What could it possibly mean? Clara's mind was wrestling with so many new and extraordinary ideas that she had to keep a firm hold on herself not to admit her ignorance and ask her mother to explain. She put out a feeler.

"I suppose it always hurts rather?"

"Such pain as you couldn't even imagine. It stands to reason when you think what has to happen before a baby can come into the world."

A wild idea flashed into Clara's mind. "*Fructus ventri tui*" it said in the "Hail Mary". She had always supposed that "womb" had no connection with the ordinary meaning of "venter". Was it possible that after all, they *were* connected? No, she must be losing her grip even to imagine such a thing. Completely out of her depth, she nodded sagely.

"Isn't it strange, isn't it terrible," her mother went on, assuming her dream voice, "that men can inflict such torment on us in the name of love? I'm sure if they had the children the world would come to an end. And the Catholic Church backs them up. Of course it's run by men."

Clara risked asking: "How does the Church come into it?"

"By making us have babies whether we want them or not. I should have thought your nuns would have told you that."

"Married people, you mean?"

"Why, naturally, darling."

Having children, then, was a matter of choice; the man's choice. "Tess" had taught her that it was possible to have them without being married and that a child was somehow the result of 'love'. Now her mother seemed to be implying that a man in some way forced a woman to have a child because he 'loved' her and that it caused her extreme suffering. But if a man had only to decide to make his wife have a child, why did some married couples pray for years for one and sometimes not get it in the end? Clara gave it up and returned to the far more interesting question:

"My three sisters. How old would they be now?"

"The first poor little thing came when you were only four. Then one when you were eight and another when you were eleven. That was the one that might have lived."

"She'd have been getting on for five now. I just can't take it in."

"There might have been a fourth baby."

"Oh *when?*" said Clara breathlessly.

"It wasn't due till December."

"*Which* December? How on earth did you know?" She was too consumed with crazy hopes to be cautious.

"This coming December. But something went dreadfully wrong. That's why I so nearly died in June."

"Boy or girl?" asked Clara in a choked voice.

"It was too early to be sure."

Here was yet another mystery. Clara felt as if an invisible stifling cocoon were being woven all round her.

"Of course I ought never to have had another," Isabel went on. "The doctor warned Daddy I might die if I did. But even the best of men is selfish when it comes to *that*. Thank goodness now there can't be any more."

"I bet that one was a boy," said Clara. "Oh well, I never really expected it." She had turned very pale. "I say, do you mind if I open the window? It's so awfully hot in here."

"But the windows are open. Both of them. Come over here and give Mother a kiss and tell her you're sorry she's had such a dreadful time."

"I expect you'd like some eau-de-Cologne on your forehead," said Clara hastily. "It really is too hot for words."

She dabbed her mother's temples as if hoping the eau-de-Cologne would act as an emotional astringent. She knew she was behaving heartlessly and that her mother had suffered enough to be entitled to a little sympathy. But she felt resentful and cheated. Forgetting that she herself dreaded the slightest pain, she blamed Isabel for cowardice. She was convinced that it was in some way her mother's fault that those children hadn't lived. Why couldn't she have done this mysterious job of having a baby properly?

But when the three of them were settled in the taxi and she saw her father's face beaming under his old Panama hat, her hostile mood vanished. Her mother, looking wan but gay, was humming to herself and Clara gave her an almost sisterly grin. The old spell had begun to work. By the time they reached Victoria they had slipped into their summer holiday parts.

At the station they went through another annual ritual. Claude bought the summer number of *Punch* for Clara, *Queer Stories from Truth* for Isabel and the latest Phillips Oppenheim for himself. They dined in the purple white and green tiled restaurant and made their usual weak joke about the suffragette colours. Claude ordered a bottle of hock and Clara, feeling considerably older than last year, asked for cider instead of ginger beer.

"Another year nearer," said Claude, lifting his glass to Isabel. It was his dream to add some rooms and another acre to Paget's Fold and retire there when he was sixty. In two hundred years his mother's family had managed to scrape together some forty scattered acres and half a dozen labourer's cottages. Always at this dinner he would talk imposingly about "the tenants". "Haywood is pestering me for a new well," he would say with a scowl which deceived no one. "I suppose I'll have to do something for the old scoundrel" or "I'm sorry Cruttenden has ploughed up the Six Berries. Never thought the fellow would be such a fool or I'd have had a clause put in his lease. One of the finest bits of pasture in West Sussex, John Hoadley tells me."

Neither Clara nor her mother could resist him in his landlord mood. Even Isabel had not the heart to reproach him for spending far more than his tiny rents in repairs, bottles of port and tobacco for "the tenants". The two dropped their private quarrels and entered into his dream as if they were grown-ups playing with a child.

"Old Squire Batchelor," said Clara. "You'll have to keep an eye on him, Mother. He'll be chewing straws and talking about 'they turnips' in no time."

"Do you think he'll even forget his Greek and Latin, Clara? Or that he ever terrified poor pupils out of their wits?"

"He'll remember two or three tags from the Georgics. And mutter them in a broad Sussex accent as he scratches the pigs' backs."

"Few people realise what a fundamentally lazy man I am, my dears. If I followed my own inclinations I should never work at all."

"Dea'est, what a fib!" said Isabel. "Why, even on his poor little holiday, we've never yet managed to stop him working, have we, Clara?"

"An hour or two of correspondence pupils doesn't count as work. I could correct Greek proses in my sleep and frequently do."

"You know perfectly well you get restless after three days," said Clara. "Own up. What's it going to be this year. Last year it was Sanskrit. And the year before—let's see ..."

"*Ich hebe meine rechte Bein,*" prompted Isabel.

"Of course. As if could ever forget!"

"Alas, my dears, *I* have. Sanskrit, alas, will have to wait till I retire." He sighed. "You know, I really think I could manage Sanskrit."

"At least no one could correct your accent," said Isabel.

"Daddy, you *have* got something up your sleeve."

"No, no. Really not. Unless you count a couple of books on archaeology which I shall almost certainly leave uncut. If they were only Oppenheims! But the great man only produces one a year."

"How you can read that nonsense!" said Isabel. "My Mudie books, that you despise so, do at least bear some resemblance to real life."

"Precisely why I have no desire to read them. Oppenheim and Le Queux transport me into an ideal world where I should be only too happy to live."

"He doesn't want to be a country squire at all," said Clara. "He wants to steal crown jewels in faultless evening dress."

"I suppose it's all very far-fetched," he said, wistfully. "But there must be some little basis of fact. After all there are such things as secret agents. And an actual Archduke was murdered less than a month ago."

He stared past Isabel and Clara with the slightly angry expression he wore when following his own thoughts.

"You know," he said seriously. "In real life, they probably choose quite ordinary people for those jobs. People no one would suspect."

"Mother, do you think he's a secret agent?"

"No such luck," he sighed. "Adventures will never come my way, And yet ... and yet ..."

"Break the vow of silence to the Crimson Arrow and tell us," said Clara.

He smiled.

"It's so patently absurd I can laugh at it myself. I suppose everyone has ridiculous fancies sometimes."

"Tell us."

"Well, fantastic as it seems even to myself ... if ever there comes an unexpected ring at the door late at night after my last pupil has gone I wonder if they have come."

"And who are They?" urged Clara.

"Representatives of a foreign power, travelling incognito. They have observed a remarkable likeness between myself and the ruling prince of ... nowhere important of course ... some obscure little Germanic State. Circumstances make it advisable the prince should disappear for a time."

"And they want you to impersonate him?"

"Well, frankly, yes."

"At great personal danger?"

"There is a certain risk involved."

Isabel smiled faintly.

"Dea'est, I never suspected you of being so romantic."

"I'm sure you didn't, Isabel. Clara, let that be a warning to you. A

125

woman can be married to a man for sixteen years and know nothing of his innermost life."

"Women have their secrets too. Don't they, Clara?"

Clara ignored her mother's meaning glance and said:

"Perhaps you really will have an adventure one day. Why shouldn't you? People do."

"Not people like me, my dear. I am the man to whom nothing sensational will ever happen."

Isabel drummed on the table.

"I'm sure enough unpleasant things have happened to both of us," she said.

"Yes, indeed, my dear," he said, meekly.

"Claude, don't you think we ought to be getting to the train? I'm beginning to feel tired and I do want to be sure of a corner seat."

Tonight they were travelling first class. They found an empty carriage and Isabel promptly put her feet up and closed her eyes. Claude was soon as deep in his Phillips Oppenheim as a priest in his breviary. By the time they were well out of London, Clara had finished her *Punch*. It was too dark to see the country and there was nothing to fall back on but her own thoughts. If those sisters had lived, they would have been in the carriage with them now. The youngest might have been asleep on her lap or asking to be told a story. But it was impossible to imagine them, to give them personalities or even names. Try as she would, she could only see three wax dolls in white coffins. She glanced across at her mother, lying with her feet up, fast asleep. The overhead light threw shadows under her eyes and on either side of her half-open mouth. She looked older than Clara had ever seen her and there was something frightened and reproachful in her expression. Had she told the truth when she said that men were cruel to the women they loved? Once more she studied her father's absorbed face. No one could be frightened of him tonight, yet how often in his presence she had felt a panic out of all proportion to anything, however harsh, he might have said or done. What was he really in himself? The brilliant, conscientious schoolmaster, driving himself far harder than any pupil? The genial dreamer of this evening? The bitter accuser in the orchard? The wonderful, yet faintly disquieting companion of the *Tannhäuser* night? Images of his face in yet other moods formed and dissolved in her mind to the rhythm of the wheels till her head grew heavy and her eyelids closed.

She did not wake till the door flew open, letting in a gale of delicious air and a broad Sussex voice shouting "Rookfield." She stumbled out, still half asleep, but as soon as she was perched on the driving seat beside Mr Joles, her eyes opened wide. It was one of the freshest, sharpest joys of the holidays, this short drive through the night with the horse's crupper rising and falling in the lamplight and hooves and wheels sounding unnaturally loud. Cool air streamed past her face, bringing drifts of sweet or pungent country smells, blowing away problems, awakening old delights. Soon she would make out the dark bulk of the walnut tree against a sky peppered with stars. In a few minutes they had pulled up at the foot of the green and there was Aunt Leah standing in the doorway with a lamp while Aunt Sophy fumbled with the catch of the gate.

Once again she walked up the uneven brick path and smelt the stocks and tobacco plants; once again Aunt Sophy said, as every year: "You must be dreadfully tired and hungry," and Aunt Leah: "Your train was remarkably punctual."

On the table stood the painted biscuit tins she had known from childhood, the decanter of Aunt Sophy's wine, the home-made cake, the pink glass dish of sandwiches, the mug of milk for herself, just as they had always stood. Once again the aunts hovered like parent-birds, refusing to eat themselves. Once again, Aunt Leah, after ceremonial coaxing, was induced to drink a thimbleful of wine and Aunt Sophy said: "Mind you don't get intoxicated, Leah. It's stronger than anything they sell at the 'Goat'."

The old clock in the shadows beyond their lamplit circle cleared its throat portentously, whirred, clicked and struck twelve. Aunt Leah said, as she had said last year, "It is only eleven by the correct time. We haven't yet been able to get the strike mended."

Clara sipped her milk and nibbled her biscuits in drowsy bliss. Nothing had changed. Here at least life was simple, secure and sweet. Nothing mattered any more. The summer holidays had begun.

Chapter 2

THE feather bed was hot and Clara could not go to sleep at once. In the dark, some of her nagging thoughts returned. So much had happened since she had last slept in this room that she wondered if even Paget's Fold could charm her back to her childhood self. With a sudden fear that the room itself might have changed, she groped for a match to light her candle but the box was empty. She fell asleep at last and when she woke, the leaf shadows on the thin red blind brought back the old sense of innocence and safety.

One by one, as a released prisoner checks his restored possessions, she welcomed each familiar object. There was the lame dressing-table with its yellow muslin skirts, the hair-tidy trimmed with pearl buttons, the patchwork pincushion on which, as every year, Aunt Sophy had arranged the pins in a huge C. A spray of ivy still grew in through the layers of faded wallpaper, the texts lettered by her grandfather still reminded her that her body was the temple of the Holy Ghost and that she knew not the day or the hour. As always on holiday mornings, the room smelt of a fresh dampness suffused with lavender, fermenting apples and frying bacon. With a rush of happiness she jumped out of bed, washed in icy rain-water and knelt down to say her morning prayers in a passion of gratitude.

Her room opened off her parents' so that when she was dressed she had to rattle the string latch and wait till they called her to come through.

Claude and Isabel were still in bed. As she stooped to kiss her mother's pale cheek and his rosy, unshaven one, she noticed how white his skin was where the pyjama jacket hung open at the neck. At Valetta Road she had never once seen him in bed. At Paget's Fold it seemed the most natural thing in the world.

In a day or two, the holiday routine was established. Every morning Claude and Clara played croquet while Isabel sat in her deck chair, occasionally glancing up from her novel to watch them. The full-sized lawn Claude had laid down some years ago still gave him a thrill of pride. Every time he looked at it, he remembered the bumpy little plot at Hamling where he had played those endless tournaments against himself. Croquet was his only game and he set about it with a methodical ferocity. He had coached Clara till she was able to beat him now and then. Isabel had always refused to learn tactics and played recklessly with total disregard for her partner if she had one. Nevertheless, having a good eye and not being above mild cheating, she beat him nearly as often as Clara. When this happened, Clara was deeply shocked, not by her father's defeat, but by her mother's frivolous attitude. This year, with Isabel reduced to a mere spectator, she and her father were able to pit themselves against each other with strict science and impeccable honour. Nor were they in the least disturbed when Isabel mocked them.

"I wish you could see your faces," she would say. "Anyone would think you were fighting a duel to the death instead of playing a game, I'm sure croquet brings out the worst in your characters."

Clara and her father would merely exchange a superior smile and whichever of them was addressing the ball would do so with an extra touch of spite.

Punctually at eleven, Aunt Sophy would trot out with a tray of glasses and home-made cakes. The aunts, who ate like birds, lived in perpetual fear that the Batchelors might be underfed. In spite of entreaties, they toiled all day in the dark kitchen, producing wonderful dishes they would never have dreamt of cooking for themselves. Aunt Sophy thought nothing of walking three miles to the market town on the hottest morning to buy special things for Isabel and they had denied themselves all the June strawberries in order to bottle them for tarts for Claude's holiday.

After lunch, therefore, it was impossible to do anything for some time but laze in the garden. Clara usually hid herself with a book in the fork of the walnut tree; a perch which had once been a perilous climb but which she could now reach in two swings. Later they would wander out over the fields. If the three went together, it was only for slow, short strolls because of Isabel. Clara had still not got over her surprise and irritation at her mother's love of the country. Her own, like her father's, was deep and inarticulate; she was shy of talking about it just as she was of religion. Isabel, however, kept up a stream of ecstatic chatter. In her high, light voice she raved about every tree and flower, taking immense pleasure in telling Claude their names which, like many country-bred people, he had never bothered to find out.

She would sit happily for hours, messing up Clara's best paintbox to make sketches of cornfields and cottages which the aunts treasured as masterpieces. Clara could forgive her mother's childish vanity about her pictures which were so bad as to have a kind of fascination. What she found almost unbearable was her caring so effusively for a place to which she had no right of blood and for which Clara had a jealous love. "She's got the whole of the rest of England to rave about" she would tell herself. "Why can't she leave Sussex ... or at least this particular bit of it ... alone?"

Her father had the same possessive, patriotic feeling but, unlike Clara, he was enchanted by Isabel's raptures. He loved this corner of Sussex less because it was beautiful or familiar than because his family had been artisans or farmers in those parts for generations. A turnip field had magic for him if he could prove it had once belonged to an ancestor's smallholding. If they drove out to a strange village, the first thing he did was to search the graveyard for tombstones of Batchelors or Hoadleys or Sayerses. If he found none, however charming the place, he was politely restless till they returned to Paget's Fold. Every Sunday after tea he would say, a little sheepishly, "Anyone care to walk round the estate with me?" Then, wet or fine, alone or in company, he would set off on a tour of his forty scattered acres. He spent blissful evenings peering at creased old ground-maps in the lamplight discussing with Aunt Leah how each patch of land had been acquired. He was delighted when Clara and Isabel called him "the man of property". "It's all very trivial, my dears," he would say, "and well I know it. Still I must admit I love to feel I have my absurd little stake in the country. As long as I stick to that, I can call myself a Sussex yeoman." Sometimes he reminded them "Claude Frederick Batchelor, yeoman of this county. That's what I want on my tombstone. And R.I.P. of course. I hope it's not heretical to feel I could only rest in peace in Sussex soil."

Those evenings had a peculiar charm for Clara. The aunts would be coaxed with difficulty to sit down and rest. Isabel would lie on the horsehair sofa under the engraving of Strafford on his way to execution and the other four would gather round the table under the yellow light of the oil lamp. On hot nights the smell of stocks and tobacco plants came in through the open window and Aunt Sophy kept jumping up to try and save the moths from scorching themselves to death. Isabel, who loved Aunt Sophy as much as she hated Mrs

Batchelor, would lure her on to tell of all the happenings in the village since last summer; the extraordinary appearance of the post-mistress at the village concert or the fiasco of the stoolball club picnic. Aunt Leah, a little ashamed of these trivialities, would try, for Claude's sake, to raise the conversation to a higher level. She would bring out her choicest scraps of historical information or pass severe judgements on the modern world. Clara would try to entice both of them to tell old stories she heard year after year and never tired of: how in their childhood they "did hear tell" of a wizard at Henfield who supped with the devil, how Aunt Leah had dressed up as a gipsy and deceived her own mother, how a young man had appeared to Aunt Sophy at the very moment he had died in India.

Listening, as if to music, to the ebb and flow of the four voices, Clara felt her whole self soften and expand. She glowed with affection for each one of them, even her mother. Enfolded, yet detached, she was conscious of her own life waiting round the corner; she was convinced that it would be rich and wonderful as theirs had never been. Every gesture, every shift of shadow as the faces swam in and out of the circle of light, quickened some faculty she hardly knew she possessed. The pendulum of the old clock beat like a leaden heart; the ribbons of smoke untwined from Isabel's cigarette; a luminous spot reflected from a wineglass shifted slowly down Aunt Leah's throat. And it was as if all these details were connected, that they were like the separate letters of a word in an unknown language and that, if only she could understand the word, she would understand everything.

Now and then she would do something which would have been unthinkable in Valetta Road: she would suddenly go over into a dark corner and begin to say poems out loud to them. She hardly knew why she did it, only that whatever they gave her, without knowing it, at those particular moments, had some connection with poetry and this was the only coin in which she could repay them. She never knew beforehand what she was going to say; usually it was Yeats or Crashaw or Francis Thompson. Sometimes, though she knew her mother was the only one could understand it, she was impelled to recite a poem of Ronsard's or Verlaine's. When she stopped, abruptly as she had begun, there was always a moment of silence. Then Aunt Leah would praise her memory and Aunt Sophy, wiping her glasses, would say, "It's stupid of me, but poetry, even when I don't follow the sense, always makes me want to cry." Isabel occasionally referred to the beauty of the actual poem, especially if it were a French one. More often she said: "You look your best when you recite. It's extraordinary how your face lights up" or "Really, you've got quite a dramatic gift. You get that from me. I always longed to go on the stage but of course Papa would have seen me dead first." Claude seldom did more than utter a deep sigh and say, "Thank you, my dear." But Clara noticed that on such evenings he held her closer than usual when he kissed her good night. Once he said, "You should have lived in the golden age, my dear. In Greece you would have been a rhapsodist." Then he added sadly, stroking back her hair, "But Wragge is in custody, Wragge is in custody."

On wet days Clara loved to walk alone and bareheaded through the lanes that smelt of wild peppermint and here and there of a fox. She sang loudly and vaguely as she walked, mixing scraps of Latin hymns with old French and English songs, breaking off only when she saw someone approaching. Then she would frown as if deep in thought and stride on very fast, swinging her stick at the thistle clumps. Recalled like this, she realised she must have looked extremely silly, if not a trifle mad. And when she returned home, with her cheeks stung red from the rain and her hair hanging in damp corkscrews, her mother's comments were far from reassuring.

Rubbing her drenched curls at the mirror, Clara had to admit that Isabel was right. She did not look wild or elfin but merely bedraggled.

"Why can't I be thin and brown and have great mysterious dark eyes?" she would ask her reflection angrily. "Can you imagine a poet looking like me? Or at me for that matter? Wood-browned pools and a beautiful name like Viola Meynell. It's not fair. I know I'd have understood him better than she did."

Comforted by hot cocoa (the aunts always expected her to catch cold if she went out in the rain) it was easier to accept the fact that she did not look a 'faery's child' and even that Francis Thompson had died without meeting her. After all, she reflected, she must be very earthly or she wouldn't enjoy food so much. As to her hated name, there was just a possibility that she might not have to keep it all her life. How lucky that she had not had the least inclination to marry Blaze. Clara Hoadley would have been even worse. Though if one loved someone, one would not mind what their name was; she would have been only too happy to be Mrs Thompson or Mrs Keats.

Another wet day pleasure was dreaming over books she had known ever since she first learned to read. There were less than forty books at Paget's Fold; many of them belonged to her great-aunts' childhood and a few had been bought over a century ago. Some had been read and re-read till they were only held together with brown paper and glue. There were odd volumes of *Beeton's Annual* and *The Gentleman's Magazine*; forgotten novels with Biblical titles like *Holden with the Cord and Shiloh;* and, what she liked best of all, the old "improving" stories for children.

"I don't see why you care for those tales, Clara," Aunt Sophy said. "They must seem so dull and old-fashioned to you."

But it was for that very reason Clara loved them. Her own childhood had always seemed a complete failure to her because there were no brothers and sisters to share it. One could not go on pretending for ever, all by oneself, that one was Lord Roberts or Joan of Arc. So she had often imagined herself a member of one of these "book" families, a large early Victorian family where the girls wore tuckers and mittens and the boys round jackets and nankeen trousers. They had a high-principled papa, stern but kindly, and a gentle, frail mamma who spent much of her time on a sofa. There was also a governess, a pony cart and a faithful old cook. They lived in a large house in the country; the boys were always tumbling off apple trees or into ponds and being nursed or rescued by their devoted sisters to whom they were grateful ever after. Sometimes there were terrible misunderstandings, only cleared up by an illness which nearly or quite proved fatal. But in the main it was a blissful life of golden summers and sparkling winters, punctuated by visits of mercy to the sick and poor and the arrival of wonderful presents from an uncle in India. Whole tracts of Clara's life, though she had never admitted this even to Nicole, had been lived in the setting of *Ministering Children* and *Les Malheurs de Sophie.* She had only to smell the brown-spotted pages with the s's that looked like f's, to see the stiff engravings of cotton mills and little girls in toques and pelerines, to be back in that enchanted world.

But, from her letters to Nicole, no one could have guessed how much she loved Paget's Fold and everything connected with it. "While you," she wrote, "are deciding between Paris and Madrid, I am balancing the giddy alternatives of a boring walk to Rookfield to buy a bar of chocolate or an equally boring walk to Bellhurst to buy a pair of shoelaces. On Sunday we shall be in a social whirl for the Vicar is coming to tea. My great-aunts will produce four kinds of homemade jam instead of two. Aunt Sophy will wear her ceremonial crochet collar and Aunt Leah will rub up her ecclesiastical history. My Papa will be painfully polite and my Mamma will either retire to bed or give him languorous soulful glances while eating chocolate cake in an abstracted, spiritual way peculiar to herself. Our dissipation may even go so far as to accompany the Vicar up to the churchyard in order to lay flowers on the graves of deceased relatives. If I don't seem much disturbed by your dark forebodings of war, it is because our local life is so dramatic that it absorbs all my attention. Only yesterday the gardener's wife was stung by a wasp and today there is a rumour (unconfirmed) that the postman's cat has had a kitten with six toes."

Clara hated herself for writing like this but the remembrance of Nicole's cynical smile compelled her to. There were a great many things which she naturally loved and enjoyed which withered at the mere thought of how they would appear to Nicole. Sometimes her conscience was tormented by this duplicity and sometimes she wondered if she hid it quite as successfully as she liked to think.

One thing had begun to disturb her at Paget's Fold and that was a real or imagined change in Aunt Sophy. During the last two summers she fancied that her favourite aunt had grown a trifle shy and even a trifle critical of her.

Long ago when Clara was very small and her parents went abroad in the summer holidays, she used to be sent down to Paget's Fold with old Mr and Mrs Batchelor. In those days she had had two people who could be relied on to spoil her: her grandfather and Aunt Sophy. Aunt Leah was severe with all young children on principle and her grandmother was less amenable when she was left in charge. It was Aunt Sophy who had smuggled in the nightlights she was never allowed at home, who let her eat sugar biscuits after she had cleaned her teeth and sat by her bed telling stories when the sun pouring through the thin red blinds made it impossible to go to sleep. In those days Aunt Leah had seemed a forbidding figure. Clara quite dreaded the Sunday afternoon Scripture lessons in the tiny parlour that smelt of mildew and where the box tree that blotted out the window threw a greenish light on Aunt Leah's white face as she spoke of the destruction of Sodom and the fate of the children who mocked Elisha. But it was impossible to imagine anyone more comforting and unexacting than Aunt Sophy with her cottage-loaf figure and withered apple face. When the strain of her own parents became too intense, Clara had often thought how delightful it would be if Cousin John Hoadley had been her father and Aunt Sophy her mother. Once when she was about six she had confided this idea to Aunt Sophy and a slow pink blush had run all over the old woman's face.

"I'm too old to be your mother, dear. Or anyone else's."

"Why? Old people are much nicer to children. I like old people."

"That's because they get soft and spoil them. Besides it's naughty to want any parents but your own," said Aunt Sophy, trying to look severe.

"I don't care," said Clara, snuggling up to Aunt Sophy, the only person she ever did snuggle up to spontaneously. "Of course I couldn't have been your little girl unless you'd been married. Why ever didn't you?"

"Because no one asked me, I expect."

"Then why didn't you ask someone?"

"Ladies don't ask gentlemen to marry them, dear."

"I'm sure Mr Hoadley wouldn't have minded if you had. Then you could have had me and a lot of other children."

She remembered that Aunt Sophy had given her a very queer look, as if this time she were really cross, but she had hugged her tighter than usual when she said "good night".

Even now that she was fifteen, Clara still liked Aunt Sophy to put her to bed; a thing she would never have allowed her mother to do. She towered now above the tiny old woman and "being put to bed" merely meant gossiping with her while she undressed. But something of their former ease had gone: there was a touch of constraint about Aunt Sophy's voice and manner.

"You're getting too clever for me, Clara. All this French and Latin and I don't know what. It makes me quite giddy. I never was clever, no more than your Granny. Leah was the one for brains."

And however much Clara might hug her and tell her between kisses:

"You're my darling, sweet, one and only little Aunt Sophy," a pucker of distrust remained on the old, childlike forehead.

It was no compensation to Clara that Aunt Leah had begun to treat her with new respect. She praised her for having done so well at school and, a mark of the highest favour, sometimes consulted her on a knotty point of history or geography. Clara did not like being ranged among the blue-stockings: still less did she like anything at

Paget's Fold to change. It was part of the order of things that Aunt Leah should be a trifle disapproving and Aunt Sophy wholeheartedly admiring. Most disturbing of all, Aunt Sophy seemed to have transferred that uncritical allegiance to Isabel. However hard Clara tried to be humble, however sharply she scolded herself for undutiful feelings, she remained convinced that she was a better person than her mother. Yet, though she reminded herself that Aunt Sophy was a very ignorant as well as a very innocent old woman, this did not alter the fact that she was usually right in her judgements. Clara could not quite rid herself of the uncomfortable notion that however much she might bluff other people and even herself, she did not succeed in bluffing Aunt Sophy.

Chapter 3

IT was several days before Clara was able to do what she loved
best of all; spend a whole day by herself on the hills. In London
or at Mount Hilary the memory of the downs often came up so
sharply that her eyes filled with tears of longing. This summer it
seemed that never before had she needed them so much.

She took as always the shortest and steepest way up the slippery
chalk path through the bostel. Stumbling over gnarled roots of beeches
she panted on without a rest till she reached the top. Once in the open,
she flung herself down on the turf where the harebells trembled above
the star-thistles and the sheep-droppings. The strong wind dried her
forehead and blew her hair out like a flag as she drew in great greedy
breaths of the smell of thyme and sea. Her eyes were greedy too as
she stared, now at the green and ochre map of the weald hundreds of
feet below, now at the distant gap in the hills which the sea closed
with a wedge of blue haze.

But she could not bear to stay still for long. As soon as she
had recovered her wind, she ran over the springy turf like a dog
let off its lead, jumping over gorse-bushes and mole-hills for the
pleasure of using her limbs. When she got to the dewpond by
Chanctonbury Ring, she took off her shoes and stockings and lay
flat on her back on the grass. In spite of the wind, it was a burning
day. As the sun climbed, the air began to dance in streaks over
the chalk as over a hot stove. The roaring wood behind her broke
the force of the wind so that it merely flowed over her in soft eddies;
the heat of air and soil seemed to pass right into her bones. She would
have liked to take off her clothes and lie there naked on the top of
the world. Underneath she could feel the solid earth; miles and miles
of it, supporting her on its grass-furred back. She could almost
imagine she felt its motion, the reliable earth that could be trusted not
to fling her off into space: at that moment she did not want to be
anything but a contented animal. She and the chalk-blue dancing over
her bare ankles were made of the same stuff and would one day be
part of this earth which had bred them both.

"Yes, really *Mother* Earth," she thought. "Mother of everything, not just human beings. And she doesn't expect love and gratitude." It was a strangely comforting idea. Shyly she turned over and kissed the ground, whispering, "Still, you know I *am* grateful."

The next second, shyness turned to fear. She sat up abruptly. "But that is how the pagans felt." She reminded herself that the earth itself had been created by God. It wasn't wrong for pagans to make gods of sun and moon, corn and sea; they hadn't known about the real God. Long before she herself had known about God, her father had taught her about Artemis and Apollo; they had been as real to her as the angels and saints had since become. But now she was a Christian she had no right even to toy with those old beliefs. Penitently she tried to think of angels, of Our Blessed Lady, of Christ Himself, but they no longer seemed real. The wind in the trees sounded mocking. Long before the Romans came, there had been a temple where the Ring was now planted. It was her father who had told her that. Devout Catholic as he was, he loved any rumour of ancient rites or haunted stones. He had said how easily he could imagine the old gods walking on the hills. And often he quoted, with a look that she now connected with the *Tannhäuser* night:

> "The pagan kingdom Wilfred found
> Dreams as it dwells apart."

Suppose it were true? Suppose there were something, old as the worlds still potent in spite of Christianity? Was it possible there were pocket, in the universe where the Christian God had no power? Fascinated and frightened by such thoughts, she got up and walked out of the orbit of the Ring on to the open stretch of down. Yet still she could not shake off these insistent fancies or temptations. What else could the legend of the Venusberg mean? Even in the Christian middle ages they must have half believed in the old gods. She had read that the Early Fathers spoke of them as devils. But she could see nothing diabolical about Artemis or Ceres or the wise Athene who watched over Telemachus as Our Lady watched over Christian children. Her father not only loved Homer as passionately as in his unbelieving days but was enchanted by any story of the pagan gods still active in the modern world. Wherever he came across such a story, good, bad or indifferent, he made a point of Clara's reading it too. Was his faith so secure that he could afford to treat them as fairy-tales or did he secretly wish they were true?

Half a mile further on she sat down again in the shelter of some gorse bushes and took out her book, half hoping to find an answer there. It was the copy of Francis Thompson's poems her father had given her on the day of her First Communion. At that time he had not read them himself and he had no idea of what they were to mean to her. She had just glanced at the book on that day, memorable because, with all its beauty, there had been the strangest sense of something just missed. It had seemed incomprehensible. Yet she knew at once there was something there for her, if she could burrow through the forbidding surface. And she had burrowed. For more than three years she had immersed herself in the poems, forcing herself to understand the peculiar idiom, learning quantities of them by heart till they had become part of herself. Nothing could shake her devotion to Francis Thompson, even though Nicole assured her he was a third-rate poet and quoted disastrous lines. Under all the turgidity and the mannerisms she found a spirit that spoke to her own and offered a hope of reconciling poetry and religion.

Her sense that the two were mysteriously opposed was something she had never spoken of, even to Nicole, for no one seemed to be disturbed by it. The great conflict for which every sermon and instruction at Mount Hilary prepared them was that between belief and unbelief, between Christian standards of morality and those of 'the world'. Within limits, a love of poetry was encouraged, but poetry and all art were subservient to the law of 'edification'. Every now and then Clara was seized by the uncomfortable but compelling idea that art had its own laws. Nicole would, of course, have agreed with her but Nicole appeared to suffer from no religious scruples. It was impossible to imagine Nicole anything but a Catholic but Clara had never discovered what religion meant to her and she would not have dreamed of asking. Clara herself was quite convinced that she would never 'lose her faith'. She was prepared to find it extremely difficult to obey the commandments when she grew up and found herself in the world faced with all sorts of temptations whose nature had been only darkly hinted. She had been well warned too against the dangers of intellectual pride but, though she was inclined to criticize and question, she could not imagine setting up her private judgement against the teachings of the Church.

What had begun to disturb her was the sense of a realm into which she penetrated now and then quite involuntarily and whose existence did not seem to be officially recognized. And this realm, though it seemed to her to be connected sometimes with truth, sometimes with beauty, seemed to have no connection with morals. A poem might be the key to it or some lovely sight or sound but quite often she would suddenly find herself in it for no apparent reason, waiting to buy cakes in a stuffy shop or on those evenings at Paget's Fold listening to the aunts' gossip. During these experiences she was not aware of 'right' or 'wrong': the words simply did not apply. How could they, since during these brief moments she was not aware of herself at all except as a kind of sensitive film? If they came from God, why were they not accompanied by a rush of fervour and a desire to be better? And if from the devil, why did they not provoke her to wicked thoughts and rebelliousness? But they seemed to have no results; if they left any wish at all, it was a desire somehow to express them. They seemed to be nothing but a sudden intensification of life and she could not control them in any way. Often she had tried to induce them, but she could not deceive herself for long; there was all the difference between flapping one's arms and pretending to fly and really flying. Sometimes she had dared to hope that this was what Christ meant when He said: "I came that you might have life and have it more abundantly." But, since she had always been assured that this meant the supernatural life of grace, something abstract and mysterious which one believed by faith but did not feel, she put the idea away as blasphemous.

Today not even Francis Thompson could help her. She ignored the pages that opened easily, pages marked by her grubby fingers as she had worked through poem after poem learning it by heart. How deeply he had comforted her once, seeing Apollo and Danaë as "types" of Our Lord and Our Lady, but at this moment these identifications seemed merely mechanical "conceits". These ways were too well-worn: she needed something new. She went on till she came to *The Dread of Height* which she had always avoided because its motto was the text that most terrified her in the Gospel. "If ye were blind ye should have no sin but now ye say: We see; your sin remaineth." She forced herself to read the poem. It gave her none of the reassurance she longed for.

"Lower than man for I dreamed higher
Thrust down by how much I aspire
And damned with drink of immortality."

There was the truth, cutting through all her poses and fancies. What use to dream what it would be like to live in the pre-Christian era? For better or worse, without having sought for it like her father, she "saw". She was a baptized Catholic: she could plead neither blindness nor "invincible ignorance". Unfaithfulness might be pardoned in others; it was unforgivable in herself. The problem came down to one thing. Was she prepared to put her whole self at God's disposal?

In the retreat she had made every year since her First Communion there was a conference she dreaded far more than those on death, judgement or hell; the one on vocations. Only one vocation was meant: the call to be a nun. Just because the idea was so repugnant to her, she had a terror that God might ask it of her. And if she refused the call, however virtuous her life, she would be like the rich young man who had kept all the commandments but refused to follow Christ. She had never mentioned the subject to Mother Lovell for fear discussion should make the idea too real. She loved "the world"; there was no doubt of that. The world meant her father, Paget's Fold, the country, freedom to read and say and eat and wear what she liked, freedom to choose her friends and even, as a faint possibility, marriage. Not with anyone like Blaze Hoadley, of course, but with some wonderful, unimaginable young man.

As she tormented herself with these thoughts, the wind came in a sudden gust, ruffling the pages of her book, as if to say: "Stop all this nonsense. You are a young human creature and it is a summer day." She realized she was very hungry and began to devour her sandwiches. Far away in the valley the spire of Parkminster monastery reared up, holding her eye in spite of herself. It reminded her inexorably of the scene in *The Conventionalists*, a book she loved and hated, where the young man is brought up by two priests on to these very downs so that he shall see that spire and ask what it signifies.

Clara knew all too well what it signified. There lived the austere Carthusians, toiling in their gardens and workshops, rising in the middle of the night for the long office in the cold chapel, scaling the heights of prayer and always, whatever they did, intent only on God. Once a week they broke their silence and went for a walk in community.

They often passed by Paget's Fold in their white habits and straw hats, chattering and laughing like a flock of schoolboys. Her mother used to say "Poor things, it's quite pathetic how happy they seem. I suppose in that awful monotonous life, even a walk is a great adventure." Clara would think, contemptuously, how little Isabel understood their real adventure. Today she realized the contempt should be not for her mother but for herself. For if she was capable of seeing, however dimly, the point of such a life, it could only be because something in herself corresponded to it.

At last her mind was so weary that she could not think any more; there was nothing but a meaningless chatter in her head that she could not stop any more than the wind. She got up and walked on listlessly in the mid-day heat. Something had gone wrong with the day. The incessant flight of shadows over the turf tired her like her own thoughts. Everything seemed to have turned hostile to her; the wind that would not stop buffeting her, the sun that hurt her eyes, the very molehills over which she stumbled. The white glare of a chalkpit became a mocking grin; the flash of a windscreen in the valley a joke at her expense. For the first time, up on the hills, solitude became unbearable. If only there were someone to share it, she might recover her old delight. Suddenly and absurdly, she began to long for that unimaginable lover to appear. She had no idea what he would look like: she only knew that they would recognize each other at once. There would be no need to talk or explain; they would simply go on together hand in hand.

All day she had seen no one, not even a shepherd. Now, suddenly, as if summoned by her thought, a man's figure appeared in the distance, right in the track where she was walking. She could only make out that he was tall, wore no hat or coat, and swung along with easy strides. Her heart began to beat madly and her whole body seemed to melt. Quickly she smoothed her cotton frock and dabbed her forehead, hoping the sun and wind had not turned her face scarlet. She turned and stood still, gazing intently at the blue haze of the sea. Her hair must be in the wildest tangle; she could only trust that it was shining in the sun. She had to hold her pose of absorbed contemplation for what seemed an endless time but at last came the thump of footsteps and her knees began to shake so that she could hardly stand. Now, surely, she could allow herself to turn round. She gave a start, like a wild creature disturbed and faced whoever was approaching with her eyes set in a dreamy stare. She found herself looking into the cheerful red common face of a man about her father's age.

"Hello, Missie," said a voice to match the face. "Nice day, eh?"

She answered, almost giggling: "Gorgeous, absolutely gorgeous."

"Bit on the hot side if you're footing it. Still there's a nice breeze."

"Yes, lovely breeze," she agreed fervently, though she was inwardly raging with shame.

"On holiday?"

"Oh yes. Yes, I am."

"Did you happen to come up from Steyning?"

"Yes. I always do."

"Started off from Findon I did this morning. Reckoning to get a bit of lunch in Steyning. Looks the best part of three miles by the map."

"It's about that."

"Long way before I can get a pint. I haven't half got a thirst on me. Spotted you quite a long way off, I did. You looked a bit peculiar standing there. Not lost your road or anything have you?"

"No, thank you," said Clara distantly. "I've known these hills since I was a child."

"No offence meant. You're a big girl now, aren't you? Know how to take care of yourself, eh?"

Clara was speechless with anger.

"Bet your Dad told you not to speak to strangers, didn't he?" he said with an insufferable grin. "Quite right, too. But you needn't mind me, my dear. I've got a girl about your age myself. Gwen her name is. Something your build, too. Fancies she's too old to get a spanking, but I don't see eye to eye with her on that. Well, so long."

She muttered something and began to walk away very fast to put as much distance as possible between herself and the odious man. Her eyes kept filling with angry tears which the wind dried as soon as they gathered. "Beastly. Everything's beastly," she said out loud, kicking at loose bits of chalk. The day was utterly ruined. She took the first track and stumbled down into the valley. There was nothing she wanted now but to get back as fast as she could to Paget's Fold. When she got to the village, it was not yet three. Pride forbade her to go home yet. A day alone on the downs was a treat to be begged and planned for: she could never admit that it had been a failure. She wandered into the post-office and bought herself a twopenny *Tim Pippin* and a copy of *Home Notes*. With these she whiled away an hour or two in a dismal little teashop. She had not enough money for an ice and spun out endless cups of strong, tepid tea till the proprietress began to look impatient. She dawdled home as slowly as possible, with intervals of sitting on gates, being careful to leave *Tim Pippin* and *Home Notes* in a ditch, though not before she had read every word down to advice on how to care for false teeth and get rid of superfluous hair.

When she got home Isabel said:

"You look a little tired, darling. Did you walk too far?"

"I'm never tired, Mother," insisted Clara, tossing her chin and her hair. "I suppose I've walked about eleven miles. But I'm not in the least tired."

"How I envy you your energy," said Isabel wistfully. "I used to be such a good walker. I wonder if I'll ever be able to again. Was it lovely on the hills?"

"Oh yes," said Clara stolidly. "Windy. But ripping all the same. I had a perfectly marvellous day."

Her father had a preoccupied expression, familiar at Valetta Road but disturbing at Paget's Fold. For a moment Clara wondered whether he might be angry with her. She could not remember having done anything to annoy him but the last few hours had left her with an inexplicable feeling of guilt. Timidly she went up to him and kissed him.

"You're not cross with me for having gone off all day, Daddy?"

He put his arm round her.

"Cross my dear? Heaven forbid. Enjoy all you can while you can. It's been a solace thinking of you up there on the hills. I'm so glad we didn't hear before you left. It might have spoilt your day."

"Hear what?" It could not be anything very dreadful for her mother looked perfectly calm.

"Germany has declared war on Russia. Mark you, that still does not necessarily mean we shall be drawn in. But there's no denying things are extremely serious."

"I rather wish there would be a war," said Clara. "It might make life a bit more exciting. I suppose I'd be too young to nurse the wounded?"

"I sincerely hope so, my dear. If it *should* happen—let's trust it will all be over long before you've even left school."

"It's such a bore being a girl. If I were a boy, I could go as a drummer or something."

Isabel interrupted:

"For heaven's sake don't let's start talking about fighting and killing. There's enough pain and misery in the world already. Of course we shan't go to war, Clara. Your father and Aunt Leah have been working themselves up all day. But Aunt Sophy and I know better, don't we?"

"I'm sure those Germans wouldn't dare," said Aunt Sophy. "The old Queen would turn in her grave. I've always heard she thought very poorly of that Kaiser though he was her nephew."

"Let's hope you and Isabel are right, aunt." He drew Clara closer and said beneath his breath: "I know just how you feel, my dear."

He kissed with sudden vehemence, saying aloud: "All the same, thank God you're not a boy."

The next day was Sunday, a day she hated in London and loved at Paget's Fold. When she pulled up the red blind, the dew was rising in mists over the meadows. The air was cool with the recovered freshness that comes between one hot day and another; smoke stood up straight from the chimneys: not a leaf stirred in the heavy August plumage of the trees. Yesterday, with its tormenting thoughts and its miasma of uneasiness, dissolved like a bad dream before the reality of this perfect morning. Washing in cold rain-water and putting on her clean Sunday clothes, she felt life beginning again, new and unspoilt. She said her prayers with devotion; asking forgiveness for yesterday's wild thoughts; asking to be made simple and contented.

Sunday had its own ritual. Before the three of them set out on the drive to Mass, they always went to the tangled beds on the little lawn at the back and picked themselves buttonholes. It was Clara's turn to choose the flowers and today she decided on roses for everyone. She selected them with special care, a red one for her father, a tea-rose for her mother and a striped York and Lancaster for herself. As she offered the rose to her mother, she was suddenly struck by her appearance. A few days in the country had revived Isabel's looks; the shadows had nearly faded from under her great brown eyes and her skin looked creamy under the bloom of powder. She was wearing a fresh shantung suit and a little toque made entirely of hyacinths. Clara found herself looking at her as if she had not seen her for a long time, almost as if she had never seen her before.

"Why, Mother," she said. "You're a really beautiful woman. But *isn't* she, Daddy? Seriously. Quite as beautiful as any of the heroines in her old novels."

"My dear," said her father, beaming, "have you never noticed it before? Unobservant as I am, it struck me the very first time I set eyes on her. Four ... five ... twenty years ago, Isabel."

Isabel took the rose, dropping her eyelids as she pinned it to the lapel of her jacket. She looked suddenly shy; a faint, almost troubled smile just lifted one corner of her sad mouth. For a moment she was not only beautiful but young.

Clara was strangely moved. Something made her feel crude and priggish and unfledged. She did a thing she had never done before, even at Paget's Fold. Stepping between her father and mother, she put an arm round each and drew them towards her.

"I think I'm jolly lucky in my parents."

Isabel said, almost absently: "Darling child." She raised her eyelids and let her soft dark stare wander up from the beds of asters and roses and the leaf-strewn lawn, to the lichened roof of the old house and the martins clipping across the summer blue.

"Oh, our lovely, peaceful Sunday mornings. And you two wanting a war. Suppose this were our very last."

"Please God, no, my dear."

She gave her most wayward smile. "Please God! It always seems to me so queer what we think does please God. Why should God be more pleased at my going to a dark, chilly church and listening to orphan boys with adenoids singing Latin words they don't understand, than if I stayed in this sweet garden and admired the flowers he made and listened to the birds?"

"Now, now, my dear," said Claude good-humouredly. "We've been into all that."

"I know you think me illogical," said Isabel, pulling down her veil, "but how do you know I don't think you illogical?"

For once Clara did not rush to back her father in this ancient fray. She merely observed: "I can hear the fly."

"Of course, my dear," said Claude, "if you don't feel up to going to church ..."

"Oh, I'll certainly come," said Isabel. "I adore that pretty drive. I'm not going to miss it when it might be our very last. Tell Daddy not to worry, Clara. I'll think about roses instead of the orphans' adenoids."

146

"Isabel, you are an incorrigible pagan."

"Oh no," she said very seriously. "I truly believe in God. And Christ and the Holy Virgin. It's all so beautiful."

"Of course it's beautiful," said Claude. "But it's something much more important than beautiful."

"I don't believe there's anything more important than beauty." She unfurled her parasol and began to step smoothly across the lawn. Claude and Clara followed her, exchanging indulgent glances. He murmured:

"*Vera incessu patuit dea.*"

Isabel stopped and swerved round. The pink lining of the sunshade threw a warm glow over her dress so that she was all rosy cream like the flower at her neck.

"That's Latin, isn't it, dea'est? Is it a prayer or a curse?"

"Neither, my dear."

"Then what does it mean? I'll make Clara tell me if you won't."

"It means that twenty ... even ten years ago ... I might have allowed myself to agree with you."

PART FOUR

Chapter 1

IN the autumn, the first of the war, Clara went to St Mark's Girls'
School. After the convent, she found it impossible to take a secular
school seriously. From the beginning she adopted an attitude of
amused tolerance borrowed from Nicole de Savigny. At first this had
been mainly bluff but, finding that the bluff worked, she threw herself
wholeheartedly into the part of the privileged eccentric. At Mount
Hilary she had been nervously anxious to conform. At St Mark's she
did not care in the least for public opinion, with the result that in a few
weeks she had established herself as one of the personalities of the
Upper Sixth.

She was helped by a piece of pure luck. Games were taken seriously
at St Mark's and she was outstandingly bad at them. Each new girl was
allotted to one of the six Games Clubs but, through an oversight,
Clara's name was left out of the lists. As she was careful not to mention
this, she managed to spend the whole of her time at St Mark's without
once playing hockey, cricket or netball though she was prudent
enough to turn up at important matches. Gym, being done in forms,
was unavoidable, but Gym had not the peculiar sacredness of games
and she managed to keep up her prestige by combining the rôles of
class clown and mistress baiter. Luckily the muscular young woman
fresh from Bedford College was as nervous of Clara's bland impertinence as Clara herself was of the vaulting horse and the parallel bars,
so the awful fact that she was a "funk" was never discovered.

In her other classes her behaviour was mildly outrageous but just
stopped short of the danger line. Within a fortnight the English
mistress had christened her "The Cat That Walked By Itself" and the
name caught on in the Common Room. Wherever she had gone a
little too far and had qualms about her report, she adopted a technique
which never failed. She conveyed to the particular exasperated mistress
the idea that she alone could subdue her. Then, for several days in that

class, she would be so alert, so obedient, so anxious to please that the storm never came to a head.

At Mount Hilary, she had worked hard and been almost invariably top of her class: now she allowed herself the luxury of letting others pass her, knowing she was good for a spurt if things became critical. The wild variation of her weekly marks gave her a footing in the two most important sets, the Brainies and the Hearties. Since she obviously wasn't a Swat and could be relied on to provide entertainment in boring lessons, the Hearties forgave her for not playing games. The Brainies accepted her on account of her essays and her French. The third set, the Swats, loathed her but, as they were despised by the other two, this was a positive advantage.

Nothing like the Swats had existed at Mount Hilary. They had minds like filing cabinets, and they worked with the nervous intensity of sheep feeding before a thunderstorm. To them Sophocles and Shakespeare were merely the raw material of 'distinctions' and 'alphas': they gazed down long vistas of exams to the goal of a post in some school exactly like St Mark's. At times the sight of their shiny noses and the anxious eyes behind their pince-nez affected Clara like a *memento mori*. Was this what her father really wanted her to be like? The Brainies also intended to have careers but they were constantly changing their minds about them. At one moment someone would decide she was going to be a writer and the next an explorer or, if women ever got the vote, a member of parliament. Clara was on excellent terms with all the Brainies but never became a formal adherent. She had no desire to cut a figure in public life or raise the status of her sex; her dreaming of careers was confined to a hope that something would turn up to save her from teaching or the Civil Service. However, she had one real friend in the set, a plain, witty Jewess who was her only serious rival in essays and the Literary Society. Apart from Ruth Philips, Clara had one other real friend and this friend outraged both the Brainies and the Hearties. She was not a Swat; Swats were at least respectable. She was not even a colourless neutral. She was quite frankly an Impossible and, to make matters worse, she was in a lower form.

Sooner or later Clara knew there was bound to be a storm over Patsy Cohen. Towards the end of her first term it broke. One afternoon during prep. four of the leading Hearties, Beatrice Wilson, Rosalind Forbes, Jean McKay and 'Blackie' Buckfield suddenly set on her.

"Spinster, we've got a bone to pick with you." They pulled her up from her desk and manœuvred her into position with her back against the wall. Clara did not resist.

"Look here, we've been holding a council about you."

"And we all agree that you're a bit queer."

"Shut up, Blackie. We agreed she was all right *herself*."

"I haven't finished, Roz. We agreed we could put up with *her*."

"But not with some of your friends, Spin." Clara was far from feeling as detached as she was trying to look. The four faces, respectively freckled, pale, rosy and sunburnt but all smelling identically of cloakroom soap, were menacing. Instinct warned her that her only hope was to be bold. She leant negligently against the wall as if she had taken up the position of her own accord.

"Really?" she said mildly. "I don't think I remember having asked you to put up with anyone. You say 'some' so I suppose you mean several."

"We mean one, and jolly well you know it," said Blackie grimly. Her thick eyebrows almost met when she frowned. "A Yid, if you want a clue."

"Not Ruth, surely?" asked Clara, looking earnest and puzzled. "I could have sworn that even you liked Ruth."

"Of course, not Ruth," said Rosalind. She was the prettiest of the four, with dark eyes and white teeth in a face the colour of a brown egg. "Ruth's as decent as can be. And we've nothing against Yids as such, provided they behave themselves."

"May I tell Ruth that? I'm sure it would be a great comfort to her."

"Come off it, Batchelor," said Blackie, lowering her head, with its dangling dark plaits, like a bull about to charge. "Cheek the staff as much as you like but you'd better not try it on with *us*."

"You see, old thing, you're a new girl," explained Beatrice Wilson. She was the most amiable of the Hearties, a full-bosomed sixteen with glazed foxglove-pink cheeks. "We've all been at St Mark's for simply years. We've sort of made an exception in your case. But we know what's done and what's not done."

"And my particular sin? Is it one of commission or omission?" asked Clara in her catechism class manner.

"Haven't the foggiest what you mean," said Blackie.

"Nor I what you mean," said Clara. "I wish one of you would come to the point."

"You must be jolly dense if you can't guess," sneered Jean Mackay. "Go on, tell her, Blackie."

Blackie cleared her throat.

"Well, for one thing, it's not done to go about with people in lower forms."

"Is there a rule about it?" asked Clara meekly. "I didn't know."

"Of course not. It's just not done."

"In my case it seems it is done."

There was a simultaneous bellow from the herd. Clara looked as if she were trying hard to follow a difficult piece of reasoning.

"You mean if Patsy were in six instead of five you wouldn't object?"

"Good lord, are you balmy? Or only pretending to be?"

"I should jolly well think we should object."

"*Patsy!* What a name for a Yid!"

"Jezebel it ought to be," said Blackie in a burst of inspiration. "Pretty good, what? She's one of the Chosen and she certainly paints her face." Her sulkiness melted into giggles at her own wit. Everyone tittered except Clara, who said judicially:

"Not paints. Only powders."

"Golly, that's bad enough," said Rosalind.

"I swear she uses rouge or something ghastly," insisted Blackie. "I vote we get hold of her and give her a good scrub under the cold tap."

"It's been done already," said Clara. "Incidentally it made the scrubber look rather silly."

"Not you, I bet."

"Oh, dear me, no."

"Tell who."

"I don't think it would be 'done' to give her away," said Clara, virtuously.

"Rot."

"We'll make you."

"All right. If you insist, it was Miss Silver."

Miss Silver was the headmistress. There were cries of "You're spoofing."

"Honour bright. Miss Silver sent for Patsy and accused her of being rouged. Patsy said she wasn't. Miss Silver made her wash her face in front of her. But no pink came off. So Miss Silver had to apologize."

"Utter swiz," said Blackie. "The Cohen made it all up, if you didn't."

"I can produce written evidence. Mrs Cohen was rather annoyed and wrote to Miss Silver. They've preserved her reply; it's really a handsome tribute. 'I confess I was deceived by the somewhat unusual brilliance of your daughter's complexion.' Patsy wants to have it framed."

Blackie, slightly deflated, growled.

"Pity she mucks up the unusual brilliance with all that powder then."

"Yes, isn't it?" said Clara eagerly. "I'm always telling her so. I'll tell her you said so, may I?" She fixed her gaze absently on Blackie's shining nose. "With such a skin as that, she really would look better without powder, wouldn't she? I can't think of *anyone* else who would, can you?"

"Filthy stuff," snorted Jean Mackay who was rather proud of her freckles. "Anyway her beastly powder's only the beginning."

"She never turns up at matches."

"She wears a pneumonia blouse with her gym tunic."

"She's always losing her school hat. Probably think it doesn't suit her beauty."

"She gives male Marcians the glad eye."

All this, Clara admitted, was perfectly true. But what exactly did they want her to do about it? She rightly guessed that no one quite liked to put it into words.

"Very well," she said boldly. "I'll spare your delicate feelings and say it for you. If I don't drop Patsy, you'll drop me. Right. Go ahead and drop me then."

Two faces were still menacing; two were puzzled.

"Can't you really see how ghastly she is?" asked Rosalind.

Clara brought up all her reserves of courage.

"Do you know," she said slowly. "I believe I've never really appreciated Patsy till this moment. She's much more amusing on the subject of all of you and, incidentally, considerably more charitable than you are about her. And at least she isn't a prig."

There was silence. Then Blackie said in a choked voice:

"Have you the nerve to suggest *we're* prigs?"

Clara imitated Nicole's shrug and faint, ambiguous smile. Her heart was thumping and her knees were so weak that she was glad of the support of the wall. They were established school powers; they were in the same form and would move up with her every year. To have the four of them permanently allied against her would make the rest of her life at St Mark's extremely unpleasant.

Jean said almost in a whisper:

"You seriously mean you'd rather chuck us than Patricia Cohen?"

Clara noticed the change of emphasis.

"I never talked of 'chucking' anybody. You four started all this silly business. Personally I think it's all very Angela Brazilish."

This went home. Even the heartiest Hearties despised Angela Brazilishness. She followed it up boldly.

"I don't in the least mind being The Most Unpopular Girl in the Sixth," she said, hoping they did not guess she would mind exceedingly, "but I propose to continue being seen in public with Patsy. What are you going to do about it?"

The four pairs of eyes consulted each other but no one spoke.

"Perhaps you'd like to hold another council? I'll leave you to it if you'll let me get out."

The four remained solidly shoulder to shoulder blocking her escape. It was Rosalind who found her tongue first.

"Look here, Spin, you're obviously as mad as a hatter. But I personally rather like the way you stick up for your ghastly Cohen. If she were a friend of mine—which of course, is impossible."

"Q.E.D."

"Don't try to be funny, Mackay. It doesn't suit you. Well, as I was saying, I'd probably do the same."

Clara watched the four exchange looks and nudges. Blackie said rather sullenly:

"I gather the general feeling is that you chaps want it to be Pax then?"

"Is it Pax by you, Spin?" asked Rosalind. Her voice was almost anxious.

"Pax by all means."

Clara had not really expected to win and the relief made her feel slightly light-headed. She risked a gesture. She drew a small battered box of *Poudre Nildé* from her pocket and dabbed her nose with a shaking hand.

"Forgive me. These emotional scenes are so trying."

"You picked *that* up from the Cohen I suppose," sneered Jean.

"Good Lord. You'll be smoking next," said Beatrice.

"At least smoking isn't *soppy*," declared Blackie. "I smoke a fag myself now and then."

"Patsy doesn't approve of smoking," said Clara, replacing the powder-box. "Afraid it might spoil her teeth."

Once again the silence became ominous. Clara cursed herself for a fool. As usual she had gone too far and spoilt everything. Then suddenly Rosalind giggled and one by one the others burst out laughing.

"Spin, you really are rather priceless. You're what La Frog calls 'im-pay-able'."

"Dare you to flour your nozzle in French tomorrow."

"Done," said Clara. They did not know this needed no courage at all.

Beatrice looked at her watch.

"I say, you chaps. Fuller's is still open. Who could do with a Pineapple Guzzler?"

"Spiffing notion. Come on, Spin, we'll stand you treat."

It was Clara's first victory over public opinion. It was also the first of many fights she was to have with various people, herself included, on the subject of Patsy Cohen.

Chapter 2

UNLIKE Ruth Philips, Pasty Cohen was not a deliberately chosen friend. Being in different forms, Patsy and Clara would probably have ignored each other but for a coincidence which Clara had not mentioned in her battle with the Hearties. The coincidence was that Patsy and her two sisters had once spent a few terms at Mount Hilary.

At the convent Clara had only known the Cohen's by sight and collectively. The three exotic little Jewesses, Vera, Mavis and Patricia, had appeared half-way through a dull term and, for some reason, had promptly become school pets. They were hardly thought of as separate identities: they were simply "the Cohens". All three were unusually short and the eldest, Vera, unusually fat. They always went about together, hopping along on their thin legs (even Vera's were like sticks) and chirping in identical shrill voices like three small birds.

Rigid school conventions were revised for the sake of the Cohens. They were all so good at mathematics that they had to do them with the highest class. With their thin legs dangling from chairs much too big for them, they looked like children, among grown-ups. Three pairs of bright eyes, small in Vera, middling in Mavis, enormous in Patricia: watched the blackboard like hawks: three high voices propounded problems which the unhappy nun could hardly grasp, let alone solve. Vera was a violinist who, at the age of twelve, had already given a recital and got excellent notices. Twice a week, a master with an international reputation came to give her a lesson, breaking one of Mount Hilary's strictest rules and upsetting school time-tables by insisting on three hours' practice. The Cohens were always getting 'permissions' sternly refused to others. They were constantly going out, dressed in identical pretty clothes, to dentists and oculists or being let off games or allowed to get up late. Throughout their brief career at the convent, they remained friendly, popular and completely unassimilated. One day, again in the middle of a term, they vanished as unexpectedly as they had appeared.

Clara had never given them another thought till one morning, as she was walking to St Mark's, she found a small figure trotting breathlessly beside her.

"You're Clara Batchelor, aren't you? I've been chasing you for days but you walk so fast. D'you remember me at Mount Hilary? I'm the youngest of the Cohens, Patsy."

Under the Marcian·straw boater, worn at an angle forbidden by Miss Silver, two enormous, brilliant eyes shone up at Clara between theatrically long lashes.

At first she could not believe that this dazzling little face could possibly belong to any of the Cohens whom she remembered collectively as sallow and beaky.

"Your hair's as gorgeous as ever," Patsy chattered on. "We used to be awfully jealous of it, being dark ourselves and not a natural curl between the three of us. In fact, except for growing, you haven't changed a bit. Would you have recognised me?"

The voice at least had not altered. It was the Cohen voice, shrill but musical. And the legs, though clothed in black silk instead of black cotton, were recognizably Cohen legs, preternaturally slim and very slightly bowed.

"Honestly I don't think I would. You've changed tremendously."

"I hope so. Except that I've hardly grown at all. None of us have. People won't believe that Mavis and I are sixteen and seventeen. But they always think poor Vera's miles more than eighteen because she's as fat as ever. Marmee makes her wear black velvet for concerts and what with that and her playing, everyone thinks she must be positively ancient. Some beastly critic actually took her for twenty-eight. Wasn't it ghastly for her? Luckily she's not vain like me."

Studying Patsy's transformed face as she hopped and twittered beside her, Clara thought she had every excuse to be vain. For Patsy now looked exactly like one of the flamboyantly pretty girls on magazine covers, the kind that subalterns were beginning to pin up in their dugouts. Her eyes were even bigger than Isabel's and did not quite match in colour: one had greenish glints in it and the other blue. The lashes of both lids were so long and dark that combined with the faint shadow under them, they made Patsy's eyes as if they were very skilfully made up. Her cheeks were very pink and her neck so white that the chalk-white powder she used only showed up as a bloom on it. At the convent, she had worn a plate on her front teeth. She must have worn it to some effect for now they were as even as any advertised smile. But what fascinated Clara most was Patsy's mouth. Rouge might have accounted for her cheeks but not for her lips. Hitherto she had supposed that coral lips were an Elizabethan convention but Patsy's exactly matched the coral brooch she wore and had the same faint sheen. She searched the vivid face for any feature she could connect with the former Patsy and found it at last in her nose. It was less obtrusive now that the childish peakiness had gone, it was carefully powdered, it was more than atoned for by those amazing eyes but it was still definitely the Cohen nose.

"Forgive my staring at you," said Clara, "but you really have grown up quite astonishingly pretty."

"No one ever thought I would," said Patsy. "Do you remember what a fright I was at the convent? All nose and eyes and rabbit's teeth. But Marmee's still the beauty of the family. You wait till you see her. Gracious, I forgot. I've been carrying a note round for days from Marmee to your mother asking if you may come to tea one Sunday. You will, won't you? Mavis and Vera are dying to see you again."

For the rest of the way they exchanged memories of Mount Hilary. Clara was slightly disconcerted to find how different the place had appeared to non-Catholic eyes. To Patsy, it had simply seemed a rather amusingly old-fashioned school run by kindly eccentrics.

"I can't think why some of them shut themselves up like that," she said artlessly. "Quite a lot were definitely good-looking even in those hideous bonnets."

But, in spite of Patsy's irreverence, it was like meeting a compatriot abroad to talk to someone who knew what was meant by 'exemptions' and 'wishings' who had eaten *goûter* under the limes and played *Cache* on feast days.

When Isabel read Mrs Cohen's invitation, her first remark was:

"Your friend Ruth Philips is Jewish too, isn't she? You seem to have inherited Daddy's passion for the Chosen Race."

"I've never thought about it one way or the other," said Clara. "Anyway the Cohens weren't friends of mine at Mount Hilary."

"I'm surprised they allowed Jewesses at the convent at all. The nuns were supposed to be so very exclusive. Especially as they're not even Catholics. I suppose money unlocks all doors these days."

"I don't think they're sensationally rich," said Clara. "After all they live in West Kensington just as we do. I don't suppose there's much to choose between Garthwaite Crescent and Valetta Road."

"Do you want to go to tea with these people, Clara? You realize I shall have to call on the mother if you do. I hope she's not another Becky Shapiro. I'm sure the name Cohen is on every other shop in the Commercial Road. But at least she doesn't write 'Yours' with an apostrophe and there's nothing vulgar about her notepaper."

Clara who, up to now, had not cared whether she went or not, became suddenly determined.

"Yes, I do want to," she said stubbornly.

"You'll have to ask Daddy. If this Mrs Cohen knew us she'd realize it was a pure formality asking *my* permission about anything that concerns you."

"I'm sure he'll let me. In fact he'll probably insist on it. You know he likes me to keep up with anyone from Mount Hilary."

They were so much back in the Valetta Road routine that Paget's Fold might never have existed. But Isabel had her revenge.

"Isn't it odd, Clara," she said sweetly, "that the very first girl from the convent who asks you to her own home should be some little Jewess you never even knew at Mount Hilary."

Claude consented without difficulty. He merely added with a sigh: "I can't help being sorry they're not Catholics. It distresses me that you have no Catholic friends. But you still correspond with that delightful de Savigny girl I hope?"

"Oh yes," said Clara with a guilty thankfulness that he could not see her own letters. She added informatively: "She's pulling every string to try and get herself sent out to some French hospital."

"Precisely what I should expect of her. All the same I'm thankful I'm in no position to pull strings if you got such notions into your head. In any case she's older than you are. But if the war went on longer than we expected and if some day you desperately wanted to join her, I suppose I couldn't in decency object."

"Oh, there's not a hope for an English girl unless she's at least twenty-one," said Clara hastily. After the excitement of the first week she had completely lost interest in the war.

She went to the Cohens not only the next Sunday but the two following ones. Very soon it became such a habit to run over to Garthwaite Crescent when she had nothing special to do that her mother complained that she preferred it to her own home.

This was perfectly true though she could never say just what it was that gave the Cohen house its peculiar charm. Perhaps it was that, for the first time, she found herself completely at home in a family. Within a few weeks she had become an honorary daughter and sister. In her present mood, the fact that it was a family of girls was an extra attraction. As a small girl she had despised other small girls and her friends had all been boys. Even during her time at Mount Hilary she had been, without her parents' knowledge, the only female member of a secret gang of boys in the lower forms of St Mark's or the higher ones of its Preparatory School, Corinth House. For, though Clara loathed games and could not face ropes and parallel bars in cold blood, she could be reckless when excited. In a black mask, with a cap-pistol in her belt she would walk along walls by moonlight or climb through the windows of empty houses without a qualm. In the character of Burglaress Bill she could do things which would have been impossible to Clara Batchelor. But, ever since Blaze had kissed her in the orchard, roof prowling and mock burglaries had somehow lost their charm. She preferred to be thought of as a girl rather than" almost as good as a boy". Until she knew the Cohens she still had bursts of playing with soldiers and trains and she continued to take in *The Captain*. Within a few weeks of meeting Patsy, the neglected regiments were gathering dust in the toy box and *The Captain* had been replaced by *Nash's*.

Garthwaite Crescent was as different as possible from Valetta Road. For one thing all the Cohens openly and demonstratively adored each other; there were no undercurrents of jealousy and dislike. For another, its doors were open at all times to all comers. At Valetta Road there were bridge parties and dinner parties but no one ever came uninvited and both Claude and Isabel detested noise. Garthwaite Crescent was always in a state of commotion. Often the front door was left ajar all day and when Clara stepped across the sill she was greeted by an agreeable babel, usually composed of the twittering of Mavis and Patsy, Vera's violin, the yapping of the two Pekes and the hum of Mrs Cohen's sewing machine. The telephone was always ringing, people, often total strangers, were constantly arriving and lingering on to several meals, the girls were always dashing upstairs to change their clothes or dashing down again, half-dressed, to try out a new record or a dance step. In spite of all this, Clara found the atmosphere as restful as a warm bath. She soon decided that this was entirely due to Mrs Cohen.

As soon as she set eyes on Lilian Cohen, she completely lost her heart. For "Marmee" was like the angel mother in the old story books at Paget's Fold. Patsy had not exaggerated when she said she would never be half as pretty as her mother. She was tinier even than Patsy, but so perfectly in scale that one never thought of her as short. Compared with her dark-eyed, ivory beauty, Patsy was a poster beside a Chinese drawing. Everything about Mrs Cohen was delicate and finely articulated from her narrow feet to her small pale face, Spanish rather than Jewish in type.

She was never idle but she did everything with a fairy-like quickness and ease. She would dart from the drawing-room to the kitchen and cook an admirable meal in less time than it would take the average person to assemble the ingredients. She would leave the sewing-machine where was "flying up" a dress for one of her daughters to sight-read a difficult accompaniment for Vera without a trace of nervous flurry. Unlike most efficient people, she never made others feel guilty about their laziness; in fact she had an enchanting gift of managing to appear lazy herself. When her fingers were flying over the keyboard or sewing so fast that the needle seemed to move in a continuous streak, she seemed to watch them with amused detachment as if they were working without any effort of hers.

Her husband and her daughters were the very centre of her life but from them her affection spread out in all directions not only to their friends and their friends' friends but to every human being who came her way. The shyest boys and girls thawed in her presence; the boorish became amiable and the most conceited cheerfully made fools of themselves for the pleasure of making her laugh. Clara might have found the Cohens' mutual adoration oppressive had it not been so light-hearted. They were gay and affectionate rather than passionate. The girls quarrelled and made up again as spontaneously as a family of kittens; no smothered resentments thickened the air as they did in her own home. As soon as she stepped into the cream-coloured hall hung with African trophies, she seemed to be enfolded in warm brightness even on the dullest day. There was nothing remarkable about the house itself although white paint, airy curtains and quantities of flowers everywhere made it far more cheerful than Valetta Road. Yet to Clara it seemed to exist in another climate, as if the Cohens had imported some of the Jamaican sun along with the rocking-chairs and the wicker tables and Marmee's plaited workbaskets.

Clara was not alone in feeling the fascination of the Cohen home. Every Sunday flocks of boys and girls from the Royal College of Music where Vera now both studied and taught and from Mavis's ballet class invaded the house. Young officers on leave made it their headquarters and brought their friends; there was a constantly changing influx of friends from Jamaica coming over to join up; French and Belgian uniforms mingled with the British. They usually began with serious music but sooner or later someone would launch into wild improvisation or jazz and people would begin to dance. This was Mavis's moment. She had remained sallow and beaky but was clever enough not to try and compete with Patsy's looks. She wore vivd amusing clothes that made her look like a sophisticated gipsy and emphasized the fact that her figure was nearly as good as her mother's. But, well as Patsy danced, she often found herself deserted in mid-floor while her partner tried to snatch even one turn with Mavis. Sometimes they extemporised burlesque opera or ballets; sometimes they merely glided sedately to the gramophone. When everyone was exhausted, they would turn out the lights and sit round the fire while Clara told ghost stories. This was a popular turn, chiefly because it gave people the chance of holding hands in the dark. There was only coffee and ginger beer unless Mr Cohen was at home and then whisky was offered by him in person only to the senior young men. But nobody seemed to mind. Their own youth and the general atmosphere of the house kept them all in the wildest spirits. Nor would anyone have enjoyed themselves half as much if Marmee had not always been hovering in the background or foreground, conjuring up food, taking her turn at the piano or knitting socks for the young soldier while she watched them dance. Sometimes they would persuade her to dance herself and, when she did, it was evident where Mavis got her talent. But after a few turns she would always slip out of her partner's arms and escape on some domestic pretext.

"I was much too fond of dancing as a girl," she would tell them. "I used to dance every night and all night. But I gave it up when I married because Julius didn't care for it."

Once a tall young Canadian tried to stop her when she made her usual breakaway.

"I'm jolly well not going to let you go. You waltz better than anyone I've ever met, even Mavis. I could dance with you for ever." And he lifted her up bodily like a child. "You're as light as a feather. I'm going to keep you up here till you promise to finish this dance."

"Put me down *at once* please," she said with such a flash of her dark eyes that he meekly obeyed.

"People were much too fond of doing that in Kingstown," she said when she was on the ground again. "It became such a nuisance that once, I'm afraid, I lost my temper and hit a young man with my fan."

In Valetta Road there were occasional storms over Clara's spending so much time at the Cohens. Her father suspected, with reason, that she was doing the minimum of homework but, on the whole, he was glad that she should have friends of her own age. He frowned a good deal over Patsy's appearance, though he privately found it attractive, and was thunderous when Clara went too far in imitation. But he liked Patsy's easy good nature and reassured himself by saying that, with such a mother, there could not be much harm in the girl. She further appeased him by always being nice to old Mrs Batchelor, asking after her rheumatism and bringing her little presents. The person who never had a good word for Patsy was Isabel. She disliked Patsy at first sight and though she listened greedily to her flattery and accepted frequent offerings of flowers and scent, she was never really won over.

Almost every day Clara had to listen to some criticism of Patsy. She looked like a chorus-girl or "something I couldn't even mention to you": she had ugly hands: her prettiness was only that of any little Whitechapel Jewess and would be gone by the time she was twenty. There were two themes on which Isabel played endless variations. "I pity poor Mrs Cohen who is really beautiful and elegant and perfectly *comme il faut* for having a daughter with such appalling style" and "I can't think what a girl as clever as you can see in that brainless little thing."

Clara nevertheless became increasingly attached to Patsy. Vera and Mavis were far more intelligent but she never wanted to idle away hours alone with either of them as she did with Patsy. Even Mrs Cohen was amazed at their devotion to each other for Patsy seemed to prefer Clara to either of her sisters and the two sometimes had to reckon with twinges of jealousy in Mavis. She said once, laughing: "Really, you and Patsy might be twins. You seem to have only one mind between you. It's rather a pity that it doesn't seem to be Clara's."

"Oh, Clara's given up trying to improve my mind. It's a hopeless job. But you must admit I've improved her looks."

"I don't think they needed any improving. Patsy, you've got far too much powder on as usual. And if you insist on wearing such a very thin blouse, you shouldn't have a safety-pin in your camisole. You should keep her in order, Clara."

At Mount Hilary, frivolity had been sternly suppressed. Clara was just at the age to respond ardently to Patsy's interest in everything the nuns had taught her to despise. She continued, nevertheless, to be coldly critical of Isabel on the score of worldly vanity.

The two girls spent hours in Patsy's bedroom, eating caramels while they tried on each other's clothes and experimented with startling new hair-styles. Patsy had inherited her mother's flair for dressmaking; she taught Clara to make blouses and trim hats. She also made her conscious of her underclothes. The first time Clara removed her frock Patsy exclaimed in horror:

"Clara, darling, you mustn't wear those beegledy cotton petticoats."

"Beegledy" was a Cohen family word which applied to everything from a murder to a drooping hem.

"Why? No one sees them."

"Well, I'm seeing one now. And don't you ever look at yourself in the glass when you're undressing? I'm always practising for when I get married. I should hate my husband to be disillusioned. I've even worked out a wonderful way of putting my curlers in in the dark. Lucky pig, you don't have to bother about them. I'll beg some bits of crêpe-de-Chine from Marmee and make you some Kirchner girl camisoles."

When Clara, on her sixteenth birthday, was promoted to a small dress allowance, she spent it entirely under Patsy's direction, often acquiring things she dared not wear at home. The two were always sending for free samples of face-creams and powders and trying out shampoos with "brightening rinses". Once, for a whole week, Patsy was nearly as fair as Clara while Clara was almost orange and it was not till the fifth frantic washing that they reverted to their normal colours. They had crises of anxiety about their figures and took to drinking lemon juice and doing strenuous exercises while continuing to eat unlimited caramels. And they discussed endlessly and earnestly the appearance of every other girl they knew and the exact degree of her success with men as if they were trying to lay down basic principles for a philosophy of attractiveness.

There was, however, another side to Patsy which Clara found equally fascinating. Life prevented no abstract problems to her. She had a touching admiration for Clara's "braininess" but regarded her as slightly demented. General ideas had not the faintest interest for Patsy; her mind was concrete and empirical. Art was simply a talent, like Vera's violin playing. What she played didn't matter, provided she did it well. Religion, like music, was a natural taste. Either it appealed to you or it didn't. Marmee was religious and Parpee didn't believe in anything and, as they were both perfect darlings, it couldn't be very important. Her ethics were equally pragmatical. She believed that everyone ought to enjoy themselves as much as possible. If something you enjoyed led to unpleasant consequences or seriously interfered with someone else's pleasure, then you did without it. Very early in their friendship she enlightened Clara's ignorance and was amazed at her first reaction of disgust.

"But why? What's there so awful about it? After all our own parents must have done it."

Clara could not explain that, to her, this was precisely the most awful part. For several days, she felt so contemptuous of her father and mother that she could hardly bring herself to speak to them. Yet, to her surprise, she did not feel the same contempt for Mr and Mrs Cohen. What shocked her most was the confirmation of her terrified suspicion that she had once been a part of her mother. She thought she would not have minded quite so much if her mother had been Lilian Cohen.

"Well, I certainly hope I never have any children," she said.

"But why?" Patsy's great eyes were open to their fullest extent. "I wouldn't mind having twenty if I could keep my figure like Marmee. Of course one looks a sight before. But they say if the man loves you he doesn't mind."

She studied herself in a long mirror.

"I shall look extra frightful because I'm so short."

Suddenly she whipped off her frock.

"I'm going to see just how beegledy I *do* look," she said, stuffing a pillow under her silk slip.

"My goodness, Clara, he *will* have to love me," she said ruefully as she glanced sideways at her reflection. "Considering it will probably be two pillows before the end. Now you try. You oughtn't to look quite so ghastly, being taller."

But Clara refused.

"I've definitely made up my mind not to get married."

"Try anyway. It might act as an awful warning in case you ever felt yourself slipping."

But Clara remained obdurate.

"I agree it would be much more fun just to go on flirting for ever," said Patsy, throwing away the pillow and pulling her scanty clothes tight so as to look her slimmest. "Still don't you think it would be awfully exciting to let oneself go and see what happened?"

"You *wouldn't*, would you, Patsy?" said Clara, scandalized.

"It's probably just as well Marmee keeps an eye on me. But sometimes I've felt a perfect beast, especially when it's someone sweet like Ronny or Colin and they're going back to the front."

"You let them kiss you, I know. Do you think your mother has any idea how many of them have?"

"Kissing," said Patsy, contemptuously. "Really, Clara, one would think you lived in the moon."

"You don't mean anyone's ever dared to suggest ..."

"Goodness, they don't have to suggest. I honestly believe you don't know the first thing about men."

"I was practically proposed to when I wasn't even fifteen," said Clara, loftily.

"Don't look so offended, old thing. I don't mean for one sec. that you're not attractive to men. But I think they're a bit frightened of you. Perhaps it's your brains."

"I sometimes think those famous brains are a myth," said Clara. "Or I have them in spasms. I'm sure I never give the least evidence of them here."

"It isn't that you show off and snub people like Vera. But no matter how you act the giddy goat, everybody will always know. Don't ask me why. I expect men will always treat you differently from the way they treat me. There's something awfully 'touch-me-not' about you."

"Well, I *am* a Catholic, after all."

"I bet that wouldn't stop them if *you* were different. I can't make you out sometimes. You like prinking almost as much as I do. And I've seen you flirt like anything in public. But I've not the faintest idea what happens when you're left alone with a man."

"I jolly seldom am. I'd probably feel rather a fool. But, in public, it's just a sort of game. It's fun trying to intrigue someone new."

"I believe you're just a cold-blooded fish. I'm glad I'm not a man. It would be pretty awful to fall in love with you."

"Do you really think so?" said Clara, half flattered, half dismayed. "Well, no one's in any danger at the moment. I've never been in love and I'm beginning to hope I never shall. I used to have romantic ideas about it but that was before I knew the facts. You've certainly cured me of my childish illusions."

"I wish you could see your expression when you talk like that. No wonder men find you a bit alarming."

"Have *you* ever been in love, Patsy?"

"I wish I knew for certain. I have the most lovely swoony feelings for at least six people, especially when I'm dancing with them. But I think there must be something more to it. I'd like to go to the limit with someone then p'raps I'd find out."

"Patsy, you wouldn't *seriously?*"

"I definitely would if it weren't for Parpee and Marmee. They'd be frightfully upset if they found out."

"I suppose it is different if you don't think it a sin."

"Marmee would think it a sin all right. The funny thing is that Parpee's just as strict, if not stricter, though he thinks religion's all rot. Do you remember that nice old French nun who used to call us pagans? I jolly well wish I had been a pagan."

"Pagan parents were just as strict. Look at what happened to Virginia."

Patsy broke into a dance-step and singing "Goodbye, Virgin-yer, I love the loveliness that's in yer".

"What did happen to Virginia whoever she was?"

"Her father killed her to stop her from being seduced."

"Do you think Parpee would go as far as that?" Patsy went on dancing.

"I love Virgin-yer's beautiful, beautiful eyes," she sang, rolling her own at Clara. "I love Virgin-yer's beautiful, beautiful skies." Anyway, if I ever did before I was married, I'd be jolly careful not to have a baby."

"But people usually do, don't they?"

"Not if they don't want to."

"They always have them in books. Look at Tess and Hetty Poyser. They certainly didn't *want* them."

"You're always reading things written in the year dot. Women aren't such fools nowadays. Of course it's always a bit risky."

Patsy stopped dancing to go into details, adding, "Of course,

Catholics aren't allowed to. I know that from my cousin Cita. She's a Catholic. All Marmee's Spanish relations are. That's how we got let into the convent."

Something flashed into Clara's mind.

"I wonder if *that's* what my mother meant when she said ..."

"What?"

"Oh, nothing. Show me that new step you were doing just now."

Clara often wondered what Ruth Philips would have said had she heard this or any of her other typical conversations with Patsy.

No two girls could have been more unlike than Patsy and Ruth. Even the fact that they were both Jewish gave them nothing in common except their devotion to their families. As a family, the Philipses had no charm for Clara. Their house was far drearier and uglier than Valetta Road and she disliked Ruth's mother and older sister who had the knack of making her feel a thoroughly useless member of society. Ruth's mother had been headmistress of a board school before she married and the sister, Miriam, was studying social welfare. Both had a brisk, cheerful sarcastic manner which made Clara feel as if she were being scrubbed under the cold tap with medicated soap. Ruth herself was as plain as Patsy was pretty and made herself look considerably plainer than she need have done. Unlike the rest of her family she did not look in the least Jewish; she could have served as a model for an unflattering picture of the typical English school girl. She was short, stocky and thick-ankled, with a round pink face and a button nose which shone as if it had been polished. Her clear lively grey eyes were obscured by round steel-rimmed spectacles which left a red furrow on her nose when she removed them and her brown hair had a dusty look and stuck out in uneven wisps. Even when she was not wearing a gym tunic, the unkindest of all garments for her dumpy body and stout legs, she favoured frocks of the same cruel cut, hanging limply from embroidered yokes. It was not that Ruth was indifferent to clothes. She chose the handwoven materials for her heather-coloured and sage-green and peat brown djibbahs with the greatest care and regarded Clara as a reactionary slave to convention. She was always mocking at her high heels and pointing out the charm and comfort of her own sandals. But Ruth's mind was as agile as her body was clumsy and, though she had no idea of line or colour in her own clothes, she had the most critical eye for both in pictures.

The two had come to know each other long before Patsy had

appeared on the scene. As the only Jewess and the only Catholic in the Sixth Form they had a quarter of an hour alone every morning during School Prayers. Almost at once they discovered so many things to discuss that they made it a habit to walk home together. And even after the incursion of Patsy, the hour or two after afternoon school remained sacred to Ruth. Clara avoided Ruth's home as much as possible and Ruth, though she was approved of at Valetta Road, was more at her ease away from it. Clara's intimacy with Patsy had grown in the setting of Patsy's bedroom, among a litter of creams and powders and open drawers of tumbled silks and chiffons. Her real life with Ruth was a peripatetic one and its background was the grey and dull red streets of West Kensington.

On summer evenings and often in winter dusks they would spin out their walk for an hour or more. Even when, after pacing deep in talk up innumerable sidestreets, they found themselves back at Ruth's home, they usually started some fascinating new hare on the very doorstep. Then they would take "just one more turn" up and down the grimy length of Smyrna Grove, losing count of the times they passed the house, until Mrs Philips called sharply from the window. They discussed art and literature, philosophy and religion; they made up satirical poems about school characters and gave cruel imitations of the staff. When either had written anything serious, she conveyed to the other that it was just possible that she might have it on her, but of course it was only the roughest draft and in no fit state to show. After pressing persuasion, the author would burrow in every pocket and, in the very last one, discover a scrap of paper. The scrap was always carelessly creased but there was never an erasure in what was written on it. Then the critic would gaze at the pavement with a concentrated frown while the author muttered the poem or the story very fast in a low fierce voice. Ruth would say:

"My God, that's good. It really does come off. I'm just wondering whether maybe you've slightly overdone the jewellery. D'you absolutely have to have chrysoprase and beryl in the same verse? By the way, just what colour *is* a chrysoprase?"

Clara, mindful of the second commandment, did not dare to say, "My God" but swore to Ruth's genius by Homeric heroes.

"By Hector and Patroclus, you've done it again. It's as good as Dryden, it really is. I wouldn't touch a word except just conceivably to vary the rhyme in the last couplet."

They had reached the same stage of mental intoxication; the fact that there was so much to read and see and to find out gave them a feeling of delicious vertigo. With Nicole, Clara had always been the follower who trailed some way behind the pioneer but with Ruth she marched side by side. At brief intervals, each in turn would discover the poem or the book or the picture which positively eclipsed all others. Oblivious of passers-by, they declaimed passages to each other or chanted them in unison as they paced the streets, their stiff straw hats askew and their satchels bumping on their backs. They had moods of noble indignation and burning idealism but Ruth's flickering wit saved them from solemnity. Her parodies and pastiches were so brilliant that Clara sometimes copied them out and sent them to Nicole. When, to Ruth's immense excitement, she won a prize in a *Saturday Westminster* competition, Clara was even more impressed by the fact that Nicole thought her entry *épatant*.

Till she knew Ruth, Clara had thought of a university as a dull prolonging of school. Soon they had both decided that their lives would not begin till they went to Cambridge. They were convinced the war would be over by the time they were ready to go up and they would be in at the dawn of a new world. All over England there must be people just like themselves, waiting to meet and set each other on fire. They vied with each other in drawing pictures of what Cambridge would be like and invented a place which was a combination of mediæval Paris, Plato's Academy and an eighteenth century coffee-house. The dons in this dream city talked like Coleridge and Wilde and the undergraduates were all brilliant or fantastic.

There was no doubt that Clara delighted in Ruth's company nor that she admired and even liked her more than Patsy. All the same she continued to spend most of her spare time at Garthwaite Crescent. Often, with her eyes still lit up with wild enthusiasms and her brain humming with tremendous lines, she would rush home, put on her flightiest blouse and slip round the Cohens for supper. Then, her pleasure enhanced if anything by a faint sense of guilt, she would fritter away the rest of the evening gossiping with Patsy, practising the tango or strumming Delysia's latest songs.

Chapter 3

CLAUDE'S first impulse had been to throw up everything and enlist. Rejected as too old to serve abroad, he had to content himself with staying on at St Mark's and accepting a commission in the O.T.C.

His attitude towards his top form became increasingly humble. By 1916 enough of his old pupils had been killed to make him shudder every time a Second Lieutenant came to say goodbye. In spite of his fierce classroom manner, he had always been devoted to his boys. Now they became so many versions of the son he would never have.

The photographs on the mantelpiece, even those of his father and Larry O'Sullivan, were gradually displaced by smooth, moustached young faces staring self-consciously under peaked caps and Gorblimeys. The originals haunted the study when they were on leave. There was nothing he would not do for them, from filling them with his best brandy ("Priceless stuff, Sir. Wish you ran our Mess.") to lending them money ("There's a slight breeze at Cox's. Only temporary, of course.") He came to dread the words "Cheerio, Sir. See you next leave," for over and over again there had been no next leave. The more attractive and promising the boy, the more likely he seemed to be killed. Pathetic little books, privately printed, began to appear on Claude's shelves among the classical texts and commentaries; "J.M.L."; "Donald"; "*Sed Miles*". Sometimes there would be a few poems or sketches by the dead boy: otherwise the contents varied little. There was the frontispiece showing him in uniform; the last holiday snapshot; a blurred head in a school group. Then came a loving memoir, his letters from the front, desperately cheerful; and lastly the inevitable note from his Colonel. John's men, Donald's men, Michael's men had been devoted to him; his courage and high spirits had been unfailing: his Commanding Officer felt his death as a personal loss.

Gradually Claude became so preoccupied with the fate of his pupils that he was almost indifferent to his family. Clara found it far easier to get her own way with him but he no longer seemed to want her intimacy. He rarely questioned her about her school work and hardly ever mentioned her future. His sense of permanence had been too much shaken for him to imagine what kind of world she would have to live in when she grew up. He no longer had a cut-and-dried answer to every question. Often when others were defending convictions he had once firmly held, he would lean his head on his hand and sigh: "I wonder ... I wonder" or remain silent.

Grief and anxiety had deepened the lines on his face: his obstinately golden moustache was beginning to turn grey. Yet something of his youth had revived through his intense sympathy with his subalterns. They were enchanted that he, well on in his forties, should be a Second Lieutenant like themselves and never tired of teasing him about his military duties which he took with extreme earnestness. "Is it true you went on parade wearing a bowler hat, Sir?" "We hear you have your water-flask filled with whisky on route marches"—"Got the long cam groove sorted out from the short cam groove yet, Sir? Wish I'd got you in my musketry class. I'd make you draw the parts of the rifle, on the blackboard and have my revenge for the parts of $\beta\acute{\alpha}\lambda\lambda\omega$." The drills and marches, a weary routine for his colleagues, were pure delight to Claude. They associated him, however absurdly, with the real thing.

For the first time since his marriage, he felt himself a man among men. Even Isabel lost much of her power over him and, for the moment, he was far less concerned about his one daughter than his twenty or thirty vicarious sons. If only he could have gone to the front with them, he would have been completely happy.

Old Mrs Batchelor had to admit that the war had greatly brightened her life. Never before had she been in such constant and flattering demand. Almost every day she attended a work party as a recognized authority on hospital shirts, sea-boot stockings and Balaclava helmets. She met other old ladies and soon came to know the details of innumerable family lives. The fact that she was the mother of "that clever Mr Batchelor" gave her considerable prestige, for Claude was well known and highly respected. She always carried a photograph of him in uniform in her handbag and everyone agreed that with his keen eyes, firm jaw and clipped moustache he looked handsome and soldierly. At times she quite lost her air of crushed resignation and became decided, even slightly daring. She replaced the chestnut curls with a grey marcelled "transformation" and trimmed her toques with aigrettes instead of purple pansies. Once she electrified Valetta Road by saying after dinner: "Claude dear, do you know I'd quite like to try a cigarette? Old Lady Robinson tells me she smokes one now and then, only in her own home of course, and finds it most soothing." And in spite of Isabel's amused looks and her own coughs, she had smoked it to the end.

Isabel, who had always detested sewing, avoided work-parties. To please Claude, she now and then put in an appearance at a Catholic one where there was no fear of meeting her mother-in-law. However, she and her friends ingeniously turned bridge into a patriotic duty by giving their winnings to the Red Cross. She also adopted a Lonely Soldier, organized drawing-room concerts in aid of various funds and became an ardent flag-seller. Quite often she allowed an admiring purchaser to give her lunch or tea and more than once she said to Clara:

"Really, darling, if it weren't for Daddy ... and of course for my being a Catholic ... I could have the most extraordinary opportunities."

Without affecting her directly, the war made Clara restless. Boys who had led the street gangs of her childhood were now leading men into battle: she could hardly open *The Tatler* without seeing pictures of girls from Mount Hilary only a few years older than herself standing beside soldier husbands on the steps of the Oratory or tending wounded "somewhere in France." Nicole was driving an ambulance; others were running canteens or acting as *chauffeuses* to generals. In gloomy moments she told herself that she was missing everything and felt that fate was very cruel not to have allowed her to be born a few years earlier.

She tried desperately to grow up as fast as possible but, in spite of all her efforts, the young soldiers she met at home or at the Cohens persisted in treating her as a child. She even went so far as to put up her hair on her sixteenth birthday, a step of which Patsy disapproved as much as her parents.

"Much better to stay an attractive flapper than a bad imitation of a grown-up," said Patsy. "I'm older than you and I'm jolly well going to keep mine down till it looks ridiculous. You're crazy, Clara. Your hair's your best point and now you'll have to wait till you're married for anyone to see it in all its glory again."

Though Clara had an uncomfortable feeling that Patsy was right, and though doing her hair became a daily torment, she remained stubborn. But, even with the upswept hair and daring hats perched on it at a perilous angle, people still refused to treat her as if she were as sophisticated as she felt. Her old friends of the Burglaress Bill days regarded themselves as seasoned men of the world as soon as they got into uniform. Though they were well under twenty, they behaved as if they were giving a "kid sister" a treat when they occasionally took her to theatres. They were never tired of telling her about the marvellous "binges" they had had in night clubs or in chorus girls' flats. She even suspected that they took her out mainly to ensure that she should go on writing to them when they went back to the front. For if, as a leave-companion, her stock was low, as a correspondent it was high. The demand for her letters was enormous. They were passed round dug-outs and, quite often, total strangers would ask her to write to them. Sometimes one of her unknown correspondents would call at Valetta Road and ask Claude's permission to take her out. In his general benevolence towards all young soldiers, he usually gave it. But Clara found these occasions disappointing. She got sick of hearing "I'd no idea you'd turn out to be so young. You write such topping letters, I thought you must be nineteen at least." She got even more sick of endless confidences about "peaches", they had danced with at Ciro's or the Four Hundred. "Do you really think a chap like me has an earthly with a girl like that? She must have simply hundreds of johnnies hanging round her." Nor was she comforted by being assured that she was "an absolutely priceless kid" and would undoubtedly be "simply fizzing" when she grew up. What deflated her most of all was their favourite compliment: "You know, you're not a bit like other girls. You're so jolly understanding. What a topping sister you'd make."

All the same Clara had to admit that it was only her vanity that was hurt. None of these young men, known or unknown, corresponded to the private image she still cherished. However much she derided, even to herself, the idea of marriage, she continued illogically to search each new face. Every time she was prevented from going to a party she was convinced that *he* might have been there. On her seventeenth birthday she was seized with something like panic in case *he* never appeared at all.

These hopes and fears were not confided to anyone. With Patsy she continued to pose as a cynical coquette and with Ruth as a free spirit.

She and Ruth never discussed marriage except as an institution and they held strong views about it.

"If you and I are really going to do something about the independence of women," Ruth would say, her spectacles flashing, "we've jolly well got to begin at home. What's the use of our setting up as a pair of bright Atalantas if we're going to stoop to pick up wedding rings?"

Yet in the very moment of agreeing that they must spurn the temptation Clara hoped very much indeed that it would be offered.

With Patsy she was equally deceptive. Though she assured her that, to her, men were merely amusements and she had no intention of ever settling down, she was anxious to know just what Patsy thought of her. On the score of looks Patsy assured her she need not worry. "You vary a lot but you've got lovely hair and a nice soft skin. Skin's *terribly* important with men, I find. And there are times when you really do look stunning." This was a great comfort to Clara who was often convinced that the reason the prince did not appear was because she was not pretty enough. Once, very carelessly, she asked Patsy whether she ever imagined an ideal husband.

After a moment's serious thought, Patsy said:

"I can't make people up. What would be the point if I could? When I want a hat, I don't imagine a hat. I go and buy the nicest one I can see. Naturally I'd like a husband as much like Parpee as possible."

"Good heavens. I should have thought anyone would want to marry a man as unlike their father as possible."

"The next best would be *your* father. I think Mr Batchelor's adorable. In fact, if he were a widower, I'd marry him tomorrow."

"You wouldn't seriously?"

"I most certainly would. I like men older than myself. Forgive my saying so, but I don't believe your mother appreciates him one little bit. I'm sure I could make him terribly happy."

Clara was so astounded and obscurely shocked that she could only laugh half-heartedly at the exquisite joke of having Patsy for a step-mother.

Since she had nobody at the front in love with her and was too young to be a nurse or a W.A.A.C., Clara refused to take any interest in the progress of the war. No one at St Mark's could have guessed that she had once slept with a hussar cap on her pillow or taken a cavalry sabre to bed instead of a teddy-bear. She would never have admitted to Ruth, who inclined to pacifism, that she still occasionally cried over her tattered copy of *The Story of a Short Life* or that she knew half the Barrack Room Ballads by heart. Up to 1914 she had been a recognised military authority; boys had deferred to her on the subject of uniforms and regimental history. But the war she was living through bore no relation to *her* wars. There were no more scarlet and pipeclay, no more plumes and cuirasses, no pitched battles and, worst of all, no charges. Nor did any of the young soldiers she knew make the least effort to arouse her interest. The last thing they wanted to talk about was their life at the front. Even when she heard that one or other of them had been killed, it did not make the war more vivid to her. Though she remembered him in her prayers, she could never quite believe that he was dead.

Her indifference to the war effort became so marked that she was nearly branded as "unpatriotic". Since she could not tend wounded under heavy fire, the form's First Aid Class had no attraction. Her knitted contributions to the School Comforts fund became so meagre that the Hearties began to grow decidedly chilly. At one point she was very nearly sent to Coventry and only restored her prestige by putting in several Sundays of voluntary work at a munition factory. Her job was to sew the little bags which held the high explosive in the heart of a shell. The finest possible stitches were needed and here her convent training made it easy for her to excel the Hearties. The last time she had had to take such exquisitely minute stitches had been when she was making altar linen. As she sat sewing in a room that reeked of glue, listening to the factory girls yelling bawdy talk to each other above the clatter of the flanging machines, it was impossible not to think nostalgically of the workroom at Mount Hilary. Perhaps, at this very moment, children she had once known were sitting demurely, under the statue of St Anne teaching Our Lady embroidery, in a room that smelt of beeswax; stitching palls and corporals while a nun read aloud the life of a saint. Then she remembered ironically that sewing, even for the altar, was forbidden on Sunday.

It was two years since Clara had left Mount Hilary. She went down occasionally to see the nuns but at longer and longer intervals. Each time she was more reluctant to go and more anxious to get away as quickly as possible.

However carefully she prepared for these occasions, leaving her nose unpowdered and wearing her soberest clothes, she never achieved the right effect. A real "Old Child" of Mount Hilary might be extremely elegant or extremely dowdy but in neither case were her clothes bought ready-made in Kensington High Street. And, though Clara left her wilder accessories at home, her wardrobe was so small that some detail was bound to betray Patsy's influence. It might be only a heel too high or a neck too low or a lingering trace of the wrong kind of scent but she knew that it "placed" her.

There was the faintest chill in the nuns' welcoming smiles: their eyes rested on her a shade too long as they stood talking to her with their bonnets inclined and their hands folded in their black sleeves. She felt the barb in certain phrases pronounced in the soft, disciplined voices: "You look so grown-up: one would hardly have recognized you" or "At least you have not succumbed to this dreadful new fashion of cutting the hair short." They spoke with such commiseration of her having to leave Mount Hilary for what they persisted in calling "this Protestant High School" that it was obvious they thought of her as a half-civilized savage who had relapsed into barbarism. "But, after all" the calm, pitying eyes seemed to say, "what could we expect? A middle-class child and both parents converts. We must not judge too harshly."

Educated themselves in convents or in their own homes, they had vague and alarming ideas about secular Girls' Schools. On Clara's first visit, Mother Lovell had said to her delicately, as they paced under the once-familiar limes:

"I suppose, my dear, you get some rather *rough* girls at your new school? And how it must go against the grain to have put up your hand and say "Please, Teacher.""

"Oh, Mother, but we never do," said Clara, stung more for her own pride than for the honour of St Mark's. "And we call them mistresses just as you do here."

"Indeed?" Mother Lovell had sounded genuinely surprised. She added with a sigh: "I suppose, with such very large classes, they find it impossible to keep discipline without at least the threat of corporal punishment. I always think it is such a mistake with girls. It tends to make the sensitive ones dishonest and only coarsens the more thick-skinned. I long to see it abolished in our own Catholic Elementary Schools."

Clara was aghast. Did Mother Lovell really suppose that St Mark's was only one degree from a Board School? She wished she could confront her with Miss Silver, fine flower of Cheltenham and Girton, almost as stately in her gown as the nun in her habit. She had tried to reassure Mother Lovell, but the nun had not sounded altogether convinced. In fact her tone as she said "Of course I don't doubt your word, my dear," had reminded Clara irresistibly of Aunt Leah when corrected on a point of fact. And she had added with gentle insistence:

"All the same, you must find it different in many, many ways from Mount Hilary. Quite apart from its being ... er ... non-Catholic, the whole *tone* must be totally unlike ours."

Clara had agreed, but she had soon given up trying to explain where the differences lay. She had discovered in this and other talks that, although the nuns were very ready to state their own ideas about her "High School" they were much less ready to listen to hers. They had made up their minds on the subject and they preferred not to have them disturbed.

In two years at St Marks', Clara still had not learnt how to manage her comparative freedom. The change from the convent discipline had been too violent. It was as if someone who had never been allowed to handle money had been given a hundred pounds to spend. In the enclosed world of Mount Hilary, every moment of her time was arranged for her; she was never on her own and never supposed to be alone with another child. It was only by subterfuge that she and Nicole had managed to snatch any private conversation. The liberty of St Mark's had been intoxicating at first but soon it became almost a burden. She felt compelled to fritter away her time simply because it was her own to squander. She missed the sharp distinction between home and school which had given a rhythm to her life. Often, when she would have actually preferred to be working, she would gossip, or linger in the cloakroom doing her hair, just because it was no longer punishable. Much of the charm of her endless tête-à-têtes with Ruth and Patsy came from the old ban on "being in twos", and the hours she wasted experimenting with her appearance were partly accounted for by six years of wearing uniform and being forbidden to use a looking-glass. The other girls at St Mark's imposed a certain discipline on themselves but, though Clara frequently made good resolutions, she never kept them for long. She was so used to obeying other people that it was almost impossible to obey herself.

All this produced at times an uncomfortable sense of dissipation. She felt she was not so much growing up as expanding shapelessly in all directions. She read omnivorously, devouring but not absorbing; never going deep into anything for fear of missing something else till her head was a chaos of unrelated ideas. All the values that had seemed so clear at Mount Hilary were becoming muddled. It was not that she doubted the truth of her religion but that it was becoming more and more difficult to make it a real part of her life. The nuns had prepared her to expect hostility and ridicule: what she found was indifference. People accepted her being a Catholic as they might have accepted her being a foreigner.

When she had first gone to St Mark's, she had rather enjoyed emphasising her difference and had clung like an exile to some of Mount Hilary's customs. She had worn her medals outside her dress and kept a small statue of Our Lady on her desk. She had even dated her homework by the feasts of the Church until Ruth had taken to dating hers by the Jewish calendar and they were both asked to stop. Eventually the statue went because her High Church friends thought it irreverent, and the medals vanished inside her frock for worldly reasons. Soon, though she never missed her obligations and went to Confession and Communion at fairly regular intervals, she kept her Catholicism to herself.

The only person with whom she ever discussed religion was Ruth. The latter greatly admired Dante and St Francis and listened with interest to Clara's expositions of doctrine. But, though Ruth was sympathetic, nothing would have deterred her from her own Jewish observances which were mainly a matter of racial piety. For her own satisfaction she was trying to work out a synthetic religious philosophy based on Plato, Spinoza and Wordsworth. Ruth was so naturally good, so incapable of meanness or spite or dishonesty that Clara sometimes wondered whether orthodoxy were so important after all. Though she brushed the idea aside as a "temptation against faith" it had an uncomfortable way of recurring. Ruth herself, Protestants like Mrs Cohen and the old Aunts, even the Seventh Form atheist, Rhoda Delaine, were far more selfless, truthful and charitable than most of the Catholics she had known. Indeed, when she considered her vanity and duplicity and how little her beliefs influenced her behaviour, she began to wonder whether she might not be insensibly growing into a hypocrite.

Chapter 4

DURING the second summer of the war, old Mrs Batchelor
said to Clara:
"There's one thing we've got to thank the Kaiser for. Have
you noticed how much your mother's temper has improved lately?
She doesn't get aggravated at every little thing as she used to."

Clara had been too preoccupied with herself to notice any change
in her mother. But, now her Grandmother mentioned it, she decided
it was true. It was quite a time since she had criticized even Patsy.

"No, she doesn't. But where does the Kaiser come in?"

"All this flagselling and so on. It's given her something to think
about besides herself. She gives way to your Daddy more than what
she used. You remember the fuss she used to make when he went off
on his marches at week-ends instead of keeping her company? I did
think it a shame. He does enjoy them so and I'm sure the fresh air
does him good. Now she quite encourages him to go. Would you
believe it, I saw her with my own eyes polishing the buttons of his
tunic?"

"Wonders will never cease," said Clara. "I'm afraid the war hasn't
improved my character. Rather the reverse."

"I'm sure there was no need for improvement, dear. You've always
had a sweet nature. Thoughtful for others, like your Daddy."

Some weeks before this conversation, Isabel had gone out on one
of her flagselling expeditions. She always dressed with great care for
these and set out in a spirit of adventure. Often the end of the afternoon found her tête-à-tête with a stranger in one of those dimly lit
tea-rooms that were springing up in the neighbourhood of Piccadilly.
Designed for officers on leave, the tables for two were set in alcoves
and the waitresses did not appear until summoned. She never told the
man her real name: he was no more than an audience before whom
she acted different parts according to her mood. She hinted at romantic
backgrounds and adopted a slightly foreign accent. Usually she im-
personated her favourite heroines; by turns she would be Paula
Tanqueray, Bella Donna, Nora or Mélissande. She would be-
wilder a simple business man by talking like Hedda Gabler or, having

attracted a Frenchman by her languid, provocative look, behave like the Princesse Lointaine.

One June day, when she had put on a new amber-coloured dress, the organizer asked if she would mind for once selling in Kensington High Street instead of the West End. She was on the point of saying she did not feel up to standing about, when the woman said:

"Forgive my saying so, Mrs Batchelor, but I don't think I've ever seen you look so lovely as you do in that yellow frock."

Isabel could not help smiling. Her mirror had told her the same but it was pleasant to have it confirmed.

"The poor High Street did so badly for the Belgians," sighed the organizer, "I promised Lady Sisson that I would put our most attractive seller there for the Winter Comforts."

After this, Isabel could hardly refuse to take the pitch outside Barker's. It was an exquisite day; she was in the mood for adventure and she fretted at being somewhere too near home to be either likely or safe for an interesting encounter. The morning passed slowly while she rattled her tin at crowds of shopping women. The few men about were so dull that she never once acceded to the request:

"I say, aren't you going to pin it on for me?"

After lunch in a stuffy teashop, she began to wonder how soon she could decently go home. As she stood hesitating, studying her reflection in a shop window and thinking how utterly wasted the day had been, she noticed a man's figure in profile reflected beside her own. The figure remained so still, with its head bent forward, that she suspected he was looking at her. She turned and met the intent gaze of a pair of blue eyes. At first sight she was dubious of the man himself. She could not quite place him. He was hatless and carelessly, even shabbily dressed; he had a sallow skin, untidy auburn hair and a reddish gold beard. The beard made it difficult to guess his age; he might be anything between twenty-eight and forty. He remained standing perfectly still, with his hands in his pockets, looking down at her from his considerable height with a faint smile and compelling eyes. The eyes were a smoky blue; at once tired and ardent. Their gaze confused her and she turned her own away.

"Ah, don't do that," he said. "I've waited so long for you to look at me, Mrs Batchelor."

The voice had an unusual intonation but it reassured her. At least this man belonged to her own class.

"Do I know you then?" she said. "I can't remember ... I have a good memory for faces."

He smiled.

"We haven't been introduced. But I have seen you four times."

"And you know my name?"

"Only your surname. I found that out the first time."

"And where was that?"

At a concert at St Mark's School. You were in rose-red with two little silver wings in your hair. Do you remember?"

She smiled in her turn.

"That dreary concert. Yes, only too well."

"You were the most beautiful person in the room. Also the only one who looked as bored as I had felt till that moment. I spent the rest of the evening looking at you and I assure you I wasn't bored at all."

"Whatever induced you to go? You don't look like a parent."

"Oh no, Madame. I am not a parent, at least as far as I know, and, if I were, I should certainly not be sending my son to an English Public School. I am a master."

"You can't be. I know them all."

"And I am not the type, you were going to add? I admit I am not the type. But with so many heroes at the front they have had to fill the gaps with what they could get. I am the temporary junior French master. My name is Callaghan."

"That's Irish isn't it?"

"Certainly. But I had a French mother. And I have a French *prénom* ... Reynaud."

"Reynaud ... what a charming name. I have some French blood myself."

"I hoped that when I first saw you. Now, since I've heard you say Reynaud, you don't need to tell me."

"It is so long since I've spoken French, I've almost forgotten it."

"I would be very happy if you would let me refresh your memory."

"I am sure you are an excellent schoolmaster, Monsieur Callaghan."

"Oh ... if you would only say Reynaud again."

"Is that necessary? You've already said you were satisfied with my pronunciation."

"I've had precious little to be satisfied with since I first set eyes on you. For three months I've had to content myself with glimpses of you in the street or through the window of a bus. I've speculated endlessly about what kind of woman you were. You always go about looking as if you were in a dream."

"Do I look like that now?"

"You look as if it would be possible to arouse your curiosity."

"Perhaps," she said coldly, to hide the fact that she was childishly excited and a little frightened.

"I've made a tactical error, haven't I? Letting you know how passionately you've aroused mine? That's the Irish side of me, always butting his head into trouble and not content till he's made an arch fool of himself."

Reassured, she smiled and asked, almost shyly: "What is it you want to know so much?"

"Your name, first of all. You'd be amused if you knew how many times I've tried to christen you. Always French names. I can't imagine you as Joan or Gertrude or Marjorie."

"What did you guess?"

"Mérode, Solange, Éliane, Isabelle."

"Isabel was right," she said, enchanted.

"Isabelle." He drew it out syllable by syllable.

"I so much prefer it in French."

An acid voice said at her elbow:

"Of course, if you're too *busy* to sell me a flag."

She turned her attention to a woman who, after asking the price of every flag, decided on a penny one and demanded eleven coppers in change for her shilling.

"Won't a sixpence and five pennies do?"

"Certainly not. I need pennies for my gas meter."

"This lady is not a machine for giving change," said Callaghan. "Hadn't you better take your shilling to the bank, Madam?"

"But I particularly want to have a flag. It is a disgrace how obstructive the flagsellers are."

"Then permit me to present you with one."

He dropped a shilling in Isabel's tin and pinned a flag on the woman's bosom.

She fluffed up her feathers but, seeing Callaghan's smile, she pursed her lips and walked indignantly away.

Isabel and Callaghan exchanged glances. She gave a sudden happy sigh.

"You'll ruin my reputation."

"If only you'd let me. But what's happened to you? With that mischievous look on your face, you're all of a sudden a very young girl. Take off that look or take off that woman of the world hat. You can't wear both. They clash."

"I'll keep my hat then," she said. "But oh, what a bore it is sometimes being *rangée*. I hate responsibility, don't you?"

"Loathe it. I've always been careful not to clutter myself up with any. Isn't it time we stopped getting in the way of all these worthy ladies and went for a walk in Kensington Gardens?"

"What about the Winter Comforts? I've hardly anything in my tin."

"Naturally. How can you convince people of the need for winter comforts? They've only to look at you to know that it will be eternally summer."

"Is it Reynaud or Callaghan who says such charming things?"

"For once they speak in unison."

For the rest of the afternoon they wandered about the Gardens or sat under the trees. Isabel was too happy to adopt any of her parts; too happy even to be critical of Callaghan's shabbiness or to mind when people stared at them. She had no idea why she should be so happy; it was as if she had discarded her ordinary life like a heavy coat. Sometimes they talked a great deal; sometimes they hardly spoke. Often they stood perfectly still and silent, looking at a flowering tree or a tramp asleep with a newspaper over his face. Things she had never even noticed became suddenly delightful or interesting. She could not say whether being with this man were like finding something new or rediscovering something forgotten.

They lingered for a long time in the Dutch Garden, staring, through one of the windows cut in the hazel leaves, at the trim bright beds and listening to the faint tinkle of water dropping from the leaden tanks.

"I'd like to see you at Versailles," he said. "You are made for a formal setting. Nature needs taming and pruning and civilizing before she's fit to come into your presence."

"Don't be too sure," said Isabel, tossing her head so that the mask of lacy shadow danced over her eyes. "In some moods, I like nature wilder than you might think."

His hand moved closer to hers on the bar of the scrolled iron gate. She was on the point of withdrawing her own but let it stay.

"But I love Versailles," she went on dreamily. "I had an ancestress at the court of Louis XVI. I should have adored that life. Those exquisite clothes and the balls by candlelight and the masquerades by moonlight."

"And the *galanteries?*"

"Perhaps even the *galanteries,*" she said demurely. "It would all have been exquisite and artificial, like a play."

"I wouldn't quite do for the part of the curled Marquis pushing the lady in a flower-wreathed swing."

He turned and faced her, smiling wryly in his beard. She could not help noticing that his shirt collar was dirty and there were buttons missing from his frayed coat.

"You haven't always been a schoolmaster, have you, Reynaud?"

"No. What would you like me to have been? Or what do you think I am?"

"I don't know," she said, vaguely disturbed at having to fit him into everyday life. "An artist, perhaps."

He frowned.

"An artist? In England that means a painter, doesn't it? If one is under forty and has a beard, one paints pictures. I'm sorry to disillusion you, Isabelle. I'm not a painter. Nor am I flattered when I'm taken for one."

A little hurt, she said softly: "I'm sorry, Reynaud. You see I've never met anyone like you."

He went on roughly, as if he had not heard her: "My father painted pictures. Damn bad ones that hadn't even the merit of selling. He died of drink."

"How horrible for you. And for your mother," she said with a shudder.

"How expensive, you should have said."

He looked suddenly bitter and remote, standing there gazing, not at her but at the neat bright water garden, with his beard stuck out at an angle and a shaft of sun showing up the stains on his coat.

"I write, if you want to know," he said abruptly. "In French, mainly. Criticism. I wrote poems when I was young like any other idiot. You wouldn't be interested. Now I've been collecting stuff on and off for years for a study of the Parnassiens. No doubt, like all women, you read nothing but novels."

"I'm afraid I do read a great many novels," she said meekly. "But I am very fond of poetry. Don't you ever write poems now?"

"No, I've got too much sense. I know my limitations."

"Are you sure you never will again?"

"You think falling in love might do the trick? Would you like me to write a poem so you could hang it like a charm on your bangle. Ah, my dear, I might be fathoms deep in love but you'll not find a pearl in a herring's guts unless he swallowed it ready made. You know no more how a poem's made than I know how your hat's confected."

She said in a troubled voice:

"I know I'm a very silly woman. But don't let's speak of falling in love, even as a joke."

"Ah, but I want to speak of it," he said. His manner had changed again. He too sounded troubled. "Or do I? I was very certain I did when I ran into you this afternoon. Now I'm not so sure."

She said, childishly:

"I've disappointed you."

" I wish to heaven you had." He went on without looking at her, "I've been making it up in my mind, all these months, just the way it would go. You see, the Frenchman fell in love with you at the concert in a perfectly normal French manner. All through those chaste madrigals you could sing with propriety before a community of nuns, he was thinking how to contrive a meeting and what that meeting might lead to by the usual well-worn steps. I know the road. I could walk it blindfold. But during the last half-hour I've been in a panic in case the Irishman might be involved too. And that hasn't happened for a very long time."

Her heart was beating painfully. She longed for him to have said: "Never." Controlling her voice with difficulty she asked: "What was she like?"

"Irish, too. Just a typical good little Irish girl. I used to hang about church doors waiting to catch a glimpse of her coming out from Mass."

"And what happened?"

"She became a nun."

"How dreadful. I can't understand what makes women become nuns."

"Can't you? I nearly became a priest myself. I had a pious mother."

" ... A priest?" she asked almost with horror.

"Don't worry. The Frenchman wouldn't hear of it. I doubt if I've been to Mass in six months."

"Is the Irishman still in love with the girl who became a nun?"

"He's enough of an Irishman to keep his thoughts off a religious. Though it wasn't the Frenchman's kind of love. It was lay my sword at your feet and put your head on my shoulder and may nor I nor any other creature ever hurt a hair of your darling head."

For a second she felt the mortal touch of jealousy and shivered in spite of the heat.

"Perhaps it was as well she went into her convent. At least she was spared disillusion."

"Och, she never had any illusions about me. If she looked at me at all it was only to tell me I was a fool. May you be spared the spectacle of an Irishman in love. I was always staring after her like a moon-calf and wanting to pull the stars out of the sky to pin up her shawl. You know the stuff ..."

"And crowd the enraptured quiet of the sky
With candles burning to your lonely face."

"Oh don't laugh, don't laugh," she said on a sharp note of pain. "It's so beautiful. I can't bear it."

"Why, Isabelle." He looked at her half-tender, half-ironical.

She turned away, feeling tears come into her eyes. After a moment she said uncertainly:

"Did you write that ... to her."

"I'd say yes if it would make you look at me this moment. You've far more the face for burning candles to than she ever had. Why do you have to keep changing? Why can't you stay the languid lady that looked as if she'd played with fire so often that the smell of smoke bored her? The Frenchman liked that. He knew where he was." Suddenly he took her face in his hands and turned it towards him. "Why do you have great dark eyes with tears in them like a stag at bay. They cry when they turn and face the hunters. Did you know that? I saw it when I was a small boy in Ireland."

She fought with all her strength to keep her face away from his and managed somehow to smile.

"It's worse when you smile. Now you look like a child trying to be brave."

"Reynaud, let me go. Please. I implore you."

"Very well." He dropped his hands and thrust them back in his pockets.

They stood for a moment or two in silence, Isabel with her hands clenched on the gate, looking at the flowerbeds through a dancing haze.

She said at last: "Let's go. Let's walk about. This garden is dangerous."

They walked twice round the pond, hardly speaking. Then, suddenly tired at the same moment, they dropped on to two chairs and sat watching the children's sailing boats. Reynaud said:

"I've got Baudelaire's passion for ships. I can't see one without wanting to get on board and sail away heaven knows where. I'd like to put you on board a ship, Isabelle, just as you are, and carry you off."

"Where to? *Au pays de Cythère?*" she risked. Out here in the open, among the children and nurses and young officers with their girls, she felt safer.

"Ah, we'd be sure to land there in the end. The Frenchman would see to that. But we might touch at another port for a while ...

> "Where beauty has no ebb, decay no flood
> But joy is wisdom, Time an endless song ...

Just as well you don't know the last line."

"Oh don't," she said. "It's everything I feel ..."

"It seems I've struck the right note," he said.

> "Faeries, come take me out of this dull world
> For I would ride with you upon the wind
> Run on the top of the dishevelled tide
> And dance upon the mountains like a flame."

"It's not fair to torment me," she said. "I used to have such wild dreams when I was a girl."

"What's wrong with dreams?" He went on with melancholy mischief:

> "Faeries, come take me out of this dull house,
> Let me have all the freedom I have lost.

For it is a dull house, isn't it? Own up now."

"It's wicked of me even to think so," she said, wringing the gloves she could not remember having taken off. "My husband loves me. He is a good man. The best of men. He's very clever. He's wrapped up in his work. And I love him. I do love him. It's not his fault I could never talk to him as I've talked to you this afternoon."

"Are there children?"

"One—a daughter."

"How old?"

"Sixteen. I was hardly older than that when I married." She had told the lie so often that she had come to believe it.

"Is she like you?"

"No. Not in any way."

"You should have had a daughter as beautiful as yourself."

"I don't mean she's not pretty," said Isabel loyally. "She's a typical, fair English girl. She's very clever, like her father. She thinks I'm foolish and frivolous."

"She sounds detestable."

"No, no, she isn't. It's just that she's never suffered. She's a strange girl. Sometimes she recites poetry with such feeling and with such a look on her face that you'd think it meant something to her. But I don't believe she has any feelings at all. She's like Undine without a soul."

"Don't let's talk about the tiresome chit. It's minutes since you gave me a thought or a look. Would you like to be run away with, Isabel?"

With an effort, she smiled.

"I've never considered the possibility."

He looked at the small white sails on the pond and sang under his breath.

> "*Dites, chère Isabelle.*
> *Où voulez-vous aller*
> *La voile ouvre son aile*
> *La brise va souffler.*"

"I expect the voyage would end in a shipwreck."

"And though that's a singularly becoming hat, it's unsuitable for a long sea trip. If the wind carried it away I couldn't afford to buy you another. I couldn't at this moment even stand you a cup of tea unless we broke into the Winter Comforts box."

"Was that your last shilling that you dropped in with such a *beau geste?*"

189

"The last, and not strictly speaking mine. Don't worry. There are more where that came from. Ushers don't get paid till the end of term you know. They're supposed to be decent citizens and have a hump to live on. It's simply that I haven't a hump so I have to use my wits."

She felt a pang of distaste.

"Money is so sordid, isn't it?" she said. "It can't buy anything worth having."

"I don't agree, I have the Frenchman's respect for money. However, an Irishman can always borrow and the Frenchman sees to it that he gets the utmost value out of every *sou*."

"Then it must have been the Irishman who wasted that shilling. I think it was that absurd gesture that made me like you."

"That's what the Frenchman hoped. He had to make an impression somehow. You must admit the shilling paid a handsome dividend."

"My flags," she said suddenly. "Whatever did I do with them?"

"Heaven knows. At least you've still got the cashbox."

"Reynaud, I must go."

"Ah, not yet, not yet," he said, rising and catching her hands so that she had to drop the gilt bag and the tin she had carefully gathered up.

"Yes. Now, at once. I'd forgotten all about time. I have to go to the dépôt ... I have to be back to dinner."

"And you've remembered you're Caesar's wife."

"You're abominably unkind."

"I'm abominably wretched. When can I see you again?"

She stood there pulling on her gloves and flushing like a girl.

"Oh, Reynaud. We can't. We mustn't. It's all so impossible."

"Are you glad it's impossible?"

"It's not a fair question."

"Could I make you love me or hate me? Or shall we leave well alone?"

"Oh leave it alone," she said pitifully. "Let's both forget."

He stood up facing her.

"If I'd kissed you, you wouldn't forget so easily."

"You've no right to talk like that. I have a husband. Oh, I'm not a good Catholic I know. I don't suppose I'm even a good woman. But I've never ..."

"You're starving for love and understanding. I could make you so happy. It's not just presumption, Isabelle. There's a whole side of you that's never had a chance. I'm the only person that even cares about it."

"Don't say any more. Let me go."

He let her go in the end, watching her till she was out of sight. Then he began moodily throwing stones into the pond until half by accident, half by design, he capsized one of the toy yachts.

She was still trembling when she got to Valetta Road. It was with the greatest difficulty she swallowed a few morsels of her dinner and managed to reply when anyone spoke to her. But no one appeared to notice anything unusual.

It was one of the evenings when Clara happened to be in. After dinner the two of them sat in the drawing-room. Clara was finishing herself a dress which meant that she was too absorbed to make conversation and kept running down to her bedroom to try it on. Isabel went to the piano and began to play. She always played erratically, with too much pedal and considerable sketchiness in the left hand. She tried the openings of several Chopin nocturnes she had played when she and Claude had been engaged but after a few bars her fingers dropped from the keys.

Clara, making one of her sudden exits, said cheerfully: "Having a lovely strum, Mother? By the way, isn't it about time we had that old piano tuned?"

Suddenly her fingers found something she had almost forgotten she knew, a polonaise which she had learnt by heart at school. She was so absorbed that, when she struck the final chord, she was amazed to see Clara standing quite close to her.

"I say, you played that jolly well," said Clara. "I had to come back again and make sure it was really you."

"You never think I can do anything, do you, Clara?"

"I didn't mean that. I've never heard you play it before, that's all. It's a brute, as I know from experience. Honestly, you play it nearly as well as Mrs Cohen. Her rhythm's better but you really put tremendous passion into it."

"Thank you, Clara. A compliment from you *is* a compliment."

"I really mean it. Play it again."

"No. You make me self-conscious."

"I'll go and listen from the bedroom."

Isabel swung round on the piano stool.

"No pet. I'm not in the mood any more."

"Sorry I broke the thread of inspiration. I must go and have another look at this skirt. I can't get the gathers right."

"I'm afraid I'm useless at dressmaking. You should have gone round to the wonderful Cohens."

"I would have, only the whole lot have gone to a concert."

"I see. I thought perhaps you were staying at home of your own accord for once."

"I often stay in. I was in last Tuesday. You were out that night playing bridge so you probably didn't know."

"I very seldom go out in the evenings. I'm sorry I missed your being in. I hope you weren't lonely."

"Oh no. I had plenty to do. I caught up a bit on my homework. Or are you being sarcastic?"

Isabel sighed.

"I suppose I ought to be glad you're fond of anyone, even Patsy Cohen. It shows you must have some affection in your nature."

"I don't think I'm so stony-hearted as you make out. I'm very fond of Ruth too. And Nicole, of course, though I'll probably never see her again."

Clara watched her mother's face; the conversation seemed to be heading towards familiar rocks. She was about to escape when Isabel unexpectedly smiled.

"Perhaps one of these days it will be a young man. You're growing up so fast; it's difficult to realize."

"Oh, there are quite a lot of young men I like too. But I'm not in love or likely to be."

"I thought the same when I was sixteen. But perhaps there's some young man in love with you and you don't even know it."

This was an interesting thought. Clara stopped glancing towards the door and sat down.

"Is that just an idea? Or are you hinting at something definite?"

"Queer things happen, Clara. You'd be astonished. Perhaps there's some young man who hangs about, just on the chance of getting a glimpse of you. For example, he might wait outside the church just to see you come out from Mass."

Clara thought carefully, but could not remember having noticed anyone. She decided she would look the very next Sunday. Her mother certainly had a rather peculiar look this evening. What did it mean?

"You're rather mysterious, Mummy. Have you got a secret or something?"

"Perhaps I have."

"Tell."

"Oh no. You are the last person I should tell."

"Does it affect me?"

"If it stopped being a secret, it might affect you more than you think."

"This is most intriguing. I do think you might tell."

Her mother shook her head, turned back to the piano and idly played the first bars of a prelude.

"Oh well, if you insist on being an oyster, I'd better go back and wrestle with that dress."

"Yes, perhaps you'd better, darling."

As Clara moved, this time rather reluctantly, towards the door, her mother said, without turning her head, "Oh, Clara, something I wanted to ask you."

"Yes?"

"You know so much poetry. I wonder if you can tell me where this line comes from. I saw it quoted somewhere or other.

"With candles burning to your lonely face."

"It's Yeats. 'The Land of Heart's Desire'."

"It's very beautiful, isn't it?"

"I used to think it marvellous. That's when I had my Celtic Twilight period and was crazy about Yeats and Synge and all that Irish stuff. Cathleen ni Houlihan; the good people, Helen with a golden nosegay in her shawl. I was quite drunk with it. So was Ruth. Now I think it's all rather tush."

Chapter 5

FOR the next few weeks, day and night, Isabel lived in a feverish, blissful dream. She went over and over again every moment of the afternoon in the Gardens with Callaghan. She even wrote down everything she could remember of it in a locked notebook, disguising it as a dialogue between "The Poet" and "The Lady". She bought a copy of Yeats' poems and read "The Land of Heart's Desire" every night before she went to sleep. A few days after their meeting she had a letter from him, an impassioned letter in French, imploring her to meet him again. After a struggle with herself, she wrote gently refusing. But she put the letter in the locked book and read it till she knew it by heart. Away from him, she could forget everything that had faintly jarred: he became the troubadour and she the imprisoned queen. Appeased by her secret happiness, she became unexacting and could even take pleasure in the happiness of others.

Clara's seventeeth birthday occurred a few days after her meeting with Callaghan. She had already given her a present but, on a sudden impulse, she went out and bought her an evening frock out of her own dress allowance.

Clara was surprised and touched. She also felt slightly guilty since she had not remembered her mother's birthday till she saw the packages on the table and had had to rush upstairs and hastily wrap up a little coral brooch which she hoped Isabel would not recognize.

"Mummy, you really shouldn't have," she said, shaking out the folds of apple-green taffetas. "It must have cost the earth. You've already given me that lovely bottle of Chaminade."

"Well, one isn't seventeen every day," said Isabel smiling. "Enjoy your youth while you have it, darling. You won't realize how precious it is till it's gone."

There was a dinner party that night in Clara's honour and she was allowed to invite whom she liked. She asked Patsy and Mavis and three young officers she had met at the Cohens. At her father's request a fourth was added, one of his favourite old pupils who was at a loose end on his last night of leave. On these rare occasions, Isabel was apt to be irritable especially if Patsy were invited. Sometimes she would sit looking bored and aloof: sometimes she would embarrass Clara by behaving as if she belonged to the younger generation and joining too enthusiastically in charades or dancing. But tonight, although Patsy flirted outrageously with Claude and the young men were too busy showing off to each other to pay her much attention, she behaved perfectly. For once Clara could not compare her unfavourably to Mrs Cohen. As she said goodnight, she gave her mother a spontaneous hug and said:

"I've had a simply marvellous birthday. You've been angelic. You really have. Do you known Tony Brinton said he didn't see how you could possibly be old enough to have a daughter of seventeen?"

Some weeks later Claude said to her:

"There's rather an odd bird among these temporary masters. He's a Catholic, though not a particularly good one, I believe. I've been wondering whether we ought to ask him to dinner. Would it amuse you to have someone to talk French to?"

Isabel felt all her blood rushing back to her heart and was thankful she was so pale by nature. She managed to ask carelessly:

"Why? Is he a Frenchman?"

"Only half. His name's Callaghan. Irish. But he teaches French and seems to have spent most of his life in France. I'd better warn you he's rather unpresentable. Has a beard and is decidedly careless about his clothes."

"Hardly the usual type for St Mark's surely."

"No. That's why I thought he might amuse you. You find most of my colleagues infernally dull, I know. Actually they were rather scandalized when Cavell took this chap on. I don't altogether approve of him myself, but there's no doubt he's intelligent and I have to admit I find him rather entertaining."

"You talk as if you saw a good deal of him."

"Actually, during the last few weeks, I have. He always seems to be in the Common Room at the same time as myself. He's rather *mal vu* by the others and seems to have taken rather a fancy to me. Now and then I've stood him a drink. He's obviously very hard up, poor fellow and I thought it might be a kindness to have him here for a meal. But that's entirely up to you, my dear."

Isabel felt slightly giddy. She had honestly done her best not to see

Reynaud again. If Claude deliberately threw him in her way, she was not to blame.

"You look dubious. Don't if you don't want to."

"I'm only thinking, dearest."

She tried to imagine Reynaud sitting at their dinner table under the eyes of Claude and Clara and Mrs Batchelor. Clara would either be distantly polite or eager to show off her knowledge of French poetry. He would sit on her own right. They would have to pretend they had never met before, yet it would be impossible for them not to exchange an intimate look. She would feel treacherous and guilty. To see him like that, in the setting of her everyday family life, would be to rub the bloom off her secret.

To gain time she said: "Is there a Mrs Callaghan we should have to ask too?"

"I discovered not. I didn't want to inflict an unknown quantity of a wife on you."

"I don't want to be horrid, dearest. But wouldn't it be better if you took him out by yourself to a restaurant? It really is getting very difficult to manage food nowadays. If we're going to ask any of the staff here, it really should be the Slaters. We've owed them a dinner for ages."

"H'm, yes. We can't kill two birds with one stone because Slater loathes the sight of Callaghan. I daresay you're right, my dear. I'll take Callaghan out for a bachelor evening some time. In any case, he's a man's man and probably ill at ease with women."

There was mischief in Isabel's smile as she said: "From your description, I've no doubt you're right." But though she smiled, her heart was in a tumult. She had deliberately thrown away her chance but it was torment to think that Claude and not herself should spend a whole evening with him.

The very next morning, as she was shopping with Clara, she saw him on the other side of North End Road. If she had been alone, she would not have had the strength not to go across and speak to him. As it was, hoping he had not seen her, she hustled Clara into a shop and surreptitiously watched his tall, bearded figure till it was out of sight.

A few nights later, Claude's ten o'clock pupil put him off and he came up to bed earlier than usual. Even at that time he half-expected to find her asleep, for when she was doing nothing special she went to her room soon after dinner. But the light was on by her bed and she was sitting up reading. She looked up with a start as he came in.

"What's the matter, Claude? Why have you come up so early? Are you ill? You look terribly white."

He sat down heavily on the end of her bed.

"No, no. I'm not ill. Only bad news again."

"Another boy killed?"

"Yes. Raymond Harrison. He was at Clara's birthday party, you remember. One of the very best."

"How terrible. When did you hear?"

"Just now. His young brother John was coming to me tonight. He rang up. Naturally he wants to be with his mother."

"Oh Claude. I'm so sorry. What a wicked, wicked waste of young lives it all is."

He leant his head on his hand with a weary gesture.

"Sometimes I feel ashamed to walk the earth, Isabel. They die so that useless fellows like me can go on rotting in comfort."

"Claude, you mustn't say such dreadful things. How can you call yourself useless?"

He said nothing but closed his eyes and shook his head slowly, as if it were a great weight.

"You feel it so much each time it happens," she said gently.

"Not enough. Not enough. One comes to take it as a matter of course."

"You were particularly fond of this Harrison boy, weren't you?"

"Yes." He sighed and repeated, "One of the very best."

"I remember thinking what a good-looking young man he was."

"Yes, indeed. He had the makings of a first-rate classical scholar. He could have done all that I long ago gave up dreaming of doing."

She said softly: "Because you married?"

He managed to smile.

"Ah no, my dear. I hadn't the stuff in me. I know that now. But I have just enough to know the real thing when I see it. And I know enough to have got him started on the right lines."

"Perhaps some day you'll find another like him."

"No. Not like Raymond. There aren't more than two or three like him in a century. It was my dream that, if I could never be a real scholar myself, I might nurse one up. Then I could have said my 'Nunc dimittis' in peace."

"You thought once that Clara ..."

"Yes. When she was a child. She showed real promise. But she lost interest long ago. I doubt if women can ever do it. Melian Stawell, Jane Harrison ... admirable up to a point ... but there's always something lacking ... either the imaginative sweep or the mental muscle. You don't get the real right thing in women any more than you find pearls in herrings."

Isabel's mind, which had begun to drift, became suddenly alert.

"Pearls in herrings. That's a clever metaphor."

"Not my own. That man Callaghan said something of the kind the other day. We were discussing Greek poetry."

"Poetry!"

"Yes, my dear. I'm not occupied entirely with '$ὅτε$'s' measurements'. Though I often feel as if I were."

She sighed and leant back on her pillows. In the light of the shaded lamp, with her eyes velvety and her acorn brown hair tumbled on her neck, she looked very young.

"That poor boy. I know it's very sad that he was so clever. But I keep thinking of everything in life he's missed. Perhaps already there was a girl who loved him."

He leant his head on his hand again and said slowly: "Yes, you're right. Hundreds of them. Killed before they had begun to live. Why should I feel the loss of one more than another? I've had the best of life. If I could give up the rest of mine just to save one, even the dullest little bank clerk, even an utter ne'er-do-well."

"Oh, Claude, you mustn't talk like that. Think of all the good you do. All the people who need you." She paused and added almost guiltily, "Think of me."

He looked at her wearily. "Do you need me, Isabel?"

She lowered her eyes. The book still lay open on her lap and they caught a line. She read out:

"Oh, you are the great doorpost of this house."

"What is that, my dear? It sounds like the translation of a line from one of the tragedies."

"No, it's by an Irish poet. Yeats. He's still alive."

"Ireland and Greece. Interesting. I've always felt there was a connection. I was saying so the other day to Callaghan and he agreed."

She asked, wondering if her face looked strange,

"You seem to discuss a great many things with this Callaghan."

198

"Yes, I suppose I do. Things I've hardly given a thought to since Cambridge. Maybe because he's Irish. Though on the outside he's as unlike as possible, there's something about him that puts me in mind of poor Larry O'Sullivan. But if there'd been a war and Larry had been Callaghan's age, he'd have got himself into it by hook or by crook. Of course Callaghan doesn't have to go. His father saw to it that he was born in Ireland so he can't be called up in France like his predecessor De Caux. And he's the kind of Irishman that loathes England. All the same, a rolling stone like that. You'd think he would have gone for the fun of it."

"Perhaps he doesn't think anything worth fighting for."

"Perhaps. It's the only thing I've got against him."

Silence fell between them. Surreptitiously she closed the book of Yeats' poems and laid it on the table beside her bed. But his tired eyes followed her movement.

"The great doorpost," he began, and broke off choked by a sudden sob. The next moment he was kneeling beside her with his head buried on her knees.

"Oh Isabel, Isabel. Without you I should be the loneliest man on earth."

Chapter 6

ONE morning in the summer holidays that followed her seventeenth birthday, Clara woke very early. The term had left her with a sense of dissatisfaction though she had done far better than she deserved in the first part of Higher Local. In a day or two they would be going to Paget's Fold. She decided that down there she would pull herself together and try to bring her life into some sort of focus.

It was still only half-past six when she had lain thinking for a long time without coming to any conclusion. On an impulse, she got up and went to early Mass; it was months since she had done so on an ordinary week-day. She made her Communion with a touch of her old fervour and walked home through quiet sunlit back-streets with a sense of freshness and peace she had almost forgotten. It took her back to Mount Hilary and, as she turned into Valetta Road, she decided she would go that very afternoon and see Mother Lovell.

The nun, as always, was delighted to see her. Standing in the red-tiled passage that always smelt faintly of incense, feeling the scratch of the starched bonnet against her cheek, she felt a rush of home-sickness for Mount Hilary. All the children had gone; the grounds were empty except for an occasional nun walking with bent head saying her rosary or a lay-sister weeding a bed. It was a golden, windless afternoon; the reflection of the trees in the lake never stirred; there was no sound but rooks cawing and the chapel bell striking the quarters.

They paced down the alleys and round the playing fields, passing the stretch of grass with the weeping ash where, in another life, she had cried over her father's letter.

"It's so long since you came to see us," said Mother Lovell. "I was beginning to fear you'd given us up. I should ... we all should ... be very sad if that happened."

Clara was about to make the usual excuses but decided to be frank.

"The fact is, Mother, I feel rather shy about coming back."

"There's no special reason for that, is there, Clara?"

"No. I don't think so. It's just that now I lead such a totally different kind of life."

"All the more reason for keeping in touch with us."

Clara was silent.

"There's nothing on your mind, is there, child? I know the world is a difficult place for a Catholic girl. From what I hear, it is still more difficult since the war. You're still living at home?"

"Oh yes, Mother."

"So many of our Old Children are doing war-work that takes them away from their families. I'm sure they do it in a splendid spirit, yet I can't believe it's good for girls to be uprooted and have to mix with all and sundry."

"I've still got a whole year more at school."

"Ah, that Protestant school. How I wish we could have kept you with us. You must feel so isolated there. But thank God you have your home and that wonderful father of yours. Your mother is a Catholic too, isn't she? Home must be doubly precious to you now."

Clara kicked a pebble.

"Nobody at St Mark's bothers about my being a Catholic. They think everyone has a right to their own religious opinions."

"There's a certain danger in that attitude, Clara. You must be extra careful yourself not to get into loose ways of thinking. Never forget that the Faith can never be a matter of opinion; it is God's revealed truth."

"Yes, of course, Mother."

"Sometimes we need to be able to show others the logical base of our faith. Father Lamb has been telling us about some wonderful sermons another Jesuit, Father Coster, has been preaching at Farm Street. Have you heard any of them?"

"I've been working on Sundays lately," said Clara. "In a munition factory."

"My dear Clara, is that necessary? I hope you don't miss Mass."

"Oh no, Mother. I go very early."

"Do you sometimes manage to get to Mass and Communion on weekdays?"

"Oh yes. I went this morning," said Clara, feeling a hypocrite but assuring herself she really would go more often.

"Ah, I'm so glad," said Mother Lovell, with real joy in her voice. "As long as you are faithful to Mass and the sacraments, there's nothing to fear. I've heard such troubling things lately since this dreadful war; children of our own, girls from the best of Catholic homes." She sighed and shook her head. They walked some steps in silence. Now and then a leaf from a lime tree dropped slowly at their feet or a pigeon called "Rouk ... Rouk" in the boughs.

As if her thought had travelled a long way in the interval, Mother Lovell went on:

"I often think of all that dear father of yours gave up in this world for the Faith. God must have had His own designs in taking you away from us just at that moment. Things often look so wrong to us until we get a hint of God's purpose and then we see that they were most exquisitely right."

She stopped in her walk and turned her beautiful pale face to Clara, patting her arm. In the sunlight a few lines showed deeper than Clara had ever seen them and the keen eyes behind the glasses were a little weary.

"Mother, you look tired," said Clara. With a sudden warmth of affection, she saw the nun for the first time as a human being with worries of her own. "Have you been overworking this term?"

"No, no, of course not. Things have been difficult for the whole Community: the war affects us even here. We have more children than ever and not enough teaching nuns. And Mother Provincial has made herself ill with anxiety over all the problems the War has created in the Order. It may be a long time before we can re-establish contact with our houses on the Continent. That means heavy burdens for years to come on the English Province. I've been acting as her Secretary so I know her difficulties."

"That means you've been doing all the work," said Clara accusingly. "What's more, I believe you've been ill yourself."

"Nonsense, my dear. The merest indisposition. Mother Infirmarian is so anxious to exercise her charity that she puts us to bed on the slightest excuse."

This was so far from true that Clara had to laugh.

"I am a pig," she said ruefully. "I haven't come to see you or even written for months."

"Dear child, if you gave no sign for twenty years, it would make no difference," said Mother Lovell gently. "All the same, it is rather wonderful your coming today. I pray very much for you always. But this morning as I was making my thanksgiving, Our Lord put you so vividly into my mind." She took both Clara's hands. "Shall we sit down for a little?"

They sat on a bench, looking through a gap in the trees across to where a statue showed white among dark bushes on the far side of the lake.

"This is one of my favourite spots," she said. "I often come and make my meditation here, looking across at Our Lady of the Lake. Often it brings to my mind those lines of William Blake's:

'Though calm and warm were the waters wide
I could not get to the other side.'

But of course we *can* get to the other side. And Our Lady is watching over us and waiting for us there."

She sat very still, her hands folded in her exquisitely darned black sleeves.

"I took a very important decision in my life, sitting on this very bench," she said. "One summer afternoon a very long time ago. Yes, a very long time, for I was not much older than you, Clara. I was a Mount Hilary child, you know."

"Yes, Mother," said Clara quietly, guessing what the decision had been.

"What a pity it is," said the nun, reverting to her practical voice, "that you can never come down for a retreat. I don't think anything helps one so much as a retreat. We all need now and then to be alone with God and our own souls. Especially in the world where there is so much noise all round us we can hardly hear God's voice. Perhaps, when you leave school next year?"

"I'm afraid I wouldn't be able to manage the summer one. It would still be term time," said Clara hastily.

"We often have one for the old children in November," said the nun. "Have you thought at all what you are going to do when you do leave? I suppose you will take up teaching like your father."

"I don't really know. If I can get a scholarship I might go to Cambridge."

"Ah yes, indeed. They expect very high qualifications now, don't they? With all this new mania for examinations, though Reverend Mother doesn't approve of it at all, she is seriously considering opening a house of studies in Oxford or Cambridge after the war, so that some of the novices can try for degrees." She sighed: "I'm afraid that just at the moment we have not any very suitable ones. And of course, if any of our own children wished to go to the University it would be so nice for them to be there instead of at one of those non-Catholic colleges," she smiled, "I think we shall have to open a house of studies specially for your benefit, Clara."

Clara laughed hoping her face did not betray that, even as a joke, the idea appalled her. Yet sitting here beside Mother Lovell, hearing a language she had half forgotten, watching a smiling lay-sister pass by, her blue apron full of vegetables, how remote seemed her own and Ruth's secular dreams. She stared at the toes of her shoes. They were patent leather ones, cracking already and dusty from their walk. She suddenly perceived how tawdry they were and wondered how she could have let Patsy induce her to buy them. Just as for months Mount Hilary had seemed dim and unreal, so now did West Kensington. Without knowing why, she sighed.

"Clara, my dear, you don't seem happy. Is there anything I can do or say that might help?"

"I'm not unhappy exactly. But everything's so confusing sometimes."

"Do you feel you've lost your way a little?"

"Perhaps. Things seemed much simpler when I was here. But then I was only a child."

"Is it that you feel you are approaching a turning point in your life and don't know which road to take?"

"Nothing so definite, really. I don't think much about the future. I suppose I'm just vaguely dissatisfied with the present. Yet I've no earthly reason to be discontented."

"No earthly reason perhaps. Only God sometimes has reasons for making us discontented. Do you remember St Augustine ... 'our hearts are restless till they rest in Thee'."

Clara sighed again, this time to try and throw off a strange sense of constriction. The long-forgotten words touched something in her which had been numbed; she felt a pang that was both aching joy and blind terror.

She said nothing. The nun laid her hand, with a touch light as a leaf, on Clara's.

"Pray a great deal, my dear. And I will pray too, more than ever. There is only one way for all of us, in or out of the world, the way of God's will. Will you come and see me again soon?"

"Yes, Mother." She was suddenly nervous and remembered with relief that they were going away. "When I come back from Sussex. Not for a month or more, I'm afraid."

"I'm glad you're going to the country. It's the best place to 'make one's soul'. God is everywhere, of course, but it's easier for us to *feel* He is there when we are quiet and close to nature."

Clara's mind went back to that day on the hills just on two years ago. Fighting down an unreasonable, mounting panic, she said rather coldly:

"I shall be glad to be in the country again. But there's nothing the matter with me, Mother. Doesn't everyone get silly moods at my age?"

"Yes, of course, my dear." The nun stood up. "I must be going in. I have to take the Novices' French reading. Poor Mother Duplessis is ill and there's no one else available at the moment."

As they walked towards the great creamy stucco house, mellow in the waning July sun, Clara asked dutifully:

"Are there a lot of novices now?"

"Only five at the moment, alas. But we have a new postulant. You'll remember her. Winifred Cruickshank."

"Winty," exclaimed Clara. "Why she's the very last person I thought would enter. If it had been May, I wouldn't have been in the least surprised."

"God has a way of choosing the unexpected ones," said the nun. "At home we were always certain that it would be my sister Theresa. No one ever suspected I would ... myself least of all."

When they reached the door, Mother Lovell said: "I've just five minutes. Shall we spend them with Our Lord in the chapel."

But Clara's panic had reached such a pitch that she had to escape at once. She pretended she had only just noticed the clock.

"Oh Mother," she blurted out, "I'd have loved to. But look at the time. I promised my mother ... if I don't catch the half-past five bus, I'll be terribly late ..."

Smiling a little sadly, the nun let her go.

"Of course I understand. I'll just come down to the lodge with you."

Once more they passed together down the red tiled corridor, pausing for a moment by the statue of the Sacred Heart. Clara could not pray: she merely stared at the flame of the red lamp almost invisible in the sunlight. Once again she smelt the incense and the beeswax and felt the nun's bonnet scratch her cheek as she kissed her goodbye. The portress came out of her cubby-hole to open the grilled door. "Goodbye, Miss Clara dear. Don't let it be so long before we see you again."

When the bolts had grated behind her, Clara remained standing on the steps, hesitating. Was it relief she felt or a sense of banishment? For no reason, her eyes filled with tears. She blew her nose violently. Then, tightening her lips and fishing out her puff, she defiantly powdered her face on the very threshold of the convent.

PART FIVE

Chapter 1

"WHAT do you think of this, Claude?" said Isabel, taking a letter from her gilt mesh bag and handing it across the dinner-table.

For once they were dining alone. It was the end of August; old Mrs Batchelor had gone down to Paget's Fold and Isabel, for reasons of her own, had come back with Claude at the end of his three weeks.

He glanced at it: "But it's written to Clara."

"Yes. It should have been written to me."

"Do you know this Catherine Lyons."

"She's one of the pious spinsters at the Catholic work party. A friend of that Mother Lovell Clara goes to see now and then. Full of good works and immensely well connected."

He read the letter and passed it back.

"I'm afraid I can't help the lady. If Clara can't suggest a young Catholic governess to look after this boy, I'm sure I can't."

"I told you she oughtn't to have written to Clara direct. Of course Clara's got the idea that she'd like to go herself."

He said irritably: "I won't hear of it. She can't leave St Mark's for another year. She's still got to take the second part of Higher Local."

"She was sure you'd say no. I expect the thought of ten pounds a term went to her head."

"Then she'd better forget it."

"Yes, dearest."

"She must write to Miss Lyons at once and say how sorry she is she knows no one suitable. Incidentally, where is Clara tonight?"

"Where she always is. At the Cohens."

"She seems to live there."

"Yes. Isn't it a pity she hasn't some other friends besides that common little Patsy?"

"I've nothing against Patsy in herself. Nor against the plain one, the Philips girl. But I wish to goodness she knew some Catholics."

"She still hears now and then from Nicole de Savigny. But she never sees her."

His face clouded. After a moment he said: "This governess idea is preposterous. All the same, the letter's a thorn in my conscience. It makes me realise how cut off from any Catholic life Clara's been since she left the convent."

"Yes. It really seems an awful pity."

He gave her a suspicious look; she was usually indifferent on this subject. She lit a cigarette.

"I'll tell Clara you said no. She'll be disappointed but not surprised."

"Surely you agree with me, Isabel?"

"Certainly it would be rather absurd for her to be just a governess. After all you've spent on her education."

"Of all the miserable, dependent jobs ..."

"You must admit this case is rather different. Miss Lyons particularly says they want a girl who can be treated like one of the family. Obviously she's suggested Clara herself to Lady Cressett."

"I'm afraid I can't follow the leaps of the feminine mind."

"It's perfectly simple. I believe the whole idea came from Mother Lovell. She's devoted to Clara and wants to do her a good turn."

"Mother Lovell? That hadn't occurred to me."

"She still takes a great interest in Clara, you know."

"Yes, indeed. She has written to me once or twice. I have an enormous respect for her.

"It's nice that Clara's kept up with her, isn't it?" Isabel puffed at her cigarette: "After all, it isn't as if you'd definitely decided on Clara's future. Or that she herself had."

He frowned. "I know I've been very remiss. But the future has become so hard to envisage. We've always assumed she should try for Cambridge next year."

"Yet only a few weeks ago, you were saying you didn't think she was cut out for that kind of career."

"She'll never be a scholar. I don't see why she shouldn't be a very passable schoolmistress. But she must get her degree."

"Couldn't she go on working for her exam. at this place, Mary-hall?"

"Possibly. But this whole notion is so extraordinary to me, I should have to give it a lot of thought. And I seem to find it remarkably hard to think these days."

He leant his head on his hand. She waited a moment before asking softly: "Don't you think Clara could do with a complete change of atmosphere? Haven't you noticed how restless and discontented she's been lately?"

"I'm afraid I'm not very observant. Anyhow she'll have a change next year if she goes up to Cambridge."

"Girls are marrying in their teens these days. Suppose she married the first young man who came along ... just from boredom."

"*Marry?* Why she's only a schoolgirl." His face stiffened. "Isabel! You don't mean there's something behind all this. Some reason why you want to get the girl away?"

"A young man? Good heavens no!"

"Thank God! For one ghastly moment I thought ..."

"*What*, Claude?"

He passed his hand over his forehead.

"Forgive me. Such appalling things happen these days."

Isabel laughed.

"Really, dearest! What about the leaps of the masculine mind?"

"I can't see anything to laugh at."

"Not even at the idea of hiding one's shame in the bosom of a virtuous Catholic family?"

Claude stared at her.

"You're talking very strangely, my dear. You were always so, how shall I say? So ultra-sensitive. One hardly dared ... Have you changed like everything else?"

"Have I changed?" She did not look at him but spoke as if asking herself the question. Stubbing out her cigarette, she said:

"You do want Clara to marry some day, don't you?"

"Yes, yes, of course," he said hastily. "Provided it's the right type. And, I most sincerely hope, a Catholic."

Isabel glanced at the letter again.

"It's only for six months, Miss Lyons says. Till the boy goes to Downside. She says that Maryhall is a lovely house and there are some charming Catholic families in the neighbourhood. Obviously she means Lady Cressett would take her about."

"You realise I should have to pay next term's fees?"

"They're nothing compared to Mount Hilary's. Do you remember how we had to pinch and scrape because you were so anxious to send her to the convent? She's losing the charming manners she learnt there, all that indefinable *cachet*. It seems such a pity. But you can't blame Clara if West Kensington doesn't provide friends of the Mount Hilary type."

He frowned and sighed. Zillah came in to announce his nine o'clock pupil. "I'll think about it," he said as he prepared to go into his study. "I can't adapt myself quickly to sudden changes."

Isabel went up to the drawing-room. She opened a book and shut it. She went to the piano, played the opening of two or three pieces idly and inaccurately, then got up and walked about the room, changing the places of ornaments. The restlessness that had come over her at Paget's Fold had pursued her back to London. It was no longer a delight to her to be left alone with her thoughts. She wished Clara were there; she would have welcomed anyone to distract her from her own imagination, even old Mrs Batchelor.

As she moved uncertainly about the room, picking up a vase or a silver box and trying it in a new position, she asked herself why she had been trying to persuade Claude to let Clara go to Maryhall. She had not meant to do more than raise the topic; she had not even been in favour of her going till they had begun to talk. She was surprised herself at the ingenious arguments she had found herself using. Was it that she wanted to be rid of Clara for a time? Or was it that she so urgently wanted a change in her own life that Clara must have it in her stead?

Change, change; how the word kept recurring. Could she have answered Claude's question? Something had happened to her at Paget's Fold. She had taken away with her the dream of the troubadour and the imprisoned queen. But down there the appeasing magic had not worked. She had discovered that it was intolerable not to be in the same place as Reynaud Callaghan. And now that she was back in London she could not resume the dream that annihilated time and space and brought them together in a fairy world. Never yet in her life had she desired a man. She had had romantic attachments and greedy private fancies. In a burst of self contempt she had burnt *The Diary of a Lost One* when *The Land of Heart's Desire* became her secret reading. But since she had come home, this too had failed her. Every day, every night she became more and more painfully aware of an aching for Reynaud's human presence.

Chapter 2

CLARA arrived at Maryhall on a perfect day in late September. All through the journey to Worcester she hugged the idea of a new life beginning. She had already spent a day with Lady Cressett and Charles and fallen in love with them and the house. The only cloud was that she had promised her father to go on working for her exam.; she would like to have started fresh, with no obligation to the past.

Patsy had said: "You're crazy and I shall miss you horribly, you beegledy thing. But I swear you'll be back long before Christmas. You'll be bored to tears. Nobody in his senses spends his leave in the country."

Parting from Ruth had been less painless.

"Does this mean you've absolutely given up the idea of Cambridge, Spin?"

"I've told you. Daddy still wants me to try for a scholarship."

"But you're not keen any more?"

"Oh Ruth, I don't know. In six months I daresay I will be again."

It was unusual for Ruth to show anger but she flushed and said sullenly: "After all our plans. I suppose you think it's freedom, being governess to some plutocrat's beastly brat."

"You're always talking about experiencing as many sides of life as possible," said Clara, angry too. "At least I'm doing something instead of just talking about it."

"Living dangerously on ten pounds a term and all found."

"As good as living dangerously in a prefect's hatband and being president of the Lit. Soc."

"We seem to be having a vulgar brawl. We've avoided that up to now."

"Sorry, Ruth. I thought you'd understand."

"Idiot." There were actually tears in Ruth's eyes behind the round spectacles. "I'd go to any lengths to stop you going."

"I'm so awful, if you only knew."

"I know all right," said Ruth with her wry smile. "Cat that walked by itself. Critical Clara, the cynic of the Seventh.

"Just for a bundle of Bradburys she left us,
Just for a title to ram down my throat."

"Go on, Sea-Green Incorruptible. Righteous Ruth the ruthless rhymer!"

"I believe at heart you're utterly conventional."

"I've begun to suspect it myself. Goodbye, free spirit."

"Goodbye, Jane Eyre."

At Worcester, Charles came galloping up the platform to meet her. He was a remarkable handsome small boy with bright dark eyes and a high colour. His manner was even more excitable than she remembered. "He's highly strung," Lady Cressett had explained. "And, I'm afraid, since his father's been at the front, more than a little spoilt."

"Your train's late," he said, snatching off his tweed cap. "Five minutes and forty-three seconds. It's got a Bear Engine. Did you know?"

He danced along beside her.

"I found the platform from the indicator. I didn't ask anyone. Nan didn't want me to meet you: she said Milburn was quite enough. But Mummy said I could. We bust a tyre. I helped Milburn jack up the car. So you see without me we'd have been late. Sucks to Nan."

When they got to the car, he said importantly:

"Miss Batchelor's luggage had better go on the rack. You can take that little case by you in front. I shall sit in the back now Miss Batchelor's come."

"Very good, Master Charles."

All through the drive he chattered at the top of his voice. Clara listened in a contented daze, watching the sallow sunlit fields and the distant flashes of the Severn through the autumn-coloured trees.

"Miss Batchelor's a funny name for a girl, isn't it?"

"They called me Spin at my last school. Short of Spinster."

"Ha, ha. Rather good. Can I call you Spin too?"

"That depends on your mother."

"I can usually make Mummy do what I like. Daddy's much stricter. They've just made him a Major. I wish they'd made him a Colonel. Jim Coldfield's father's a colonel and Jim swanks about it like anything though he's only temporary. Look at that plane. It's a Sopwith pup. Milburn, it *is* a Sopwith Pup, isn't it? I told you so. I'm making a new model plane, Spin. You can help me finish it if you like. Nan's in a wax because I spilt glue on the table. I expect that's why she tried to stop me meeting you."

"Nan's been with you since you were a baby, hasn't she?"

"Yes. Of course I'm much too old to have a nurse. Nan's supposed to see to the linen and be a kind of maid to Mummy now. But since I had pneumonia last year, she's taken to sleeping in my room again. I put up with it because she's quite useful when I have nightmares."

"Do you have them often?"

"No, but they're whoppers when I do. I walk in my sleep sometimes too. I'm terrifically highly strung. It's awfully bad for me not to have my own way." He spoke with extreme gravity as if he were an elderly invalid discussing his symptoms.

"What happens if you don't?"

"Well, sometimes I get frightfully excited and don't quite know what I'm doing. The doctor says it's a kind of brainstorm. Once Nan took away my best engine and locked it up and I jumped into the pond and I didn't know I'd done it till I found myself flopping about in the cold water."

"Did Nan always let you do what you liked after that?"

"Well, not always, no. She has fits of being frightfully strict as if I were still a baby. Sometimes I have to put my foot down and tell Mummy. She's a perfect dragon about tidiness. I hope you're tidy. You'll get into awful rows with Nan if you're not. She used to get fearfully cross with Miss Stephenson, my last governess, for leaving things lying about in the schoolroom."

"I'm not terribly tidy, I'm afraid."

"Never mind. I'll protect you. I didn't protect Miss Stephenson because I was bored with her and wanted her to go. I can usually get round Nan because she adores me. Unless she's in one of her regular right-down royal waxes." He glanced at Milburn's old-soldierly back in its green livery and lowered his voice to a hoarse whisper.

"Mummy's sister, Aunt Monica, says she's a domestic tyrant and Mummy ought to get rid of her." He added aloud, "No one could possibly imagine Maryhall without Nan."

Clara could not help feeling slightly apprehensive though Lady Cressett had forewarned her. During her visit a fortnight before, Nan had remained in the background. But she retained a sharp image of a small, thin woman with smooth red hair, a pale bony face and downcast sandy lashes. Lady Cressett had warned her too that Nan was apt to be jealous of anyone Charles liked. "That didn't arise with poor Miss Stephenson, because Charles never took to her. He has taken to you, quite violently."

They turned in by the lodge and the house came in sight round the curve of a drive bordered by yew hedges. Clara gave a happy sigh; the place was as perfect as she remembered it. Maryhall was a small Jacobean manor house of plum-coloured brick, built in the form of a hollow square enclosing a flagged courtyard. It stood on a slight swell with lawns dotted with clipped yews sloping gently away from a low-walled terrace. Beyond it rose a semi-circle of woods, their leaves bright as a pheasant's plumage in the sun, and far in the distance lay the blue mass of the Malvern Hills. When the engine stopped, she could hear the cooing of the pigeons in the stable yard and the clap of their wings as they flew up from the cote. The door of the house opened and a collie burst out, barking frantically and hurling itself on Charles as he jumped out of the car.

"Down, Hero, down. Don't be such a silly ass." The dog crouched on its haunches, grinning. "Come on, give the lady a paw."

The dog looked doubtfully from Charles to Clara; allowed himself to be patted but did not offer his paw.

"Fool dog," said Charles angrily slapping Hero on the muzzle. "Do as your master tells you. Give your paw, Sir."

"You'll never train him like that," his mother called from the doorway. "Leave Hero in peace, and Miss Batchelor too. Miss Batchelor, you must be dying for your tea. Come along in and don't let yourself be bullied."

Lady Cressett was a big, strongly-built woman of thirty-eight with a settled look that made her seem older. Charles had not inherited one feature from her pale, Flemish type of face with its long nose and large lustreless grey eyes. Her greying brown hair was piled up in a modified version of the pompadour that had been fashionable when she was a girl; it was arranged with the utmost neatness and skill but it made no concessions to vanity. Everything about Theresa Cressett was plain, good and built to last from her well-cut, well-pressed tweeds to the brogues that shone like chestnuts. Her person, like her house, gave the impression of being kept always in perfect repair. Clara, in a crimson velour coat that had seemed both smart and countrified when she had bought it, with her hair blown into wild tangles under a crimson tam o'shanter felt once again that she looked all wrong. But Lady Cressett smiled at her with her peculiarly attractive expression and Clara forgot to be self-conscious. She had been charmed the first day by that smile. It was at once shy and humorous and it conveyed that the person she found slightly ridiculous was Theresa Cressett.

"I ought to ask if you're tired after your journey," she said as she took Clara's arm and led her upstairs. "But you look so young and bonny it doesn't seem to make sense. I do hope you're not going to find life too dull here."

"I've been counting the days till I came," said Clara fervently. "I've remembered everything. Even the smell of the house."

"Dear me!" said Lady Cressett, "I've never noticed. I hope it's agreeable."

"Heavenly. Beeswax to begin with like Mount Hilary."

"That must be my furniture polish. I get it from the Carmelites. I hope it doesn't smell like a convent."

"Oh no. The rest's quite secular. Woodsmoke and some mixture of herbs, rosemary's one I think. And somewhere in the background the sense of a very delicious cake being baked in the oven."

"Well, let's hope today's delicious cake is waiting for you on the tea table."

Charles came clattering up the shallow oak stairs behind them, swinging one of Clara's suitcases.

"Hurry up and come down and let's get tea over," he shouted. "You needn't bother to take your coat off. I've got heaps of things still to show you outside."

At the top of the stairs Nan was waiting. She wore a spotless white silk blouse, a dark skirt and a tiny muslin apron. Her thin lips smiled quite pleasantly as she said:

"Good afternoon, Miss Batchelor. I hope you had a nice journey."

But as Charles continued to shout and tug at Clara's sleeve, her smile vanished.

"Come and wash your hands at once and stop pestering Miss Batchelor," she said sharply and seized him by the shoulder. He tried to escape but, though she was only a few inches taller, her thin wrists were strong and she marched him off down the passage.

"I've given you the little blue room you said you liked," said Lady Cressett, opening a door.

Clara exclaimed with pleasure, wondering at the same moment why it should be called the blue room since there was nothing blue in it but the carpet and one bowl. The walls were whitewashed between the irregular squares of dark oak, there was a patchwork quilt on the narrow old four-poster and the curtains at the casement windows were embroidered with many-coloured silk flowers, once bright, now faded.

"It's nice looking out over the hills, isn't it?"

Clara had been too busy mentally inhabiting the room to think about the view. She glanced through the two diamond paned windows to the distant line of the Malverns and said:

"They're higher, but they make me think of the downs."

"Your people come from Sussex, don't they? I hope you're not going to think the Midlands 'sodden and unkind'."

"How could I? I know in my bones I'm going to love this place."

Left alone, Clara put her outdoor things in the wardrobe, determined to be as tidy as possible. The water in the copper jug, though tepid, was deliciously soft; the linen towel smelt of lavender. There was no time to re-do her hair. She stuck in a few pins and hoped for the best, hoping too that her covert skirt and hastily knitted jumper looked sufficiently countrified. From now on she was determined to be an entirely different person.

As she came out, Charles bounded at her and butted her with his newly-brushed head.

"Come on slow-coach. Tea, tea, tea."

She had meant to make a dignified entrance but he rushed her helter-skelter down the slippery stairs, making such a clatter that Hero and Lady Cressett's Scotch terrier barked in excited sympathy.

The tea-table was drawn up by a log fire that burned pale and clear in the late sunlight. No one could have guessed it was the third autumn of the war. There were hot scones and girdle-cakes, home-made jams, shortbread and even a jug of cream.

"At least we can feed you properly," said Lady Cressett. "We get plenty from the farm even when the hospital's had first turn."

Clara was hungry and was unable to stop herself from eating an enormous tea; the kind of tea she used to eat at Paget's Fold when she was a child.

"Thank goodness, you can eat," said Lady Cressett. "I was afraid you would be worrying about your figure."

"I ought to be," said Clara ruefully; "If I go on like this, I won't have a figure to worry about."

"Charles will give you plenty of exercise if you let him."

Charles, for a boy of ten, ate surprisingly little. He kept pulling at Clara's sleeve.

"What's the matter, Charles? Can't you let Miss Batchelor have her tea in peace?"

"Women dawdle and chatter so over meals. The light's going fast and I've got lots of things I want to show Spin."

"Spin?"

"Need I call her Miss Batchelor? They called her Spin at school. Short for Spinster, see?"

"I get the point, Charles. But Miss Batchelor mayn't like it. They called me Porky at the Sacred Heart. I shouldn't like it at all if the name had stuck."

"Porky! Porky!" yelled Charles. "I shall call you Porky, Mother."

"I rather think you won't, my son," said Lady Cressett tranquilly and Charles subsided.

"I don't mind what he calls me if you don't," said Clara.

"What about discipline? I must say I find it hard to call you Miss Batchelor myself. You look such a baby."

"I do hate my surname so."

"Why? It's such a nice old English name. But I'd rather call you Clara."

"Oh, please do."

"Can I call her Clara too?"

"Certainly not, Charles. At least not in lesson times. Otherwise she'll never be able to keep you in order. I hope your father's let you into lots of professional secrets, Clara."

"Secrets, what about?"

"About how to make ruffianly little boys behave and learn their lessons, Charles. Clara's father is a very famous schoolmaster."

"How boring. Why isn't he in the army like mine? Or a submarine commander? Or a ..."

"That's enough, Charles. If you've finished your tea and Miss Batchelor's nice enough to let you drag her about, you'd better say your grace."

"Namerfather," began Charles hurriedly.

"Say it properly."

He said it properly. His mother and Clara crossed themselves.

"You'll have dinner with me tonight, won't you, Clara?"

"Can't I stay up her first night?"

"No, you cannot. There's no chance of peaceful conversation with you around."

Once out of the house, Charles rushed Clara from the stables to the paddock, from the walled garden to the keeper's lodge. She had seen most of the estate before but now he showed her everything as if it already belonged to him. Though half the men had gone to the war, nothing looked neglected. The turf was shaven, the hedges clipped, the cowstalls on the home farm freshly white-washed. The two old hunters were as carefully groomed as if they were just going to a meet. Everything suggested order and security; a life that moved to a regular rhythm. Clara drew deep breaths of the wonderful air, distinguishing the smells of burning leaves, turned earth, sweet drifts from late roses and the faint dankness that steamed from the river as the sun waned.

As they walked she rubbed a sprig of rosemary between her fingers and sniffed it.

"I suppose rosemary's for remembrance because it's got such an unforgettable smell. I'm sure I shall think of Maryhall every time I smell it."

"We've got masses of it. Especially in the walled garden. I like it best as stuffing," said Charles. "What do you think of Maryhall, Spin? Not a bad little place as places go, eh?" His voice was so grown-up and proprietorial that Clara nearly laughed.

"I'd hardly call it small, Charles."

"It's not a great show place like Crickleham. But the Hughes-Folletts have only rented it. Maryhall's been ours for hundreds of years. And this size is easier to keep up properly. Of course Mummy and I have had a fearful time keeping it apple-pie with Daddy away. He's most frightfully particular. So am I." To prove it he shouted at a one-armed boy who was picking apples.

"I say, Johnson, there's a pane cracked in the little greenhouse. You'd better jolly well tell Baines to get it mended. The Major may be home on leave any day."

"Very good, Master Charles."

"I expect Archie will come over one day soon."

"Who's Archie?"

"Archie Hughes-Follett. The people I told you about. He's jolly decent."

"Your sort of age?"

"Oh, no. Quite old. Older than you even. He's in the Inns of Court, waiting to get his commission. But he's home on sick leave. He had an accident. Old Archie's always smashing himself up. Mummy sometimes asks men over to shoot. But old Archie finds shooting a bore. He prefers playing with me. He comes over entirely for me."

"What do you play at?"

"Oh, frightfully good games. Spy and war mainly. We make them up. The grown-ups think Archie's rather a dud. His father did."

"Did?"

"He was in the Scots Guards. He got killed early on."

"Poor Archie."

"He didn't mind much. He couldn't bear his father."

"Oh. I suppose his mother minded?"

"Dunno. Anyway she's got Archie just as Mummy would have me. My father's in the Coldstream. My grandfather was too. I hope this war goes on long enough for *me* to get a commission. Of course Daddy'll want me to be in his regiment. But I want to be in the Flying Corps."

"You can't get a commission till you're eighteen. Do you really want this war to go on eight more years?"

"Beastly long time to wait. I can't really remember much before I was four. And that's only six years. Practically my whole life. I s'pose it wouldn't let me off school, even."

"Then you'll stand for a bit of peace, perhaps?"

"As long as they have another decent war when I'm grown up. With simply millions of planes fizzing about everywhere. And *enormous* bombs. Like the one I've invented that can blow up Worcester Cathedral in one bang."

"I didn't know you invented bombs."

"I invent everything," said Charles superbly. "It was me that invented tanks among other things. I could fly an aeroplane as easy as winking. I've got a chart with all the controls. Milburn lets me steer the car sometimes. I do it jolly well. And a joy-stick's a million times easier. Are you warlike, Spin?"

"I would be if I were a man."

"War's dull for women. Mummy hates it. Of course Daddy's frightfully bucked to be doing some real fighting at last. I have to pray every night he won't be killed."

"Then I'm sure he won't be," Clara's mind strayed for a moment.

This boy, Archie Hughes Follett, was older than herself and his father had been killed in the war. His father must have been about the same age as her own.

"Oh yes, I hope not," said Charles cheerfully. "Of course lots of chaps' fathers do get killed. If he did and got the V.C. they'd give me his medal, wouldn't they? And I'd be Sir Charles. Though I suppose even then I wouldn't be allowed to do just as I liked till I was twenty-one."

Clara decided not to be shocked.

"What is it you want to do most?"

"Have my own aeroplane, of course. The south paddock would do for a landing field. Actually I've fixed up a windsleeve already. I'll show you how to land, shall I?" He whirled round, making a noise like an engine and working an invisible joy-stick. "You must keep her nose in the wind. Like this." He frowned with concentration. "Whoa, steady there. Ah, there she bumps." He relaxed into a grin of triumph. "Nearly pancaked. Were you windy?"

"Not really. Considering it was the first time I'd been up."

"I'll take you up with me whenever you like. I daresay I could train you to be an observer."

"I'd need a lot of practice in map-reading." Remembering that she was now a governess, she added: "We might plan some air-routes when we're doing geography."

"Beastly old lessons. Still it would be better than exports and imports. I can learn things when I'm interested but I'm very easily bored."

"Intelligent but lazy, your mother said."

"Shut up, Spin. There's a grey squirrel." He threw a stone and the squirrel vanished in a silver streak.

"Glad you missed him."

"Just like a girl. We're supposed to wage war on grey squirrels."

"I know. I'm glad all the same."

"I wasn't aiming properly." He indicated a gate into a field. "That's the way we go to church when we don't take the car."

"How far is it?"

"Half a mile by the fields. Longer by road. We only take the car on Sundays. But Mummy walks over to Mass nearly every day. She's awfully holy."

"I thought she was. What about you?"

"Not at the moment. In fact Father Samson says he sometimes

wonders if my baptism took properly. But I might suddenly decide to be a saint. Lots of the saints were naughty when they were young."

"Do you think one can be a saint just by deciding to be?"

"I could. I can do absolutely anything if I want to."

"Saints don't boast."

"I haven't decided to be one yet. Two in the family's enough."

"Two? Who's the other? Not Nan?"

"Of course not. She's not even a Catholic. I said *family*. Mother and Aunt Monica. They each say the other is. I don't see how Aunt Monica *could* be with that temper. Besides, she's a suffragette. She threw a rice pudding at Daddy once because he said something rude about suffragettes. Still she did try like anything to be a nun. But they wouldn't have her."

"Why?"

"Mother says it's her headaches and Aunt Mon says it's her temper. *I* think it's her face. She's the ugliest woman you ever saw."

Dusk was falling when they returned to the house. Nan called from a lighted upper window:

"Come in at once, Master Charles. Your bath's been ready this ten minutes."

"Botheration," said Charles, breaking into a trot. "That probably means a Wax. Calling me Master Charles usually does. P'raps you'd better not come and talk to me while I have my bath. When she's in a wax, it's wiser to let her have one to herself."

"She doesn't still give you your bath, does she?"

"Not *give*. I let her be my lady-in-waiting. Actually it saves a lot of fag to have someone to scrub my back."

Clara avoided Nan and slipped into her own room. Her bed had been turned down and on it lay the black velvet dress she had worn at her grandfather's funeral, converted by herself and Patsy into a semi-evening one. One of her two treasured pairs of Milanese stockings lay beside it: she noticed that a hole in one had been exquisitely darned and guessed that Nan must have done it. All her things had been unpacked and ranged in the great drawers they did not nearly fill. Nan must have done that too. She was filled with shame at the thought of Nan's pale disapproving eye examining her scanty and carelessly mended underclothes. Why had she not spent some of her father's cheque on snowy lawn instead of letting Patsy persuade her into that crimson coat? The old tweed one she wore at Paget's Fold would have looked much better up here. And why had she been such a fool as to slip in Patsy's parting gift, a jade green camisole with *"Dieu, que les hommes sont bêtes"* embroidered on it in black? There it lay, carefully folded, on the top of the lean pile. She had barely finished dressing when Charles' voice sounded imperatively from the night nursery.

"Spin ... Spin!"

Hastily thrusting the jade camisole out of sight, she hurried up the passage and found his door ajar.

"Come and say goodnight to me," he said. "Nan's having her supper."

He was sitting up in bed, his face glowing and his hair tousled from his bath. In his pyjamas he looked far more childish.

"Read to me till the gong goes."

While she was finding the place he said:

"Have you got any brothers?"

"No, worse luck."

"You seem to like boys' things."

"I always played with soldiers instead of dolls. But I'm rotten at cricket and so on."

"I don't like games except the ones I make up myself. I've got heaps of soldiers. Shall we have a battle tomorrow?"

"Certainly. Want me to read now?"

"No. Changed my mind. You know, I desperately want someone to play with. Archie's only on leave by accident and Miss Stephenson was much too old. It's a nuisance being an only child, isn't it?"

"It certainly is."

"Rather fun if you were my sister, wouldn't it be?"

Clara nodded carelessly. She was thinking it would be the most delightful thing in the world. She looked at the firelight playing on the checkered walls, at the statue of Our Lady with its lamp and flowers and wondered how it felt to have such a childhood and to grow up with a definite place to fill."

"I wouldn't mind an older *sister* because I'd still have Maryhall and be Sir Charles. It might be better if I married you. You're not so frightfully old. Mummy's older than Daddy. She told me so. Yes. I might quite likely decide to marry you when I grow up."

Clara laughed.

"I notice it's you who are to do all the deciding."

He said in his most precocious voice: "Nan says I shall be a very good catch."

The gong sounded.

"I must go. Goodnight, Charles."

"Aren't you going to kiss me?"

"Don't boys hate being kissed?"

"Oh, I'm used to it," he said, with a provocative look.

She kissed a cheek that felt like a peach and smelt of Wright's coal tar soap. Suddenly he pulled her down and covered her face with wet, explosive kisses, giggling helplessly between each.

"Charles, you little beast, let me go. I've just done my hair."

She extricated herself and he dived under the blankets, rolling one dark, brilliant eye at her.

"Oh my," he choked, "Lovey Dovey. Be-yootiful Spin. Goodnight. Sleep tight. Mind the fleas don't bite."

"Goodnight, Charles Cressett," said Clara severely.

Chapter 3

CLARA and Lady Cressett dined by candlelight, waited on by a parlourmaid. Lady Cressett was also in black velvet, long-sleeved and just low enough to show that her plain face was set on a handsome neck. She wore a small string of perfectly matched pearls and pearl studs in the large lobes of her exposed ears. Her expression, mild as it was, was less placid than Clara had at first supposed. Occasionally her forehead puckered in a nervous twitch. During dinner they talked about Mount Hilary, which Lady Cressett knew well; then the conversation turned to farming. Clara tried to remember everything Cousin John and Blaze had told her—she wanted desperately to emphasize all the country side of her life. At one moment she feared she had overdone it for her hostess asked her if she was fond of riding. But, mercifully, she added before Clara had time to answer:

"I'm afraid you won't get much chance here. My husband won't let anyone ride his hunters except himself and the groom. I don't ride myself, and I have to admit I'm thankful that Charles doesn't seem keen. It's foolish to be nervous, I know, but when one's a hen with one chick ..."

They had their coffee in the drawing-room. Freed from the hovering parlourmaid, Clara relaxed and let her eyes wander at will. The panelled walls were painted a greyish-green touched here and there with gilding and each piece of furniture, old or new, had that inimitable air that comes from being acquired in the century it was made. The room was a whole; the modern chintzes did not quarrel with the lute-backed chairs and the tapestry screens because everything had been chosen by people of definite tastes for their own use or pleasure and no one had tried to impose a scheme on it. Though no two rooms could have been more unlike, Clara was reminded of the old aunts' extraordinary dining-room which had grown in the same haphazard way.

"Do you mind if I wander about?" she said when she had finished her coffee. "There are so many things I want to look at."

"Wander as much as you like. I love people to look at our things."

Clara examined the miniatures on the walls, tracing Charles' dark eyes and high colour back through two centuries; now his eyes stared languorously under Byronic curls; now sparkled under a powdered wig.

"The Cressett type persists, doesn't it?" said his mother. She indicated one of the old portraits. "That boy with the lace collar and the bird ... he was a page at Charles the First's court. We sent Charles to a fancy dress ball last year dressed like that. He was the picture come to life. It was rather uncanny."

"I love old things and family histories," said Clara. "I'd like to know the whole life of every single one of these people. People look so final and definite in pictures. I'd like to know how it felt to *be* them. Whether they woke up one person one day and someone quite different the next."

She wandered about the room, stopping now and then to pick up something or ask where it came from. A painted spinet had belonged to an Italian Lady Cressett, a snuffbox had been a present from the Young Pretender, a breviary taken from the body of a guillotined priest had been left by a Marquise who had taken refuge at Maryhall during the Terror. All the while she was contrasting these things with the traces of her own ancestors at Paget's Fold. In almost as many centuries they had left no more than some clumsy pieces of furniture, a few paper silhouettes cut by travelling pedlars, an inlaid workbox or two and a handful of worn silver spoons.

"I wish you could infect Charles with some of your passion for the past," said Lady Cressett when Clara at last sat down again. "He only cares about the future. And the future for him means aeroplanes, submarines and goodness knows what more mechanical means of destruction."

"I suppose all small boys are like that. Even when they're lucky enough to have always lived in a house like this."

"This house seems to fascinate you. I love it myself so much, I can't help being pleased."

"I've never been in just this kind of house before. When I was little I used to dream about such places and pretend I lived in one."

"Then you must look out for a nice young man who has one and marry him."

"I can't imagine marrying anyone," said Clara rather gloomily. "I expect I'll be an old maid."

Lady Cressett laughed.

"At seventeen there's still reasonable hope. And I can't say you look the old maid type to me."

"I can't imagine even being in love. If I were, I'm sure the person wouldn't be in love with me."

"Don't let that stop you from marrying him if he'll have you. I'm old-fashioned. I think all women should marry or be in convents and the sooner they can find a man or an Order to take them on, the better. People will tell you that the important thing is that your husband should adore *you*. But they're wrong." Lady Cressett's forehead twitched. She changed the subject to planning Clara's day with Charles.

"You've got your own 'homework' to do, haven't you? So you'll probably prefer to have your dinner in the schoolroom most nights so that you don't have to waste time changing and so on."

Clara realized that this was an order. Her face must have fallen for Lady Cressett added at once:

"I hope you'll often manage to keep me company all the same. And you must always come down when Charles does or if there's anyone you specially like staying or coming over for dinner. I do so hope you won't be dull. All the young people seem to have gone to the wars," she sighed. "I feel so useless. There's nothing I can do but keep Maryhall going and roll bandages and knit socks. And I'm afraid I thank God every day that Charles is only a child. I know women who have sons as well as husbands out there."

"You must be anxious all the time," said Clara shyly.

"Yes. Especially these last weeks. I'm pretty sure things are bad where he is. I'm afraid we all hate the sight of the telegraph boy. We're so lucky, being Catholics. When I think of all those who haven't got that, I'm ashamed of myself."

They were both silent. Then Lady Cressett said:

"Your parents must be missing you tonight, Clara."

Clara realized guiltily that she had never given them a thought.

"I frankly dread Charles' going to Downside. An only child leaves such a hole in a house."

"Perhaps the war will be over soon and you'll have your husband home."

"Not for a long time, I think. And when the war's over, it won't be the world I knew. You're young enough to find change exciting."

"When I was really young I never wanted anything to change. But ever since I left Mount Hilary, I've been restless. I suppose it's the war."

"Or growing up. Did you like your Protestant school?"

"Yes and no. I felt rather a fish out of water."

"Then we must put you back in the river again."

"I don't seem to belong anywhere," said Clara in a burst of frankness. "I love this house. I know I'm going to be terribly happy here. But I shan't belong."

Lady Cressett looked at her thoughtfully.

"You're what's called introspective, aren't you? You worry about things and analyze them. Why not take them as they come?"

"I'll try," said Clara.

"I do so want you to feel at home here. There'll be snags of course. You mustn't let that son of mine tyrannize over you. He can be very unkind when he's in a bad mood. You're sensitive; one sees that in your eyes. And then there's Nan. She's difficult with strangers but she's a wonderful woman. She'd go to the stake for her loyalties. Remember that she's not a Catholic and try to make allowances for her."

"I know she's devoted to you all."

"Nan's very pious. But she's proud. She comes from Herefordshire where they're so proud they starch their stockings. We hope she'll be a Catholic one day. But my sister Monica says she'd be too proud to admit she'd been wrong before. So you'll just have to come out strong in charity and patience in your dealings with Nan."

"I'm afraid I'm remarkably weak in both."

"What a golden opportunity, as the nuns used to say when the porridge was burnt. But don't be a martyr and suffer in silence. Come to me if you have any trouble. You're the ruler of the schoolroom now and I'll back up your authority." She stood up. "High time we were both in bed, don't you think?" She patted Clara's cheek. "God bless you and happy dreams."

Sleepy as Clara was, she said her night prayers properly for the first time for weeks. As she lay on a pillow that smelt of lavender, listening to the faint creaks and rustlings of the old house and breathing the sharp country air, the last two years seemed to drop away from her. God had given her another chance. A new life was beginning, clean and uncomplicated. And this time, she firmly assured herself, she was not going to make any mistakes.

Chapter 4

IN one way, Clara's life at Maryhall turned out the reverse of what she had expected. She had thought it would be the beginning of being grown up; instead, week by week, she found herself slipping further back into childhood. She became so completely absorbed in Charles that she entered into his world as if she had been ten years old herself.

Finding that his birdlike mind could not attend to anything for long, she turned lessons into a game. She drew dragons and submarines and aeroplanes which had to be destroyed by good marks and, by making every subject a battle, she forced a little knowledge into his unwilling head. Some of her father's talent for teaching was in her blood. Sometimes, warmed by Lady Cressett's praise, she even wondered whether he had not been right in wanting her to take up teaching. Then she would remember the rigid figures of the mistresses at St Mark's, the plain, tired faces under hair that was either wildly untidy or scraped into a meagre bun, the high-collared blouses adorned with fountain pens and enamel brooches and hastily put the idea away. Even becoming a nun could hardly be worse than that.

Her real life with Charles began when lessons were over. All day long they played with the utmost seriousness. She learnt far more from him than he from her. He forced her to master the internal mechanism of submarines and locomotives. For days on end they lived in different characters, carrying on the impersonation even at meals. Sometimes Clara was Wing, the intrepid commander of a destroyer, sometimes Jenks the comic fireman of the Scottish Express, sometimes Golden Eagle, the wise but cautious old Indian chief, reluctantly admiring the exploits of Fox Tail, the disobedient young brave.

She surprised herself by the thoroughness with which she threw herself into these various parts. Very soon, like Charles himself, she came to resent ordinary life as an interruption. When Nan, on the stroke of half-past six, would ruthlessly demolish a submarine made of chairs or sweep the deployed armies into the toybox, Clara had to make an effort not to give away the fact she was just as furious as the boy. Often on her lonely evenings in the schoolroom, instead of tackling her set books, she found herself thinking up some elaborate game for the next day or working out new strategies to defeat Charles in battle.

Milburn had built them a Robinson Crusoe hut of willow branches in one of the shrubberies and there the two of them spent hours as Indians, shipwrecked mariners or pirates. Every part of the grounds had a place in their secret geography. The copse was an equatorial forest, the paddock a landing field, the walled kitchen garden a harbour and the hollow rose garden that had once been a cockpit a shell crater.

Lady Cressett was amused and bewildered by Clara's enthusiasm for these childish games. Sometimes, on the nights they dined together or as they walked over the misty fields to early Mass, she tried to fathom it.

"Either you're a wonderful actress or some part of you really is ten."

"I was rather elderly and precocious when I really was ten. I suppose it's all coming out now."

"I simply can't realize that you never had any brothers."

"Perhaps that's why I like small boys so much."

"It's not much fun for the only child. I never realized how badly Charles needed a companion till you came."

Clara was often on the verge of bringing out the never mentioned and never forgotten thing her mother had told her but never actually did so.

"You must marry early and have a large family while you're still young enough to play with them."

"I like children. But I can't see any attraction in babies."

"Can't you?" Lady Cressett sighed. "I like them almost best when they're tiny. I should like to have had a succession of babies in the nursery. It's queer how the Lord sends them to those who don't want them and not to those who do. However, I assure you that babies turn into children in no time, if that's any comfort to you. It seems only yesterday since Charles was in long clothes."

The weeks slipped by in a kind of dream. Clara was so absorbed in her life at Maryhall that it was only with the greatest difficulty that she could bring herself to answer her parents' letters or Patsy's wild, gossiping scrawls. Only her fear of her father, attenuated though it was by distance, made her do some part of the programme of work she had promised. She was much more conscious of Charles' displeasure than of anyone else's; there were moments when she realized that Charles had more power over her than even her father had ever had.

She had no illusions about the boy. She knew he was spoilt, lazy, selfish and tyrannical. But she loved him as she had never loved any creature before. He knew his power and used it. Whenever she looked like escaping, he had some trick to bring her into subjection again. Sometimes he would sulk with her for a day or two and fall back on Nan, deliberately excluding her. Nan, as she had been warned, was jealous and disapproving. None of Charles' former governesses had thrown themselves into his life in this peculiar way. Nor had Clara's good resolutions about tidiness lasted long; often she was as untidy as Charles himself and took Nan's scoldings as if she had been another child. Sometimes Nan would try to restore Clara's lost dignity. She would mend and press her clothes, do her hair for her when she dined downstairs, emphasize the fact that she was a young lady of seventeen and not a tomboy of ten. Drooping her sandy lashes and covering her hatred with an appearance of respectful interest, she would ask Clara about her plans for the future. Clara knew well that Nan lived for the day she herself could not bear to think about, the day when she would have to leave Maryhall. Nan could afford to wait; she would always be part of their life. She would have her place there when Clara would be a fainter memory to Charles than Hero the collie.

When Clara was out of favour and she was in and the three of them sat in front of the schoolroom fire in the interval between Charles' bath and bed, she would pull the sleepy Charles on to her lap. Murmuring "Nan's boy. Nan's own lamb," she would look across at Clara with a smile of triumph and pity. But when the balance of Charles' favour dipped the other way, there were moments of bitter tension.

One night when Clara was just going to bed and had taken off her dress and let down her hair, there came an agonized cry from the night nursery.

"Spin ... Spin ... Sp-in!" The sobbing wail rose to a shriek.

Clara hesitated. Then she remembered that Nan had a cold and was not sleeping with Charles. She huddled on her dressing-gown and ran along the passage. When she put on the light, she saw Charles sitting up in bed with his face distorted with terror. His eyes were wide open but she realized that he was still fast asleep in the grip of his nightmare.

She put her arms round him, soothing him while he continued to rave. When he woke from the bad dream, he clung to her frantically and would not let her go. At last she got him quiet enough to promise to try to go to sleep on condition she stayed with him. She turned off the light so that there was only the weak glow of the dying fire and the red bead of the lamp in front of Our Lady's statue. She took his hot hand and began to talk softly to him, reminding him that he had a guardian angel, perhaps St Michael himself with his sword and armour, and telling him old legends of Our Lady she had heard from the nuns. Just when his eyes had closed again and his hand relaxed in hers, the door opened and Nan came in with a candle. She too was in her dressing-gown and her red hair hung in two plaits on either side of her thin white face.

"What are you doing in here, Miss Batchelor, keeping the boy awake? Do you know it's gone eleven o'clock?"

"Charles had a nightmare," said Clara, keeping her temper. "He called out so I came to see what was the matter."

"I don't believe you," muttered Nan. "You came in here when my back was turned and frightened him with your silly stories. You ought to have more decency at your age."

"Please, Nan," whispered Clara. "I've only just got him to sleep again." But Charles, roused by their voices, was awake again.

"Go away, Nan," he screamed. "I had an awful dream and I called out for Spin. I called out for Spin, not you. I want Spin."

Nan's white skin turned a ghastly yellow. The candle shook in her hand, sending waves of shadow over a face clenched in hatred.

"Very well, Master Charles," she said very low, "I will go away. I will go away and never come back."

Charles looked so terrified that Clara rashly interposed: "He doesn't know what he is saying. He didn't mean it, did you, Charles?"

"Yes, I did," he said with nervous defiance.

"I must go back to bed now. And you must go back to sleep." But he clung to her.

"Stay with me, Spin. Make Nan go away. Beastly old Nan."

"You'll be sorry for this, Master Charles. And you'll be sorry too, Miss Batchelor. I shall have something to say to her Ladyship in the morning."

Nan's eyes were glittering. "It's a downright wicked sin. You worm your way in here. You work on that poor child's feelings. It's a shame and a disgrace. You're not fit, you've no right ..." She continued to rave at Clara, her voice rising more shrilly at each sentence.

Charles stared, frightened and fascinated. Clara was trembling all over but she kept enough grip on herself to say nothing. To her relief, the door opened and Lady Cressett appeared. With her greying brown hair tied loosely back and her long blue robe she looked like a Flemish Madonna. At the sight of her Nan stopped short.

"What is the matter? Is Charles ill?"

Both Nan and Clara remained silent. She turned to Charles who began to explain volubly.

"I see, darling," she said quietly. "Nan, I think you had better go to bed. You too, Clara. I'll stay with Charles for a little."

Nan and Clara left the night nursery by opposite doors. Back in her room Clara was too shaken to go to bed, even to finish undressing. She sat huddled on the edge of a chair, feeling at once humiliated and exultant. Absurd ideas raced through her head. At one moment she imagined Nan's dismissal and Lady Cressett imploring herself to make her home indefinitely at Maryhall. At another she thought of leaving secretly next day and began to compose a letter of renunciation. When there came a soft tap at her door, she started guiltily. It was Lady Cressett.

"I saw your light on. May I come in for a moment?"

"Oh, please do." She jumped up and offered Lady Cressett her chair.

"No, I won't sit down. Clara, my dear, you look quite ill." She put her hand under Clara's chin and turned her face up. "You mustn't be so upset. You're far too sensitive."

"Am I?" said Clara wretchedly.

"I quite understand what happened. You don't know Nan's little ways as I do. She'll be all right tomorrow. I guarantee that. You do realize it's only because she's so devoted to Charles, don't you?"

"Yes."

"You'll try to forgive her for being so rude to you?"

"I'll try. But she does hate me so."

"No. That's an exaggeration. She sees that Charles is very fond of you and the two of you have things she can't share. She's bound to be a little jealous. If I blame anyone, I blame Charles."

"I expect it was my fault," said Clara childishly, her lip beginning to quiver. "It always seems to be."

"Listen, Clara, I don't blame you in the least, not in the very least for what happened tonight. But do you mind if I say something to you?"

Clara shook her head, unable to speak.

"You're very fond of Charles, aren't you?"

She nodded.

"It's very touching. And, as Charles' mother, I can't help being pleased. But for your own sake and perhaps even for Charles' ... I wonder if you aren't even a little too fond."

Clara flushed. A wave of heat ran over her, drying the threatened tears. Suddenly she found her tongue.

"Oh, please. It's not wrong, is it? It can't be. You don't know how completely selfish I've always been. I've had friends I've been fond of, yes. But this is the first time, the very first time in my whole life I've cared for anyone more than myself."

Lady Cressett bent down and kissed her.

"You poor child. Of course it's not wrong. But just because you love the boy, don't always give in to him. I know how terribly hard it is to be firm with people one's fond of. I've given in myself and let myself spoil Charles. I don't know what his father will say when he comes home. Will you ... how can I put it ... be a little more on the grown-ups' side? Will you help me, Clara."

Put like that, Clara could only say: "I'll try. Truly I'll try."

Lady Cressett patted her cheek.

"I know you will. You're so very young yourself, aren't you? Now go to bed and forget all about tonight."

"Is Charles quite all right now?" she ventured.

"I left him sound asleep. He always sleeps like a top after one of these nightmares and wakes up extra rampageous."

As she moved towards the door, Clara noticed that she was very pale and that her forehead kept twitching.

"You're terribly tired," she said, penitently.

"We're both tired. Things look all out of proportion at this hour of the night. God bless you and sleep well. But don't spend all your love on that scamp Charles. Keep a little in reserve for later on."

When she had gone, Clara went obediently to bed but it was a long time before she could get to sleep. In spite of all Lady Cressett's kind-.ness she had a sense of uneasiness and foreboding. However gently, however tactfully, she felt she had been warned of some danger.

Chapter 5

URING the days that followed Nan's explosion, Lady Cressett kept Clara more than usual in her own company. She took her to visit various houses or sent Charles into Worcester with Nan while Clara helped her in the garden or rolled bandages at the Red Cross depôt.

One Saturday she said at breakfast: "It's high time I took you over to Crickleham. It's our show place in these parts. We might run over this morning as you've no lessons."

"Can I come too?" said Charles promptly.

"Certainly not. What about Father Samson and catechism?"

"Bother catechism. I haven't seen Archie for ages."

"I was thinking of bringing Archie back to luncheon if he's well enough. But if you're going to be silly ..."

"All right," said Charles. "There's nothing to see at Crickleham, Spin. Just a house and a lake and some boring old swans. It'd be all right if it belonged to them but they've only rented it. Why don't they buy a decent house of their own, Mummy?"

"I daresay Mrs Hughes-Follett will when her lease is up. They had a place of their own in Dorset but the Captain sold it because he wanted somewhere with fishing. They only took Crickleham while he looked round for something."

"Well, he's looking round purgatory now. They can go where they like."

"Yes, Charles."

Crickleham was a perfect cream-coloured Palladian house like a glorified version of Mount Hilary set among dark trees and smooth lawns. Charles had mentioned the lake but not the shallow white bridge reflected in it nor the yew walks with statues in their bays nor the fountain copied from Versailles.

The inside was decorated with great richness and comfort, even with taste, but it had the impersonality of all houses that have been let furnished to a succession of tenants. The few possessions the Hughes-Folletts had brought with them, mainly the late Captain's fishing-rods and trophies, only emphasized the fact that it was not their real home.

Clara liked Mrs Hughes-Follett at sight. She was a plain woman who had the courage to dress admirably. Her figure, though tall and straight, was not remarkably good; there was nothing about her that could be called beautiful except her slim wrists and ankles. Yet she was the most elegant person Clara had ever seen. Like Lady Cressett she wore a tweed suit, a wool jumper, ribbed stockings and heavy brogues but, whereas Lady Cressett's, excellent as they were, merely suggested practical necessity, hers were a work of art.

Her son Archie was as unkempt and untidy as his mother was immaculate. When he came slouching into the room in the private's uniform of the Inns of Court, he looked like an enormous overgrown schoolboy dressed as a soldier. His dark red hair had grown long during his illness and, with his tunic unbuttoned and his hands thrust in his pockets, he was a most unmilitary figure. Instead of boots he was wearing an old pair of tennis shoes with their laces untied.

"You must forgive Archie," said his mother. "He hasn't been on his feet long. Not that you were ever a model for the *Tailor & Cutter*, were you, old boy?"

As they walked round the grounds, Clara found herself paired off with Archie. When they were first introduced he had glanced at her with suspicion like a shy child being introduced to a grown-up. Though he was well over six foot and, in spite of his slouch, firmly built and muscular, his face had an unfinished look. He had large, irregular features and deep-set dark blue eyes whose expression reminded Clara at once of Blaze Hoadley and Charles' dog Hero.

At first he was obviously so ill at ease that Clara thought it kinder not to make conversation. She watched his mother's figure moving some distance ahead of them along the yew walks and marvelled that a grey tweed suit should look as right in this setting as hoops and panniers. Archie not only looked completely out of place but seemed quite unmoved by the beauty of Crickleham. At intervals he removed one hand from his pockets and jerked a thumb in one or other direction, muttering:

"That's the belvedere over there," or "That's the maze. Too easy to be much fun."

At last Clara had to laugh.

"It must be an awful bore having to show people over this park. I suppose you've done it hundreds of times."

"You're right. Especially when Papa was alive. He expected me to be a ruddy guide-book."

"You needn't bother for me."

"I say, d'you mean it?"

"Of course."

"Don't think I'm being rude and all that?"

"Not in the least."

He stopped in his stride and surveyed her. Then his brow cleared and he let out a long whistle.

"You're the first sensible girl I've met. I thought, being Charles' governess, you'd want all the historical details." He stared at her with growing interest. "I must say I've never seen a governess in the least like you. You know you're pretty enough to be on the stage. In fact, you distinctly remind me of one of the girls in *The Bing Boys*."

This was evidently a high compliment and Clara was sorry to have to admit she had not seen *The Bing Boys*.

"What rotten luck. I've seen it six times. Couldn't you take a day off and buzz up to London with me and do a show?"

"Afraid not."

"Shame. I don't care how often I see it. I simply can't decide which is the more priceless, old George Robey or old Alfred Lester. And the songs are absolutely top-holibus." He began to sing:

"If you were the only girl in the world,
And I were the only boy-ee."

"Oh, I know the song," said Clara. "We were always singing it in London. All the errand boys whistle it. What an awfully good voice you have."

"Queer, isn't it?" said Archie simply. "Can't think where I got it from. Mamma plays the piano marvellously but can only chirp like a sparrow and Papa hadn't a note of music in him."

He sang on with great fervour, but obviously no personal reference:

"Nothing else would matter in the world today,
We could go on loving in the same old way."

There was no doubt about the beauty of Archie's voice. It was a rich tenor with no quaver in it and a peculiar quality that suggested a stringed instrument.

"Do you ever sing any other kind of music? I heard a tenor at

Covent Garden once singing *Tannhäuser*. I'm sure his voice wasn't half as good as yours."

He gave her his suspicious look again.

"Classical music? I had enough of Mendelssohn and Bach and all that stuff when I was in the choir at Beaumont. I wouldn't half mind going into musical comedy. But I'm miles too tall. You've got to be able to do fancy dancing too. Papa would have had a fit. And even Mamma wouldn't exactly chortle with joy."

They walked on a little way in silence while Archie contemplated the flapping laces of his large and shabby tennis shoes. Suddenly he said very gloomily:

"I might have known you'd be brainy."

Clara felt that, at all costs, she must dispel this gloom. It was impossible not to like Archie and, without knowing why, to be sorry for him.

"Charles is always talking about you," she said. "All our best ideas come from you. We haven't been able to think up a really good Schweinhund for days. And we need you terribly at the moment. The secret telegraph's broken down."

He brightened at once.

"Wants a new battery probably. So you know about Schweinhund? D'you mean you actually play those kid games with Charles?"

"We do it all the time. They get so real that, even when Charles isn't there, I find myself going on with them in my head."

"But this is absolutely priceless. A grown-up girl that doesn't think it's all bilge. Some governess! I've been in bed for weeks, you know. I'd have been bored stiff if I hadn't been able to think up some new stunts for Schweinhund."

After that he talked as volubly as Charles himself. Suddenly he said:

"I'll show you a secret. I was saving it up for old Charles but I'll let you in on it first."

He led her to a remote rock-garden. There among the boulders and the tiny cascades he had fixed up an elaborate miniature railway.

"All electric," he said, proudly. "These are the Alps." His dazed, puzzled look had vanished and his face was alight. Running his trains, commanding Clara, he was no longer an overgrown schoolboy but a man. She played, as fascinated as Archie himself.

"Let's have an accident. The first on this line."

The railway had become so real to Clara that when the locomotives crashed into each other and a tiny coach came uncoupled and toppled over a precipice eighteen inches deep, she felt a shock of horror.

Mrs Hughes-Follett's voice sounded in the distance.

"Archie! *Archie!*"

"Come on," said Archie. "Let's run for it. Quick. I don't want her to find it." He seized Clara's hand and pulled her along with him as he ran.

When they reached the terrace where his mother and Lady Cressett were standing, Clara was flushed and breathless.

"We thought you two must have got lost in the maze," she said. "Good gracious, Archie, what have you been doing? You've run the poor girl off her feet."

She turned to Clara, smiling. "And what have you been doing to my son, Miss Batchelor? He looks cheerful for the first time for weeks."

Chapter 6

ARCHIE came back to lunch at Maryhall that day and for the rest of his sick leave he was constantly appearing on his battered motor-bicycle. All Archie's possessions quickly acquired a battered look. Some part of his own person was usually bandaged or in sticking-plaster. From babyhood he had attracted accidents and misfortunes of all kinds or been the innocent cause of accidents to others. China and glass seemed to smash at his approach and his motor-bicycle, skilled driver as he was, was constantly charging him into walls or flinging him into ditches. The fact that he was convalescing at Crickleham was due to a grenade having exploded, through no fault of his, killing another man and quite severely wounding Archie himself.

Lady Cressett was fond of him and encouraged him to come over and make a third in Charles' and Clara's interminable games. Occasionally Charles would be jealous of the two older ones since he regarded each as his personal property. Occasionally Clara was nervous, in case Charles should try to imitate Archie's recklessness. But, luckily, Charles had an extreme dislike of hurting himself and was quite satisfied with warning them of the alarming things he was just about to do in plenty of time for one or two of them to stop him. Clara noticed that, though Archie did not care how much he bruised and scratched himself, he watched over Charles almost like an anxious mother. He was nearly as devoted to Charles as she was herself and it made a bond between them. Only once did she ever see him angry with the boy and that was when Charles, who had been in an abominable mood all the afternoon, burst out:

"You're always butting in on everything, Spin. Can't you see men sometimes want to be alone together?"

Archie had boxed his ears and said furiously:

"Shut up, you little bastard. Sorry, Clara. Apologize at once or I'll leave this very sec. and take Clara with me."

Nevertheless she did sometimes leave them to play together, though she loved the absurd adventure games as much as ever and hated to lose a moment of them. Remembering the night of Nan's outburst, she would try to conciliate her enemy by offering to clear out the toy cupboard or even to darn Charles' socks. Sometimes her offers were grudgingly accepted; more often they were declined with frigid politeness. Once Clara nearly lost her own temper when Nan, in an unusually affable mood, said:

"I expect you'll be glad when Mr Hughes-Follett goes back to his regiment, Miss. He's put your nose out of joint, hasn't he?"

However, if she left them for more than half an hour, Archie always came in search of her. And on this particular occasion, when he burst into the schoolroom, crying: "*There* you are, you deserter! Come right back, will you? Charles and I can't carry on another sec. without you," she could have hugged him. When he came over to say good-bye, he was as downcast as a boy going back to school. Clara and he and Charles wandered sadly about their old haunts, too low-spirited to play.

"If you ever get sent to the front, Archie," said Charles, "you'd better jolly well look out or you're sure to get yourself blown to smithereens."

"I expect I'll get chipped about a bit. But it's never fatal with me. Mamma says I must have used up at least six lives already."

"You won't be going yet?" asked Clara, anxiously.

"No fear. Got to get my commission first. If I ever do. You'd better pray for me, Clara. I haven't hope of another leave till I get the ruddy thing. Gosh, what a priceless one this has been. I loathe going away."

Charles hung on his arm.

"P'raps I'll write to you, old man," said Charles kindly. "I don't absolutely swear, though. I find letters very exhausting, don't I, Spin? You see, I *have* to write to my father every Sunday."

"I'd be jolly bucked, Charles. Don't worry about spelling and all that rot. Can't spell myself."

It was getting late. Nan called for the third time from the house, this time so imperatively that Charles said, "Damn" and slouched off with his best imitation of Archie.

"Walk down to the lodge with me, Clara," he begged. "I left the old bike there. The Major's as touchy as my late Papa on the subject of gravel."

He walked so slowly, in his unwillingness to go, that Clara was afraid she would be late for dressing. Miss Catherine Lyons, to whom she owed her coming to Maryhall, had arrived during the afternoon and she was to dine downstairs. Looking up at the tall, disconsolate figure in the creased uniform she felt intensely sorry for him. His hair had been cut very short and his whole appearance suggested a convict rather than a soldier. Though the two were totally unlike, she could not help being reminded of Blaze in his Sunday suit.

"We shall miss you awfully, Archie," she said.

"Truth and honour?" he asked gloomily.

"Truth and honour."

"It's asking an awful lot. You wouldn't write to me now and then, would you?"

Clara had a faint pang, remembering all the young soldiers whose letters had remained unanswered since she came to Maryhall. But she assured Archie she would write. He brightened at once.

"That's really priceless of you. I'd be hugely bucked if I got a letter from you. Only don't expect a brainy reply, will you? I know you're frightfully brainy however much you like fooling about with Charles and me."

"I'm beginning to think it's all nonsense about my brains. I did have some once but I think they've just vanished."

"Theresa Cressett said you were working for a scholarship to Cambridge or something. So you must be pretty hot."

"Cambridge," she said and stopped. It came over her how completely she had changed in the last two months. She had forced herself to work a little on her set books but she had not, of her own accord, read anything but boys' adventure stories and books on ships and engines. "Don't mention Cambridge."

"Sorry, old thing. Have I dropped a brick?"

"I just can't imagine how I ever wanted to go there. I've completely lost interest in all that kind of thing."

"So you don't want to be a female blue-stocking after all?" he said, eagerly.

"I definitely do not. I don't think I want to be anything. In fact, I hate thinking about the future at all."

"So do I. My Papa was always heckling me about what I was going to do and all that. Thank God for the jolly old war. At least it saved me from having to make up my mind. Isn't it a bore having to grow up?"

"I used to want to grow up as fast as possible," said Clara. "Especially since the war. I felt as if I'd miss everything otherwise. But, since I've come up here, I don't care. What is there to grow up *for*."

"Exactly," he said. "You and me and Charles. Why can't it go on for ever?"

"Do you hate being in the army, Archie?"

"Not really. Not this amateur sort of thing. I couldn't have stuck the regulars. I like some of the chaps I'm with and of course I like any kind of an old scrap. All the same it gets my goat, the idea of killing people. Especially since I saw—well, never mind."

He had never referred to the accident on the parade ground before. Clara said gently:

"It must have been awful for you. And you nearly got killed yourself."

"Why can't we have battles like ours where the dead get up and go off to a whacking great tea? Not that I'd mind being dead personally. Solve the problem of the old future once and for all."

"Do you really feel like that?"

"Sometimes. Don't you?"

"I admit I don't like thinking about the future. It seems completely unreal."

"What, you too?" he said eagerly. He stopped in his walk and turned to her. "I suppose you think I'm a pretty rum sort of chap?"

"I never met anyone quite like you, no."

He studied her with his puzzled dark blue eyes.

"If you ask me, Clara, we're both a bit queer. You're miles beyond me, of course, but neither of us seem to quite belong anywhere, if you see what I mean. Or to know where the hell we're going."

She saw only too well and was not altogether pleased; there were times when, fond as she was of Archie, she wondered whether he might not be suffering from arrested development. Then he struck his forehead with his large, nicotine-stained hand.

"There are so many thoughts in here that can't get out," he said. "You don't know how lucky you are being able to express things."

His face was so wretched that Clara forgot her hurt vanity.

"What sort of thoughts, Archie?"

"I think about you a lot, for one thing. Did you know that?"

She shook her head as they walked on.

"I've never had much use for girls. Nor they for me. Of course

I take a chorus girl out for a binge now and then, like anyone else. And I like hearing backstage talk. But they expect you to get sentimental and give 'em a diamond wrist-watch. I can stand for the wrist-watch but not the billing and cooing."

They were at the lodge at last.

"Goodbye, Archie. I must rush back or I'll be frightfully late."

"Goodbye, Clara, old thing. You will write, won't you?"

She nodded and began to run back up the drive. A moment later she heard him running after her.

"I'm a giddy idiot," he said, as he caught up with her. "I forgot this. Whole point of my asking you to come all this way. I wanted to give you something."

He thrust a small revolver into her hand. She knew it was one of his most treasured possessions.

"Archie ... I couldn't possibly take it," she panted, keeping up her run.

"I'll chuck it in the river if you won't. I want you to have it. Better not use it. No licence. Don't tell Charles. He'd be green with envy."

"But you love it."

"That's the point. Cheerio!"

He dashed away again and Clara dared not waste any more time by going after him. When she got back to the house she made sure it was not loaded. She wished he had not given it to her. It was too cherished a possession and she had an odd feeling that it committed her to something. Next time she saw him she would make him take it back. Meanwhile her one concern was to get dressed as quickly as possible. She thrust the revolver under a pile of underclothes and forgot all about it.

Chapter 7

MISS Lyons stayed only for a long week-end and when she had gone Lady Cressett's sister, Miss Monica Underwood, came for a fortnight.

She was a vividly ugly woman, with no resemblance at all to her sister Theresa. Her skin was swarthy, her mouth crooked, her thick eyebrows almost met over her nose and the witchlike impression was increased by a mass of short wiry black hair standing up all round her head. She was as lively as Lady Cressett was calm and she gave several displays of her celebrated temper.

The explosions were violent and often comic, but they were quickly over and followed by such rueful kindness to the victim that it was almost a pleasure to be attacked by her. It was certainly a material advantage for she always gave the object of her rage a present. By the end of her short visit, Charles' toybox had received several handsome additions and Clara herself a pair of silk stockings. Father Samson brought on a storm by attacking Christabel Pankhurst. The next day Aunt Monica hurried over to confession in the pouring rain, armed with a box of cigars.

"I brought it in case of emergency," she explained at the breakfast table. "I knew sooner or later I'd fly out at a man. If your parish priest insists on talking politics, I'd better bring a whole set of vestments next time."

But Aunt Monica's greatest "occasion of sin" was Nan. She was constantly driven to fury by Nan's self-righteousness and by her treating Charles as if he were still a baby. "I wish you'd get your animal instincts straightened out, woman," she roared once. "Are you trying to be that boy's mother or his wife?" Nan remained coldly dignified throught these assaults. Miss Underwood, as one of the family, was privileged: she classed her tremendous tempers and her tremendous headaches together as signs of her being "not quite right".

Aunt Monica was more contrite when she lost her temper with Nan than with anyone else. "She's a maddening female," she said to

Clara once, "but what hell nurses must go through. A mother does at least get something. But a Nanny's lucky if her beloved baby remembers her enough to send her a Christmas card."

During the second week one of her fearful headaches came on. For the best part of three days she lay in a darkened room in the farthest wing. Clara, accidentally passing her door, heard a sound that she never forgot coming from inside: a moaning that was unlike any human noise.

On the morning she got up again, Clara walked with her round the walled kitchen garden. It was a still, frosty day in late October. Clara picked a sprig of rosemary, breathed on the fine fur of crystals till they melted, and sniffed it as they walked. It reminded her of her first walk with Charles. She thought, as then, that she would never smell its fresh, sharp scent without remembering Maryhall.

Miss Underwood's face was still drawn from the pain and her swarthiness had a greyish cast. She kept stopping to take a deep breath of the keen air and shaking her head, as if to test that it was safe to move it again. As they passed along the wall nearest the stables, one of the hunters whinnied and she whinnied back.

"I like horses in their proper place," she said. "I can't say I care for them galloping behind my eyeballs."

Clara asked timidly if nothing could be done about the headaches.

"I really don't know, my dear girl. At intervals my family drag me to some new doctor who has some new theory about them and some new cure that doesn't work. My own theory is that, for one reason or another, God wants me to have them."

"Surely God couldn't be so cruel."

"God isn't cruel," said Miss Underwood with a strange look. "We are."

Clara said with a shudder: "I don't know how you put up with such pain."

"I don't put up with it. I swear like a trooper and think of the crown of thorns."

"There's one thing that repels me in the lives of the saints. They talk as if they enjoyed suffering."

"My dear girl, don't ask *me* what the saints mean. Presumably one would have to be one to understand what they're driving at."

"I'm afraid I'm terrified of pain and suffering."

"So was Our Lord."

"Yes, but I'd run away. I know I would. I'm the most arrant coward."

"Well, sooner or later it'll catch up with you. And the funny thing is that, sooner or later, you'll be extremely thankful that it did."

"There, you see. You're talking just like the saints."

"Rubbish," said Miss Underwood so violently that Clara was afraid she was going to explode. They walked some yards in silence. But when she spoke again it was in a reasonable, almost apologetic voice.

"I suppose the whole problem's somehow connected with love. You dote on that nephew of mine, don't you? Say he broke his arm. You'd probably rather you felt the pain than he did. Which isn't saying you like pain *as* pain."

"It's so much easier to imagine doing things for the love of human beings than for the love of God," sighed Clara.

"D'you think so? I know it's in St John, loving one's brother whom one has seen, et cetera. Personally, I tend to dislike my neighbour on the least provocation and to tell him so. I wish I could be like Tess."

"Lady Cressett's wonderful, isn't she?" said Clara. "She really seems to love everyone. I know someone else who's got just the same angelic nature." She was thinking of Lilian Cohen.

"I assure you she didn't start life with an angelic nature," said Miss Underwood. "When we were children there wasn't a halfpenny to choose between us. If I grabbed the poker, she grabbed the tongs."

She pushed up her wiry hair and exposed an old scar on her left temple. "That's a little memento of Tess's angelic nature. Now she's as calm as a mill-pond except for that nervous twitch. I call it the tombstone of her temper."

"Do you mean she just fought and fought until she conquered it?"

"No. I think something else just grew until there was no room left for it. Call it grace. Call it the love of God. I'm no theologian. In my opinion, Tess is much more of a saint than a great many on the official list. And I do *not* say that because she trudges a mile to Mass every morning and plays Lady Bountiful to the parish."

They walked a few steps in silence. Then Miss Underwood asked abruptly:

"Ever met Charles' father?"

"No. I know he's very handsome from his photographs. I suppose he's very charming, too."

"All the Cressetts are charming when they want to be. But he doesn't waste much of his charm on Tess. He treats her like an efficient housekeeper and makes the hell of a fuss if she isn't efficient enough."

"Lady Cressett's awfully fond of him, though, isn't she?" said Clara uncomfortably.

"Devoted to him. And to the boy. Humanly speaking she'd break her heart if anything happened to either of them."

"Is Sir George fond of Charles?"

"Extremely. Charles is himself all over again. He was madly keen to have an heir. It's an old baronetcy and would die out otherwise. But if Charles had been a girl, heaven help us. Tess can't have any more, you see."

Clara was deeply shocked.

"Can it mean so much to a person, the idea of a title going on?"

"George is a snob, of course. But he's got a tremendous feeling about this place. It's his one permanent passion. I'm sure his idea of heaven would be permission to haunt Maryhall. And the notion of Maryhall without a Cressett would be purgatory ... or worse."

Clara sighed.

"And I've always thought of them as such an ideally happy family."

"So they are in a way. It's Tess who keeps the whole thing going."

"She's always saying how happy her life is. And encouraging other people to get married."

"Good people always assume everyone else is as good as they are."

When Aunt Monica had gone, Clara had moments of acute depression. After that conversation in the kitchen garden, though she admired and liked Lady Cressett more than ever, some of the charm had gone from Maryhall. She had made great efforts to be more of a governess and less of a wild playmate, with the result that Charles complained that she was getting as bad as Miss Stephenson. On the days when he was bored or sulky, she was horrified to realize how dependent she had become on the affection of one small boy.

November was grey and stormy. Sometimes, at night, as she sat in the schoolroom, with the wind howling outside, she felt lonelier than she ever had in her whole life. She took to writing long letters to Ruth and Patsy and even to Archie Hughes-Follett.

Chapter 8

EARLY in December the house was thrown into commotion by the news that Sir George was expecting leave. Preparations began at once: everything indoors and out was reviewed and put in still more perfect order. A few days later a telegram came and, for the first time, Lady Cressett's fingers did not shake as she opened it.

"He arrives in London tomorrow," she said. "He's got ten days. I'm to go and meet him and stay in town for a couple of days' shopping."

In private she said to Clara: "You'll have to keep an eye on Charles. He'll be wild with excitement. He's quite capable of ordering one of George's young trees to be cut down to make a bonfire for the hero's return."

As if she guessed Clara's misgivings, she added:

"I know you can keep him in order. You've been much less of a fellow-conspirator lately."

As soon as his mother had gone, Charles' spirits became irrepressible. After weeks of dampness, the weather had cleared to blue sky and east wind. Clara invented an energetic outdoor spy game to keep him amused till tea-time. It was a success and, as they walked back to the house, he tucked his arm under hers.

"You're a decent old Spin," he said. "Sorry I ragged you and said you were like Stevie. You aren't a bit."

After tea he ordered her to read to him.

"Get Mummy's *Times*. I must be up in the battle news for Daddy."

He curled up on the floor in front of the schoolroom fire while she read him the day's despatches. It was like their first happy weeks. Now and then she glanced down from her paper at the dark head resting against her knee. Once she ran her finger down the pencilled groove at the nape of his neck.

"I like it when you do that, Spin. It gives me a nice shiver."

He begged so hard that she broke the rule she had imposed on herself since the scene with Nan and went to say good night to him in bed.

"You're O.C. now Mummy's away," he said. "She told me so. Only it's a secret. Nan, you know."

She nodded.

"All right. Only you'll have to behave yourself."

"Don't worry. I promise not to grease the back-stairs. Heard from old Archie lately?"

' "I had a letter this morning. He's got his commission." '

"Good egg. That means he'll get leave. Not that I'll have much time, with Daddy here. But why didn't he write and tell me?"

"Because you never wrote to him, I suppose."

"It takes so long writing things down. Anyway nothing exciting's happened. I wish a German aeroplane would crash in the garden and I could take all the crew prisoners."

"Perhaps it will."

He looked at her mysteriously.

"Do you know?"

"No. Only guessing."

"Perhaps you've guessed right. Perhaps it'll be tomorrow. In the kitchen-garden."

"What, have you intercepted a message?"

"Shan't say." He lowered his voice. "Anyway there's a brand new type of anti-aircraft gun concealed in the gooseberry bushes."

"Your invention?"

"I stole the plans. Of course I improved them a lot. It works by compressed air, and ..."

"Shut up. Schweinhund may be in the cupboard."

She tiptoed over and opened it.

"All right, Sir. No one there."

"Sucks to you. I knew he wasn't. I happen to know he's piloting this plane. He's in Berlin at this moment, probably getting blotto with the Kaiser."

"Why didn't you tell me?"

"You don't tell me everything. You've been keeping up a secret correspondence with Archie. Is he sweethearting you, Spin?"

"Don't talk rot. Good night, Charles."

"Tuck me in. I'm an orphan boy tonight."

She did so. Charles rolled his eyes.

"Beloved Spin," he groaned in a deep bass. "Say thou wilt be mine." Then he squeaked. "My own darling Archibald, I will."

"Shut up, idiot."

"Fancy tucking up a lot of little Hughes-Folletts. All with big feet and carroty hair."

"Good *night*, Charles."

"Holy water, please. Must keep the devil away."

She made the sign of the cross on his forehead as his mother always did.

"God bless you. Now really, truly and finally, good night."

"Good night, Spin. For ever and ever, amen."

That night Clara went to bed happier than she had been for a very long time.

Next day after lunch, she and Charles went down to the keeper's lodge to see a new litter of puppies.

"This one's Hero's child all right," said Charles, picking up a black and white one. "It's the spitting image of him as a puppy."

At that moment there was the chugging of a motor bicycle in the lane.

"It's old Archie," shrieked Charles, dropping the puppy back in its basket. "I'd know his engine anywhere."

A moment later, Archie dismounted at the gates.

"Golly! Do I have to salute you?"

Archie was resplendent in Second Lieutenant's uniform. It was still too new for him to have reduced it to the usual state of his clothes, though there were already spots of oil on the slacks.

He inserted himself between the two and put a long arm round each.

"Gosh, it's good to see you chaps. I hared straight over to celebrate. Your father hasn't arrived yet, has he?"

"No. Mummy's in London with him. I'm in charge."

"Good egg. Can we have tea in the schoolroom?"

"Of course. But it's ages to tea. I haven't worked off lunch yet. What shall we do?"

"What time's that German plane due, Sir?" asked Clara, speaking across to Charles.

"Jove, I nearly forgot. About three pip emma. We'd better dash to the kitchen garden and give that gun crew their orders. On their way to the kitchen garden, Archie said: "They're beginning to use parachutes quite a bit. Wonder if the German blighters have got 'em."

"If they try and use them, we'll shoot them down in the air. Good egg," said Charles.

"I don't think that's fair ..." Clara began.

"Rot, Spin. Don't be soppy. They'd do it to our chaps. What can we use for a parachute?"

"Umbrella?" suggested Archie.

"Spiffing," Charles dashed off at top speed.

"Bring mine," Clara shouted after him. "Doesn't matter what happens to it."

In a few minutes Charles was back, panting and brandishing Clara's umbrella.

For once, no one was working in the kitchen garden. Clara, mindful of her responsibility, insisted that the aeroplane crashes took place on the gravel paths and not on the beds. Time after time Archie, as the German crew, was successfully brought down by the secret weapon in the gooseberry bushes. After at least his tenth leap from the eight foot wall, grasping the open umbrella, he rolled over on the gravel, groaning "Ach, mein leg, mein leg, it gebroken is. Verdammte Chute, nicht open gut." This was a great success and after that he had to keep pretending to injure himself. Once he stayed crumpled up and motionless for so long that Clara was afraid he really had hurt himself. But when she bent over him he whipped out an imaginary revolver and shot her. "Schweinhund the last word has, so. Hoch der Kaiser."

Suddenly Charles shrieked, "It's my turn, I'm going to do some jumps."

"Not from that wall you're not," said Clara, ceasing to be Wing the gunner. "It's much too high."

"Rot. Archie's done it thousands of times."

"Archie's nearly as high as the wall."

"Don't be governessy. Give us a leg up, Archie."

"Nothing doing, old man, Clara's right. You might easily damage yourself."

"Soppy Archie! Soppy Spin!" yelled Charles in a fury. "Go and play Pa and Ma by your silly soppy selves. I'm jolly well going to jump. I will and I shall."

Before they could stop him, he had dashed away with the umbrella to another path that ran from a door in the wall between stone copings. Behind the copings on either side were thick bushes of rosemary.

Clara gasped: "Archie! For mercy's sake stop him."

"Don't worry. He can't possibly get up on that wall."

Neither of them had noticed that someone had left a ladder leaning against it just at the place Charles was making for. In a flash he had scrambled up, kicked the ladder away and was dancing on the parapet, brandishing the open umbrella.

Clara opened her mouth to call him but Archie clapped his hand over it.

"Shut up," he whispered. "You'll only make him do it. Bluff's the only hope. Stay where you are."

He ran till he was only a few yards from Charles.

"Just a sec, old chap. Let me get up too. Must do it scientifically."

"I know how! I know how!" bawled Charles, beside himself with excitement. "Get out of my way."

Before Archie was near enough to catch him, Charles clutched the umbrella with both hands and made a wild, sprawling jump. Clara saw Archie lurch forward to try and break his fall but he was too late. She heard a thud and saw the umbrella shoot away and land upside down on a rosemary bush. Now Archie blocked her view so that she could not see what had happened. He was bending down; then he fell on his knees and remained perfectly still. If they were still playing, why did neither of them speak? If Charles was hurt, why didn't he cry? He usually made a fuss over the slightest graze. Her knees began to tremble so much that she could hardly run the twenty yards to where they were.

Archie was crouching over the boy, hiding the top part of his body from her. All that she could see was Charles' bare legs and brown shoes sticking out wide apart on one side and on the other the open umbrella rocking very slightly to and fro on the bush.

As she came behind them, Archie just turned his head. His face was grey. He said thickly:

"Get back indoors. Phone for the doctor."

She tried to push Archie away and look. But her strength was gone; she could only tug feebly at his tunic.

"Go *in*, will you? Get him to come at once."

In a daze of terror she stumbled back to the house. There was no one in the hall where the telephone stood. She found the doctor's number, was told he was expected back shortly and left an incoherent message. Then she heard Nan moving in the passage upstairs. She could not face telling Nan yet that Charles had been hurt and tore out of the house again, running at top speed back to the kitchen garden. It was a long run and her knees were giving way; she had to stop and get her breath. The effort of breathing calmed her a little; she was able to think. Then she realized the whole thing had been a hoax. She walked on slowly with a huge sense of relief. By the time she reached the open door of the kitchen garden she had forgotten her fear and was furious with the two of them. She stopped and listened but there was no sound of voices or laughter.

She went into the garden. Far away to the right, in the path that led to the other door, the two figures were still in the position she had left them a quarter of an hour ago. As she hurried towards them Archie got up and came towards her. He grabbed her by both shoulders and turned her round so that she had her back to Charles.

"Is the doctor coming?"

She stared at him. She had forgotten the terrible look he had had. It was still there. Her mouth went dry.

"Then he really is hurt?"

"Clara, you've got to know. Hold on to yourself, dear. It's just as bad as it can be."

"What do you mean?"

He said very quietly. "He's dead, dear. Instantaneous. He didn't suffer."

She heard nothing but the word "dead" and felt an appalling sensation half pain, half nausea, between her shoulder blades. Then she turned cold and began to shake all over. She said, with her teeth chattering:

"It can't be. It's not possible. Un ... unconscious. Let me look."

She tried to break out of Archie's hold but he would not let her go and she was too weak to struggle.

"I know the difference," he said. His face worked. "Oh, Clara, it's all my bloody fault."

The misery in his voice steadied her.

"But Archie, it's only a little drop. It's barely eight feet. It couldn't kill anyone."

"His head caught against the stone. He broke his neck."

"I don't believe it."

This time she was stronger than he and before he could stop her she was kneeling beside the body. She saw it clearly but it had no more relation to Charles than a dummy dressed in his clothes. Her mind no longer took in anything at all.

From the house the gong sounded for tea.

Archie pulled her to her feet. She did not resist.

"Try and understand what I'm saying, dear. We must go in now. We must tell Nan."

Part of her consciousness came back. She clung to him, almost screaming. "Oh no, oh no!" She could not grasp that Charles was dead, but she realized that something fearful and irrevocable had happened.

"Try to remember. You 'phoned the doctor, didn't you?"

She made a great effort to close the gap that seemed to have opened in her head.

"The doctor? Yes. I 'phoned the doctor."

"And he said he'd come?"

"Somebody said he would come. Yes, that's right. When he got back."

Archie forced her to walk in the direction of the house, half pushing, half dragging her along beside him. He shut the door of the kitchen garden behind him, locked it and put the key in his pocket.

"Why did you do that?" she said, vaguely.

"Never mind."

It seemed to Clara that they were not moving at all but that the house was steadily advancing towards them. Familiar things went by like a film; the cockpit where a few late roses bloomed, clipped yews, the faded blue face of the stable clock. A sense of extreme lassitude came over her. She could hear Archie talking from very far away.

"I'm going to leave you outside while I go in and tell Nan. I've got to tell her first, see? It was my fault. She's got to understand it was my fault. I'll see you through, Clara. I won't leave you alone with her."

The words meant nothing to her. Suddenly she stopped. She had caught sight of the willow hut in the shrubbery.

"Look, Archie."

"What is it?"

"There's a notice on it."

A piece of paper was pinned to the hut. On it was printed in huge crooked letters: BEWEAR.

"Oh, God, the poor kid," said Archie.

"What does it mean?"

"We shan't ever know."

PART SIX

Chapter 1

CLARA woke the next morning in a strange bed in a very large room. Her head felt empty yet heavy, as if it were full of some dense gas. She could not make out where she was nor how she came to be there. The curtains were drawn but there was enough light to distinguish chairs and mirrors and the rail at the foot of the bed.

There was a lamp by the bedside. After a long time her mind took in the idea that, if she were not dreaming, this lamp could be turned on. It was difficult to keep this idea in focus and still more difficult to communicate it to her hand but, after an interval, she managed to switch on the light. Then she lay back with closed eyes, exhausted by the effort. When she opened them again she saw a huge, luxurious room in which nothing seemed to have any connection with her. Over the bedrail hung a fur-trimmed dressing-gown; she herself was wearing a silk and lace nightdress which did not belong to her. At last, on a gilt-backed chair, she made out a pile of clothes, neatly folded, which she recognised as her own. With great difficulty, as one tries to piece together the fragments of a vanishing dream, she managed to clutch at some vague memories. She realized she must be at Crickleham and rested for a long time on the triumph of this discovery. Now she must try and find out why she was at Crickleham. The fog in her mind thinned a little. She remembered sitting in the sidecar of Archie's motor bicycle. Then, very slowly, the fog cleared, a patch at a time and each clearing revealed an image until at last the whole hideous dream was connected up; every detail vivid. But what puzzled her was that the dream ended with a fact; the fact that she had woken up in someone else's nightdress in this great, soft unfamiliar bed.

There was a tap at the door. She called "Come in." It was Mrs Hughes-Follett. Clara watched her move noiselessly across the thick carpet and seat herself on her bed. She said very gently:

"Have you been awake long, Clara? How do you feel?"

"My head feels so strange. How did I get here?"

"We put you to bed here last night. The doctor gave you something to make you sleep."

"The doctor? Have I been ill?"

"No dear. You just needed a good rest. Don't try and think. Just relax. Could you manage a little breakfast? It's nearly eleven o'clock."

"No, thank you. I'm not hungry." Clara sat up and pressed her hands to her temples. "Oh, please, do help me to remember. Why am I here?"

"You've had a very bad shock. You must just be quiet and take things easy. Don't force your mind."

Clara shook her head.

"No, I must get it right. Nothing seems real. I can remember a horrible dream. Only it doesn't seem like a dream. What day is today?"

"Thursday."

"Then yesterday was Wednesday. These things happened on a Wednesday. I went into the hall and rang up the doctor and they said: 'Wednesday's his day at the Malvern hospital.' Was that right?"

Mrs Hughes-Follett was very pale. She gave Clara a long, pitying look.

"Yes, dear. Quite right. But let it come gradually."

"No, no. I must know. Everything."

"Are you sure you feel strong enough?"

"I'm quite well. It's just my head. I can't get things clear. Please, please help me."

"I will. You've got to be very brave. Archie brought you here last night from Maryhall. Can you remember that?"

"That was the side-car. Yes. There's a blank after that."

"You were worn out and no wonder. The doctor wanted you to come here and rest. The worst's over now, Clara. We're going to look after you for the next few days."

Mrs Hughes-Follett took her hand.

"Clara. Don't strain it. But do you remember at all before Archie brought you over?"

The touch unlocked something in Clara's head. She said:

"Charles is dead. I must go and tell his mother."

"Hush, dear. She knows."

"Who told her?" said Clara wildly. "I ought to have told her. I was left in charge. It was all my fault," she began to sob.

"Cry, dear. It will do you good," said the other, laying a cool hand on her forehead. Through her dry, tearless sobs she heard a soothing voice saying:

"It was a dreadful thing to happen. It wasn't your fault. Archie told me all about it. The little boy didn't suffer. It was a terrible shock for everyone."

"I'm not fit to live," moaned Clara. "Oh, why wasn't I killed?"

"Hush, Clara. You mustn't talk like that. Try and be a little calmer. We all have something very difficult to bear some time in our lives. We're all very, very sorry for you. Lady Cressett wanted you to know that."

"Lady Cressett? How can she ever forgive me?"

"She knows it wasn't your fault."

Suddenly Clara remembered something. She said with horror: "His father?"

"You won't have to see his father."

"Have I seen him?"

"No, Clara."

"What happened? Did I run away?"

"No, dear. Archie took you away. I know it's painful but would it help to tell me what you remember?"

"Yes, please." Clara pushed her hair and rammed her knuckles into her temples, trying to force her mind into focus.

"The doctor came. Yes. And a policeman. I had to answer a lot of questions. First me and Archie. Then me alone. They wouldn't let me see Charles again."

"No. When there's an accident like that, they have to take the person away."

A vague, terrifying memory came back.

"Nan," she said. "Something about Nan."

Mrs Hughes-Follett's voice was unnaturally calm.

"Yes, dear. Nan can't hurt you."

"What did Nan do? She screamed. Then someone got hold of her. But she got away and ran upstairs."

"Nan was beside herself. She didn't know what she was doing. Try and understand that."

"It's getting clearer now. Somebody phoned to London. I wanted to stay, didn't I? I knew I ought to stay and tell his father and mother."

"Yes, but the doctor said no and Archie brought you back here. I think you've remembered enough, dear."

"No ... there's a bit still missing. I must get it," said Clara obstinately. Suddenly she was aware of a slight pain in her left wrist. She looked at it and saw it was bandaged.

"Why have I got a bandage on my wrist?"

"You hurt yourself. Just a little cut. Nothing to worry about."

"Now ... now I remember. I went up to my room. And Nan was there. In the big cupboard where my clothes are. She had a pair of scissors and she was cutting pieces out of my clothes. No. That must have been in the dream."

"It wasn't a dream, Clara. Nan was hysterical. I tell you she didn't know what she was doing."

Clara touched the bandage.

"Did she do this?"

"Yes. We must be thankful it was no worse. Luckily Archie came in in time."

"Did he? I don't remember that. I just remember Nan and the scissors."

"Don't think about it. She would have been horrified if she'd realized."

"I don't blame her," said Clara wearily.

She lay back and closed her eyes, suddenly limp and exhausted. Every piece of the puzzle fitted now. There was nothing left to do but to try, inch by inch, to admit the intolerable facts. Charles was dead. She had wrecked his mother's happiness; destroyed the whole beloved fabric of the life at Maryhall. It was inconceivable that she herself could go on living, waking up morning after morning, finding this load of grief and remorse still there. She knew she was still too numb even to begin to feel its full weight. On the very edge of her consciousness one more appalling thought began to take shape. Sooner or later, she would have to tell her father.

She said in a painful whisper: "If only ... only he had let Nan do it. How can I go on living?"

She heard Mrs Hughes-Follett say almost sharply: "My dear girl. You mustn't talk like that. Hasn't there been enough suffering? Do you want to make more? Poor Archie has been through hell over this. Can't you give him one thought?"

Clara roused herself with an effort. She said with shame:

"Archie was so good to me. You don't know how good." She began to cry weakly. The tears oozed under her closed lids and crawled down her cheeks. She felt the cool hand on her forehead again.

"There, there, Clara. Realize you're among friends. I want you to know that Archie is very, very fond of you. Will you let him come and talk to you when you're feeling a little more yourself?"

Chapter 2

ISABEL was having her breakfast in bed, as usual, when Claude burst into the room without knocking. There was a letter in his hand and his face was mottled. Her heart began to beat violently. She had only one thought: "Reynaud."

"Read that," he said, flinging the letter on to her tray. Then she saw that the writing was Clara's. She said:

"Why does she write from somewhere called Crickleham Park?"

"You'll see why," he said grimly.

When she had read it, she said softly: "Oh, the poor child. The poor, poor child."

"The Cressett boy. Yes, Horrible."

"I meant Clara."

"*Clara?* Good God!"

"But, Claude, think what she must have been through."

"I've no sympathy to spare for Clara. I'm thinking of that boy's parents. It was her fault. She admits it."

"Can't you see she was half out of her mind when she wrote this?"

"She must have been quite out of it to be so criminally careless. She was left in charge. She admits she let the boy play this idiotic game."

"But Claude, you know what boys are. You know how she loved the child. I'm certain ..."

"She wasn't engaged to love him. She was engaged to look after him." His lips were white. "I suppose you realize there will be an inquest. Clara will have to give evidence. By God, if I were the boy's father, I'd have her up for manslaughter."

"Claude ... how can you be so horribly unfair?"

"Unfair, am I?" he shouted. "D'you expect me to like having my name dragged through the police courts? It may not be a name to boast of, but at least I've made it decent in my profession."

"You talk as if she'd deliberately ..."

"She failed in her duty. Her elementary duty. If after this she imagines that any fourth-rate school ..."

"Oh, what does all that matter? Can't you spare one thought for the child's feelings?"

"When has she ever thought of mine? Or yours either, for that matter? If my daughter's publicly disgraced, I had better hand in my resignation. As for Clara, the best thing she can do is to change her name and be thankful if she's allowed to serve behind a counter."

Never before had she seen him in such a state of uncontrollable fury. She fought down her repulsion and let him rave on. At last she said:

"Claude, aren't you letting your imagination run away with you? We don't even know that anyone *is* going to blame her."

"She blames herself. She'd have wriggled out of any responsibility if she could. Therefore I blame her, too."

"What can we do? Should I go up there and see her?"

"Most certainly not. I absolutely forbid you to do any such thing. I shall write to Clara. And I assure you it will be a letter she won't forget."

"Claude, I implore you, no. Not till you've calmed down a little."

"I shall write what I please and when I please," he said loudly. "I shall also write to Lady Cressett. They shall see one member of this family has some sense of shame."

"Then I shall write too. You can't stop me. I shall write as one mother to another."

"You seem to ignore the fact that the boy had a father. What must he be feeling? His only son."

"I'm not denying that it's terrible for his parents. But we know the little boy was spoilt and disobedient. His mother told Clara so when she first went there. Was that Clara's fault?"

"She wasn't alone. You forget that. There was some young man or other about. Instead of looking after the boy, she was fooling about with *him*. As a result the boy breaks his neck. I ask you, was that Clara's fault, or was it not?"

"I don't see how we can possibly tell till we know just what *did* happen."

"The whole thing's perfectly obvious to anyone who knows Clara. The very day of my father's funeral I found her in the orchard carrying on like a servant girl with Blaze Hoadley."

"That old nonsense!" she said contemptuously.

"You find it nonsense, eh?" he said savagely. "I should have supposed ..."

"I think you're being utterly cruel and unfair. I didn't think you could be so heartless to your own child."

"Heartless, am I? Because I have an elementary sense of justice?" He hung over the brass bars of the bedstead like an animal half out of its cage. She could not bear to look at his grey, blotched face and stared instead at her breakfast tray, at the half-eaten toast and the pale scum of milk on the cooling tea. A clock struck a quarter past nine.

"I must go to school," he said. "I shall have more to say about this disastrous business at lunchtime."

She was filled with such horror of him that she could not bring herself to say goodbye and he went out slamming the door. Clara's pathetic, half-crazed letter still lay on the bed. She read it again, handling the paper as if it were a bruised creature that could be hurt. She had known these blind rages of Claude's before, but she could not understand this one. She read Clara's letter again. It was addressed to Claude alone; there was not a single mention of herself in it. A keen pain ran through her. She thought how many times Clara had shut her out like this. Everything had always been for her father; her mother was lucky to have an occasional crumb. She wondered how Clara would have felt if she had overheard the conversation between her parents. She had been going to write her a tender letter. But a great rush of bitterness came over her, making her tremble. She got up and dressed in frantic haste. She did not know what she wanted to do. She sat down at her desk and tried to write. Twice she began: "My darling little Clara," with a hand that shook. But love and hate had reached a pitch where she was impotent. At one moment she saw Clara white and tearful as she must have been when she wrote to her father. At the next she saw the cold eyes and the small contemptuous smile and knew that any tenderness of hers would only make them more contemptuous. She had a bitter impulse to describe, word for word, her conversation with Claude: Clara should see who really cared for her when it came to a crisis. But would Clara believe her? And, if she did, would her daughter ever forgive her? Would she ever forgive herself?

She sat at the desk, lighting cigarettes and throwing them away half-smoked or nervously twisting her wedding-ring. In the end she wrote nothing but "I'm so terribly sorry for you, darling, and long to have you home." It was still only half-past ten. She looked round the dreary dining-room. Never had she hated it more. She could not bear the thought of staying in the house; at any moment her mother-in-law would appear, trying to find out, as she always did, what had been in Clara's latest letter. She ran up to her room, put on her outdoor clothes and went out, with no idea of where to go or what she meant to do. It was cruelly cold; the wind buffeted her through her veil and swirled dead leaves and old newspapers round her ankles; her hands were icy in her muff. Tears formed in her eyes and dried again as she walked blindly, taking any turning at random. Suddenly she stopped, finding herself in a street she did not know. She looked at the name and saw it was the one where Callaghan lived. She could not remember the number of the house where he had rooms. Whichever it was, he would not be there now; he must have left for St Mark's an hour ago. There could be no danger in just walking past the houses; it was an obscure comfort to know that one of those shabby doors must be his.

She had not gone more than a few yards before a man came running down the steps of a house just ahead of her. Before she had time to cross over, she was face to face with him and the next moment she was weeping in his arms.

Chapter 3

CALLAGHAN held her for a moment or two without speaking. Then he said: "We can't stand here. You'd best come inside." He helped her up the steps. When he dropped her arm to fumble for his key, Isabel had to clutch the railing to keep herself upright.

"Put your muff up and hide your face," he muttered. "Every window in this house is full of eyes."

He jabbed his key into the lock at last and almost pushed Isabel into a dark hall that smelt of oilcloth and stale cooking. Whispering to her to walk quietly, he led her along a passage and opened a door with a broken china handle.

"You'll have to forgive this. It's the only room I have," he said as he shut them in together. "Will I lock the door? Better not." Raking some books off the only armchair and thrust Isabel into its sunken seat.

Then he knelt beside her and pushed up her veil. "For God's sake will you stop crying and trembling and tell me what's the matter?" She was no longer weeping but her breath came in choking gasps so that she could not speak.

He clutched her shoulder, hurting her. "Here ... wait."

He got to his feet and stumbled about the room, slamming open a cupboard and flinging a pile of papers off a desk.

"Praise be, there's a finger left."

He came over to her with a smeared tumbler with some whisky in it. "Drink this."

The smell made her feel sick. She tried to push the glass away but he held it against her mouth.

"Oh, come on, now. It'll pull you round."

She managed to swallow a mouthful: some spilled down her chin.

"No more," she coughed. "It's horrible. It burns."

"Then I'll finish it. If I'm seeing phantoms, I'll keep up the illusion that you're sitting in my chair."

He drank the rest in one gulp and sat down on the bed. The shock of the whisky brought Isabel's mind into focus. She became aware of the shabbily furnished room; of Callaghan, still in his overcoat, sitting on the unmade bed holding the empty tumbler; of the smell of whisky, dead cigarettes and unwashed sheets.

"I must go at once," she said. "I never meant to come here."

"I believe you," he said. "But stay where you are. You're in no state to move."

"I am better now," she said, trying to keep her voice steady. "I shouldn't be here. Nor should you. You must have been on your way to St Mark's."

"To hell with St Mark's. I was late as it was. They're used to my not showing up. I've got the sack anyway."

"Oh, Reynaud, I'm sorry."

"I can't say that I am. It's strange to hear you speak my name again."

Outside in the street she had not looked at his face. Now in the harsh light, smirched but not softened by the dirty window pane, she compared it with the one she remembered. It was sallower than ever; the lids of the heavy blue eyes were swollen and the whites yellowish. She was conscious of all the disorder of her own; she had studied it for too many years to need a mirror to tell her how it must appear in that cold glare. Yet she did not pull down her veil to hide her reddened eyes and the tracks of tears through the powder. Almost proudly, she exposed her ravaged face for him to see if he wished. But he was not looking at her. His eyes were wandering moodily about the room as if seeing it for the first or last time. She let her gaze follow his, searching for traces of Reynaud himself among the neutrality of the lodging-house furniture. At first she found them only in the French books scattered on chairs and chest of drawers and heaped in crooked piles on the floor. He had not even bothered to take down the landlady's pictures—"Wedded", "The Bath of Psyche" and a faded photograph of the Taj Mahal in a frame full of empty sockets which had once been inlaid. Gradually she found other traces: a torn dressing gown on the door, shoes in the fender, ties and collars dangling from an old gas bracket. Above the mantelpiece, littered with crushed cigarette packets, hairbrushes and empty bottles, two photographs were tacked on the wall with drawing pins. They had evidently been torn out of books; one she recognised as Verlaine; the other was a boy with tight lips and fine arrogant eyes. These eyes seemed to be looking at her with such contempt under the high forehead and dishevelled hair that she turned away to glance again at Callaghan.

Their silence had lasted several minutes. It was a relief to her that he showed no signs of breaking it. There was a kind of weary content in inhabiting this room with him. She turned her eyes slowly back to the wall above the mantelpiece as if to defy the fierce, dishevelled boy. Then she noticed a third, very small picture, pinned up askew behind one of the bottles. It was so dusty and curled at the edges that she could only make out the blotches of crude red. It might have been an old Christmas card. She wondered with a pang of jealousy why he kept it.

"Well, my dear, have you taken in my surroundings? It's not a place I'd have wished you to see. But what could I do when I find you wandering like a lost soul almost on my doorstep?"

She was calm now, as if the weight of her heart kept her steady. He looked across at her, questioning. She looked back, taking in his weary eyes, his air of shabbiness and dissipation; trying to read his expression in which she seemed to make out bewilderment, triumph and anger. They stared at each other for a long time till she dropped her aching lids. She had seen all she needed to see: she had no more illusions. Everything confirmed what she had suspected ever since her return from Paget's Fold four months ago. There was no humiliation, no misery she would not accept simply to be with Reynaud Callaghan.

She said, quietly and reasonably, as if she were giving evidence.

"I had no idea of coming here. I was walking without thinking where I was going. I didn't know I was in your street till I looked up and saw the name. Then I meant to turn back. But it was too late."

"How did you come to be walking in any street on a morning like this. You're not the sort of a woman that wanders about in an east wind for the pleasure of it."

"I had to get out of the house. Something rather horrible had happened."

As she spoke, she felt as if she were lying. The scene with Claude had become so remote and unimportant that she could not remember the details. She looked down, confused, and saw the letter she had written to Clara in such a passion of tenderness sticking out of her bag. She realised that she had forgotten all about Clara's misery. Nothing mattered but the fact that she was here in this room with Callaghan.

He asked:

"A quarrel, do you mean? You and Claude?"

"He lost all control of himself. He was cruel and unjust."

"And why was he so angry?"

"Because of a letter. He ..."

Callaghan interrupted sharply:

"Something to do with you and me?"

"No."

"Thank God for that. I was afraid maybe ..."

"You needn't be afraid," she said, sharp in turn.

"You know Claude and I see each other now and then?"

"Yes. He talks about you. He admires you."

"The more fool he. I had a morbid fancy to make his acquaintance. I came almost to like him. He's by no means so dull a dog as I once hoped. And he's a decent man, a generous man."

Isabel said bitterly:

"He was neither decent nor generous this morning."

"What man is when he's enraged with a woman?"

"Even with his own daughter?"

"A daughter's worse than a wife. You can't work off your rage by making love with her."

"What an appalling thing to say."

"I'm sorry. I forgot you had romantic notions about human beings."

She sat silent and wounded.

"I've a genius for hurting you, haven't I, Isabel?"

She said very low:

"It doesn't matter."

He sighed and frowned.

"I've a terrible head on me this morning. I can't think straight. What were you saying about a daughter? I didn't know you had one."

"I told you I had. I told you that day."

"Maybe you did. It's not the kind of thing I'd remember." He stared into the empty tumbler and threw it on the floor. "I'm sorry, my dear. I can't concentrate on anything, even you, without a drink. And they're not open yet."

He lit a cigarette and began to smoke in quick, nervous puffs.

"I'd better go," said Isabel, making a weak movement towards her muff and handbag. Her lips had begun to quiver again.

He dropped his cigarette and stood up.

"No, no. I'm a swine, but don't leave me like that. And don't begin to weep again for I can't bear it." He stood up and began to move towards her. "Talk, talk, talk ... that's all that you and I have ever done. What's the use of all this welter of words?"

She said: "No ... stay over there" with such agitation that he sank down on the bed again and looked at her with a trace of his old smile. He picked up his cigarette. He had lit it badly and it was drawing on one side only so that the ash fell on his coat collar. "My dear, I'm beginning to wonder if you haven't a drop of Irish in you somewhere. You fall on a man's neck in the open street but you won't let him within range of you inside four walls. I'm almost suspecting it's the first time you've been in a man's room."

"Yes."

"I believe you. Yet that's not how you struck me the first time I set eyes on you. What kind of a woman are you?"

"How should I know? A bad one, I suppose."

"It's ironical, you'll admit. Here we are, alone together for the first time—in a room like a pigstye—you looking like Niobe with her hat awry and me with the spleen and a hangover. Winter Comforts ... d'you remember."

She managed to smile.

"Of course."

He turned his head away so that she saw it at just the angle she had seen it at a particular moment in the Dutch Garden. The reminder was so sharp that she could almost feel the sun on her neck and hear the drip of the lead tanks.

"Well, it's winter all right," he said morosely. "And precious little comfort I'm being to you."

They looked at each other once more and Isabel had the strangest sense that they had been together for years. When she spoke again, it was almost with the practical anxiety of a wife—

"Reynaud, what's this about your leaving St Mark's?"

"They've chucked me out, that's all."

"But why?"

"General behaviour prejudicial to discipline. In other words, drunk and disorderly." He waved his cigarette stub at Verlaine "I'm no more cut out for an usher than he was."

"Where will you go?"

"God knows. Out of this bloody country if possible. Ireland, maybe. I might even enlist. They give you free board and lodging. Not to mention burial."

She clasped her hands.

"Oh, no ... no."

"Why not? You could divert some of those belly bands and Bala-
clavas to me. After all, they owe me a shillingsworth."

"Have you no money at all?"

"My end of term salary will just about meet my arrears of rent and
my chits at 'The Three Kings'. They may give me a term's money in
lieu of notice. I doubt it."

She said fiercely, "If only I had anything of my own."

"Why? Claude provides for you doesn't he?"

"Yes. But I have to ask for every penny."

"Then be thankful you haven't a taste for whisky at twelve and six
a bottle."

"Are you deliberately trying to hurt me?"

He smiled at her.

"Aren't we merely discussing money in the abstract?"

"You know very well we're not."

"What's on your mind, Isabel?"

She said, without looking at him:

"If there were anything in the world I could do. Anything at all."

"Not just money?"

"Not just money," she said in a dry voice.

He considered her long and closely.

"What do you mean? Or believe you mean?"

"Do I have to say it?"

He lowered his head and rested his chin on his hands.

"I'm no good to you, Isabel. You frighten me, as a young girl would.
You look old today. The first time I've ever seen you do so. It only
brings home to me how much of a child you are, how much I'd hurt
you. I'd hate myself for hurting you and you for being hurt."

"I'm prepared for that," she said. "I would deserve to be hurt. Clara
wouldn't miss me. But Claude ..."

"You're not seriously suggesting leaving Claude."

"What else?" she said proudly. "You don't think I'd consider it any
other way?"

He stared at her.

"Leave all and follow me. ... Is that it? I don't know whether to
laugh or weep. Have you any idea of what you'd be committing yourself to? Have you ever lived in a room like this? The two of us together,
we'd be lucky to get as good. I ask you, have you ever so much as
seen a man in drink?"

"Yes."

"How long ago?"

She answered at once.

"Eighteen years."

"And you were so revolted that you've never been able to forget it."

"The man wasn't you."

"Isabel, Isabel. You're crazy, but you're superb. You can thank your guardian angel that I was drunk myself last night and I'm feeling the consequences. Otherwise ..." He snatched another cigarette and lit it. She noticed how his hand shook. "But it wouldn't do, my dear, it wouldn't do. It wouldn't be an *embarquement pour Cythère* at all. It would be my father and mother all over again."

She said quietly:

"At least there would be no children."

"Are you telling me you've thought the whole thing out? In a moment I'll believe you came here deliberately ... that your weeping and wandering were all play-acting. Is that it?"

"I thought nothing out. I've told you nothing but the truth."

"I can't fathom you at all. I doubt if I could even if I had the use of my head. I called you crazy just now. Yet you speak as if you were in your right mind."

"I am, Reynaud. Perhaps for the first time in my life."

They exchanged a long, almost impersonal look. It was Callaghan who looked away first.

He said heavily:

"No, my dear, no. Go home and forget me."

"Forget! That's an insult."

"It wasn't meant so. I'm thinking of you."

"Men always say that."

"Och, let's not quarrel. I won't deny I'm thinking of myself too. But it's the truth that I'm concerned for you. If you knew me at all, you'd know the fact that I'm trying to be honest with you means more than a lot of sweet words about love. I'm in no mood even for the thought of love at this moment, as you can see. But tonight, when I've a little drink in me again, I'll be cursing myself for letting you go. For don't think I haven't wanted you all these months."

Her heart turned over with misery. She drew a fierce gulp of breath like a drowning person coming to the surface. They sat for some moments in silence. Then, with an effort she had not believed herself capable of making, she stood up.

"I'm going now."

He came slowly over to her and put both his hands on her shoulders. At that, her eyes which had been as dry as sand suddenly filled up and the tears ran down her cheeks without a sob.

"Oh, Isabel."

He laid his unshaven cheek against her wet one. Then he lifted his head and looked into her streaming eyes. His face was blurred by her tears: she smelt the whisky on his breath as they exchanged their only kiss.

As they drew apart, she forced herself to smile at him.

"Don't do that," he said roughly. "It's worse by far than when you cry." She saw that there were tears in his eyes.

"Ah, no ... no," she said and turned away her face to encounter the cold stare of the boy pinned up beside Verlaine. To avoid it, she glanced beyond, looking for something, anything to distract her from her pain. She was like someone slipping helplessly down a cliff face, impatient, now that hope was gone, for the final drop yet clutching at any cranny. Suddenly it became of enormous importance to know what was painted on the crumpled card behind the whisky bottle. She would never be in this room again. In a moment she would have lost her last chance to find out. Straining her eyes she saw that it was a tawdry holy picture of the Sacred Heart.

"Of all things—to find that *here*."

He followed her look.

"Are you shocked?"

She did not dare admit that she was.

"I thought ... you didn't believe in all that."

"I'm Irish enough to go a long way before I'll put a holy picture in the dustbin."

"It seems ... well ... superstitious to me. I suppose because I wasn't brought up a Catholic."

"*Does* your faith mean anything to you, Isabel?"

"I'm a wretchedly bad Catholic. I know that. But it does mean something. It was one of the things I was prepared to give up."

"Had it occurred to you it mightn't give you up? Do you think, just because you're a convert, you can drop it like a dress you're tired of? You're wrong, my girl."

"Haven't you dropped it yourself?"

"I've dropped the practice all right. As to the rest ... don't ask me. All I know for certain is that it would have been one more torment between us."

He pulled her veil down over her face.

"Now go, my dear. We'll do no good by talking. I've not much resolution. There ... now I'll think of you as having taken the veil."

"I'm not like her—She was lucky. Did she give you that picture?"

"She did."

Isabel said, with sudden hysteria:

"That's why you kept it. Nothing to do with religion. Oh, you are hateful."

He said quietly.

"I'm more hateful to myself than I can ever be to you."

"Reynaud, forgive me—I don't know any more what I'm saying."

"Will you take the picture yourself? As a token?"

"No, no I couldn't!"

He smiled.

"Not even to relieve me of the responsibility of it? As you say, it's out of place."

She shook her head.

"As you wish—Will you pray for me now and then if you've a mind to?"

She sighed.

"Is there nothing you don't mock at?"

He touched her shoulder.

"I'm not mocking at all. I believed you when you said you'd do anything in the world. Well, that's what I'm asking you. Will you do that?"

She looked into his eyes and nodded.

"If you want me to. ... But my prayers ... what good could they do? Wouldn't they be almost ... blasphemy?"

He gave her a strange, slow smile.

"I think not, my dear. I couldn't pray for myself even if I wanted to. I'm too proud. But you're humble. Did you know that? Now go."

Chapter 4

ALL the way to St Mark's Claude's fury possessed him as completely as his grief had done on the day of his father's death. Every resentment he had ever felt against Clara surged up violently. It seemed to him that all her life she had done nothing but frustrate him. It came over him with force how much he had come to hope, without realising it, from her going to Maryhall.

His first doubts had been dispelled by a letter from Mother Lovell praising his wisdom in allowing Clara to have some months in the 'ideal Catholic atmosphere' of the Cressetts. Her own letters had built up a picture for him of a way of life he could never know himself but which was everything he had wanted for her. Lady Cressett had written saying how fond she was of Clara and how she hoped that she would often come to Maryhall when she was no longer Charles's governess. He had begun to dream of her marrying some young Catholic squire and having a country house of her own. Since he could never have a son, he had begun to look forward to the idea of a grandson. Now Clara had disgraced herself and destroyed the whole fabric of his dream. If Charles Cressett had been that grandson, he could hardly have felt more bitterly towards her.

When he arrived at the school, he was shaking all over. He could not control himself: he was in terror of how he might behave in front of his form. His rages in the classroom were merely for dramatic effect; none of his pupils had seen the real thing. During school prayers he went into the cloakroom and splashed his head and wrists with cold water to try and sober himself. He was calmer, but still trembling, as he snatched his gown from the peg and walked up the stone passage adorned with dusty plaster casts. Apollo and Antinoüs, Caesar and Socrates stared at him from blind sockets. The familiar smell of the school; ink, chalk, men's old clothes and mildewed books soothed him a little. By the time he turned the handle of his form-room door and heard the muffled stamping as the boys stood up, he had mastered himself. That morning he gave his lessons with unusual patience.

Back in the Common Room his anger began to throb again. Someone said to him: "That rotter Callaghan hasn't turned up again this morning. I had to take Lower French. I hear Cavell's sacking him at the end of term. High time too." Callaghan's absence was an added irritation. As he hung up his gown, it struck him that Callaghan was the only person whose company he could have endured that morning.

He walked home slowly for once, loathing the prospect of Valetta Road. If it had not been unprecedented, he would have lunched out. He was actually on the point of telephoning when he remembered that he must take a firm line with Isabel. After their conversation in the bedroom he could no longer trust her. He was filled with bitterness against her, too. She had not even attempted to see his point of view; he would force her to realise what he was suffering.

When he got home, he was exasperated to find that she had not yet come in. His mother, for once, was lunching out. There was no one to sympathise with him; no one on whom to vent his anger.

Zillah, seeing his thunderous face, said:

"I'll bring your lunch up at once, Sir. I'm sure the mistress won't be long."

"Did she mention she was going to be late?"

"No, Sir. She went out very early, before Cook had time to give her the shopping list."

"I'll wait."

He waited twenty minutes. He almost forgot his fury with Clara in his new grievance against Isabel. Had she defied him and done something idiotic, such as going up to Worcester? The third time Zillah suggested bringing his lunch he spoke so roughly to her that she did not return. At last he heard the front door bell. The fact that Isabel must have forgotten her latchkey was a final, absurd irritation. He stamped down the passage, wrenched upon the door, tight-lipped with rage, to find himself glaring into the frightened eyes of Patsy Cohen.

"Mr Batchelor ... I'm so terribly sorry ... I didn't want to disturb you ..."

"Who do you want to see, Patricia?"

"You," she stammered. "I'll come back later ... I didn't want to interrupt your lunch."

"I haven't begun my lunch. My wife has not returned yet. What do you want to see me about? Is it urgent?"

"Yes, but ..."

He had never seen Patsy pale before. It entirely altered her appearance. "You'd better come in," he said harshly.

He hustled her along the passage into his study and shut the door.

"Sit down," he commanded, almost pushing her into the great faded green armchair. She collapsed into it; her tiny body in the fur coat almost lost in its depths; her slim silk legs sticking out in front of her like a doll's.

"Well, what is it?"

She could not speak at first. She ran her tongue once or twice over her lips. Against her unusual pallor they looked brighter than ever. At last she brought out:

"It's Clara. We had a letter. We're so terribly sorry for you all."

"Do you mean to say she's told you about this appalling business? I'm surprised she should be so anxious to spread the news."

"She's so frightfully upset."

He said grimly: "So she should be."

Patsy was trembling but she went on:

"I know how frightfully upset you must be too. But please, oh please don't be angry with her. She's so afraid you will be. She keeps saying it was her fault. But I'm sure it wasn't."

"I'm afraid I disagree."

"But her letter ... Marmee said she'd never seen anything so pathetic. It was absolutely unlike Clara. You could hardly read the writing even. Surely you realise ..."

"Realise what?"

She just doesn't know what she's saying. The shock must have done something to her brain. She's got the most dreadful ideas. That she's disgraced you ..."

"She has disgraced us all."

"I'm sure it wasn't her fault," wailed Patsy. "I'm sure Mrs Batchelor knows it wasn't."

"No doubt you mean well, Patricia. I should have had more respect for Clara if she hadn't sent you to get round me."

"She didn't. She didn't." Patsy was on the edge of tears. "I came of my own accord. I wish I hadn't. I never dreamt ... you were always so kind."

"You flatter me," he said, with a savage smile. He stood over her, with his hands in his pockets, glaring down at her. After a moment Patsy said in a shaky voice:

"I know you've had a fearful shock. I expect you're not yourself any more than she is. I'd better go."

"No, stay, Patricia. There are one or two things I have to say on this subject."

"Yes?"

"No doubt Clara has always described me as a brutal father?"

"Oh, *no*," said Patsy, gripping the arms of the chair. "Never. She adores you. Can't you see that's why she's in such a state? She just doesn't know how to face you. She feels you'll never trust her again."

"She is perfectly right. As for this affection you speak of, I can't say I have seen many signs of it."

"Clara finds it awfully hard to say what she feels."

"Really? My own impression is that she feels remarkably little."

"That's not true. I *know* it isn't. She's just one of those people who bottle everything up."

"So you know my daughter better than I do?"

A little colour came into Patsy's cheeks.

"Perhaps I do in some ways. After all she's my best friend. She's just the opposite of me. I blurt everything out. I expect it's just because I'm shallow."

He considered her, sitting there like some bright-eyed, smooth-furred animal.

"Shallow, are you Patsy?"

He took a deep breath and said in a less bitter voice: "I think you don't understand the situation. But you've stood up pluckily for your friend. Loyalty's a rare thing. I can never be quite indifferent to it, however mistaken."

Patsy blinked away her tears.

"I know I'm a little fool. But I'm awfully fond of Clara. And I know you are too, whatever you say."

He said nothing, but continued to stare at her. Her eyes, still wet, were more brilliant than ever and the long lashes had caked into points so that they seemed framed in soft black thorns. At last he gave her a wry smile.

"Men are rather partial to little fools when they happen to be remarkably pretty."

She bit her coral-coloured lower lip that was a trifle swollen from crying, but did not answer.

"I'd like to ask you a question," he went on.

She whispered: "Yes?"

"You like men, don't you?"

"Yes, of course."

"You'll probably get married one of these days. Suppose you had a son. And suppose that son were killed through someone's criminal carelessness. How would you feel then?"

"I'd feel awful of course. But I do believe I'd be a bit sorry for the person. Think what they'd be feeling."

"I'm afraid I can only think of one thing at this moment: what that boy's parents must be going through."

... "You keep talking as if she'd done it deliberately."

"Deliberately or not, what does it matter? The boy's dead."

"It's awful I know. But surely, surely. ... Suppose it had been Clara herself."

"Let's stick to facts," he said, almost wearily. He shook his head and sighed. "As if there weren't enough slaughter in your generation. This boy was young enough to have survived it."

Patsy regained a little confidence.

"I expect I sounded rather heartless—I didn't mean to—It's just that one's got so used to people being killed suddenly."

He considered her for some moments without speaking. His harsh expression relaxed but something in his face made her uneasy—

"Young men you know ... friends of yours ... have been killed, have they Patsy?"

"Yes. Several."

Again he considered her. When he spoke again his voice was low, almost confiding—

"You said just now that you liked men. Evidently men like you, too. Are you kind to them ... the boys who go out there?"

Nervous again, but in a different way, she drew herself further into the chair and asked:

"What do you mean?"

He said, still more softly:

"You know very well what I mean. Or do you think I am too old to understand or ... or ..."

Suddenly he swooped down and grasped one of her silken ankles, muttering in a thick voice:

"You're made to attract, aren't you? Made to make people forget?"

He fell on his knees and leant over her, his face close to hers.

"Please don't—*please*."

"You're not frightened of me *now*, are you, Patsy?"

She wished frantically that he would be cold and angry again. His face was so near her own that it was out of focus. His breath, smelling of tobacco, came in gusts against her cheek. She drew as far back as she could, pressing her head against the chair so that a little fold formed under her soft chin.

He pulled her fur coat open and kissed her neck, almost groaning: "So white, so soft."

She was trying to push him away when she heard the front door open. In a moment he was on his feet again. His face was convulsed. She watched him force it back, with a fearful play of muscle, into a face that she could recognise.

"My wife," he said.

He looked suddenly so old and unhappy that her revulsion turned to pity.

She whispered.

"I understand. I do understand. I won't remember."

He turned to her blindly and seemed about to speak but said nothing. Instead, with an astonishingly swift movement he dropped on one knee and kissed her shoe. The next moment he was opening the door. She recovered herself enough to murmur: "Clara. Promise you won't be too hard on Clara," before he had gone. She heard light steps in the passage, then his voice, saying humbly:

"Ah, there you are, my dear. I was getting anxious."

Even through her numbness, Isabel noticed the change in Claude's voice since she had last heard it. She stood in the dark hall waiting for him to question her. He merely asked solicitously if she had had anything to eat.

"I don't want anything—I'll go straight up to my room. I'm rather tired."

"Can you wait one moment?" he implored. "There's something I must say to you before I go back to school. It's almost time I left."

He led her into the dining-room and shut the door. She stared at the bleak white tablecloth and the undisturbed knives and forks and said:

"You haven't had your lunch. Why?"

"Like you, I'm not hungry. But sit down. You look exhausted."

"Can't we go into the study?"

"There's someone in there."

Some constraint in his voice made her look at him for the first time.

"Claude—you look ill. You've not had any more bad news?"

"No, no, my dear. But it's about Clara that I wanted to speak."

There was a sound of light footsteps in the passage: then the front door softly closed.

"Whoever it was has gone," said Isabel. "Do let's sit in the study. I really can't bear this room."

He glanced at the black marble clock.

"I'm late as it is. This won't take a moment."

Then he saw that she was shivering.

"What a brute I am. Come along: it's warmer in there."

He took her into the study and seated her in the great green chair while he poked up the fire. Isabel, trying desperately to drag herself back to the present, said:

"This chair's warm. Do your pupils usually sit in it?"

Stooping over the fire, with his back to her, he answered:

"It wasn't a pupil. It was Patricia Cohen."

"Whatever was she doing here?"

"She wanted to see me. She had had a letter from Clara."

Isabel felt a stab of jealousy which brought back her old pain and made the present all too real. Far from obliterating the new one, it made it sharper still.

She said bitterly:

"So she could write to *Patsy*. But not a word to me."

Claude turned and faced her, stammering:

"But my dear ... my dear. That other letter ... Obviously meant for both of us."

"I read it. You forget that. I wasn't so much as mentioned."

"The child didn't know what she was writing. You said so yourself—you said ..."

"You didn't believe me, did you?" she broke in passionately. "I was the one who tried to find excuses for Clara. You wouldn't listen. You were unjust ... more than unjust...heartless. And now ..."

"I know, Isabel," he said wearily. "You don't have to tell me. I realise it now. Can you ever forgive me?"

His face was so wrung with misery that she could not help pitying him. But standing over her, looking so abject, he filled her with distaste, almost contempt.

"This is rather a violent change, isn't it? Is Patsy Cohen responsible for it?"

He winced.

Isabel went on ruthlessly:

"Clara should be extremely grateful to Patsy. She's done what her own mother so utterly failed to do."

"Isabel ... please. I deserve every hard thing you can say ... and more. Can't you accept the fact that I've seen that I was wrong and you were right?"

"It hardly seems to matter now."

He sighed. "Not to you perhaps. But it is going to matter to Clara."

She said coldly: "Did you write her that letter? The one you suggested this morning?"

"Thank God, no. Isabel ... if you knew how I loathed myself."

He sounded so wretched that she softened a little.

"Well, what do you propose to do?"

"I leave it all to you. I will go absolutely by what you say. One of us must write at once. Or should we send a telegram?"

"I wrote her a note," said Isabel. Then she frowned and added as if to herself, "Yes. I did post it after all."

"Thank God, again. Oh, my dear, where would I be without you? Where would Clara be?"

"It won't mean anything to Clara," she said. "Naturally, I couldn't speak for you. So it won't mean anything at all."

"I implore you ... Isabel. If Clara realised what a father she has ... I don't deserve to have a daughter—I don't deserve either of you."

His face and voice were full of such despair that for the first time she felt guilty. She said slowly:

"You're being too hard on yourself. Don't people—sometimes— say things ... do things ... that no one would expect them to do? Things they didn't know they were capable of themselves?"

He muttered "Yes ... yes, indeed."

"Clara doesn't know. She won't ever know. So she can't be hurt."

"You're too good to me."

He leant forward and caught her hands, snatched them up as if to kiss them, then let them go. "No. I'm not fit to touch you."

She leant back in the chair, pushing her hat askew.

"I'm not good," she said wearily. "We'd better be practical, hadn't we? About Clara, I mean."

He said humbly:

"Will you help me? I can see how worn out you are—that's all my fault too—But I have to get back to my grindstone ... I shan't have a moment before the country post. ..."

"You want me to write another letter?"

"I hardly dare to ask you—But you would know how to put it ... to say how sorry I am for what she's been through ... that, of course, I'll write myself tonight."

"Yes." She stood up. "I'll do it now. Then I must get some rest. I'm terribly tired. Zillah can post it."

"My poor girl. You should never have gone out at all on a morning like this. I've been so full of my own concerns I've not so much as asked you where you have been all this time."

"Nowhere in particular."

He put his hands on her shoulders and she gave an involuntary slight start.

"You've been nearly driven out of your mind. How can you ever forgive me for all I've made you suffer?"

She forced herself to look at him and the two pairs of tired eyes considered and questioned, each aware of something unspoken in the other.

Claude said at last:

"She will be all right. At that age ... one can recover from what seems unendurable."

She gave him the faintest smile ... "At that age—Yes."

Suddenly, he took her in his arms.

"Oh, my dearest. I thought you would never smile at me again."

Chapter 5

IT was two days since Charles's death. Clara and Lady Cressett walked in silence along the border of the lake at Crickleham. There was neither sun nor wind: the air was damp and cold. By the water the bushes were knee-deep in fog; the statue of a nymph stood as if on a cloud among the dripping laurels. They seemed to be walking in a dream. Clara had no more tears; only utter desolation. She was no longer even afraid. Nothing mattered any more. It would have been a consolation to walk like this for ever, never to have to speak again.

"The boy is with God," said his mother at last. The words came as a shock to Clara. She had not been able to comfort herself with the thought that Charles was in heaven.

"Yes," she murmured. Then as the pain began once more to stir under the numbness. "How can you even bear to speak to me?"

"Clara, you must stop blaming yourself. It couldn't have happened if it hadn't been God's will."

"I can't believe that God *could* want …" she said. Her voice sounded loud as a blasphemy in the stillness.

"No. Everything that happens. Everything," Lady Cressett's voice was dry from weariness. "We don't understand. We don't see why. We can only pray."

"I've tried to pray," said Clara. "I can't. Nothing seems real."

They spoke at long intervals. Clara watched her own shoes moving over the gravel and the dead leaves.

"God wanted the boy," Lady Cressett said. "He took him while he was innocent."

Clara noticed that for all her calm she could not bring herself to say Charles's name. She muttered:

"What you've been through … I daren't think. If only you'd be angry with me."

"I have been angry," said Lady Cressett. "I couldn't control it … the feeling. I could only try not to will it. You weren't to blame. Or no more than the rest of us. When I was able to think of anything besides myself, I knew you must be suffering even more." Clara glanced for the first time at her face. It was haggard and twitching and there were red veins in the eyeballs.

"You're so much too good to me," she said wretchedly.

"You're very young. The first terrible thing that happens to us ... we just don't understand it. Clara, I don't want to hurt you. But there are one or two things I feel I must try and say."

"Yes," said Clara, feeling her cowardly heart sink.

"Archie came to Maryhall last night as you know."

"Yes."

"Remember, I believe everything that Archie said. That's a very brave young man, Clara. I just want to know ... it did happen as he said ... didn't it? You tried to stop ..."

"But so did Archie. So did Archie. If he's blamed himself, it's not true. We were both there."

"Yes, he said that. But other people ... you understand, Clara?"

"I don't care what they do. I wish they'd put me in prison."

"There's no question of that, Clara. But, you must face it, they may say something harsh at the inquest. That will hurt. I know you don't deserve it. But Nan will be a witness. She has tried to convince his father. I am sure for your own sake you would rather not see Maryhall again just now. But in any case ... my husband, well, you understand?"

"Yes," said Clara, with dry lips.

"I packed your things. I've brought them with me in the car."

"*You* packed them?"

"Yes. I know what Nan did. I don't listen to what she says. Can you forgive her, Clara?"

"Yes."

"That is very good. You were always generous. But ... and I'm afraid I have to say this ... apt to be reckless sometimes. Perhaps you can guess what I found when I was packing your clothes. It was empty, yes. But it should never have been in your possession. Anyone in charge of a child ..."

"Archie's revolver," said Clara, almost in a whisper. "I'd forgotten it. Truly, truly I never wanted to take it. I begged him not to give it me."

"I'm sure you did. But you have enough influence over Archie to have been firm. If I hadn't been the one who found it and if it had come out at the inquest ... well, I don't think I need say any more. It's with your other things. No one knows but the two of us."

Clara broke out:

"Oh, why do you try to let me off? I deserve to be punished."

"I am very fond of you Clara. I know how you loved him. Then there are others who are fond of you, to be thought of. Your father and mother. And Archie.

"Yes."

"If you have heard how he spoke of you, how he stood up for you."

"He was so good to me that day. I can't ever forget."

"It's quite likely he saved your life, Clara. Nan must have been quite beside herself. She is very strong."

"I almost wish she had killed me. I do wish it."

For the first time there was anger in Lady Cressett's voice.

"That is wrong, Clara. But I'm sure you don't really mean it. You can't realise what you're saying. Think of Nan having to live all her life with *that* on her conscience."

They walked in silence again. Then Clara said:

"Always the same. I think of no one but myself. Why should you, why should anyone care what happens to me?"

After a pause Lady Cressett said: "Archie's not what one would normally call a strong character. But all this, the really splendid way he came out, made me realise something."

"What was that?"

"That if there were someone in his life he really cared for, he might be very different."

Clara said hesitantly "Yesterday he ... he asked me to marry him. And I said no."

"Was that because you couldn't think of anything like marriage just now? When these sad days are over ... for we do get peace, Clara, even after what seems unbearable at the time ... mightn't you think again?"

"Oh, I don't know, I don't know," she sighed. "I can't even imagine the future."

"You must make an effort one day. It's hard now, I know. But I have thought about you so much. There's all your life ahead."

Clara said in a choked voice: "I would give it all up—all. Just to know that he ... Oh, why couldn't it have been me?"

"I know, Clara, I know," Lady Cressett spoke very quietly. "But we have to go on living as long as God wishes us to. Our lives aren't our own to dispose of."

"What ought I to do with mine?" said Clara, desperately. "I've been utterly selfish, utterly useless. Always. There's something that haunts me, something I've always been terrified I ought to do. I've shut my ears. I was so afraid *that* was what God wanted."

"Do you mean become a nun?"

"Yes. How did you know?"

"Wouldn't it be likely to be the first thing you'd think after a blow like this."

"Then you see what I mean? What's the use of feeling sorry? I want to *prove* I'm sorry. I want to be punished."

For the first time Lady Cressett smiled.

"The old Clara, all or nothing. Have you ever had the idea of becoming a nun before?"

"Yes. Because it was the one thing in the whole world I was most frightened of. So I thought God must want it."

"Then you must have wrong ideas of God. God is not a harsh father, expecting us to do impossible things against the grain of our natures. Hard things, ah yes, often. But even those, out of love, not out of fear."

Clara asked anxiously:

"Do you truly think I haven't a vocation? That I oughtn't to try?"

"Try by all means. But I don't think any Superior in her senses would take you if you tell her what you've just told me. As to having a vocation, of course you have one. We all have. Vocation is only a name for God's will for us. And so often it is nothing spectacular; just the ordinary duties of life as they come along. For most women, marriage."

"I can't imagine marrying."

"How often you've said that. All girls do."

"Don't you see?" said Clara desperately. "Less than ever now. I'm not fit."

"You're being morbid. That's what I most feared. That you would turn in on yourself. Can't you see, Clara, that this is just another form of selfishness? God never sends us suffering, even the bitterest without a reason. Isn't he perhaps giving you a great opportunity now, the chance of really devoting yourself to making someone else happy?"

After a long pause, Clara asked: "You think I should have said Yes?"

"My dear, that's not for me to say. It is something for you to think about and pray about. All I know is that you and Archie have been brought together in a very strange and tragic way. Archie isn't a very happy person, as you know. There's so much latent good in him but he might so easily go to the bad. His mother worries herself sick about him sometimes. He's never cared for a girl before. The two of you might bring out the best in each other. There would be a home and children and best of all, the bond of both being Catholics. Don't think I'm trying to influence you, Clara. I've no right to do that. I'm only suggesting that you should weigh all this up very carefully and try to find out whether that might perhaps be God's way for you."

When Lady Cressett had gone, Clara walked for another hour in the park thinking over this conversation. Yesterday, when Archie had asked her to marry him, she had been almost too dazed to take it in. All that she remembered sharply was the misery of his face when she had refused him. Yesterday there had been no past and no future; everything was blotted out by the huge fact that Charles was dead. She had written incoherent letters to her father and to Patsy; she could not remember a single sentence of either. But now, since she had seen Lady Cressett, the torn edges of her life had begun to come together again. It was at once a relief and a new suffering; the future stretched blankly ahead, thousands and thousands of days when she must get up, wash, dress, eat, fill up the day, go to bed. Suddenly she realised that by now her father must have got her letter. In less than a week she would be at home again. At the thought, her heart almost stopped. The thought of home was like going back to prison. Never again would he trust her, never again would she be allowed to escape. And she would be utterly alone. There would be no one who had ever seen Charles, no one who knew what she had felt and lived through the last two days. She wandered aimlessly along the misty alleys, losing herself, finding herself back at the tree or the stone bench she had passed a few minutes before. Soon she found she was completely lost. She stood hesitating not knowing which direction to take. Then, in the muffled silence, she heard a faint metallic clashing and whirring. She followed the sound and found herself in the rock garden where she had gone that first day at Crickleham with Archie. He was there, crouching over his miniature railway, absorbed and forlorn. He did not hear her at first; then, just as she was moving away, he looked up with a start, clutching a toy engine in each hand, and turned red.

"I say, old thing. What a swine you must think me. The fact is ... I just had to do something to take my mind off, well, everything."

"I don't think you a swine at all," she said. "I know just how you feel."

"You were absolutely right, Clara. Now you see just the sort of fool I am. I don't know how I ever dared," he said, wretchedly. "I suppose it was somehow thinking we were in it together that gave me the nerve. Just forget it."

"Do you want me to?"

"Of course. I've been awake all night thinking what a bloody fool I was to think for one moment that you ... Oh, Clara," he threw the engines down and turned his tired, unhappy face away.

"Archie."

"You don't need to do any explaining."

"Archie, would it make a lot of difference to you if I'd said yes?"

"Oh God, don't torture a fellow. Difference!"

She went up to him, took his head in her hands and turned it towards her. At first he only stared at her blindly. Then, as he took in what she meant, she forgot everything else in the sight of his transfigured face. For the first time in her life, for one moment, she had made another person completely happy.

PART SEVEN

Chapter 1

CLARA travelled back to London the day after the inquest. It had been even more horrible than she had feared. She had steeled herself in advance for the questions she would be asked: the comments that might be made. What no one had prepared her for was the presence of Sir George Cressett. All through the ordeal she had been aware, not of the inquisitive or sympathetic eyes that kept glancing at her but of the pair that remained steadily averted. In spite of herself, she was constantly compelled to look at him, to verify each feature and to torment herself with his appalling likeness to Charles.

As she sat in the train, trying to obey Mrs Hughes-Follett's last words "Try and think only of the future, my dear', her still dazed mind kept reverting to the day before. Archie had been wonderful. If she were never to see him again, she would like to remember him as he had stood up in the court, straighter than she had ever seen him hold himself, going to such lengths to take all the blame that at one point the Coroner had said drily: "I might almost suppose this young man is trying to get himself indicted for manslaughter." Yet, touched and grateful as she was, all Archie's protectiveness had been no comfort to her. The only thing that had given her the strength to get through without breaking down were some words in her mother's writing on a sheet of paper she kept clutched in one hand. "Daddy sends you all his love and sympathy in your terrible trouble darling. He will be writing himself tonight."

She had that other letter with her now. It had arrived just before she left Crickleham. Yet, oddly enough, it was that first message in Isabel's writing that had meant the most. Perhaps because the reassurance had come when she most needed it, perhaps because all she had so desperately wanted to know was that he was not angry with her, his own letter, long and loving as it was, seemed almost as flat as the confirmation of a telegram.

Every station she passed seemed to put Charles's death further away in time as well as in space. The pain and horror were still there but they no longer made an impenetrable wall between her and ordinary life. As the train approached the outskirts of London, she began to think almost with pleasure of Valetta Road; even to imagine what it would be like to see Ruth and Patsy again. Then she realised that something, not the ache to which she was growing accustomed as one grows accustomed to the loss of a limb, was nagging her mind. How was her father going to take the news of her engagement? He must have got Mrs Hughes-Follett's letter by now. When Archie's mother had told her she was writing to her parents, Clara had hardly taken it in. She had been too dazed to connect her acceptance of Archie with anything that affected her father. Now she grasped that this might be an even worse shock to him than the other. Might it not seem one more proof of her utter heartlessness? He knew that Archie had been with her in the walled garden. He would suppose that they had been too occupied with each other to notice what Charles was doing. Suppose he were to remember the garden at Paget's Fold and his finding her with Blaze on the day of her grandfather's funeral.

The train was drawing into Paddington. She realised with horror that he might be on the platform to meet her. He had said he would, if he could get away from St Mark's in time. In a panic she pulled off the diamond ring Archie's mother had given him for her to wear and thrust it into her pocket.

As the train slowed down, she leapt up and looked out of the window, peering anxiously through the dusk. There were not many people waiting: she strained her eyes to pick out any man of her father's height and build. Then she saw her mother walking alone up the platform. Her relief was so great that she stumbled out of the still moving train and ran to her. In a moment she was in Isabel's arms, almost sobbing words she had never intended to say—

"Oh, Mummy ... I'm so awfully glad it was you."

In the business of dealing with her luggage, she had time to collect herself. Ashamed of her outburst, she sat stiffly beside Isabel in the taxi though she let her mother keep her arm through hers. They drove back to Valetta Road almost in silence. Isabel asked none of the questions she dreaded—she said little beyond how glad they were to have her home again.

There were two letters waiting for her in the hall, one from Ruth and the other from Patsy. She took them to her room, meaning to read them at once. But the sight of the room itself drove everything else out of her mind. How small and shabby it seemed after the rooms she had grown used to in the last months, yet how inexpressibly dear. There were her books and her few pictures, things for which she had once cared passionately and had now almost forgotten; there was the scratched desk where she had done her homework and even written poems. Without removing her hat and coat she began at once to pull open drawers and cupboards, identifying and rediscovering old possessions. In a few moments she was so much back in the past that she almost resented the few changes in the room; a chair in a different place, the new blue bedspread that had replaced the faded Indian cotton, even the vase of flowers on the dressing table. She had already reduced it to something like its old disorder when her mother tapped on the door saying:

"Your tea's getting cold, Clara. Come along. You must be starving."

Tea was laid by a blazing fire in the drawing-room: a magnificent tea with all her favourite cakes. She had the oddest sense of having awakened from a very long nightmare. For a few minutes she ate and drank in silence. Presently her mother said:

"You know, darling, you look better already. You looked so terribly white and ill at the station."

"I think I must be a little mad," said Clara. "All this ... do you know what it keeps reminding me of?"

"What, pet?"

"Coming home from Mount Hilary for the Christmas holidays. The first tea at home after a bad term."

Her mother smiled.

"At this moment, you don't look any older than you did at the convent. It's impossible to realise that ..."

Clara interrupted, frowning:

"I just can't fit things together yet. Something seems to have got jammed in my head. It's as if I were two people and one of them had never left here at all."

Isabel said gently:

"I know how you must feel. Don't try and think things out. Don't talk if you don't want to."

Something unfamiliar in the way her mother spoke made Clara look at her. It struck her that Isabel seemed older. It brought home to her the fact that she had been away. Was she merely noticing lines and shadows that had been there before but which one only perceives on a familiar face after long absence? Isabel looked as if she had been ill or suffered some painful experience. Then she guessed that this must be connected with her own. And at once her nagging preoccupation returned. She asked abruptly:

"Will Daddy be home soon?"

"Not for another half-hour. He was so disappointed not to be able to get away in time to meet you."

"Mother ... there's something I must ask you before he comes back. Has he ... have you both had a letter from Mrs Hughes-Follett?"

"Yes, darling. This morning."

"And he's read it?"

"Of course. We both have. I didn't say anything about it on purpose. I thought you'd rather wait till Daddy was home to talk about it."

"Is he angry?"

Isabel gave her a peculiar look and paused for a moment before answering:

"Angry? Why should you expect him to be angry? Naturally he was surprised. We both were. We hadn't been prepared for anything of the kind and you're so young."

Clara gave a sigh of relief.

"I was afraid Archie would be one more nail in my coffin."

Her mother smiled but her eyes remained troubled.

"Darling ... what a very strange way to think of the young man you're going to marry." Her face became serious again. "I've thought about nothing else all day ... trying to take in the idea that you're engaged ... or want to be. It isn't just that you're so very young. But you never gave us the least hint in your letters. You hardly mentioned this ... this Archie except as someone almost ... well ... absurd."

"He's been anything but absurd the last few days," said Clara defensively.

"Oh, my darling child," Isabel exclaimed. "I didn't mean to hurt you. I know how you hate showing your feelings. Forgive me ... I've been tactless and stupid. But I can't help being bewildered—the idea's so very new and strange."

"It's rather new and strange to me," Clara said.

"Yes. Of course," said Isabel almost absently. She seemed pre-occupied with some worrying thought. At last she said hesitantly:

"You must know that I'm longing to hear all about it ... about Archie, I mean. But not if you don't feel like it now."

"What did Mrs Hughes-Follett's letter say?"

"It was a very charming letter. I'd show it you, only Daddy took it to St Mark's with him. She must be a very nice woman."

"Yes. She was awfully kind to me. I stayed there, you know."

"I know, darling." As if fearful of coming too near the subject neither of them had mentioned, she asked at once what she looked like.

"She's not good-looking but she's always most exquisitely turned out and *soignée*. Just the exact opposite of Archie."

"Ah ... of course it's Archie I really want to hear about."

But here Clara had no glib description ready. She said haltingly. "Well ... he's tall. He's got red hair. And he's frightfully good at mechanical things. I've told you already he's awfully untidy. Oh, yes... he's got a rather wonderful singing voice—Really good enough for opera."

"Is he artistic, then? That should be right for you. You're so artistic yourself."

For the first time since Charles's death, Clara laughed.

"Oh, Mummy—Archie artistic! You can't possibly know how funny that is."

Isabel looked almost hurt but then she had to smile. Once Clara had begun to laugh, she could not stop at once.

"Well ... the only thing that matters is that he should make you happy. It's so lovely to hear you laugh again."

When Clara had recovered, she said:

"I'm no good at describing people. But Archie really is difficult. You see he doesn't seem in the least like anyone I've ever met."

Her mother said hopefully:

"That's because you're in love with him."

Clara frowned.

"But Archie *really* isn't like other people. Everyone admits it. Even his own mother."

"She said he'd never shown signs of caring for anyone before. And that he was absolutely devoted to you. She seems very fond of you, Clara."

"Yes. She seems frightfully pleased about the whole thing," said Clara with such detachment that Isabel looked thoughtful. She said after a pause:

"It seemed to mean a good deal to Daddy ... her being so obviously anxious to have you for her daughter-in-law. I was glad too ... but it seemed perfectly natural to me."

"I suppose ... well, they are an awfully old Catholic family. One of the oldest. And Archie's the heir."

"So is my family, the Maules, very old," said Isabel with a touch of sharpness. "And, like all old families, it must have been Catholic once."

"I know, Mother, I know. Only I mean ... those sort of people ... well they all live in big country houses and so on. And the Hughes-Follett's are quite alarmingly rich."

Isabel resumed her thoughtful look.

"All that, naturally, weighs with Daddy. Most of all, of course, the fact of their being Catholics."

"You sound as if *you* didn't approve of something."

"Don't misunderstand me, darling. Of course ... I should be delighted if you made what's called a brilliant marriage. But you're such a child ... not even eighteen. And his mother implies that you're thinking of getting married quite soon."

"There's no point in waiting, is there? I should have thought the sooner the better. I've made up my mind."

Isabel said almost harshly:

"Marriage isn't a thing to be rushed into, even these days. I know you'll say there's a war, that he'll be going to the front. But you've known each other such a short time. And marriage lasts for so long."

"Not always, nowadays."

"Clara ... darling ... don't even let yourself think about that."

"I didn't mean it about us. Archie's got a charmed life."

"Let's hope he has. But oh, darling, if you'd only wait a little—if you'd be engaged even for a year."

"I told you. I've made up my mind," said Clara stiffly.

Isabel stiffened, too.

"You're as obstinate as your father. I suppose you realise that you're too young to marry without our consent."

"Well, from what you say, it doesn't sound as if Daddy is going to object."

Isabel lost her self-control. She said bitterly:

"It never seems to occur to you that you have two parents."

But Clara was not attending. She had caught the click of her father's latchkey and was already half way to the door.

Chapter 2

CLAUDE had kept that evening clear of pupils and, after dinner, Isabel left him alone with Clara in the study. The subject of her engagement had been discussed between the three of them when he had returned from St Mark's. It seemed to Clara that it had gone almost too smoothly; there was something unnatural in the way he had glossed over all Isabel's hesitations. She found herself wishing that he would make some objection, however faint. She had never known him so compliant, so anxious to please her since she had returned home from Mount Hilary after that last summer term. Towards the end of the family conference, she and her mother had said almost nothing while he continued to talk about practical details with such enthusiasm that he might have been the person most deeply concerned in the whole affair.

"In all the circumstances ... it would be better to have a very quiet wedding. You would wish that, wouldn't you? Of course you will have a Nuptial Mass. The Oratory is not our parish church but I should so much like you to be married there. There was a priest I met there once who impressed me so much. I wish I could remember his name. I should so much like him to marry you. But only, of course, if you and Archie have no preference of your own."

To hear him talk of Archie only increased Clara's sense of unreality. She could not yet manage to connect Archie with her family or Crickleham with Valetta Road. She was almost appalled to see how much she had set in motion by a single gesture. He had asked her to put on her ring again.

"Even though their engagement will be private for the time being, I think she should wear it, don't you, Isabel? Certainly among the family. I will tell my mother not to broadcast the news just yet. But I may let Granny into the secret, mayn't I, Clara? It will give her such enormous pleasure. And, if I may say so, what a superb ring it is!"

At one point Clara had glanced at the heavy glittering stones that looked so out of place on her chapped, unmanicured hand and wished she had never seen them. For a moment they seemed nothing but an unwanted responsibility, like Archie's revolver.

Now that she was alone with her father for the first time since her return, Clara thought that he too looked older. Though his skin was still rosy and he held himself more stiffly upright than ever, there was an indefinable air of brittleness about him. She noticed too that, when he filled his pipe, he did so with slower, almost fumbling movements, unlike the quick ramming she remembered so well.

He turned to her with such a fond, happy face that she was obscurely disturbed.

"My dear ... I hardly know what to say to you. To think that ... after such tragedy ... this should be the outcome."

Once again she felt her old sense of inadequacy. She said lamely:

"You're really pleased about it then?"

"Pleased, my dear? Pleased is an understatement. This is one of the greatest moments in my life. I could almost say my *Nunc dimittis*—in perfect peace.

She looked at him, a little frightened by the strange elation in his face and voice. He said more soberly:

"I know your mother thinks I am being rather rash ... that I ought to insist on your waiting. And from every ordinary point of view, she would be perfectly right. But I cannot bring myself to look on this from the ordinary point of view. To me, it is like a dispensation ... I might almost say a direct answer to prayer."

She said faintly:

"It is all rather extraordinary, isn't it? I can't quite believe it myself."

"It must be difficult, I know. The shock of happiness after the terrible trial you've been through. I ... that is to say we, of course, have been so worried about you. Now you must think only of the future."

Clara said nothing. She was trying to attach some meaning to the words "shock of happiness".

He pulled at his pipe, staring in front of him at the bookcase filled with black files. Those files had been there ever since Clara could remember. How often she had read their neat labels ... "Responsions", "Little-Go", "Fair Copies G.P." and the mysterious one marked "Haec Olim" ... as she sat anxiously beside him while he scored her proses in red ink.

"Do I seem heartless," he said, "to talk only of this? My dear ... don't think I've forgotten the ... other thing. I know how deeply you have reproached yourself. I know you must still be very much affected by it. Your mother felt that there was some reserve ... that, even allowing for all you had been through ..." He hesitated and cleared his throat. "I said it was only ... and it does you credit, my dear ... that your own happiness was clouded by thinking of someone else's grief."

Clara could only make an incoherent sound.

"Don't think I want to reopen that wound. But there's just one thing I want to tell you. I haven't told your mother yet. I don't quite know why."

"What is it?"

"I had a letter from Lady Cressett this morning. A letter that touched me most profoundly. She must be a very wonderful woman ... almost a saint."

"Yes."

"She could rejoice in your happiness ... at a time like this. That made a very great impression on me. Perhaps you wonder ... I am sure your mother did ... why I asked so little about Archie. But I felt that if a woman like Lady Cressett who must know him very well ... and who so obviously has a real affection for you ... so evidently approves."

Clara stared at her ring.

"She does very much want us to marry—yes."

"But for that," he said, "I think I should have insisted on a much longer engagement. I could not have borne the idea that it might seem too sudden ... even callous ... to Lady Cressett. Now I see no reason why you should not be married, as you naturally want to be, before Archie goes to the front."

"He thinks it will be about three months—less perhaps."

"So soon?" He sighed. "You are both such children." He glanced involuntarily at the subalterns on the mantelpiece. "Please God ..."

Abruptly he stood and came over to her, clumsily smoothing back her hair.

"My dearest child," he said. "You've hardly so much as smiled this evening when you should have been so happy. Try and think of all the joy ahead. Such a wonderful new life beginning for you."

His face was so tender and sorrowful that she forced herself to smile. She said, speaking almost naturally:

"You know, Daddy ... I can't imagine it properly. It's been so restful coming back to my old one. Just at the moment, I feel quite content with that."

He kissed her.

"Oh, don't think I want to lose you. If you knew how I used to dread the very idea of your getting married."

He sat down in the great green chair then half rose again.

"My dear ... you should be sitting here. Whatever am I thinking of?"

"No, do relax for once, Daddy. Do you know, I've hardly ever seen you sitting in that chair."

"I used to at Cambridge. Somehow I never seem to have had much time to since."

"It's funny, isn't it? I might have gone to Cambridge myself."

"Yes. I wanted that so much once. I had such ambitions for you."

"I've always been a disappointment to you, haven't I, Daddy. I didn't mean to be, but ..."

"My dear, never say that. If you knew how this surpasses all my wildest dreams for you." His face lit up again with that almost frightening elation. "To think that you are making a Catholic marriage—to think that there will be children growing up in a real Catholic atmosphere—all that, as converts, your mother and I could never give you. And the other aspects—I should be lying if I said they did not count."

"I suppose we shall actually have money some day," said Clara. "It seems very queer."

He smiled.

"Very queer indeed to anyone in this family. I know money is not everything but there's no doubt it makes life very much easier. Yes ... I can't deny I'm glad of that. Though I feel ashamed that you should have to go to your husband empty-handed or very nearly. But what delights me so much is that you should have the background I always longed for for you. You know my feudal temperament."

She said hesitantly:

"I'm afraid Archie's not awfully feudal. He rather hates that sort of thing."

"Then perhaps I shan't find him too alarming. But I expect it is just temporary with him. At his age, he is restive. Poor Larry was the same. But he reverted to type. I'm longing to meet my son-in-law."

She said in sudden panic:

"We're not married yet."

He looked at her ruefully.

"My dear ... forgive me. I can't help anticipating. But it means so much to have something to look forward to. After all the tragedy, the

298

devastation of this war ... to have good news instead of bad. I'm getting old, Clara. And I find that makes one live in the future ... not in the past as I had always supposed. In the future of others ... that is."

"Oh ... Daddy ... I can't bear you to talk like that."

"Nonsense, my dear," he said with his old smile. "It's a very healthy sign."

She said tentatively:

"You're not ... ill or anything are you?"

"Certainly not. A little weary, that's all. I've overdone things a trifle lately. Who hasn't? My doctor wants me to cut down on pupils. And maybe ... now that I know your life is so happily provided for ... I might consider it."

Suddenly, without the least idea she was going to, Clara began to cry. They were not violent tears but they brimmed over and crawled down her cheeks without her being able to stop them.

"My dear," he said in consternation, "whatever is the matter? Whatever have I said?"

She said unsteadily:

"I can't bear it when you talk like that."

Misunderstanding, he said:

"I didn't mean to alarm you, my child. I assure you I am as sound as a bell. I assure you, nothing short of assassination is going to stop me from living to be a grandfather."

But Clara's tears continued to run though she made violent efforts to check them. He leapt up from his chair and stood over her, with his hand on her shoulder.

"Clara," he said at last, in a voice of such terror that she managed to control herself. "You're not worried about anything else ... you're not regretting anything?"

Through the blur of her tears she saw his face. Its expression was so like Archie's on that morning she had found him playing with his trains that once again nothing mattered except to wipe out that expression of blind misery.

She stood up beside him and threw her arms round his neck.

"Darling Daddy. Of course it's all right. Truly, truly it is."

Pain and relief struggled in his face.

"You're certain my dear?"

She put a finger at each side of his mouth and pushed up the corners of his mouth.

"Smile! Oh please smile!"

He did so at last. Then he turned away, fished out his handkerchief and blew his nose violently. Clara did the same. She caught sight of their two heads in the smoke-dimmed mirror behind the rows of photographs. "We're a pretty pair," she said, with a hysterical bubble of laughter.

"Your mother will never forgive me," he said. "I should have seen that you were worn out. Goodnight, my dearest child and God bless you."

"Goodnight, Daddy. And don't worry about anything ever again."

They embraced stiffly, at arm's length, like acolytes giving each other the kiss of peace.

Chapter 3

THE date of the wedding was provisionally fixed for the middle of March. As the days drew on towards it they seemed to Clara to gather speed till they ran together in one continuous streak. There was an interval of light during which she visited shops and dressmakers, opened parcels and, if Archie were on leave, went to a nightclub or a theatre; then an interval of dark, sometimes blank but more often filled with disturbing dreams. Most often they were of Charles, alive and nearly always in his most mocking mood. Occasionally she dreamt of the wedding. She could not get to the church in time or, when she arrived, another bride was walking up the aisle on her father's arm. Once she waited a long time at the altar but no bridegroom appeared; then she realised that Archie and her father were drinking champagne together at the restaurant they had gone to on the Tannhäuser night. Once ... and this was the most painful dream of all ... the bridegroom was not Archie but Charles. He was wearing the brown blazer and grey shorts he had worn in the kitchen-garden. Horror and joy overwhelmed her. She cried out: "Oh, Charles, I thought you were dead," and was about to embrace him when he said, "Don't touch me, Spin. Someone cut my head off and Nan sewed it on again. I have to wear Hero's collar to hide the join."

One morning she woke up and realised that she was to be married in less than a month. What brought it home to her was the fact that Mrs Hughes-Follett was in London and was giving a dinner for her and Archie that night. The thought of this party, at which the bridesmaids and the best man were to be present, shocked her out of the state of blank light-headedness in which she had drifted for weeks. Up to now she had been almost detached from the girl who received congratulations, tried on dresses and wrote letters of thanks to total strangers. She saw Archie only at rare intervals and seeing him, if anything, increased her sense of unreality. He regarded the preparations for the wedding as a boring convention on which parents insisted and took no interest in concrete plans. It was enough for him that, once the war was over, he and Clara would be together always and be able to do as they liked without anyone interfering. Meanwhile he was so pathetically happy to be with her that she had nothing to do but let herself be adored. He asked nothing of her at all beyond accepting his devotion; even his love-making was confined to an occasional rough, but respectful, kiss or holding her closer than usual if they were dancing to a sentimental tune. He showered her with expensive and incongruous presents, ranging from a pearl necklace to a giant Meccano set. At first he had made desperate efforts to "improve" himself, asking Clara to tell him books he "ought" to read or suggesting they went to a serious play instead of a revue. But Clara preferred to adapt herself to Archie's tastes and found a certain pleasure in doing so. In his company she was spared any necessity of thinking and thinking was the last thing she wanted to do. Often their engagement seemed to her no more than one of their old make believes played in the setting of Ciro's and the Berkeley. Often indeed, when they were alone together, they dropped back into characters from the Schweinhund game, finding it a huge relief from having to think of things to say to each other.

One thing at least was almost painfully real: her father's persistent and ecstatic happiness. He had taken Archie straight to his heart as "one of the very best". Things which he might have criticised in a boy of his own class he saw merely as charming foibles against the glamour of Archie's background. When Isabel once remarked that she did not think him nearly intelligent enough a husband for Clara, he insisted almost angrily that courage and kindheartedness were far more important than brains. He was fascinated by Archie's physical recklessness and his genius for understatement. He even seemed anxious in case Clara did not appreciate him enough. "Archie may not be a brilliant talker," he would say, "but he's something far better. He's the kind that gets the V.C. and then apologises for 'stunting'. I've dealt with young men all my life and I know the right thing when I see it. You're very lucky, my dear." There were even moments when Clara was almost jealous of her father's affection for Archie which Archie whole-heartedly returned. She knew how much he had hated his own father but he was so devoted to Claude that he gave him almost as many presents as he gave Clara. Often he insisted on Claude's accompanying them to theatres and even night-clubs and the only concrete plan he seemed to have for the future was that Claude must retire and live with them. When Claude smilingly refused Archie would persist obstinately: "What's the good of my beastly money, sir, if you won't let me buy you out of that ghastly treadmill."

The only breath of chill air in the warm, drugged atmosphere of approval in which Clara had lived ever since she returned to Valetta Road was her mother's attitude. Since that first evening, Isabel had never again suggested deferring the marriage. She remained strangely remote, dealing with the preparations efficiently but without enthusiasm. Archie was rather in awe of her: she was perfectly polite to him but there was no sympathy between them. Clara resented her mother's behaviour, not because she cared in the least what she thought or felt, but because it made her uneasy. There were times when it nearly provoked her to stop and think when all her instincts warned her that to do so might be dangerous.

This particular morning, however, she found herself nearer to thinking than she wanted to be. There was something uncomfortably definite about the idea of this dinner party tonight. It was as if she had been putting off learning a part in a play which she never imagined would be produced and found herself faced with the dress-rehearsal. She put off getting up as long as possible and dawdled in her bath till the water was cold, unable to face the day. When she was half-dressed, she wandered over to a shelf and began idly pulling out some of her old books. She stood for several minutes turning over the pages of her worn copy of Francis Thompson's *New Poems* and trying to find any connection between her present self and the Clara who had once cared so passionately for poetry when her eye caught the words "The Dread of Height". All at once she experienced a burning pang of shame and disappointment: she remembered the hot noonday on Chanctonbury Ring and the horrible man who had called her "Missie". The next minute she remembered all the absurd things she had been dreaming when she had first caught sight of a man's figure in the distance; her sense of loneliness and bewilderment, her sudden longing for a lover who would share her most private thoughts.

She flung the book away and snatched another at random without looking at the title. She let it fall open of its own accord and found herself reading:

> "Je trône dans l'azur comme un sphinx incompris
> J'unis un cœur de neige à la blancheur des cygnes."

It was the Baudelaire Nicole had given her just before she left Mount

Hilary. It was natural it should open there; she had learnt the poem by heart in those dreary weeks of her mother's illness before that sense of blankness and unreality had descended on her. She shut the book and sat down on her unmade bed. Was she not in the same state of hypnotised lassitude at this moment? But there was nothing she could do. It was too late. She was like a person gliding with shipped oars towards a waterfall.

In spite of herself the poem continued to write itself out unfalteringly, line by line, in her head. She was almost frightened to find that she remembered it so clearly. Suppose that other things she had forgotten or tried to forget should resurrect themselves as vividly? To distract herself, she turned her mind to Nicole. They had not corresponded for months until lately she had written telling her that she was going to be married and Nicole had replied that her brother had known a small boy at Beaumont called Archie Hughes-Follett. "He doesn't seem to remember your fiancé except in a surplice or in splints. He says he had an angelic treble and a fiendish capacity for getting into scrapes." The thought of that letter gave Clara a faint comfort. By marrying Archie she would at least be able to move in Nicole's world; they would be able to meet, to visit each other's houses. Fond as she was of Ruth and Patsy, she had not tried to recapture their old intimacy since she returned to West Kensington. At best they had been poor substitutes for Nicole. She was seized with a passionate desire to see Nicole again and hear her husky voice. If she could see Nicole often, would it matter so very much that Archie would rather hear "The Bing Boys" ten times than "The Magic Flute" once? Then the faint comfort gave way to a new despair; she imagined how Archie would look to those critical green eyes and thanked heaven that she was in France and could not be invited to the party tonight.

The gong had gone long ago. By the time she was dressed and down in the dining-room her father had left for St Mark's and there was no one at the table but her grandmother. Isabel, as usual, was having breakfast in bed.

Mrs Batchelor greeted her with:

"I'm glad you've had a nice lie-in, dear. I expect you'll be up late with your grand party tonight. Quite an occasion, isn't it? It makes you realise that the wedding's quite close on us now."

Clara let her chatter on while she sipped her half-cold tea. She had heard it so often before that she did not need to listen. Nearly every day since her grandmother had been told of the engagement she had listened to her marvelling at Clara's good fortune, at the impossibility of imagining her "little girl" as a married lady, at Archie's being such a nice, unaffected boy "not a bit what you might expect considering it's such a grand family and he might even come into a title one day, Lady Robinson says."

But this morning, some unexpected words caught Clara's attention.

"You know, dear, I've just discovered such a peculiar coincidence."

"What's that, Granny?"

"The date of the wedding. I do hope it's not unlucky. March fifteenth."

"Why?"

"Well, dear, I don't suppose it would mean anything to you. In fact I'd almost forgotten it myself till I was looking at an old diary—but it's the anniversary of the day your poor Grandfather died."

Clara said nothing. Mrs Batchelor gave her an anxious glance and said hastily:

"Oh dear, I hope I haven't said anything to upset you. I'm sure I didn't mean to. After all, when you come to think of it, it's really very nice, isn't it? To think how sad we all were that year and how happy we shall be this."

Clara still remained silent and her grandmother gave her an anxious look.

"Dear me, Clara, you don't look quite yourself this morning. Have I said the wrong thing again? You haven't had any bad news?"

"No. None."

"I'm so relieved. I was so afraid for a moment that perhaps you'd heard that Archibald wasn't able to get leave after all and the wedding would have to be postponed."

"I don't think there's the least likelihood of that, Granny," said Clara, getting up and leaving the room rather abruptly.

The routine of things that had to be done carried her through the morning; she had an appointment with the hairdresser; one or two accessories had to be bought to go with the new dress she was to wear tonight. As she chose a pair of silver sandals, without first asking the price as she had done hitherto all her life, it struck her how easily she had acquired expensive tastes. Her father had been almost extravagantly generous with money for her trousseau. Occasionally she felt guilty, suspecting that he would have to drive himself harder than ever to recoup himself. But she salved her conscience by telling herself that this extravagance gave him pleasure, that very soon she would be off his hands for life and that, once she was married, she and Archie would find a way to make him accept money from them. For some reason the guilt was stronger than usual this morning and at the last moment she countermanded the sandals in favour of a cheaper pair. The assistant, who had been all smiles and flattery, froze at once. "Of course, Mademoiselle sees that there is no comparison in *quality*. However ... if Mademoiselle wishes." There was such scorn in her voice, in the very set of her shoulders as she tied up the parcel that, for the first time, Clara realised what it would mean to be rich.

She lunched with Archie and his mother at the Hyde Park hotel where Mrs Hughes-Follett was staying for a few days and where the party was to be held that night. All through the meal Clara found it difficult to concentrate on Mrs Hughes-Follett's animated talk about the dinner and the wedding and several times missed her cues. Once, as she tried to improvise an answer to a question she had not heard, she saw her future mother-in-law looking at her anxiously.

"Clara, dear, are you sure you're quite well? You're looking very pale."

Clara hastily assured her that she was perfectly well though a little tired.

"You've been overdoing things. There's always such a lot of running about and arranging, even for the simplest wedding."

"I can't see why two people can't get spliced without all this fuss," said Archie gloomily.

"Surely you can put up with a little fuss for once," his mother said with a touch of sharpness. "After all it's only a couple of bridesmaids and hardly anyone except the family and very close friends. After all one must have a congregation at a Nuptial Mass." She said kindly to Clara:

"You'll find all the trouble has been well worth while when it comes to the day. It's such a tremendous ceremony, Clara. You said you'd never been to a Nuptial Mass, didn't you? That wonderful moment ... I've never forgotten it ... when the bride and bridegroom go right up on to the altar. ... The only time in her life a woman does."

"Rot. Church chars do," said Archie, "and the pious old girls who arrange flowers." The prospect of the party, which he regarded as waste of precious leave, had made him sulky as a schoolboy.

"It's not in the least the same thing."

There was an uncomfortable silence. At last Clara managed to say: "I do feel stupidly tired. I think I'll go home and lie down or I'll be a wreck this evening."

"Very sensible, dear," said Mrs Hughes-Follett with relief. "*No ...* Archie ... you can stay here and keep your old Ma company for once. If you go with Clara you'll only persuade her to rush off with you somewhere instead of resting. Just go and get her a taxi."

"No, please," Clara implored. "I'd rather walk. I need some air." It had suddenly become desperately important for her to be alone.

She got away at last, unaccompanied. She walked fast, with no idea of what she intended to do, along Knightsbridge and into Brompton Road. When she came to the Oratory, she stopped and surveyed it— its Romanesque dome and colonnades which called for sunlight and blue skies looked gloomy in the grey February afternoon. It was there that she and Archie were to be married in a few weeks' time. On an impulse she walked up the grimy steps, empty except for a cripple selling Catholic papers, and went in.

The great dim church was almost empty too; a few people, mostly women, were kneeling in prayer at side altars. But there was none of the peace and silence she had expected. Men in green livery were busy unrolling a red carpet and shifting benches with a noise of thunder. Clara knelt down at the back and began to pray automatically, as she did every time she entered a church, for Charles and his mother. But, though she buried her head in her hands, she could not concentrate. The shattering roar of benches being dragged over bare wood echoed back from the stone walls with a menacing sound. She looked up and saw two red velvet *prie-Dieu* being placed right in front of the high altar. At the sight of them she suddenly realised the huge commitment of a Catholic marriage. She was not going to take part in a play but to do something irreparable. By accepting Archie for life there, in the presence of God, she was going to renounce all hope of ever finding her true love. It was as if, having worked out a smooth solution of a problem, she found she had misread the question. Panic seized her. She wanted to cry out: "I didn't understand. Give me time! Give me time!"

She began to pray frantically for light and guidance, for some sign from heaven to show her what she might do.

A moment later, a hand fell on her shoulder. She raised her head from her hands and looked up wildly expecting she knew not what:

a miraculous intervention, an angel. It was one of the green-liveried men, whispering loudly. "Sorry to disturb you, Miss. We want to shift this bench."

She moved quickly away, angry and hurt. It was as if God had deliberately mocked her misery. Her first impulse was to run straight out of the church. But where could she go? She could not face the thought of returning home or wandering aimlessly about the cold streets. She began to walk hesitantly up the side aisle, pausing at the chapels with their stands of guttering candles. The Sacred Heart and St Joseph, each had its sparse collection of praying figures. The third was Our Lady of Sorrows. Only one woman was kneeling there, motionless and almost invisible in the shadows, her face hidden in her gloved hands.

Clara approached the black and white marble altar almost on tiptoe. It had a forlorn and deserted look as if it were seldom used. There was an air of perpetual mourning about it as if it were devoted only to Requiem Masses. Above the altar was a sombre painting of Our Lady as Mater Dolorosa, indifferent enough, yet conveying an impression of almost inconsolable grief. As she stared at it, something seemed to calm the fever of her own troubles; she began to think remorsefully of Theresa Cressett.

Kneeling down on the hard bench in the centre of the chapel she prayed, not with fierce importunacy but humbly and soberly. She asked forgiveness for whatever share she might have had in Charles's death and for the grace to make true reparation for it, to accept whatever penance God sent and not, self-willed, to inflict her own. She implored Our Lady to console his mother and then, gradually detaching herself from her private griefs, widened her petition to include all bereaved mothers. For a little while she felt an extraordinary peace descend on her: she lost all sense of time and space, conscious only of a penitent joy in the renewal of her relation with Our Lady which she had neglected for so long. How simple life would be, she thought, if she could be always in this state of calm and humble recollection; she would be patient, kind, unselfish, strong. But even in the very occurrence of these thoughts, the spell was beginning to break. She had not enough of the habit of prayer to be able to keep herself at bay for more than a few moments. Already she was becoming aware of the discomfort of the hard wood against her silk-clad knees. The men had stopped moving the benches but sounds intruded themselves again;

footsteps, resonant whispers, the dropping of coins in a box. With the return of normal consciousness, her old preoccupations surged up more violently than ever. Once more her mind was in utter confusion. She stretched out her clasped hands towards the altar, muttering under her breath, like a litany, "What shall I do? Refuge of sinners, Comfort of the Afflicted, my darling Mother Mary, what shall I do?" But now the chapel seemed empty. It was as if Our Lady, whose presence she had felt for those seconds, had withdrawn, leaving only the mediocre painting of a woman with eyes upturned in grief. Clara put her hands over her face and began to cry, at first quietly, then uncontrollably, like a child. She felt someone take the place beside her on the double bench and shifted further away, without looking up. But the person moved closer to her. Presently she felt an arm round her shoulders and someone gently lowered her hands and drew her wet face against fur that smelt familiar. Clara let her head stay where it was, too exhausted to be surprised, while her mother's voice whispered:

"My darling child. My poor little girl."

They stayed so awhile till Clara was calmer. As they drove back to Valetta Road, Isabel seemed disinclined to talk. It was Clara who kept saying with childish obstinacy:

"But how did you come to be in the Oratory, Mummy? That's what I can't make out."

"I go there quite often," said Isabel.

"You're not a bit the sort of person who drops into churches at odd times," Clara persisted almost peevishly. "I'm sure you never used to."

"No. I never used to."

"Whenever did you take to doing it?"

"Oh ... quite lately ... a few months ago."

"About the time I came home?"

Isabel answered in a muffled voice.

'I daresay. Yes ... it was about that time. What a lot of questions!"

"Sorry. Just one more ... However did you know *I* was there?"

"I was in that chapel when you came and knelt there."

"I remember noticing someone. Of course I never thought of its being you. Otherwise ..."

"Otherwise what?"

"Oh, nothing," said Clara uncomfortably. "Is that your usual haunt ... Our Lady of Sorrows?"

"No. Actually it's the first time I've ever gone into that chapel. I usually go into the first little one on the left. The Sacred Heart."

When they reached the house, Isabel, with unusual authority made Clara go and lie down on her bed. She moved quietly about the room, putting away Clara's outdoor clothes; then she drew a chair up close to her.

Finding herself alone with her mother in her own room, Clara was seized with a panic of embarrassment.

"You've been an angel," she said, "but I'm quite all right now. Do go and have some tea. You must be pining for it?"

"Do you want some, darling? If so ..."

"No, really, thank you. I think I'll be sensible and try and get some sleep. There's this party ... I'd almost forgotten it ..."

"I'm afraid we must talk first, Clara dear."

She knew it was inevitable but protested feebly: "Not now." Her mind was splitting up into disconnected strands. She fixed her aching eyes on the silver dress hanging over the chair. Only yesterday it had seemed of enormous importance: perhaps in a few hours it would seem so again. At one moment one was on one's knees imploring the grace to submit wholly to the will of God, however painful: the next one was in a rage because a hem line drooped a quarter of an inch. How did all these things fit together? What was important? What was real? She closed her eyes and said in a whisper:

"I must have been a bit hysterical."

"Rubbish," said Isabel so sharply that Clara's eyes sprang open again. "Are we going to face facts or not? Because if not you may just as well go to sleep. You *have* been asleep, more or less, in any case, for the last three months."

Clara had never heard her mother speak so incisively. She stared at her as if she were a stranger. Isabel said more gently:

"You don't really want to marry Archie, darling, do you?"

Clara gasped:

"But I *must*. How could I break it off now? It's far too late ... Besides ..."

"Do you love him or don't you?"

"Oh, Mummy ... I don't know. Does it really matter very much?"

"Matter!" said Isabel with such scorn that Clara was almost frightened. She said defensively:

"You said yourself once that it was better not to have romantic feelings when one got married. Anyway I *am* very fond of Archie."

"Yes. As you might be of a nice dog."

Clara sat up on the bed. "You've no right to say that. You're being horribly unjust. I know you hated Archie from the first."

"I don't hate him," her mother said quietly. "I'm very grateful for all he did for you. I'm very touched by his pathetic devotion to you. But I've never for one moment thought he was the right husband for you."

"Surely that's for me to say."

"Certainly. If you loved him."

"I wish you'd stop harping on that. Daddy thinks he's the right person. You know how terribly pleased Daddy is about it."

"I know darling," Isabel spoke all the more softly as Clara's voice rose. "And I know how difficult that makes it for you."

Clara looked at her mother. She had never known her in this mood of gentle firmness. Even her face was subtly different, as familiar faces are in dreams. She said, almost pleading:

"Mummy, I couldn't. It would break Daddy's heart."

"It would be a terrible disappointment to him, yes. But if he knew that you weren't happy ..."

Clara clutched her temples. "I've always disappointed him—always. You don't know. You don't understand. And now ... for the very first time ... no, Mummy, it's impossible."

Her mother looked down and sighed. After a moment she said hesitantly:

"Clara ... you're far too young to realise this. But you'll find one day that you can't make people you care for happy just by giving them what they imagine they want."

"Imagine? But he *does* want it."

"What Daddy wants is not this actual marriage but his idea of it."

For the first time, Clara stopped to think.

"I wonder. You might be right. But Archie ... Archie really would be unhappy."

Her mother clasped her hands together: her face was sterner and older than Clara had ever seen it.

"Unhappy? If you and Archie get married, Clara, the best for both of you would be that he should go straight to the front and get killed."

Clara leapt up, furious.

"How dare you! Of all the wicked, vile things to say. I used to think you were soft and sentimental. I believed you were fond of me. I used to feel guilty because I wasn't fond of you. Now I see you're as hard as nails. I don't believe you've ever cared for anyone ever."

"No?" Isabel had gone deathly white and the knuckles stood out on her clasped hands.

Clara sat down on the bed and burst into nervous sobs. Between them she said frantically.

"You're right ... I'm not fit... No one ought to have anything to do with me ... I just destroy all the people I care for. No one should be fond of me ever."

Once again she felt Isabel's arm round her shoulders.

"Hush, my darling ... it isn't true ... it isn't true. You've tormented yourself about Charles haven't you? She spoke on quietly, almost hypnotically through Clara's convulsive sobbing. "You thought you could somehow make up for it ... forget it. My pet ... the only way we can make up is by bearing our own unhappiness."

At last the sobs died down and Clara relaxed against her mother's shoulder. They stayed thus a long time. Then Isabel said:

"I had to be cruel, darling. I had to give you a shock that would make you wake up."

Clara asked childishly:

"Why didn't you long ago?"

"How could I? I was so frightened for you ... after all you'd been through. I thought that you might stay in your half-awake state all your life and it would be safer not disturb you. But then ... when I saw you in the chapel ..."

Clara nestled up to her as she had not done since she was a small child.

"Mummy, was it me you've been praying for all these months?"

Isabel hesitated a moment before answering:

"Of course I've prayed for you. But for ... well ... other people too."

Clara smiled.

"I should hope so. Selfish to the last, aren't I."

Isabel hugged her.

"Mother ... I've just remembered. This party tonight. What am I to do? I can't possibly go."

"I'll telephone and say that you are ill. If I do it now ... there will be time for Philippa to put the other people off."

"Do you think she'll have any suspicion? Still, she did say I wasn't looking well at lunch."

"I hope she does have suspicions. It will make it easier all round."

Already Clara was beginning to realise what she was going to have to do. She even had a pang of childish disappointment at all the pleasant things she would have to give up. She said, despising herself for her cowardice:

"Mother ... I don't know how I'm going to break it to Archie. ... You couldn't possibly ...?"

"No, darling, I'm afraid that's something you'll have to do yourself. Shall I ask him to come round tonight."

Clara sighed and set her teeth.

"Yes."

"That's a brave child. I do know how hard it's going to be. But I'll manage all the horrid practical details for you."

Clara looked at her mother with admiration.

"You know, you *have* changed. You never used to be like that ... so ... so definite and thinking things out."

Isabel smiled.

"Well ... people change. There's another thing I've been thinking about. I wondered ... when this is over ... if you'd like to go to Paget's Fold for a little?"

"Paget's Fold?" said Clara eagerly. "Oh, I would. It's the one place where I feel I could bear to be at the moment. I never thought of it ... yet the moment you said it I knew it was right. However did you know?"

"I suppose I went by my own feelings. It's not just that it's so peaceful there—or that the old aunts are so sweet. But things seem more real down there. One finds out what is important and what isn't."

"I know just what you mean," said Clara. She added naïvely: "Isn't that odd? I never imagined you and I could ever feel the same about anything."

"Very odd," said Isabel with sweet irony.

Clara considered.

"You know ... you are different. Even your face and your voice. I thought there was something different about you that day I came

313

back from Maryhall." It was the first time she had managed to bring out that word. She guessed that Isabel, with this new alarming, yet reassuring sharpness, had noticed it too.

"Why were you the only person who understood about Archie and me?"

Isabel smiled.

"I wonder."

"It's so strange," Clara sighed. "It's as if I saw you for the first time as a real person."

"Perhaps I wasn't real to anyone. Even to myself."

"But that's just how I feel," said Clara. "How do people become real? Does one just change as one gets older? Or did something definite happen to you?"

Isabel did not answer at once. At last she said, very low: "Something did happen. Yes."

"I wish you'd tell me."

She looked at her mother eagerly and Isabel met her look with a strange, transfiguring smile. It brought back all the beauty to her weary face and added something to it that Clara had never seen and could not fathom. Confronted with that smile she felt a raw and ignorant child. Her mother slowly shook her head:

"Net yet, Clara. Not for a long, long time. Perhaps never."

ANTONIA WHITE

was born in London in 1899 and educated at the Convent of the Sacred Heart, Roehampton and St. Paul's Girls' School, London. She trained as an actress at the Royal Academy of Dramatic Art, working for her living as a free-lance copywriter and contributing short stories to a variety of magazines in the 1920's and 1930's.

Antonia White was the author of four novels: *Frost in May* (1933), *The Lost Traveller* (1950), *The Sugar House* (1952) and *Beyond the Glass* (1954). Her other published work included a volume of short stories, *Strangers*, and the auto-biographical *The Hound and the Falcon*. She also translated over thirty novels from the French, among them many of the works of Colette.

She died in London in 1980.